The Unwelcome

The Unwelcome

Jacob Steven Mohr

**COSMIC EGG
BOOKS**

Winchester, UK
Washington, USA

JOHN HUNT PUBLISHING

First published by Cosmic Egg Books, 2021
Cosmic Egg Books is an imprint of John Hunt Publishing Ltd., 3 East St., Alresford,
Hampshire SO24 9EE, UK
office@jhpbooks.net
www.johnhuntpublishing.com
www.cosmicegg-books.com

For distributor details and how to order please visit the 'Ordering' section on our website.

ISBN: 978 1 78904 559 8
978 1 78904 560 4 (ebook)
Library of Congress Control Number: 2020933429

A CIP catalogue record for this book is available from the British Library.

Design: Stuart Davies

UK: Printed and bound by CPI Group (UK) Ltd, Croydon, CR0 4YY
US: Printed and bound by Thomson-Shore, 7300 West Joy Road, Dexter, MI 48130

We operate a distinctive and ethical publishing philosophy in
all areas of our business, from our global network of authors to
production and worldwide distribution.

To Steve and Marie Filizola, who knew I could.

OTHER BOOKS BY JACOB STEVEN MOHR
The Book of Apparitions 1731453876
Daughter of Man 1629898805

The more we get together, together, together,
The more we get together, the happier we'll be.
'Cos your friends are my friends and my friends are your friends.
The more we get together, the happier we'll be.

Raffi

The past is never dead. It's not even past.

William Faulkner

Not about to see your light,
But if you wanna find hell with me,
I can show you what it's like.

Danzig

Prologue: Names

The imposter waited in the empty world.

The air smelled like snow. The sky over the little hunting cabin was the white of chalk dust, and the skeletal fingers of the bare trees grasped up into it, reaching hungrily, dark against the clouds. The woods stretched out for miles in every direction, but the cabin crouched in a small clearing off a gravel lot at the edge of the narrow, winding road that threaded through the trees like a vein of ore. Here there was no sound but the hollow groan of the wind and the subtle creak of the trees moving in its grip and the noise of the imposter's own lungs working the cold air. He could see his breath. The imposter puffed out through chapping lips, watching white steam whirl and vanish in front of his numb face, marveling at the sensation of it. He was perched on the cabin's front porch, the wood cold through the seat of his jeans, his chin propped on folded hands. He cocked his head to one side and he listened, his eyes half-lidded.

There were bodies in the forest, and he could hear their voices.

The imposter had wondered before if the world had always been empty. But he could not imagine it otherwise. He had wandered until wandering sickened him in the belly, and the unending vacancy of things had been the one constant across years of hypnotizing solitude. But he supposed the possibility remained. Perhaps he had arrived too late to witness the center draining out of the world or perhaps he had simply missed the signs. It did not matter. Now the world yawned hollow. Depleted, barren.

The bodies numbered four: three female, one male, college students all. They were deep in the shaded valley to the north now, moving slowly away, towards the water. Their voices bumped against one another in his head like marbles in a pouch. The imposter listened to them with feverish intensity, parsing

1

the different sounds, separating them like a sieve. Man, woman. Frightened, anxious, vicious, brutal. The names he strained away; these did not matter, either. They were extraneous data. Meaningless, like labels pasted onto empty jars. The bodies were flesh, and flesh did not have names.

But *she* was among them.

That girl—*Heart-Brecker*.

The imposter moistened his dry lips irritably. Her voice was hard to separate from the soup of noise inside his head. Once this had been easy, like lifting a melody from the crash of a waterfall. Once he would have known her voice from a chorus of a hundred others. But she had mingled with the bodies, clinging to them stubbornly, aping the movements and habits of flesh. He felt his rage and his desire rise in him like magma, semisolid and too hot to touch. He imagined her as he had known her, naked, or perhaps wrapped loosely in the sheets of the bed they once shared. He pictured her writhing under his touch as the backdrop of the empty world boiled away into a void like a night sky, and his face slashed open in a pale, joyless grin. He would take no pleasure bringing her to heel. But he would do it, because he loved her.

He would do it because there was nobody else.

Now he turned his attention to the vehicle idling just off the lot, partially hidden behind a threadbare shrub next to the rusted-out mailbox. The imposter had pretended not to see the Jeep arrive, but in truth the sound of the engine and of the tires grinding the asphalt beneath them had given the game up long before the vehicle actually rolled into view. Now he could see the driver from the corner of his eye: a great mountain of a body crammed behind the steering wheel. The skin stretched across the broad, freckled face was pale and blotchy, and two dark, piggy eyes stared out from beneath the heavy singular brow that hung over the face like a low-flying cloud. The lips were broad and fleshy and seemed to have no real shape of their own, and the hands gripping the wheel were enormous paws tipped with thick-knuckled fingers. A swamp creature, the imposter mused. A museum model of a Neanderthal or the Megatherium. Something ancient and primitive and monstrously strong.

A peculiar nameless unease settled over him. He knew this body was called *Cormac*, but this meant as little to him as the fact that the vehicle the body drove was called *Jeep*. And yet he could not discard the name. He had used it to summon this body here, being the body called *Riley*, just as he had been the body called *Ben*, and before that, *Alice*. Their names tumbled in his head like dice, clacking against one another. Suddenly their voices became overwhelming. He tried to shake the feeling away, but it was like strong ropes thrown across him, pulled tight by the weight of names, of voices, of *flesh*. He could not silence them; he could not escape the sound of the screams. It was like being drawn down into a great quagmire. It was like drowning or already being drowned.

The imposter's insides squirmed with disgust. How did he let this happen? How had he allowed things to come this far? The big body inside the Jeep swung the driver-side door out and emerged behind it, broad enough almost to darken the sky. At last the imposter allowed himself to turn his head, taking in this interloper fully, noting with some small glee the look of bewilderment on the other body's milk-colored face. He wondered what it would be like to wear that face, however briefly. He thought again of the other faces he had peered through that day alone, and the day before, and before and before. He considered his own features, hanging from his skull like a heavy wooden mask, smiling and yet expressionless in the same go. Then he thought of *her* face, hidden partially behind the fanned-out sweep of her hair, twisting away from him into the darkness, and his teeth ground together like stones. His hand flexed around the handle of the hacksaw, then he stood up slowly, as though he had nowhere in particular to be.

"Hey!" he called out in a cheerful voice. "*You're* not supposed to be here..."

The big body looked up, startled, seeing the imposter striding across the gravel towards him, but no fear registered on the broad face. There was only dull confusion, mixed with perhaps a kind of relief the imposter would never learn the source of. The thick lips moved and sounds poured out, and the imposter responded, though he could not remember what words he said. But he remembered putting his hand forward to shake, and the feeling of that ape-like paw wrapping around his hand as though it would crush it.

Then the terror did come... and the imposter felt it, really *felt* it rushing up within the other body like the start of some terrible, wracking climax. The center of things collapsed and drained out from under like the pull of quicksand. He put the hacksaw in the other boy's hands and watched him lift it towards the exposed neck without any hesitation. But of course there would be no hesitation. It was inevitable, the imposter knew. Inexorable, like rot, like decay.

It was too late to correct course now, too late even to scream.

After all—by then, neither of them was really there at all.

Chapter 1

Confession

Kait Brecker always became somebody else when she closed her eyes.

The horror sprang up behind her shut-tight eyelids—and suddenly she would be *replaced*, wearing somebody else's skin and teeth and hair and treading the curving, shadow-haunted corridors of another life. It was always the same, this conversion. The face and features were different, sometimes in some obvious way, sometimes subtly, but the *feeling* never changed. It was cold and sharp, like a needle in her vein.

It was a Sunday within the dream, and the wind was breathing winter's cold overtures down the back of her neck as she watched a handful of brittle brown leaves tumble around and around the yellow bowl of the Armistice College "Front Lawn." The air was full of noise. Here gathered protesters—the usual gang, waving pasteboard signs and chanting slogans in singsong. Or here were lovebirds, in pairs, along the duck pond railing, pawing lecherously at each other while their orange-and-black striped scarves whipped in the cold wind. Or there, in the center of the lawn, a scrum of brawny seniors lobbed a Frisbee back and forth across the wide grass plot, hollering jubilantly, their bodies blurred with motion. She did not know why she was here, seeing all this. This was not her body, not her life.

But she would see him soon. She always saw his face in the dream.

She could almost picture him already: here, there, somewhere, always on the periphery. Sway-backed and limp-shouldered and grinning ear-to-ear, with his thumbs thrust into the front pockets of his jeans. He was waiting for Kait. Waiting for her to look up, to see him and smile.

5

But she would not look for him this time. This body would walk briskly across the dry, crunching grass, and Kait, riding along inside the hollow bones, could peer out through the holes in the skull at the crowded world as it swept by. Past the grass and past the pond, thrilling in that dream-winter's bracing shiver and in the lovely, weightless sensation of that new, fresh skin, free of the intolerable burden of *being Kaity Brecker*. And when Lutz popped into frame like he always did, she'd be ready, ready to look past him, too, just another part of the world outside this body, outside this new Kait Brecker's life.

She could avoid him forever, in the dream. She could look down at her splayed hands and read alien histories in the lines on the palms, stare into the mirror's reflection and only see the pale blur of a stranger's face. But even this was poison under her skin. She had wished for it, this crowded, faceless world, but she knew it could not last. It was an eggshell, a balloon about to burst, a cotton-candy memory that would melt in her mouth. She knew it wasn't real, any of it—but it stung worst of all because she knew, deep in her dream-bones and dream heart, that this sharp and lovely dream, it would *never* come true—

* * *

"...can't lighten up for one second. You'd think she..."

"...might *hear* you, Ben, *please*..."

"...and thank you, I might just *let* her hear, might do her some *good* to..."

The voices dragged Kait bodily from the rolling depths of sleep, and when she opened her eyes the memory of where she was hit like a hangover. She was sprawled across the back seat of Ben Alden's station wagon with her seatbelt slashing across her trachea, camping gear piled high around her. She'd crammed her balled-up Armistice College sweatshirt against the passenger window for a pillow, and one of her sneakers had lost its foot and tumbled down among the bungee cords and takeout containers on the floor. The light said early morning, a deeply unholy hour—but Ben was driving, and that meant it was Ben's show. Ben wanted to make Simmes Creek by five and maybe the cabin by five-thirty, and tough shit to the late risers in the party.

"...*know* that's not true. She's just..."

Next to Ben in the front passenger's seat, Alice Gorchuck's dense thicket of ginger curls wobbled atop her head, and when her voice trailed off, the four white ribbons knotted into her hair waved like surrender. Kait felt a fist close around her heart. She'd heard this argument before. There was no mistaking it. From the jagged break in Ben's voice and from Alice's pleading responses, they could only be talking about *her*, Kait, good old Heart-Brecker herself.

But it wasn't the real Kait Brecker they were talking about. No—she knew it was this new model, the lurching, sulky creature she'd woken up inside. This was the rough beast thrilling the airwaves today. This was the Kait that Ben Alden hated.

The Kait that Lutz Visgara had loved.

"...the sun doesn't shine out of her ass, the better..."

Ben talking—a sharp downswing on the last syllable, capping his point as neatly as a Magic Marker. Ben, buttoned-down Ben, who wasn't a lawyer yet but already dressed like one, though today he'd ditched his steam-pressed shirts for a cabled sweater and slim canvas pants. Ben couldn't argue like the high-powered Washington lawyer he wanted to be or even like a sly southern one, with a drawl and an *Ah-Objeect!* and thumbs pressed up under his suspenders. But he had the cadence down pat. His voice wasn't loud, just insistent, like a drill on half-power, driving in screw after screw until your head was full of holes and sawdust. It worked—especially if you were Alice Gorchuck and didn't want to fight in the first place.

"...a whole weekend like this. You know she doesn't..."

"Mrrfah." Kait made herself heard with what she hoped was

7

a convincing stretch-and-grunt. For extra effect, she kicked the back of the driver's seat and blinked sleepily at Ben's forehead, visible in the rearview mirror. "We there?" she asked.

"Kaity!" Alice cried out, whipping around in her seat. "You're awake..."

In no time at all, she'd slipped loose of her seatbelt and was kneeling with her chin hooked over the plush headrest, peering down at Kait, an avalanche of curly red hair framing her heart-shaped face like tumbling flames.

"Ooo. Lucky me." Kait stretched again, for real this time, and began the laborious task of sitting upright. "How far to Riley's?" she asked.

Alice remained swiveled, watching her, unabashedly wide-eyed. But if she was searching for some tell that the conversation had been overheard, Kait gave none. Instead she did her best to smile, though her face did not seem to remember the correct sequence of movements. Her headphones, slung around her neck, belched white noise and tinny little guitars.

"We're here," Ben answered testily.

The station wagon puttered to a stop in front of a brown condo-style apartment building, and Kait hauled herself upright just in time for a curvaceous shape to bounce into view, lugging a monogrammed camping tote over one bronze shoulder and a pillow with a pink pillowcase under the opposite arm. The shape rapped sharply at the window near Kait's head, and she caught a glimpse of black-and-orange nail polish as the offending knuckles retreated.

"Halloo!" Riley sang out.

"Halloo," Kait parroted dubiously.

She unlocked the passenger door, and it immediately sprang open, dumping loose backseat detritus out onto the street. Riley slid in beside Kait, dragging her tote and pillow with her and filling the air with the thick stink of perfume. Kait winced, feeling crowded. Riley Loomis wasn't *fat*—to be precise, she was probably the least "fat" young woman Kait could think of in that instant, with the kind of figure Lutz insisted on calling the "Goldilocks proportions." But her personality, like her perfume, was gaseous, and in the backseat of Ben Alden's wood-paneled war chariot, Kait was already feeling quite smothered.

"You'll never believe the dream I had about Spencer Kittredge last night..." Riley began in a cheery voice — and before Kait could blink, out tumbled a charmless saga of tabloid filth that began with a mysterious self-locking closet and ended, improbably, with the entire Armistice College wrestling team. Kait sniffed and turned towards her window, but the two in the front seats snorted and clapped, egging Riley on while she mimed the escapade with her hands. Then Ben cranked the music and gunned the motor, and David Lee Roth started howling about how he'd been to the *edge*, baby, and the station wagon jolted forward.

Kait re-buckled her seat belt and bent forward, rubbing the bridge of her nose between her fingertips. Was it big breasts that made you go slutty? Or were they just a symptom of this larger disease? She squeezed her eyes shut — a headache knocked just above her left ear, and she knew the noise and motion of the car would soon turn it into a barnburner. The old Kait, the pre-Lutz Kait, would never have asked a question like that, but now the pain in her head filled her up with black, oily thoughts. She sank lower in her seat, scowling to herself and briefly considered returning to sleep. But no, she decided — better to engage with the madness as long as humanly possible. Observe the breeders in their natural habitat and stay wary for signs of aggression...

She kneaded her forehead. *Enough.* That was Lutz-talk, Lutz-rubbish, Lutz's voice coming in hot over her internal intercom. And it was unfair, at least to Alice, who had at last turned from the back seat and was peering at her pink lipstick in the pull-down mirror over her head, her left hand resting delicately on

Ben's knee.

Alice, sweet, apple-cheeked Alice. How long had they known each other? It was a struggle to recall, a fact that unsettled Kait's stomach. Ten years? Twelve? Hadn't they been children on a muddy playground together in some distant past—or was this, too, another false memory? No, this much held true, surely: Alice Gorchuck had been her friend. Her jump-puddle, mud-kneed friend. Back when her hair was candy-orange instead of dyed crimson, back when she'd been genuinely fat instead of merely pleasingly plump. But other than these two outliers, little had changed about the Alice she'd once known. There was no Alice-Mark-Two. Only this perfect prototype—*imitated but never duplicated.*

A memory clunked loose. The two of them on a futon in front of a blazing television set, wrapped to their necks in bulky comforters and gorging on sugary Halloween plunder. Kait still wore her poofy pink princess dress, the tiara and scepter both broken and hucked in a rhododendron bush down the street, and Alice's black witch-hat crouched askew atop the pile of her orange curls. A Fairly Odd Parents marathon was playing, and the girls clapped chocolatey hands over their sticky lips to stifle giggles. It was after midnight, and they were supposed to be asleep, of course, but the devastating combination of Nickelodeon cartoons and high-fructose corn syrup and this righteous, hot-blooded friendship kiboshed that idea entirely. They were eleven. The rumpus room was warm and dark, and outside the window the bright full moon was as big as a god. Life was rockin'.

Then the memory flipped over, like a postcard. Another Halloween night, another year. But now it was Lutz by her side, not Alice. She was eighteen years old, and she had only been dating this new crazy boy a few short weeks. *Lutz Visgara.* Not a name a normal human being should have—but then again, what was normal about Lutz? No declared major, no job, no gaggle of sweaty gym ape friends to crash around downtown with... No other friends at all, seemingly, save for a cousin or a stepsister who lurked in his apartment sometimes whom Kait was instructed to call "Jill". Sheepish good looks, lop-eared and grinning, game for anything; for Kait, Lutz would forever call to mind a baby lamb caught between the paws of a hungry predator and saying, *Well, looks like you've got hold of me, big fella. What happens now?* With that same oafish grin.

Except it was Kait who got caught. He took her—not with passion but with shrugging shoulders and a sardonic eye-roll that condemned the whole wild world to flaccid mediocrity. But not Kait. No, Kait was immune. That's what had bound them. He'd seen the twist in her nature, he told her once, clutching her hands in the middle of some wet empty cobblestone street on the bay side of downtown. The same crazed wildness that lived in him, the staring, alien *thing* they hid from the rest of the world. The thing that made them strangers in the crowded world. The thing that made them *better*. She pretended not to understand at first—*Oh, just what every girl wants to hear, you big dork*. But she was eighteen, and his words tugged at the tiny bell inside her, and it was a bell that could not be un-rung.

That was the first time he kissed her, right in the middle of that rain-slick street. A taxi laid on the horn, bathing them in the gaze of its headlights. Lutz flipped the bird, and Kait mirrored the gesture unconsciously and kissed him back hard. It started to rain, only a drizzle at first, like a fine curtain, and in the blast of the headlights the droplets seemed to hang in the air around them as though time had surrendered to their power. Kait remembered all this, that the glow of the headlights and the gentle press of rain and Lutz's lips and hands on her felt almost exactly like the touch of heaven. So that was the beginning of it, their first night together—they tumbled into his apartment, she recalled, fumbling off their clothes, clinging to each other like wet leaves cling to cold glass. And when the rain began to pound

11

against the windows, it drowned out the sounds of her ecstasy like a hand clamped over her mouth.

Then they flipped the *world* the big one—and they kept it up for four straight months.

So, that Halloween: a Big Moon night, a witch's night, like that one so long ago. She and Lutz were not in costume. Indeed, neither of them were wearing much clothes at all. They were on the couch, the television blasting AMC's twenty-four-hour marathon of *Invasion of the Body-Snatchers*. Somebody knocks; Lutz answers, drunk enough not to bother with pants, just a pillow clutched over his nethers. And lo, there appears Alice, holding Kait's half of their paired costumes. But *Kait's not there, no, Kait's not home, no Kait here that I know of,* says Lutz, sloppy drunk and leaning in the doorframe, the pillow laying forgotten on the carpet by his feet. And now Kait's behind him saying *Oh, I'm sorry-sorry-sorry, I ca-aaa-an't, maybe next year, I forgot, really I did...* But she's giggling, too, giggling because Lutz is laughing—actually laughing at this wide-eyed girl on the doorstep, holding one half of a Thing One-Thing Two costume set and wearing the other, her hair all teased up in proper Seussian style...

And Alice had been wearing Thing Two. Alice picked out the costumes and she gave Kait Thing One, and the little girl who lived inside the hollow bones of Kait Brecker knew, still knew, that Thing One was the best *Thing—*

But Lutz had laughed and so Kait had laughed, and Alice stood there in her ridiculous red jumper and her ridiculous cloud of blue cartoon hair, a slack look on her round face. And behind her, the moon's huge pale eye stared down, huge like you imagine God's eyes as huge.

The memory twisted once more, and so came the third night. Not Halloween, but a Big Moon night just the same, with a big black sky full of cold starlight. This was the night that drove the wedge between Kait Brecker and Lutz Visgara; it was the cold womb that birthed the squirming terror lodged in her heart.

This new Kait slunk across campus, darting shadow to shadow, furtive as a mouse in a wheat field even if there was no one to observe her flight. She felt dozens of eyes on her. She knew enough now. The knife was still twisting in her.

Her feet led her there. To the doorstep. And the moon made her knock—*and eat your shame, Heart-Brecker, choke it down, eat it whole like a good girl.* So there she stood, January's breath cracking in her bones, when Alice Gorchuck opened the door.

Alice—suddenly a vision in a lumpy Armistice College sweatshirt and green converse sneakers. A bowl of popcorn under one arm, half full, crumbs and butter smeared on her chest. Eyes wide with surprise, disbelief. Dull noise of a television in the background, a male voice laughing along to the canned laughter of a sitcom.

"Kait..." she had whispered. "Kaity, your makeup's runnin'..."

"I'm sorry." Kait wiped at her face, rubbed her ear, wiped her face again. "Alice," she said, "I need... He... I think..."

Then it was like a dam bursting. She surged forward into Alice's arms, tears running hot down her face, cooling on her cheeks and on Alice's buttery sweatshirt. Folded into the big girl's arms, Kait felt the weight of four months crashing against her bulwarks like waves crushing the coast to pebbles, and when her friend whispered, "What happened?" close by her ear, it nearly split her open. "Kaity... Tell me, please..."

Oh, the plea in that voice. The affection, the tender desperation. It would have been so *easy*, too, to fall back on obedience—to tell all, to make a full confession...

But: "What did he do to you?" There was no answering that. Maybe the old Kait could have managed it, but there was nothing she could conjure now that would satisfy, that would stand up to even the slightest scrutiny. Alice led her by the hand into the flickering den, lit by what sounded like *Friends* reruns. Kait wouldn't look—she was too occupied avoiding the eyes of

13

the strange boy in the argyle sweater-vest coiled against one arm of the foldout futon couch. Alice sat her down, fetched her a drink, *No please, just water, nothing strong,* while this boy, Ben Alden, watched her like a butterfly squirming under ether. Alice sat her down on a folding camp chair and found a spot beside Ben for herself, and they both looked at her expectantly.

So Kait confessed her sins.

But she had to be careful. The knife was still in her; a wrong utterance could push it deep. So she chewed her words, spitting them out like cherry pits, keeping the dark red juice for herself, already learning to savor misery.

And Alice fell for it, didn't she. Buried her in that endless hug again, didn't she. Cried real tears with her, rubbed her eyes, cried again, cursed Lutz's name with a zealot's passion— if words were lighting, her ex-beau might've been struck dead where he stood. And when this communion was over, she clapped her hands and invited Kait—no, *Kaity,* she'd said Kaity, hadn't she?—to run away with them for the weekend. This boy Ben's family owned a lake house up beyond Simmes Creek in the mountains, deep in real backcountry. And Kait could come with them, get away from her problems, find solace at the bottom of a bottle for a while. And in the ultimate act of self-immolation, Kait had actually said *yes—*

* * *

The car jostled over a bump in the highway; Ben groaned, Alice and Riley yelped, and the mix CD in the deck skipped from "Ain't Talking Bout Love" to "No Time" without anybody noticing. Kait was bumped to the side, and in that instant she caught a glimpse of the entire interior of the car in the rearview in one brief flash. Her gaze flicked from face to face, from Ben to Alice to Riley to *her,* Kait. And for a moment, she almost recognized them all.

"Thank you for inviting me," she whispered. Then, a little louder: "I'll make this up to you, really I will." And she closed her eyes again.

I'll make this up to you if it kills me.

Chapter 2

Girlfriend

I wonder what she's thinking about.

Alice squirmed beneath her seatbelt. The sun was climbing off the horizon, reflecting a blade of white light off the rear windshield of the Fiat leading Ben's station wagon. She squinted and shielded her eyes with one hand, then twisted down the sunshade on her side with the other. The mirror in the sunshade's belly reflected the back seat of the station wagon in glorious widescreen: Riley texting, blushing and biting her lower lip at something on her phone; Kaity with her headphones on and nodding silently to something with lots of big guitar in it, her eyes shut and the hood of her sweatshirt up. A dozen anxieties clawed: what if Kaity had heard Ben before? Was her friend having second thoughts about the trip? What if she was pissed royal at Ben?

Or pissed royal at her.

Alice forced herself to glance away. Kaity's face was inscrutable. Like somebody had slammed her shut like a door or a book. She adjusted the mirror again; Riley glanced up from her phone, leaned across to the center of the back seat, and pulled a face at her reflection. Alice stuck her tongue out and forged a giggle. When had this happened? When had her friend disappeared behind the clouds? Oh, there had been a time when even a slow lift of the eyebrows could have passed like a secret handshake between them, but now? Now Kaity's mind was a cave in the mountains, something hidden and strange. Now the book was closed to her.

"What're you doing?"

Ben's voice cut through the music and through her thoughts —
Kaity's eyes flicked up, and Alice quickly averted her gaze again.

"Oh. Just checking my makeup. You know."

"You know I can't drive with those things down."

"What...?"

Ben smiled apologetically. "The sun-flaps. I know it's silly—it's just a thing with me."

Alice blinked. "I know that, but the sun's—" She pointed out the front windshield. "We've been driving straight into it."

"Your makeup looks fine."

"Ben, I can't *see*."

He sighed, giving her a glance before turning back to the road. "Look," he said. "I'd let you borrow my sunglasses, but I've got to drive. And I can't drive with those flaps down." His fingers drummed the steering wheel. "Close your eyes, if it helps. We'll be driving through trees soon. That should block the sun."

Alice shrugged and swung the sunshade up flush with the ceiling. Ben smiled, leaned over, kissed her cheek without taking his eye off his driving. "This is going be fun," he said. "I think you're really going to love this place."

"I'm sure I will." His sunglasses had crushed against her ear when he kissed her, and she massaged the lobe between her fingertips. *Just a thing with me.* Well, you put up with a lot of funny *things* for the people you loved. That's how Alice saw it. And if she didn't love Ben Alden now, she had a gut feeling she was well on her way there. Or would be, after the trip was over. If she could work herself up to it.

Riley snorted and tapped Alice's shoulder, thrusting her phone screen in her face with a giggling "Lookitthis"—and as Alice turned her head to look at the cartoon on the screen, she glimpsed Kaity sitting forward in her seat and glaring with all her might at the back of Ben's head, as though she could melt through his scalp with her stare. Then she caught Alice's eye, grinned, shrugged, and went back to her music. Yeah, you put up with a whole lot of things for the people you love, but that's how you knew you loved them, wasn't it?

And Alice Gorchuck would do just about anything for Kaity Brecker.

It'd been over a year since the Halloween party, but Alice could still see the ghostly strands of toilet paper dangling from the trees in the frat house's front lawn, hanging in great parabolas alongside the strings of cheap orange lights, ethereal and almost floating, half-shrouded in thick gray mist belching from the rented fog machine on the brick front porch. Music and flashing lights spilled from the front door, and Alice's hands were starting to sweat. She'd felt braver than a jungle cat when she had picked out her costume, but bravery is a fine thing when you're in the costume shop two weeks before the party, not when you've got to walk into the lion's den wearing a corset and fishnet stockings for the first time.

There was a caved-in and rotting jack 'o lantern squatting next to the fog machine, and whenever the clouds cleared Alice could feel its drooping eyes taking her measure. Her chest felt like a windup toy cranked past its limit—this was long before she'd discovered the soothing sorcery of Ativan, so the only cure for this awful tightness in her midsection was to get back in the car, tear off this ridiculous getup, and make an Alice-blanket-burrito on the couch until this whole stupid holiday blew over. But Kaity had squeezed her shoulders and adjusted her wig and grinned at her through about a pound of mottled-blue Bride of Frankenstein face paint.

"You look badass," she'd assured her. "You're a big beautiful badass, Alice Gorchuck."

"Kaity, I don't know—"

"You're going to kick a criminal amount of ass at this party. They'll call five-oh for sure this time. And throw away the key."

"*Kaity*—"

"We've sold our souls, Alice. We... Tell me again. Tell me who we sold our souls to."

Silence as Alice chewed lipstick. Kaity persisted:

"A-L-I-C-E, who'd we sell our souls to?"

Finally a sigh and a slow helpless grin. "We sold our souls to rock 'n roll," she admitted.

Kaity nodded solemnly, her plastic bolts bobbing. "Bought and paid for," she intoned. "C'mon, Thing Two—we owe it to ourselves to burn this place to the ground tonight."

Only then had Alice allowed herself to be led up the drive, through the door, and into the pulsing, bassy maw of the party. And though the fist in her stomach never quite unclenched, Kaity's hand on her shoulder put honey in her blood. Time seemed to blur, and as Alice slowly drained the plastic cup of dubious punch in her hand, the noise and motion of the evening eventually swirled and melted into a single wave of sensation that lapped against her over and over again—a forceful tide, but never powerful enough that it threatened to bowl her over. And when inevitably red-and-blue lights flashed on the lawn and the cry of COPS began to sound over the music, it was Kaity that propelled her out the back door, over the high wood fence, and led her by the hand out into the maze dark streets beyond, into the night, to safety.

"I have to whizz," Riley announced brightly.

Ben shrugged and pulled off the highway, coming to a bumpy stop at a gas station with a lot half-covered in loose gravel. "Everybody else go while we're here," Ben said. "We can't stop again after this. If it's dark by the time we hit the county line, we'll never find the cabin. No street lights," he added in an aside to Alice, who was unbuckling and hunting under her seat for her purse.

"Ben used to come up here as a little kid," Alice said, twisting to face Kaity. "He was telling me the other day. With his family. And their uncle—what was it? Teddie?—would get up in the middle of the night and drive out so he could turn the porch light on for the rest of the family to find. He'd be dog tired the rest of the day, but it was the only way anybody could find the place in the dark without GPS."

Kaity pulled her headphones off her ears and shook her hair out. "Sounds like a swell guy," she replied, offering a wan smile.

Ben grunted and swung his door open. "Yeah, well. Uncle Teddie runs a meth lab now, I think," he announced. "Let's shake a leg, huh?"

Alice climbed out of the car and stretched and looked around. Though the waystation was just off the highway, it was the only building around seemingly for miles: to the north, the road became a bridge that curved out of view, while to the south was a long straight stretch of two-lane that drew to a point on the horizon. Behind the gas station was an empty gray field that looked as if it had once been farmland, and beyond that a stand of trees visibly swayed. A big cold wind began to slap Alice's hair around, and she tugged her jacket tighter around her shoulders and fumbled for the zipper.

"Jesus," Riley was saying as she hot-stepped towards the door. "Where'd this bullshit come from?" Kaity stood and stretched audibly before shuffling inside after her, with Alice and Ben close behind.

The bathrooms were singles. Ben did his business and pushed back into the wind to put gas in the station wagon, while Alice and the other two girls made a line outside their door. Riley emerged first, shaking out her splayed fingers like she was drying her nails. "No hot air," she mused. "Or paper towels. Place is a hole. Listen—I'm going for smokes. You want anything while I'm up there?" Kaity shrugged and locked the bathroom door behind her. "Alice, anything? Snacks, booze…"

Alice's eyes went round. "Do you think you can?"

"Well, so long as I get cooperation," came the reply, accompanied by a sly grin. Alice followed her gaze to the pimply teen picking his nose behind the checkout counter. "Let's see what's in *his* wallet."

Riley flounced off, but motion outside the convenience store drew Alice's gaze. Ben leaning against the rear bumper of the station wagon: he waved, then mimed pulling up his sweater sleeve, checking a nonexistent watch, and going into what looked like a seizure of disbelief. He waved her outside, but Alice crossed her legs and rocked back and forth before smiling apologetically. Ben shrugged and slouched off towards the driver's seat.

"Alice!"

Something tapped her elbow, and Alice turned: there stood a beaming Riley with a cardboard box in her arms and a plastic bag slipped over the crook of one elbow. "Hope you like Bud," she scoffed, adjusting her grip to tug the neckline of her shirt back up. "All they had. Plus," she whispered, leaning in, "they're *Mitch* here's favorite, apparently."

"What's that on your hand?"

Riley shifted her grip, revealing a ten-digit number scrawled in blue pen across the back of her hand and wrist. "Oh, I'll wash it off when we get to the cabin," she said. "Listen, let's get this stuff in the trunk before Lover Boy's manager comes out and tells us some bad news."

Alice glanced at the bathroom door. "You go. I still have to… you know."

"Suit yourself." Riley hefted the box and pushed the door open with her back, then banged on the station wagon's trunk. The trunk swung up, and Alice watched her friend heft the big box inside as another car pulled up near. The bathroom door creaked behind her and Kaity appeared, flicking water off her hands with a brisk one-two motion, then wiping her palms on her jeans. There were streaks under her eyes, hidden by a rub of the palm against her cheek and a wide yawn.

"Your boyfriend is an asshole," Kaity mumbled through the last of the yawn.

"What's that?" But Kaity was already gone, ambling off behind a rotating display rack of cheap sunglasses towards the front counter.

Alice watched her disappear. For a moment, something tight and cold rose from her chest into her throat, but she forced it down with a burst of will. This wasn't Kaity's fault. This wasn't Kaity at all—some afterimage, perhaps, something stripped down and flayed. Something hurting. This was something that had been done to her.

And Alice would never forgive Lutz Visgara for that.

She pulled the bathroom door shut, then forced the rusty lock to slide home with a grunt. In between that cold January night and now, how many times had she imagined it? How many nights had she lain awake, staring at the popcorn ceiling of her dorm room and tried to guess at the horrible thing Lutz must have inflicted upon her friend? And though they were no more than fantasies, how many times had the images she conjured soaked her pillow in sweat, driven the breath from her body as she trembled in the grip of some terrible sympathy? The plastic seat was cold against her bare thighs. She focused on this sensation, trying to ignore the pictures flickering across her mind. She had envisioned this scenario so many times that it began to bring with it a kind of shame—as though she was keeping Kaity's pain alive through sheer force of imagination alone. Alice thought again of the wet streaks under Kaity's eyes, and her hands moved, without her permission, to her face. She rubbed her eyes, ground the knuckles against them, her fingers coming back glistening...

The crash shocked her back to reality. A noise like something breaking, then Kaity's muffled curse—Alice was already hiking up her pants and hobble-jumping towards the bathroom door. She was fumbling with the rusty lock when something stopped her in her tracks.

"What the fuck are you doing here."

Kait's voice, stern and cold—how she always sounded when she was scared out of her mind. Alice pressed her ear to the door, squeezing her eyes shut, her mind racing. Then:

"Oh, come on, Heart-Brecker, don't be like that."

Alice's eyes flew open. Kaity spluttered something incoherent and angry, but before she could finish, *that voice* rang out again in a laugh, a stop-and-go, hiccup-y kind of laugh. Alice had heard that sound before—like Cindi Lauper yelping her way through "Girls Just Wanna Have Fun" mixed with a toad's wheeze.

"C'mon, at *least* say you're surprised to see me," Lutz Visgara said. "It doesn't even have to be a *good* surprise…"

Alice burst through the bathroom door and there he was, standing in the store doorway with his shoulders slumped forwards and his hands thrust into the pockets of a brown hoodie jacket. His face was hidden behind a jutting box of candy bars and a rack of trashy romance novels, but she could hear the grin in his voice—that crooked fault-line smile he fished out for every photograph she'd ever seen of him on Kaity's social media. The knees of his tight blue jeans were muddy, and what little she could see of his hair was windblown and piled high on his head like an eighties heartthrob. She caught herself holding her breath, and she let the air out of her lungs in a shuddering *whoosh*.

"Just tell me how you found me."

Alice swung her gaze: Kaity was backed against the sliding glass doors at the back of the store where the beers and cold drinks were kept. On the ground beside her lay an upturned rotating sunglasses rack—maybe a dozen pairs were scattered across the peeling tile at her feet, a few with the lenses popped out and crushed underfoot. Her eyes were serious and her mouth was set in a sneer, but her cheeks had gone the color of butcher paper and the fists at her sides were trembling. Behind the store counter, the pimple-faced sales clerk's round eyes flicked from Lutz to Kaity to the mess on the floor, his mouth hanging half-open, not speaking.

"I didn't," Lutz replied, walking forward. "I'm as surprised as you are, honestly. Maybe I should ask you if you're following *me*, huh?"

"Get bent." Kaity's mouth twisted. Her eyes met Alice's, standing in the doorway of the bathroom with the door cocked against her sneaker heel. Kaity mouthed something across the store to her, then turned back to Lutz. "I don't, I don't care how you got here. Just go. Just—"

"Kait, that's unkind," Lutz answered jovially, stretching out the pockets of the hoodie. "I miss you. It's been *weeks*. Try to think of how I feel."

"I don't give a shit how you feel."

He had almost reached her. To Alice, watching him in the big fisheye mirror above the cashier's counter, he looked almost tiny against the dingy white tile of the floor. Like a Q-tip with legs—much smaller than Alice herself. But he was slouching forwards, stalking Kaity like a hyena sniffing up to a wounded animal, and she found herself frozen in the doorway, one hand on the cold steel knob and one twitching helplessly by her side. She couldn't move, couldn't *speak*—her breath was beginning to catch inside her, the sweating hand on the doorknob squeezed as tight as her heart, tight as a constricting noose.

"Then at least tell me why you thought you had to run so far away," Lutz said, his voice hoarse with emotion. He was gone from the fisheye mirror, his body now blocking Alice's view of Kaity, blocking her friend's path to the door.

Kaity made a strange sound, halfway between a scream and a frightened gasp—and then Alice was *there*, across the store and by her side, her body positioned directly between her friend and Lutz. Whatever had gummed her up before was gone, and she stared down at Lutz with wide, cold eyes, while her every heartbeat pounded in her head. Lutz didn't meet her gaze at first, bobbing his head back and forth trying to see over first her right shoulder, then her left. But when he couldn't manage to see Kaity *through* her, he at last let his eyes settle on Alice's. *Thank*

God, she thought through the haze of her anger, *that I was born a big girl.*

"You're Alice, then," Lutz said, trying to force a smile. "I think Kait introduced us—didn't you, Heart-Brecker? That one Halloween? Hey, remember—"

He tried to dart around Alice's left side, but she moved to intercept him, nearly pinning him to a three-stack rack of bagged chips. Kaity made a strange noise behind her.

"She doesn't wanna talk to you," Alice said.

Lutz frowned, then managed to twist that into a smirk. "Look—you're being a good friend," he said. "I get that. Ex-boyfriend shows up out in the middle of nowhere... I know how it looks. I understand the situation. But I *need* to talk to Kait right now. You can have her back when we're through, Thing Two."

Alice's face flushed, and to her great surprise the edges of her vision actually tinged a dull blood-red for a second or two. "She told you to get bent," she replied, her voice deep and strange in her ears. "So get bent."

The bell over the store entrance jangled; Riley peered in the doorway, her eyes flicking from Lutz to Kait to Alice and back to Lutz. "Kaitlyn, honey," she called, her voice even, "come on out to the car, okay?"

Kaity put a hand on Alice's shoulder and started to sidle past, picking her way through the broken sunglasses on the ground, though one broken lens did crunch under her heel. Lutz wheeled towards the door, towards Riley, his eyes and mouth wide open. And as Kaity passed him, his hand flew out of its jacket pocket and snatched at her wrist. "Heart-Brecker, *stop*—"

Alice's fist struck him on the cheek, just beside the nose and above his top lip. It happened so fast: his fingers wrapped around Kaity's arm, then her own fingers were balled into a tight fist and striking out, and then Lutz was splayed out on the ground, flailing among the broken sunglasses as Kaity ran for the door.

"You *bitch*," he was sputtering, "you colossal pig *bitch*..."

25

But he was laughing, actually *laughing* through the bubbling blood flowing down under his hands. "You actually—*urghh*—you actually broke my nose. Do you believe that? Jesus Christ, I think you broke my *nose*."

"Leave us alone," Alice told him, staring in disbelief at her stinging knuckles. "We're on vacation." Then she strode past the gobsmacked cashier and out the door to the car.

Riley pounced on her the instant she neared the station wagon. "That was *so* badass," she crowed, skipping around the back of the car to clap Alice on the back. "You laid him *out*, girlfriend. You—hold on."

Her expression hardened as she gripped Alice by the shoulders and spun her around to face the store entrance. The door opened, and Lutz shambled through, a fistful of paper towels mashed to his nose. "Jeezy-pete, did *you* lay a number on him," Riley murmured in Alice's ear as he shuffled off around the back of the building. She released Alice, who turned around, surprised by the contemplative look on the other girl's face.

"Maybe we should hit the road, huh?" Riley said, regarding her coolly. "Looks like we've done all the damage we can do here." One orange-and-black fingernail tapped the station wagon window: inside was Kait, hiding in her headphones and hood once more, eyes squeezed shut as she bobbed noiselessly to the music. Alice nodded and tried to smile back. Her heart was still between her ears, but the roar of her blood was dulling to a hoarse whisper now.

Riley winked and skipped around to her side of the station wagon, and Alice climbed into the passenger seat beside Ben and reached for her buckle. "Are we done here?" Ben sighed, rubbing an eyelid with two fingers. "Everybody get their business sorted?" But before Alice could answer, he'd already started the car and cranked the music back up. Riley started singing along to "Run Through the Jungle," and at the chorus Ben's colorful baritone joined in, trying his best to harmonize.

"Oh. By the way. Here." Kaity tapped Alice's shoulder, tossed a plastic shopping bag into her lap. "For the rest of the drive," she said in a whisper that cut through the music.

Ben, still singing, trundled the station wagon out of the gravel lot and back onto the side road, and Alice rustled open Kaity's gift: a pair of ruby-red sunglasses stared back at her from the bottom of the bag. Alice smiled and slipped them on, her heart feeling like a gooey candy-apple in her chest. It was a cheap, brittle set of glasses, tight around her ears and across the bridge of her nose, and the lenses fogged up every time she exhaled. They could not have cost more than five dollars.

But that didn't matter. Not to Alice Gorchuck. She turned back in her seat, stealing a last glance at Kaity's nose and mouth nodding silently under the flap of her hood, then turned bravely back into the sun. They were just right. They would always be just right.

Chapter 3

Skin

The sun screamed across the sky, and before long it trespassed the western horizon, throwing long fingers of shadow across the road in front of the station wagon. Kait smooshed her cheek against the cold glass, staring sidelong at the bare trees and empty gray fields whipping by in arrhythmic blurs. Powerlines did their dip-and-rise dance on their poles, and in the far distance, the pale form of a Simmes Creek water tower rose against the sky like an enormous fist, raised to strike the world a blow. Across the back seat from her, Riley had her window cracked and was trying to smoke a cigarette through the narrow slit between the glass and ceiling. Frigid February road winds blew her long blonde hair around like a checkered flag; to Kait, it looked like a huge moth with big blonde wings had mistaken her face for a lightbulb and was trying to dash itself to pieces against her cheeks and neck.

Kait shook herself, made fists with her eyelids, shook herself again. The hours between then and when he'd shown up in the gas station were a damp and shaky blur, but the Polaroid image of Lutz coming through the door—just *appearing* there, like a magician's final showstopper trick—made her fingers tremble and her stomach knot every time she called it up. There had been no fanfare, no creeping dread or tingling suspense to herald his entrance. He simply arrived, just as he *always* did, breezily and utterly careless, like he owned the joint or didn't give two shits who did. Right back inside of her world and inside of her life with a crooked smile and a wave. *Hi there, didja miss me?*

In a moment of acute panic, Kait wondered if she could ever look at a door the same way again, without fearing that Lutz Visgara would just waft through whenever he wanted, wherever she went. After all—how, exactly, had he found her? What had given her away? Could he do it again? Did he know where she was right now?

But the feeling passed as quickly as it had come, bubbling away to nothing in the pit of Kait's stomach. She was better than that, wasn't she? That was the point of tagging along on this fucking trip. Wasn't it? To prove she could be better? That she could keep herself in line?

But who are you going to prove it to? wheedled the dark little voice inside of her. *There's nobody here but us, Heart-Brecker. And we both know it'll take a whole hell of a lot more than a change of scenery to cure you.*

"Cure me of what?" she snarled back, almost out loud but without moving her lips.

The voice chuckled. *Of you, silly. Always of you.*

"Shit, that was our road," Ben groaned. He turned down the music, bumped onto the shoulder, and pulled a sloppy U-turn onto an unmarked dirt road leading straight on into thick forest. "Won't be long now—Riley, dammit, put that out, this isn't my car..."

Riley smirked at Kait before flicking the smoldering butt out the window. Kait tugged her hood off her head and shouldered her headphones, then scrubbed fog off her window and pressed her nose to the glass. There were no leaves on the trees outside, but they stood close enough together that their branches filtered out the sun's fading light almost entirely, forming a wall of sheer darkness only a couple dozen feet beyond the edge of the road. And as the station wagon trundled deeper and deeper into the woods, the shadows constricted into a narrow tube around the vehicle until there *were* no woods anymore, just the twin yellow ovals of the headlights pushing back endlessly against the black.

"Alice, Kaitlyn, check it." Cranked to max brightness, Riley's phone screen lit up the back seat like a flashlight blasting in Kait's eyes. She squinted into the antiseptic glow as Alice craned her neck around to see Riley's home screen, cluttered with social media alerts and with a photo of a fat orange cat as her background.

"What am I looking at?" Kait asked in a monotone. Her headache, forgotten through the afternoon, was beginning to resurface, pulsing like a kick-drum just behind her right ear.

"Who's *Cormac*?" Alice cooed.

Riley flipped her phone around and flicked a text alert away. "None of your *business*, sweetie," she scolded, slapping Alice playfully on the shoulder. "Anyway, lookit." She tapped the upper left corner of the screen. "No bars... Data service's getting spotty... And there's the small matter of that *it's dark as shit outside...*" She grinned wickedly, holding the lit screen under her chin. "I think our Benjamin Alden's brought us out here to kill us. Oh-ho-ho-ho."

"Thwarted again," Ben deadpanned. "And I only needed a few more square inches of skin to finish my Buffalo Bill suit. *Oh-ho-ho-ho.*" Alice and Riley giggled, but Kait felt a muscle tighten in her midsection. She tried to smile, but the most her face could manage was a lip-twisting grimace. Pain twinged in her head, flashing like a warning.

"But give it to me straight, is Ted Levine not a *hunk* in that movie?" Riley said, rolling her window up at last. "Honest to God. I'd let *him* kill me. Wear my skin, I don't care. I just want to *look* at him."

Kait's face went rigid, the Halloween half-smile frozen on her face. "Buffalo Bill was not a *hunk*," she said, her voice shaking.

"That's so gross, Riles," Alice agreed, but she was stifling a laugh just the same.

Riley tapped her phone a few times, then showed the rest of the car a picture of a stringy haired man with eyes like glacial ice. "But you can see it, right?" she urged. "In the eyes? Man, talk about *intensity*—"

Kait's hand lashed out, snatched the phone out of Riley's

hand and pressed it, screen-down, against the seat between them. Then everything in the station wagon seemed to freeze. Riley and Alice stared, their expressions terrifyingly unreadable in the darkness. A silent moment passed. Then two.

"Kaity...?" Alice began.

"What're you all looking at back there?" Ben asked.

"Buffalo Bill... James Gumb... killed women," Kait said, every word quivering. *You can stop talking now.* "He kidnapped them..." *Stop any time.* "Kept them in a well for weeks..." *Just shrug and say you were wrong.* "And then he took their skins." *You didn't know what you were saying.* "He wore them like *costumes.*" *Still not too late, Heart-Brecker.*

But no, onward, forward to the big finish:

"...and you, you want to *fuck* him."

Too late. Now, let's see what you've won...

Slowly, almost warily, Riley retrieved her phone, tugging it free of Kait's grip. Kait folded her arms, her face stiff as a mask and hot as a stove. "So you did see the movie," Riley said at last. She mirrored Kait's posture, her arms folded across her chest, the phone buzzing dully in her left hand. "Guess I figured you wrong—I had you pegged as more of a chick flick kind of girl."

"Yeah," Kait said, staring at her knees in the dark. "You had me wrong."

"Then let's talk about it."

"There's nothing to talk about."

"Kaity—"

"Don't call me that," Kait snapped. "I told you not to call me that anymore."

Alice leaned forward to protest, but Riley put a gentle hand on her shoulder. "Hey, you heard her," she said. "There's nothing to talk about. Let's leave it, huh?" Alice tried to shrug the hand away, but Riley leaned in quickly and whispered something in her ear. The two girls stayed frozen like this, locked in a strange half-hug, until Alice nodded silently and slowly returned to her normal sitting position.

"How much further, Ben?" she asked.

"That's it up ahead," came the reply. And indeed, the station wagon came to a stop in a small grassy lot in front of a one-story cabin, the narrow front porch all lit up in the headlights' forceful beam. Ben threw the E-brake, popped the trunk, and swung his legs out on his side. Riley threw open her passenger door and thumped the roof with her fist.

"All ashore who's going ashore!" she sang out. Alice climbed out silently without so much as a backwards glance. Kait felt like crying.

Too fucking late, Heart-Brecker.

By the time Kait emerged from the station wagon, the others had almost finished tussling their bags and backpacks out of the trunk. Kait's things—one small airport suitcase, a parachute duffel, and a pillow with no pillowcase—were piled on the ground by the back bumper. She mutely gathered them up in her arms and followed behind Riley as Ben led the group up the porch steps and hunted for the key along the top of the doorframe, using his phone as a makeshift flashlight. The temperature had dropped again, and Kait pulled her hood's drawstrings, constricting her field of view to a misshapen oblong. She tried not to shiver; her headache was getting worse by the second, and even the impact of her footsteps sent bolts of pain scurrying across her skull.

At last Ben got the door open. "Let's get some lights on," he said, holding the door open for the girls. Riley and Alice stumbled through, but Ben stopped Kait at the door with a jutting shoulder.

"You listen to me carefully," he told her through a toothy smile, his voice so friendly it was almost sing-song. "I don't get it. Why you're here. Alice begged and begged me to bring you along, but..." He sighed, glanced over his shoulder, returned his gaze to Kait. "Look—do you want to be here or don't you? I honestly can't tell."

Heat rose in her stomach. "I want to be here," she said, but her hands curled into fists inside of her baggy Arm-C sweatshirt sleeves.

"Then *cut that shit out*," Ben hissed. "Back in the car... I can't take any more of that. This whole thing was supposed to be for me and Alice, but if you make this suck for me, so help me God, I'll make it about *you*. I'll turn it around on you so fast it'll make your head spin. Now, look me in the eye and tell me we're not going to have any more problems here on out. Tell me, *Ben, it's gonna be smooth sailing.*"

The heat was a cauldron boiling inside her; her fists shook at her sides, and she had to grind her teeth to keep her face from twisting into a rictus of disgust. It'd be so easy, she thought. Alice had shown her the way not a few hours before, to *deck* this ass, with his cabled sweater and his Patrick Bateman horn-rimmed glasses... To wipe that fucking *grin* off his face, at least, that smug, lopsided grin that suddenly reminded her of Lutz, *so very much like Lutz...*

But then she thought of the silence in the back of the station wagon, of the way Riley had stared at her pityingly in the dark. Of the tears in Alice's voice when she turned away, how her shoulders had trembled. One finger at a time, her fists uncurled and her brow smoothed. Her teeth still ground in her jaw, but she was able to look Ben in the eye without sneering.

"Aye-Aye, Captain," she said, clicking her heels and throwing up a snappy salute, nearly dropping her pack in the process. The two stared at each other a long moment, and when Ben finally frowned and broke the look, Kait realized she'd been holding her breath.

"Fine. After you," he said, propping the door for her as well.

Kait squeezed past him with a sigh of relief. The interior of the little cabin was already warming up with two bodies moving around inside; Alice had disappeared through one of the two bedroom doors, and Riley had dumped her bags across the cracked leather couch that faced an empty fireplace and a huge oil painting of an America Indian waving solemnly. The floors were old hardwood, but an impressive array of braided rugs covered nearly every inch, like moss on a forest floor. A sliding glass door with thick tan curtains over it led out the back of the cabin—presumably to the lake Ben hadn't stopped crowing about before they left—and above this, a ten-point buck's head gaped at them from a fixture on the wall.

Kait looked around, scanning near the low ceiling, and spotted several sets of antlers set in the walls, one of which had been converted into a light fixture near the little kitchen area. A hunting cabin, then. Ben hadn't mentioned that—but Ben hadn't told her much of anything about the trip. And Alice, she imagined, couldn't have known. But it was just as well. If they were really going to do the whole rustic thing for three nights, they might as well go whole hog.

"Kaitlyn! Yo!"

Kait's headache flanged. Riley was waving her over from one corner of the leather couch, sitting with her long tan legs kicked over one broad sofa-arm. "Got a weak signal." She beamed, showing Kait her phone. "But I still bet they won't deliver us pizza out here, huh?"

Kait shrugged, resisting the urge to massage her temples. "We should get our stuff to the bedroom, right?" she said, easing her backpack to the ground to rest her shoulder. "Make some room out here for when we start eating."

Riley's eyebrows jumped up. "Oh. Oh, no, don't worry about that. The bedroom's all yours. This couch is just fine for me."

Kait's heart sank, though she couldn't place why. "I mean..." she began. "I wouldn't make you do that. I know we don't know each other that well, but I'm sure there's room enough for both of us, and it's not for very long..."

"Trust me—you don't wanna bunk with *this* Loomis," Riley

assured her. "I snore. I drool. I toss and turn. You're better off shacking up with Rudolph over there." She angled her head at the deer head on the wall. "Don't worry," she continued warmly, though her smile didn't reach her eyes. "We'll still have plenty of time to hang out. We just won't be getting as friendly with each other as Benjamin and Alice, right?"

Kait shrugged and grabbed her pillow and duffel, then tromped over to her bedroom door. She'd known all along she wouldn't be sharing a room with Alice, but she hadn't figured on getting... *penned up* like this. But that would solve everybody's problem real nicely, wouldn't it? Nail some boards over the door from the outside to keep good old Heart-Brecker from ruining their good time. She opened the door and tossed her things onto the double bed inside. Fine, then—Riley could have her couch. There wasn't enough room for three people in the bed anyhow.

Riley, Kait, and Buffalo fucking Bill.

She crept from the room just in time to see Alice and Ben emerging from the opposite door, Ben's arm around her shoulder and hers about his waist. "We were thinking of going down to see the lake before we start cooking," Ben announced to the room. "Or at least, before we get too deep into the—Holy Mother of God, *where did that come from?*"

Kait followed his pointing finger: right above her head, a wooden rack was fixed to the wall above the bedroom door holding a long, well-polished hunting rifle. How had she not noticed it before? Dangling above her like the Sword of Damocles itself? This *was* a hunting cabin, after all—it stood to reason the place should be armed to the teeth. Kait took a step towards it, sweeping her eyes up and down the weapon's length. It was a beautiful piece: smooth wood stock, polished so bright it almost looked like horn, and a black, oily muzzle. Whoever had owned the rifle had taken immaculate care of it, or had never handled it at all. Kait wondered if the gun had even ever been fired.

"Who's the hunter in your family, Ben?" Alice asked. "You

didn't mention it before we got up here."

"I... don't know," he replied slowly. "I haven't been here since I was a kid. The place looks completely different than I remember." His head cocked to one side, like somebody admiring a display of pinned butterflies, though his eyes were wide and his brows held high.

"Maybe it's your famous Uncle Theodor's?" Riley offered from the couch.

"Oh-ho, I doubt it. Ted's a big gun control nut. He used to push for those neighborhood-by-neighborhood buyback programs you'd hear about sometimes. He'd go house to house with his kids made up like corpses to raise awareness about school shootings."

"I assume," Kait put in, not taking her eyes off the rifle, "that this was before your Uncle Ted went to the meth."

Kait didn't turn around, but she knew Ben was rolling his eyes. "Yes. That was before he went to 'the meth'."

"I wonder if it's loaded," she said.

Everyone went quiet. Kait turned around to see the other three staring at her, equal mixes of shock and fear on their faces. Alice and Riley's eyes were round, but Ben looked as though he'd bitten into something sour—or something with a bug in it.

"Of course it's not *loaded*," Alice broke the silence with a nervous giggle. "Nobody would leave a loaded gun above a bedroom door—would they?"

"That's a good point," Ben replied. "Why the hell *is* it above the bedroom door? Seems morbid, right?"

Riley righted herself on the couch and crept up behind the rest of the group. "Benjamin, you should check," she said, grinning maliciously.

"Check what?"

"If it's *loaded*, silly!" she explained, clapping him on both shoulders. "We can't have a loaded gun just floating around the cabin while we're here—especially once we get our drank on. I, for one, am yet unconvinced you're not trying to make a skin suit out of us."

"Ha-ha-ha. Yeah, I'm not going anywhere near that," Ben said. "I don't know the first thing about guns. *You* check if you're so damn antsy about it."

"Oh, don't look at me," Riley protested. "I'll put a hole in the ceiling for sure." She looked at Alice, but the redhead only threaded her fingers together and edged away.

"Well, we should move it, at least," Ben suggested. He took his glasses off and began to clean them. "Maybe put it outside…?"

"There's no way the thing's loaded," Alice repeated.

"I'm so not touching it," Riley added.

Kait looked from face to face, her brow furrowed, toying with the idea—it had been a few years since she'd handled a gun, but her hands still remembered, could feel the quick movements of her wrists and fingers, feel the well-oiled wood and iron responding to her touch. But those hands did not feel like her hands now, nor were those memories *her* memories. What would it mean to call upon them now? Could she wield them like a tool—or would trespassing that life feel like just that, a trespass?

Or like walking across a grave?

"Have we got a towel we could wrap it up in?" Ben mused. "That way nobody'd have to touch it, and we could move it without—"

"For heaven's sake," Kait said at last. And before she could talk herself out of it, she strode to the doorway, stood on tiptoe, and slung the big rifle down from the rack.

A collective gasp of horror rose up, Ben in particular giving a very satisfying and unmanly yelp, but Kait ignored them. The gun was heavier and slipperier than she'd figured, and it nearly slid out of her hands as she juggled its weight, but once she got a handle on it she turned the weapon over in her hands, staring down the length of the barrel and inspecting it from all angles. "Winchester Model 94," she murmured, the corners of her mouth twitching. "Lever action. And that's *eighteen* ninety-four—they don't manufacture these anymore." She shouldered the gun and looked down the iron-sights, testing the balance of the weapon, keeping her trigger finger well above the guard.

"Betcha it shoots, though."

"Maybe we should think about putting that back?" Ben began, but Kait swung around, careful to keep the barrel of the rifle pointed towards the floor. The other three in the room jumped back a step, Alice letting out a bleat. Kait's heart was pounding, but something propelled her forward with irresistible strength, her hands moving quickly and surely across the gun's oil-slick mechanisms.

"You wanted to know if it was loaded, didn't you?" Kait hooked two fingers through the lever and pulled; the ejection port slid open, and, sure enough, a fat gray bullet slid into view. *I'll make it about you.* "Well, shit, look at that. It is." *I'll turn it right around on you.*

She dumped the bullet and pulled the lever three more times. *Chu-kunk, chu-kunk-chu-kunk.* Three more bullets tumbled out, hitting the floor around her feet with sharp thuds against the rug. *Tell me we're not going to have any other problems, Kait.*

The fourth click came up empty, so Kait slammed the chamber closed with a satisfying *chunk.* "And now it's not." *The bedroom's all yours, my dude.*

"Kaity—"

"And don't we all feel so much safer?"

Come on, Heart-Brecker—don't be like that.

She cradled the rifle and took three steps forwards towards Ben, kicking aside the little pile of bullets before thrusting the gun into his arms. Ben jumped and tried to push the weapon back, but Kait kept him and the gun at arms' length, though it took all her strength to keep her arms locked. Ben stared. They *all* stared, but Ben stared hardest of all, and this time he did not look away.

Tell me we're going to have smooth sailing here on out.

"Here's your smooth sailing, Captain," Kait said. Then she stooped down, snatched her pillow off the floor, and retreated to the darkness of her bedroom.

Chapter 4

Boyfriend

"What did you say to her?"

Steam rose in Ben's face, fogging up the lenses of his glasses as he stirred the rotini pasta around in the boiling pot. Alice leaned against him heavily from behind, knotting her hands across his stomach and propping her chin on his shoulder affectionately. Her cloud of auburn hair tickled at his ears, making him flinch away at first, but he corrected himself and leaned into the hug, nuzzling at her with his cheek.

"What do you mean?" he said.

"When we were walking into the cabin," came the soft reply. "I saw you two talking in the doorway there. What did you say to her?"

"Oh, that." Ben stopped stirring, then began again, counterclockwise. "It was nothing. It was quick, at any rate. Just, ah, exchanging gossip?"

Alice broke the embrace, coming around to lean on the kitchenette counter next to him. The condensation on his glasses rendered her form totally inscrutable: a vague cloudlike shape reclining against the marble countertop beside him, but her red hair bobbed atop her head in a manner that struck Ben as disapproving. "Well, whatever you said's got her cheesed off."

Ben sighed. "I'd rather not talk about it." A pause—he glanced sidelong at the Alice-shape to his right. "She's difficult to talk to," he said at last.

"She's really not, I promise."

"Well, she's difficult for *me* to talk to."

"Why, Ben?" A hand emerged from the blurry form, gently slid his glasses off his face one ear at a time; Alice scrubbed the fog off with her sleeve and returned them, equally gently, to their perch. "Look, she's really nice—honestly. You just don't know her like I do."

"Oh, I know that," Ben replied. He could see her clearly now, but though her form was crisp the precise expression on her face still eluded him somehow. Her features were smoothed, but there was something in her eyes he couldn't place. Sadness? Anger? Confusion? He wanted to reach for her hand, but instead he just stirred harder, sloshing the boiling water around in the pot. "You're right," he said. "I don't know her like you know her."

"So talk to her."

"I only know her like I know her."

"I mean it!"

"Jesus, Alice…"

"I want the two of you to be friends."

Boiling water splashed over the lip of the pot and sizzled on the red-hot burner. "Then what should we talk about?" Ben asked. "About Lutz? Probably not. Classic rock, then? Or, or *slouching*? What about being a total—"

"Ben." A warning. He ignored it.

"She pisses me off so damn much, Alice. All she's done is sulk and snipe at me from the back seat and bitch about my driving."

"She hasn't—"

"I know she was thinking it." Another slosh of hot water, another vicious sizzle. "She hates me. When I backed off that curb a little funny in Mette? She *smirked*, Alice. I saw her in the rearview. I won't be *smirked* at."

"She doesn't hate you. She just—"

"Just what?"

He watched her consider the question, rolling words around in her head with her tongue in her cheek. "She just needs some time to get right again, is all," she replied at last with a drop of her shoulders. "She's had a bad couple of—well, you've heard the story. But she'll get there, I know she will. I just want the old

Kaity back."

"I know that," Ben said. He loved Alice Gorchuck. He knew it was too soon to say that kind of thing aloud, but shit, there it was. He loved her, and the knowledge that he loved her stuck pins in him every once in a while, whenever he thought about her or when she looked at him in a certain way. That was the genius of love, wasn't it? It hated to be ignored. It couldn't stand silent acknowledgement—it demanded *notice,* like a cat pawing at your laptop keyboard or kicking breakable things off the desk or a high mantelpiece.

And Ben had only ever been in love once before, a silly quick thing late in high school, when he was eighteen and she a little younger than that. They'd loved each other with that hot-burning, jealous kind of love you only know how to produce when you're young and stupid, but eventually the affair broke apart under its own weight and she cut off all her hair and moved up to Massachusetts, and Ben never saw her again. He'd liked it, though, while it lasted—feeling silly like that. Like a hard pasta noodle sliding down into boiling water and softening up, expanding, curling cozily into the bottom of the pot. That's how Alice made him feel—but damned if he could say it, especially in front of this Kait girl.

Ben twisted the heat dial, bringing the pot down from a rolling boil. "But why has it got to be my time? Our time," he corrected hastily. "Did I ever tell you about the time my father brought my mother to this cabin? This was way back, you know, before they—"

"You told me that story," Alice replied, grinning at him. "You—here, let me stir that a while. You know where the sauce is in the big cooler." She took the spoon from his hand and nudged him out of the way of the stove with her hip. "Do you think we've got enough water in here? Look, the noodles are making an island."

"Well, it's a good story," Ben said.

"I know."

"I like that story."

"I like it too!" Alice replied. "But we're not your mother and father, are we?"

Ben watched the pasta swirl. "You're right."

Because my father would never have brought along Kait Brecker.

With a low chuffing sound like a jungle cat, Kait stalked out of the bedroom and flopped backwards over the top of the couch, righting herself clumsily next to Riley, who slid over to give her room to sit. Alice watched her pass by, and Ben watched her watch. Color rose in her cheeks, which rankled—but why? He couldn't get it straight in his head. Again he wanted to reach for Alice's hand, to feel the cool assurance of her touch, to know that she was *there* and, by the simplest leap in logic, that *he* was there as well. He craved that anchor—but Alice was stirring the boiling pot with one hand and waving hot steam from her eyes with the other, so Ben looked out across the living room at the open doorway that led into Kait's bedroom. He stared a moment, then two, blinking.

"Alice?" he said at last.

"Hrm?"

"What happened to the hunting rifle?"

"What do you mean?" she asked without looking up from the pot.

"I mean," Ben replied, grinding his teeth a little, "that stupid gun's not on the rack anymore. Kait unloaded it, I put it back over the door—remember? But now it's gone."

"Well, I didn't do anything with it..." Alice frowned, then she turned the burner under the pasta down to low and stepped out into the living room, "Jeez, you're right—hey, Kaity?"

"I took care of it," came the sullen reply from the couch.

A muscle in Ben's leg twitched. "Now, hold..." Alice caught his eye and held it. "What do you mean, you took care of it?" he began again, almost lilting.

Kait's face appeared over the couch-back. "I mean," she replied, "I took care of it. Stowed it back in the bedroom so we wouldn't have to look at it anymore. The bullets, too—they're in a baggie in a dresser drawer. S'that okay?"

"Yeah, that's fine, I guess..." But Kait had already flopped down behind the couch and turned her music back up. Ben could hear tinny little guitars from across the room.

"See, Kaity took care of it," Alice said, trotting back to the kitchenette. She fished an oven mitt shaped like a beluga whale's head from a low drawer and took the pasta pot off the stove, ferrying it gingerly over to the sink to drain.

"That's right," Ben said through his teeth. "Kaity took care of it."

"Ben? The sauce?" Alice asked from the sink.

"Soup's on!" Riley sang out.

Riley appeared at the threshold of the kitchenette with Kait close behind, and soon the space filled up with before-meal chatter. *How many cups? Where are the clean plates? Not the breakable ones, the plastic'll do fine...* Then they were all around the little dining table just off the main living space of the cabin, tucking their knees and trying to avoid kicking each other in the shins. Ben ate ravenously. Driving always famished him—and though the tomato sauce was out of a jar and the Italian bread was all but stale, the meal was quite delicious, especially on such an empty stomach.

But when his plate was clean, he realized the mistake he'd made. The others were eating instead of talking, leaving him little to do but stare across the table at Kait. Kait eating, chewing noisily, slurping Coke and occasionally peeking up at him through the curtain of her bangs. Her headphones were slung around her neck, and though the sound was turned down he could still hear what sounded like Danzig blasting from them. He pulled his gaze away and found a window to stare out, but only the dark wall of the night greeted his wandering eye, so reluctantly he returned his attention to the table.

Riley, seated to his left, let out a rattling belch. "Whoof! Good *eats*, Benjamin," she said, punching him playfully in the arm while the others applauded, even Kait. She shoveled in another bite of his pasta, laughing around the fork at a private joke.

Ben sighed and stared into the leftover red sauce on his plate. Where had things gone wrong? He thought back to January, tried to picture the exact placement of the pieces on the board. There— the scene was coming together. He and Alice were sprawled out on the beat-to-shit hand-me-down sofa in her apartment, their limbs tangled together in comfortable knots. A pretty picture, the two of them, snuggled under a striped throw-blanket with the TV blazing—playing some old sitcom his parents used to love. Getting cozy and horny all at the same time, kissing and laughing, kissing and laughing again...and when a knock at the door startled them out of lip-lock, it was Alice who wanted to ignore it. *It's so late, it's so cold, they'll give up eventually, come back to me, Ben, keep me warm...*

But, no, Ben had shrugged off the blanket and tried to stand, prying loose from her protesting arms: *we'd better see who it is, it could be important, plus they're not going to quit knocking, listen to them go at it...!* And so finally Alice had laughed and pulled him down to the couch, then rose herself and padded over to the door. A slow creak—the knocking stopped. The sound of muffled sobs cut through a gap in the laugh track. Ben half-rose, looking to the doorway. Then:

"Kaity?"

Ben had it figured down to the second: it had taken no more than twenty-seven seconds, not even a full minute, for the wheels to come off his precious little life. Alice reappeared at the entrance to the den, leading by the hand a trembling, red-eyed twig of a girl with brown hair and fat, poofy bangs and thick black eyeliner running in two parallel lines down her tear-streaked face. She didn't look at him, only waved blindly in his general direction as Alice steered her into the room, but instantly the whole atmosphere seemed to change—like in the theater when the stage crew swaps out the yellow filters for blue and the orchestra switches to minor key.

Ben shoved over on the couch, and the quivering girl circled around and plopped down heavily next to him, more heavily than her slender frame should have permitted. The sounds she was making were awful: the body-wracking sobs he'd heard from the hallway had bubbled away to little hacking baby-bird cries, and the lines of her makeup joined her eyes and the corners of her mouth like a kabuki mask. Pity stirred in his heart—and yet, he could not help imagining her face splitting open along those black lines, just unfurling like a big sad flower before wilting, drying up, crumbling away. The television flickered in the background, gone to commercial, now mercifully on Mute.

Then Alice said something like, "Could you give us just a few minutes, Ben," and he'd gotten up silently, numbly, barely thinking as he re-tucked his shirt and bobbed off to Alice's bedroom. He could hear them talking down the hall—Alice's voice soft and soothing, the new girl's low and scraping and full of anguish—but it wasn't until he closed the door and flopped down across Alice's big double bed that the sobs started in again, louder than ever. And that's when it occurred to him: his high school girlfriend had begun dating another girl a few days after she arrived in Massachusetts, a childhood friend who'd moved up there only two years before.

This was how Ben Alden met Kait Brecker.

He got the story out of Alice later, little by little, but the more she told him, the less sense the whole strange situation seemed to make in his mind. He'd seen Kait around campus a few times but didn't know her by name until that night, but Lutz he *knew*—from an Honors course his freshman year and a couple of debate club meetings the year after that. And he'd liked Lutz, he remembered, even if they'd only ever spoken a scant handful of times. It wasn't hard to read the guy: noisy, goofy, probably bullied a lot through junior high (for being called *Lutz Visgara*, of all the fool names), learned he was funny once he got to high school—voices, impressions, the whole class-clown spectrum. Loud and inappropriate at times, sure, but good-humored about it, even gracious when he wanted to be. He reminded Ben of a Looney Tunes character—an animated llama, perhaps, or a lop-eared lamb. Something gangly and wobbly and slender and wholly harmless.

So to hear Kait's story now, filtered through Alice's own star-blind fury...well, it almost bordered on madness. He couldn't dismiss the idea—and yet, he could not bring himself around to full-throated support either. He could no more believe Lutz capable of such behavior than he could accuse his own father or the family dog. And it was like his father had said: *Benji-Boy, the truth is always floating out in the middle of things—which means that both sides are always lying, at least a little. That's a lawyer's whole job. To catch the other side in their lie and make them pay for it. And never stop making them pay.*

But here was a new scenario—one that Ben could not simply lay by and observe. There were new pieces moving on the board in patterns he couldn't fathom. Ever since that cold January night, Ben could not remember a day when he hadn't been put in a room with Kait Brecker somehow. She seemed to cling to the undersides of his days: there she would be, walking arm-and-arm with Alice to a class, or here, sliding in beside him and Alice for lunch at The Barn, or here again, sprawled out on the couch watching BBC documentaries when he came over to Alice's apartment for a late dinner and a cuddle. Ben and Alice became Ben and Alice and Kait, and there seemed to be nothing Ben could do to shake her. So the cabin trip couldn't come soon enough. They'd been planning it a month, and Ben clung to some fool hope that when he and Alice got back from Simmes Creek, Kait would have her shit *sorted* somehow, or at least she'd have found some other friendly harbor to dock her ship at—

* * *

"Jesus—he's choking!" Riley cried out suddenly.

Alice's chair clattered to the floor as she jumped to her feet. Kait let out a bleat and started to rise as well, but Ben was already coughing and wiping at his face and waving them away. "I'm fine," he tried to splutter before Alice pressed her water glass into his hands and made him drink. He could feel Kait's eyes on him, and his cheeks burned as a little water dripped down his chin and soaked into the collar of his cabled sweater. "I'm fine, really," he managed to say at last. "I wasn't choking. I don't know what happened."

"But you were all red!" Alice said, still standing over him, one hand between his shoulder blades, worry-lines creasing her forehead. "And your eyes were starting to bug out. I thought…" She paused, looking around in confusion. "Well, I'm glad you're all right."

Ben looked from face to face around the table, then down at his hands. His right fist was clenched around the handle of his fork: The knuckles were white and taut, and his fingernails were biting into his palm. But he felt oddly numb, as though something thin and slow and warm had slipped down inside of him and curled, like a long pasta noodle, in the pit of his stomach. Even Alice's hand on his back felt strangely feverish, but this thought seemed to come from a long ways off, like the hum of a distant motor. Finger by finger, he watched his grip relax until the fork clattered out on the table, but he could hardly feel the movement of his hand at all.

"Jesus," he said at last. "I think that settles it. It's time we got into something a little stronger than water."

"Hear, hear!" Riley agreed, pounding a fist on the table. She rose and headed into the kitchenette, then began rummaging in the cooler. "Ben, do we have anything to open these with?" she called out.

"Ben's got a corkscrew on his pocketknife—right, Ben?" Alice had moved around the table to stand behind Kait, her hands on the other girl's shoulders. She kept leaning against Kait, and her hands kept straying downwards, threading fingers through Kait's brown hair or scratching at her hairline or between her shoulder blades. And that *smirk* was back, twitching on Kait's lips, almost invisible, hidden behind the bell of a headphone.

But Ben could see it. It was all he could see.

Look for the lie, Benji-Boy, said a voice from the rear of his mental theater—his father's? his own? *Look for the lie. Make her pay for it. And never stop making her pay.*

"I'm glad you're all right too," said Kait, her eyes gleaming.

Ben nodded mutely, and Riley returned with a bottle of Yellow Tail in one hand and a box of beers under the opposite arm. "Ben? The wine screw?" she asked.

Never stop making her pay.

"What's got you goofy all the sudden?" Riley remarked, thumping the drinks down on the table in front of him. "I swear to God, Ben, if you don't make quick with that pocketknife, I'm going to go after this with my teeth, really, I will."

A big grin had spread across his cheeks like a plague. "Guys..." he heard himself say, and suddenly a laugh shot out of him like a burst of gunfire. "Guys, I'm just... so... *happy* to be here with all of you." And then the warm thing inside him wrapped great strong arms around him and pulled him down and down.

Chapter 5

House Rules

Riley drummed long fingernails against the table, watching Benjamin's clumsy fingers fumble with the corkscrew. He was half-crouched, the bottle gripped between his knees, beginning to sweat a little along the hairline. Across the table from Riley, Kaitlyn had wet a forefinger in her mouth and was running it along the rim of an empty wineglass, producing intermittent whines and squeaks, while out in the den, Alice had some kindling piled in the fireplace and was starting to fool around with the starter fluid. Riley stifled a sigh and cast her gaze out the dark back window of the cabin, suddenly abominably bored.

Aw, shit, she thought, watching dim reflections lope and flex in the glass pane. *These crazy kids are gonna hurt themselves out here.*

An itch skittered across the back of her wrist, and Riley swatted at it idly as though it were a bug, weighing her options. The Yellow Tail continued to get the best of Benjamin, but she resisted the urge to yank the bottle from his hands and dispatch the cork herself. The look of grim determination on his face quickly giving way to frustration told her everything she needed to know: she could no sooner help him here than she could change his oil or fix his computer. So instead she folded her arms and leaned across the table conspiratorially.

"Benjamin," she began in a low, insinuating tone, "don't look now—but I think your girlfriend's about to burn this shack to the ground."

"Hrm?"

Benjamin looked up, his cheeks flushing mightily—*the color of tomato-guts,* Riley thought. *All mashed up and left in the sink near the disposal.* She had to squash a grin behind her hand to say,

"Can't you give her a hand or something? I'll give this a go while you're gone."

She reached across the table for the wine bottle, palm up in supplication, and after a brief hesitation Benjamin slid it to her with a reluctant grunt.

"It's not a *shack*," he muttered under his breath, but Riley watched him tromp across the den and sink down next to Alice, placing a steadying palm against the redhead's back. She could hear them murmuring to each other from across the room, his mumbling baritone mixing with her high whisper in a kind of domestic harmony.

They're cute together, she admitted to herself. Real Norman Rockwell, and all that.

Turning away, Riley folded away the corkscrew attachment on Benjamin's Swiss Army knife and flicked out the big main blade. "Corkscrew won't do you much good," she stage-whispered to Kaitlyn with a sly wink, "not unless you get rid of the wrapper first—but we won't tell *him* that, will we?"

Kaitlyn wrinkled her nose but made no other reply, still running her finger around the rim of her wine glass. Riley shrugged and ran the point of the knife expertly around the neck of the bottle, tearing the wrapper off whole before rapping the point of the neck against the corner of the table and—*thok!*— popping the cork, easy as lying. She then cast a glance over her shoulder at the happy couple kneeling by the hearth, then pulled the bottle up to her lips and took four long swallows of wine.

The Merlot splashed across her tongue, and almost instantly she felt the stress-points throbbing at the base of her skull and along her lower spine start to unclot. The smell of burning wood began to waft across the room; Riley's boredom faded into a kind of blue cheer, and she picked at the label wreathing the bottle. Though she couldn't lay hands to hard proof yet, she was beginning to piece together why she had been strung along on this little shindig. She and Alice knew each other, sure—they'd taken two freshman classes together and been to maybe a dozen of the same parties up and down Frat Row—but they weren't *friends*, not like Alice and this Kaitlyn girl were friends. And Benjamin she'd only met twice, in planning for this excursion.

But when Alice had texted her, begged her to drive up with them—*you'll love it Riley, I promise. Ben says it's so beautiful in wintertime, plus we can get as drunk as we want, there's nobody around for a dozen miles*—she'd jumped at the chance, thinking maybe this time, this time it's really going to happen, this time it's all gonna come together.

But it didn't take her long to tease out the truth. There was powerful tension here, knit into the air, hanging like fine filaments, ready to trip up, to ensnare, to *sever*. So it was smart, really, what Alice had done. Introduce a Riley into the equation—as a buffer, as a *lubricant*, as a slick silk liner between what Riley had quickly come to realize were warring factions. And, yes, it *was* a war. Riley couldn't see quite yet where the battle lines were drawn, but you didn't need to know the names of the generals to see the bombs falling. Or perhaps her intended role was simpler than that. After all: you don't invite a party girl along unless you're looking for a party.

Instant fun: Just add Riley.

But it was just as well. None of her usual crowd were throwing her kind of get-together anymore, and the Omega Lambda keggers were getting a little grab-assy, even by Armistice College standards. Still, Riley wished she'd been given more warning that this was going to be a working weekend—or, at the very least, more time to prepare herself.

She stared across the table at Kaitlyn, who caught her looking and held her gaze. The girl's brows furrowed, music shrieking from the fat blue headphones around her neck, but she would not look away. An expression fluttered across her features— Curiosity? Disgust? Boredom?—and Riley found herself wishing strangely that she could snatch that emotion away, press it down, examine it under glass with a microscope. The flash of anger she'd felt in the station wagon had long faded, and with the wine inside her Riley began to regret benching herself on the couch for the trip—or was it Kaitlyn she'd benched? She could see *two* Kaitlyns, now, one shimmering overtop of the other, and a piece of her yearned to apologize, to split open along the breastbone and say, *here I am—another trembling soul, just like you!* But instead she let a grin slide across her lips and reached forward, plucking the wineglass from Kaitlyn's grip.

"I think this place is trying to destroy us, Kaitlyn," she told her, pouring a half-glass from the bottle. "And the only defense is to get as wasted as humanly possible."

She slid the glass towards Kaitlyn, who eyed it suspiciously. "Your mission, should you choose to accept it," Riley added, waggling her eyebrows.

To Riley's great surprise, Kaitlyn shrugged, snatched the glass up and drained it in one go, a dark streak trickling from one side of her lips when she set the empty glass down again. "Whatever," she mumbled—but a smile bloomed on her face almost in spite of herself. Blossoms of color rose on her pale cheeks, and Riley watched with glee as her eyes glazed slightly as she peered across the common area at the couple crouched by the fireplace. "Damn, that's... actually really good stuff."

"And it gets better," Riley promised. She stood, circumventing the table to stand beside the other girl. "Look," she said, splashing a little more Merlot into Kait's empty glass. "I know things started off weird here—but this sort of jamboree can be a whole lot of fun, if you let it. You've just gotta loosen up a little."

Kaitlyn glanced down at the glass, then across the room: Benjamin and Alice had retreated to the leather sofa, and he had pulled Alice into his lap, his chin resting low on her shoulder. "I don't feel loose," she replied a little thickly.

Riley patted her shoulder, then grabbed the bottle off the table, starting towards the den. "You'll get there," she called over her shoulder. And when she heard Kaitlyn's chair push back, she strode the rest of the way across the common area and tapped Benjamin on the back of the skull with the bottle.

"Whaddaya want?" he grumbled through a grin.

She took one last swig of Merlot, then handed him the now half-empty bottle. "There. Loosened it for you. I mean," she corrected herself with a giggle, "you loosened it for *me*." She could feel the wine starting to take her, egging her forward, but she pushed the feeling down—*Not yet, honey, not yet*—and watched him pour a half-glass for Alice, then himself.

"Drink up," she purred. "We're playing Truth or Dare."

The next few moments passed in a kind of honeyed blur—not from the booze, but from sheer anticipation boiling her blood. Riley guided the other three into forming a circle, cross-legged on the rug in front of the hot fire, and while they were settling into position, she hefted the case of Budweiser onto her shoulder and brought it over to the hearth. She was almost giddy, a fact that annoyed her faintly, but the fact was:

Riley Loomis *loved* Truth or Dare.

She'd always adored the game, ever since her eleventh birthday party, the first time her parents let her have a sleepover for her school friends. But when she discovered alcohol in tenth grade (a bottle of '99 Cabernet left out from one of her mother's mommy-group functions serving as her date to the dance), her appreciation for the sport evolved. Through high school and into college, Riley found herself at party after party, walking alone in a sea of bobbing, faceless bodies. Again and again, she felt a kind of mask drop down over her face as the booze in her stomach—stolen from pantries or bought from gas stations or grocers with a good fake ID—took hold of her, and soon the stories Sober Riley heard of her drunken doings the night before began to scare her. Most of her associates had danced on a table or two after a few cans of PBR, but nothing like the tall tales the frat kings swapped like baseball cards over groupchat—screenshots of which occasionally found their way to Riley's phone by way of a concerned friend.

But she couldn't stop: either she'd worn the mask too long or the fit was too tight, but something had changed in the way people looked at her. Even her friends' eyes seemed to slide over her, and boys' glances always missiled in on the parts of her that talked the loudest. Even Riley herself felt changed — like her skin was crawling across her bones every second she didn't have a beer in her hand or, later, a cigarette between her lips. So in time, Truth or Dare became less a game than a tool to her, a pry bar she could lever against her own failures of self, something to tear down the human walls that kept her at bay and uncover the faces that hid beyond them.

And Riley badly wanted to see the faces of her friends tonight.

"Alice asks first," she instructed, popping the tab on her first beer. "Alice pooped last, so she goes first. House Rules."

"You've got no way of verifying that," Alice giggled, "*and* it's not your house. But, sure. Ben — Truth or Dare?"

"Oh, God, Truth." Benjamin shivered. "You've told me about Riley's dares, and I'm not doing anything to a banana."

Kaitlyn booed through funneled hands, but Alice swatted her playfully on the knee and asked earnestly, "How many years have you been coming to this cabin, Ben?"

Now it was Riley's turn to caterwaul. "This *is* your first time playing, isn't it?" she moaned. "Here's a tip, girlfriend: never ask questions you know the answers to already."

"But I don't!" Alice protested, blushing a little. "I was curious."

"At any rate, it's a boring question," Riley returned. "Drink. House Rules."

Her rules were simple: no question was out-of-bounds, and no challenge was off the table — but simultaneously, no player should feel compelled to answer a particularly prying Truth or fulfil a dangerous or embarrassing Dare. The catch was, if you demurred, you had to take a shot of the strongest liquor at the party, or pound a beer, in this case. If you failed to answer truthfully or complete a dare fully and to the satisfaction of all — or, God forbid, asked a boring question for Truth, the greatest sin of all in Riley's eyes — the same penalty applied.

Riley tossed an unopened can of Bud into Alice's lap, who stared at it like Riley had tossed her a slug. "House Rules, huh?" she said.

Riley waggled her eyebrows at her across the circle and swigged from her own can. "I don't makes 'em," she replied. "I just enforces 'em."

Alice shrugged and held the cold can against the hollow of her neck but didn't drink. "How 'bout it, handsome?" she asked.

Benjamin rocked back, looking between Riley and Kaitlyn into the fireplace. "That's a tougher question than you think," he began, casting his eyes towards the ceiling. The firelight flickered there, throwing warm light across the surface of the ceiling in rough, lively ways. "I've never asked my parents directly ... but I'm fairly certain I was conceived here."

Kaitlyn coughed, clapping a hand over her lips to avoid spitting a mouthful of wine, while Riley watched Alice flush mightily and collapse into nervous giggling. "I only meant, I've been coming here a long time," Benjamin continued, going tomato-red again. "I didn't mean —" But this only made Alice and Riley laugh harder.

"Please tell me it wasn't my bed," Kaitlyn deadpanned.

"Or this *couch!*" Riley smacked the seat at her back with a balled fist. "Christ — there's probably not a safe sleeping surface in this cabin. The whole place should be condemned."

Alice made a show of shaking her hands off as though they were covered in slime, then wiped them with exaggerated slowness on the back of Kaitlyn's sweatshirt while the other girl squirmed away, trying not to laugh.

"That's not what I meant," Benjamin repeated, ducking his

shoulders as though he would turtle his head and neck between them.

"Then what *did* you mean, Ben?"

Kaitlyn had fought Alice off at last and was leaning forward, lips pursed and eyes narrowed. Her head tilted coyly to the side, chin jutting, and Riley watched that same strange expression crawl slowly across her features. She seemed to be studying Benjamin, with eyes as hard and cold as marble. Riley felt recognition jolt through her. She'd seen this expression before— at a dozen or so late-night soirees, just before the first punch got thrown. Her shoulders and stomach tightened reflexively. *Where had this come from?* Riley wondered. How had she missed this building? Should she say something? *Do* something?

But to her great surprise, Kaitlyn broke the moment's tension, rocking back on her bottom and draining the wine in her glass. Benjamin took the opportunity to plow ahead.

"I had my first Christmas here," he began, speaking too quickly, mushing his words together. "Or at least, it was the first one I could remember at all. It was after breakfast, and the rest of the family was coming through the front there. I remember, 'coz cold air kept sweeping in every time somebody came in with another suitcase. Me and my father were by the fire—right where you and Kait are now, Alice—opening a few last presents, and we didn't have a trash can for the wrapping paper, so we were just—" Benjamin lifted a hand from Alice's leg, mimed a weak throw, "—chucking it into the fire and watching it curl up and burn. And it was so warm there, but I remember being terrified my father would grab one of my gifts and torch it by mistake."

Kaitlyn let out a titter, while Alice cooed and snuggled closer to her beau. "Once he reached for this Superman sweatshirt my Aunt Amanda gave me," Benjamin said, "and I got so spooked, I grabbed it and hid it under my pillow in my room."

Benjamin lifted his wine, staring into the dark purple-red

liquid in the glass. "I wish I still had that shirt," he said. "I wish I could remember more of that day, but that's all I've got. Just those few seconds. But that's it: my first happy memory. That's why I brought you here. I was always happy at this cabin—and I'm happy right now."

He found Alice's hand and threaded his fingers through hers, and Riley felt a sudden and powerful urge to applaud, but instead she pressed her hands to her heart and smiled, trying to thaw her analytic gaze.

"Well, shit," she said. "I didn't know that was gonna be a *cute* story."

There's your face, Benjamin.

Riley shrugged, mock-ruefully. "I take it back, Alice," she continued. "It wasn't a boring question. And that means—" She snatched her half-empty beer off the side table and hoisted a salute. "—that *Riley* drinks."

And drink she did, pouring what was left in the can down her throat while the others cheered. The applause warmed her, but as the Budweiser settled in her stomach, Riley again found herself staring over at Kaitlyn, watching her eyes flick back and forth—from Benjamin's face to Alice's, back to Benjamin's, and finally to Riley herself.

This time Riley averted her gaze, smiling inwardly. She thought she understood, or could be made to understand in time: Kaitlyn's face looked like a cliff of ice collapsing into the ocean. The melting ice was cool and fresh and sweet—but something of enormous beauty had to be destroyed to make it. Riley realized she was watching some manner of tremendous struggle playing out in the little movements of the other girl's eyebrows and cheeks and lips, the nature and scope of which she could only guess at. What could Kaitlyn want so badly?

And what inside her was she so willing to kill to get it?

Riley frowned, reaching blindly behind her for the torn-open box of Budweiser. She'd find out. Maybe now, maybe later—

but she'd learn the truth eventually. This is why she played the game. She cracked open a fresh beer, and the carbonation hissed angrily, foaming a little at the aperture. This might turn out to be an interesting weekend, after all.

* * *

The game proceeded smoothly from there—from Benjamin back to Alice, to Riley, to Kaitlyn, back to Riley, and to Benjamin yet again—and by ten-thirty or so, spirits were high and the mood was getting woozy. Benjamin had his shirt in his lap, dared by Riley and Alice as a team to play the rest of the game topless, and his neck and shoulders were reddening slightly with his back to the fire. Riley had expected him to refuse the dare, but Benjamin had surprised her, grinning cheekily as he stripped off both sweater and plaid button-down in a single smooth movement. The transition mussed his hair and set his glasses askew, but all Riley saw were the blocky shoulders and the long, smooth muscles of the upper arms. The effect was transformative, as though a bulky football mascot had removed its huge foam head to reveal not a sweaty geek but a young Ryan Gosling, and Riley, five beers in and drinking straight from the bottle of Merlot now, was finding it difficult not to stare.

But it wasn't just Benjamin's physique that caught her eye. As the game wore on, Kaitlyn was becoming more and more visibly agitated. She answered one Truth but swatted away two Dares outright, slugging down her penalty beers bravely but with perceptible disgust. Riley guessed she was used to fruitier drinks, or hadn't been a big drinker to begin with.

Or she just hasn't got a stomach for the stuff, she mused. *Jeez, if she's a lightweight, I almost feel bad. This isn't a game for greenhorns.*

But the night seemed to be getting to Kaitlyn. When it was her turn to choose, she always turned to Alice, sometimes going whole minutes without even glancing at another face around the circle. Her Dares were tame and half-formed, but her Truths were stranger: each question seemed calculated, probing—but never after any strange story or kinky secret. Instead she asked after little things in Alice's life, small, personal stories that seemed of no consequence even to Alice herself, who answered gamely but seemed confused by the other girl's line. *Don't you remember?* she would say. *You were there, Kaity.* Or, more often, *We were there together.*

And all the while, Kaitlyn was getting drunker. She weaved her head in a kind of figure eight, eyes closed, legs folded in front of her, the sides of her head tapping first Alice's shoulder, then Riley's. She seemed to be collecting herself, working up the courage to ask one last big Truth—but now it was a race between her stomach and her heart, to see if she could work up the gumption before she passed out in Riley's lap. For her part, Riley went easy on her, steering easy questions and cheap dares her way whenever she could. Now more than ever, she wanted to know what was moving the clockwork behind that thin, frowning face.

And then, at last, the moment seemed to be upon them. Kaitlyn soldiered her way through a middling dare—to pose provocatively with the stuffed buck head from the wall while the rest of the group took pictures—and after she had rubbed the fur off her lips, she stood on tiptoe to return Bambi to his hook, slurring, "I'll call you," to hoots and laughter from the others. Then she swiveled, bouncing on her toes with her hands behind her back. Her mouth smiled, but her face was a hard white mask as her eyes swept across the three bodies by the fire, until at last she said, "Alice."

"Truth," Alice began to say, but before the word could form, Benjamin hollered, "Just you hold on a moment." His voice was thick, and he struggled into a half-crouch, leaning against the sofa as he turned to face Kaitlyn. "You've given Alice four in a row," he protested. "Lob one at me. Or Riley. Or—"

"Let her ask," Riley hissed with a ferocity that surprised her. Her head felt as thick and heavy as a medicine ball when she adjusted her position on the rug. She felt the mask beginning to slip down over her eyes; she shook herself, but her head kept swimming and spinning.

"All I'm saying," Benjamin continued, "is that there should be a, a House Rule for this sort of thing. No monkey-in-the-middle, or something like that."

"Do you feel left out, Ben?" Kaitlyn had come across the room and was leaning on the back of the couch, her head cocked coyly, propped up on a curled fist.

"Yeah. That's it," Benjamin replied. He got up, sliding onto the middle cushion of the sofa; he was grinning, but his voice was like hard wet sand on a beach. "That's it," he said again. "I'm just feelin' left out over here."

"How can you feel left out?" Kaitlyn demanded, reaching for the beer she'd left on the side table. "You're, you're *dating* her aren't you?"

"I'm just sayin'," Benjamin repeated, "that there should be some kind of rule." The muscles in his chest tightened and slackened, tightened and slackened.

"Let her *ask* already." Here it was again: strain hanging in the air like twine held tight between two fists. Riley felt caught in a loop. What was wrong with them? Couldn't anybody talk to each other in this room without baring teeth? Riley felt a strange and sudden urge to cry out, to *scream*, but her lips hung dead from her jaws, her voice imprisoned behind the mask.

"For th' love of God..." Kaitlyn clapped both hands to her cheeks, smushing her face between them. She turned again to Alice, but Riley didn't hear what she said next. A deep vibration jangled across her right hip, and she clapped her hand to her pocket before rolling to one side to retrieve her phone. Four words flashed across the screen, and a bolt of panic struck her, even through the cotton in her head.

GOT AN ADDRESS FOR ME?

"Hold on," she said, half under her breath. Fuck, fuck, fuck—how had she forgotten? How could she possibly have been this stupid?

A second message appeared under the first:

WON'T MAKE IT TIL TOMORROW AFTERNOON. DON'T WANNA GET LOST IN THE DARK HAHA.

"Benjamin?" Riley began, quickly hiding the phone in her lap. "Would you remind me what the address of this place is again?"

A cold line of sweat wriggled down along the back of her neck while Benjamin looked down at her from the couch, firelight licking off his glasses.

"I don't think I ever told you the address," he replied. "Why?"

"I'm just—" Riley began, then stopped herself. No. This was her mistake. And he'd only demand an answer anyway. "Look, I didn't know what this was when I got invited," she said.

"Riley, who was that on your phone."

She sighed and made a point of meeting his glare head on. "His name is Cormac Kasdan," she said evenly. "He's from school. He's captain of the swim team and—"

Again she stopped herself. This was ridiculous: she felt like she was back in high school, about to bring a boy home for dinner for the first time. *He's very nice, Mommy, really. He gets good grades and goes to church and he's got a dick like an Italian sausage. You'll love him.*

" —and I've invited him to meet us at the cabin tomorrow," she concluded, feeling a little out of breath.

Benjamin blinked. "You didn't," he said. And when she gave no response, he slapped his knees and leaned forward to stand up, but only rose halfway before he sank onto the couch, then, "Well, I guess that's—no. No, it's *not* all right. Goddammit, Riley, *why?* What were you thinking?"

"Like I said," she replied, "I didn't know what this was when Alice invited me. I thought the whole thing was going to be bigger—"

"Oh, of *course* you did." Benjamin heaved to his feet, walking unsteadily towards the back door. "And where is this complete stranger supposed to sleep? Huh? In Kait's bed? On the couch with you? What?" His back was turned, but Riley could see his bare shoulders shaking with anger. "At any rate, no, he can't come here—not that you asked."

"He's already coming," Riley said indignantly. "I told you, he's from school. Left after we did. He's staying with a friend in Virginia, and tomorrow—"

"Then tell him to turn around."

Benjamin's voice was cold, and she could see his face reflected in the glass window of the sliding door, warped and twitching.

"No!" The word came out almost at a scream. "I'm not just..." Anger was rising from her gut, hot and solid and heavy as molten lead, filling her up and turning her blood to steam in her veins. She sputtered drunkenly, making horrible sounds.

And then, in the reflection, she saw Benjamin's face again. The mask dropped down, and rage took her like the first belly-sucking plunge on a roller coaster. His shoulders were shaking and his features were contorted, but it wasn't from anger.

Benjamin was *laughing* at her.

"You're not what?" he asked without turning around. "You're not...?" He cocked his head, but when again she made no reply he half-turned, his face red with mirth. "I'll tell you then. Truth? Okay: What makes you think I wanted you here in the first place?"

The silence that followed crushed like a wave. She could feel every tiny muscle across her trim frame tightening, compressing like springs coiled within her, just as surely as she could feel three pairs of eyes drilling into her as she squeezed her eyes shut. A second passed, then another. The world took a breath and held it.

"You're right," Riley said. "I'm not supposed to be here at

all."

"Ben, *please*," Alice's voice said from somewhere behind her, but Riley was on her feet, stalking through a red haze towards Benjamin. She saw the dim form of Alice following after, but she waved it away before planting her feet right behind where Benjamin was standing.

"I didn't *want* to be here," she hissed. "I didn't *ask* to be here. But you begged me to come—God knows why. Because you didn't *trust* yourselves, I guess, because..."

"Both of you, stop!" Alice had appeared behind her and tried to position herself between Riley and Benjamin, but Riley shouldered her out of the way. "Riley, please don't do this," Alice begged, but the words were coming up, pouring out like thick bile.

"Because of *her!*" She pointed one shaking finger backwards, straight at where she knew Kaitlyn was sitting at the hearth. "Because you couldn't stand to be alone with her—either of you. I don't know what happened between you all, but it's got you all twisted up on the inside—hasn't it? And now you can't stand to be in the same room as each other, but for some reason you can't stand to be apart, either. So you didn't bring along a fourth wheel, Benjamin. You hired a *babysitter*."

Kaitlyn let out a gasp of anger, and to Riley's right, Alice made a strange wet sound but made no more attempts to stop the confrontation. Riley's fists were shaking by her sides, but in the reflection, Benjamin's twisted-up face was still laughing, laughing, laughing...

"When Alice texted me," she said, "I was so fucking happy..." Now Benjamin faced her, laughing no longer, but studying her coolly. Somehow this was worse—*Yell at me!* she wanted to scream. *Call me names, call me a bitch, a slut, a drunk.* Anything but laugh, anything but that blank, alien face.

"I thought somebody had *seen* me, you know?" she continued. "Seen who I was, or *past* who I was, and thought, that girl should stick around some. Why did you ask me to come here?" Every new word that came out was slow and heavy. Speaking felt like dredging the bottom of an ocean with a weighted net, dragging through sand and thick silt and the crushing weight of water. "I'm no good for this. I'm sorry—I can't do what you want from me. I can't *fix* you."

At this, Benjamin tilted his head, seeming to consider the words. "Then we're both disappointed," he said, shrugged, and began to laugh again.

Then Alice let out another strangled cry, and this time, Kaitlyn parroted the sound. Riley heard her leap to her feet, as well as the sound of beer hissing as it spilled, followed by the thump of bare feet on floorboards. "Alice!" Riley heard her say.

But Alice was gone. The door to Kaitlyn's room banged open—Riley caught a glimpse of a cloud of retreating red hair, as well as Kaitlyn herself in pursuit. Then she and Benjamin were alone in the den, alone with the dying fire. Benjamin had stopped laughing: he looked strangely stunned, unsteady on his feet, and his eyes darted back and forth from the slamming door to Riley's face and back as though he didn't know where he was.

"What happened?" he mumbled through what sounded like a mouthful of peanut butter. "Where'd they go? Where's Alice?"

"She's gone," Riley murmured, similarly thick-voiced. Ice-cold panic filled her like a foot in a sock, pushing inside in the wake of her spent rage. Her entire body trembled, shivers running in sheets down her arms and the backs of her thighs, and her lips felt thick and dry. She'd done this. She could see it all clearly. Another night gone sour, just when things were going so well—because of her. Only she knew what the buttons did when you pushed them—and Riley had pushed them all. If only...

Yes—'if only.'

But it's always 'if only' with you, isn't it? If only you hadn't drunk so much. If only you'd asked how the punch was mixed. If only you hadn't kissed him. If only you'd just said 'no' for once in your life.

If only you'd kept your big mouth shut.

She felt Benjamin's confused and searching eyes on her as she brushed past him, slid open the cabin's back door, and stumbled out into the frigid air, her hand brushing against his bare flank for only the briefest instant. The night was starless, but the waxing moon was visible through the bare trees and rendered almost amorphous by the clouds. Riley leaned against the cabin's back wall, a cigarette finding its way between her lips as she patted the pockets of her jean jacket for her lighter. But the Zippo was inside, left on the breakfast nook table or buried deep in her purse, and Riley wouldn't, couldn't, go back to fetch it. Not with them. Not with Kaitlyn and Alice huddled in a bedroom picking her corpse clean with their whispers. Not with Benjamin and his sad, puzzled eyes waiting for her in the den.

His *strange* eyes.

How had it happened? She had seen his face, hadn't she? Teased it out of him, the way she always did? But he had laughed at her, *mocked* her, transformed like a banana shedding its peel— and then somehow reverted, collapsing inward, looking as lost as a lamb in an empty field. How had she missed that?

How had she gotten it all so *wrong?*

Riley patted her pockets once more but, finding no lighter, flicked the cigarette away into the darkness beyond the back porch. A low sob rang out into the night, and after a few moments there was nothing she could do to hold the tears back.

But some time later—how long, she couldn't tell—she shivered and ventured a glance through the sliding glass door into the lit den. No sign of Benjamin, and the fire was all but ashes in the hearth. He was in his own bedroom, she figured, or gone to comfort the other two girls. The coast, at least for the moment, was clear.

She put a hand on the door handle, then paused. She didn't want to walk back inside only for all three to come through the door and confront her at once, but she didn't have any choice. She could not stay out here in the cold forever. Sooner or later, she was going to have to face the music and dance.

But just as she was about to throw open the sliding door, Kaitlyn burst out of her bedroom with a clatter. Her eyes were wide and rolling like a spooked horse, and before Riley could duck back out of sight, Kaitlyn zeroed in on her and half-sprinted up to the door, slipping and sliding on her stocking feet.

"Riley!" she hissed through the glass. "You've gotta come inside. Right now."

"I'm coming—" she began to say, but not before the other girl yanked open the door and practically dragged her through by both arms. Riley stumbled against the doorjamb, stubbing a sock-clad toe on the wooden partition, but the pain was numbed by the cold and drink in her belly. "I said I was coming in," Riley mumbled, a little irritably despite the tear-streaks still gleaming on her face. "No need to get grabby."

"Did you hear anything out here?" Kaitlyn asked, ignoring both her and her tears.

"What?" But Kaitlyn was barely listening; she twisted her neck around, casting frenzied glances first at her bedroom door, then Benjamin and Alice's, both closed tight. Then she grabbed Riley by the lapels of her jean jacket and pulled her closer, so close their faces were nearly touching and Kaitlyn was breathing Budweiser in her face.

"He's here," she slurred. "He's *inside the cabin.*"

"Who?" Riley asked. "What are you talking about? Where are Benjamin and Alice?"

"I heard him," Kaitlyn moaned, again ignoring her. "You gotta believe me. He knocked... on my door. Just now. He *talked* to me. It wasn't his voice but, Goddammit, I *know* it was him."

She tugged Riley's jacket, pulling her even closer, almost like she would try to climb into Riley's lap. "You believe me, don't you, Riley?" she whispered. "You know I wouldn't lie about something like this, don't you?"

"To be honest, I don't know," Riley replied, trying her best to free herself from the other girl's grip. There was a funny feeling stirring in the pit of her stomach, warm and heavy like a good meal or a shot of bourbon. "Now, girlfriend, you'd better tell me what's going on," she said, "or I'm gonna lose it. *Who's* here? Who are you talking about?"

Kaitlyn opened her mouth to reply, but before she could speak, Benjamin's bedroom door creaked open an inch or two. Kaitlyn turned her head, staring into the deep shadow beyond the door, but nobody emerged. The doorway remained empty. But when she finally spoke, the words that fell from her lips seemed burdened with unspeakable horror, and even though to Riley it was the name of an utter stranger, the words still made the warm thing inside her twitch and coil.

"My ex," Kaitlyn said in a voice like powdered glass. "The boy from the gas station."

And then, in an even softer voice:

"Lutz Visgara."

Chapter 6

Jill

Kait held her breath. She watched Riley blink once, twice, three times, and then the other girl's stunned expression melted into a mixture of concern and exhausted relief. For a split-second, Kait felt relief wash over her as well—but then she saw the pitying twist of Riley's lips as she smiled fondly at Kait, and panic bloomed inside her once more, bursting like a balloon in her stomach. A thought fluttered through her head like a bat through a cave:

She thinks I'm crazy.

And if I didn't know better—I'd say she had a point.

"Oh, Kaitlyn," Riley began in a mothering tone. "This is all my fault."

"What are you talking about?" Kait yelped. Her hands were still clenched in fists around the lapels of Riley's denim jacket, but the taller girl took hold of her wrists and gently eased her grip away. "Don't talk like that. This hasn't got anything to do with you."

"But it does," Riley persisted. "I pushed you to drink. I didn't know your limits. And now... Well, *listen* to you."

"I know it sounds impossible..." Kait hissed.

But it's true, she wanted to say. She had *heard* it, clear as the blast of a car alarm. She and Alice had been in her dark bedroom, with Alice curled up and shaking oddly on the bed and Kait standing awkwardly in the corner, trying to comfort her. It was a dance they'd done dozens of times as children, but tonight the words had refused to come to the surface. The best she'd managed was a friendly pat between Alice's shoulder blades, but she couldn't shake the feeling that something had changed in the equation: Alice wasn't crying, exactly—just kind of trembling,

69

making no noise. Kait had never seen her do this before, and the sight almost disgusted her, though she couldn't name the reason.

And then, across the silent room, somebody had knocked on the door.

"Are you all right in there, Heart-Brecker?"

The sound struck at her marrow, and for a single, terrifying instant Kait feared she might actually crack in two. The voice was all wrong, but the cadence, the musical bounce of the words, could only come out of one person. And that name: *Heart-Brecker*. This was a sobriquet that belonged to Lutz and Lutz alone. She remembered hating the nickname at first—and then for four months, she hadn't been able to hear it often enough. But to hear it here, in this darkness? It was enough to freeze her heart, to turn her intestines to jelly, even as her head continued to spin and throb in the grip of the beer she'd drunk.

Just beyond the door, the voice heaved a deep sigh, and Kait heard what sounded like a forehead tapping against the wood. "You're busy in there, I can tell," said the voice behind the door. "Well, I can wait. Come on out when you're ready to talk seriously." And then she heard retreating footsteps and the sound of a door creaking, and the presence vanished into thin air.

Kait couldn't count the long seconds she waited, frozen on her knees next to the bed. Alice had stopped trembling, but she made no sound, gave no sign that she had heard the sound that had struck Kait so. So at last she forced herself to her feet with a tremendous thrust of will and exploded through the door, determined to catch her ex slinking away—but she'd seen only Riley, slinking *in*, and Ben was nowhere to be seen.

"Kaitlyn?" Riley began again, now in a slightly more jovial tone. "How far away are we from that gas station?"

Quick-blooded fury flashed behind Kait's eyes, mixing and pooling with her panic. But as she cast a furtive glance over her shoulder, all she could do was repeat, "I know it sounds crazy." Her own bedroom door was snugly shut, but Ben's was still hanging ajar, oozing darkness.

"And how far are we from the closest town?" Riley continued. "The closest... anything?"

"*I know!*" Kait snapped. "I did the math. I know how this sounds. But—"

"How does it sound, Kaitlyn?"

Kait balled her hands into fists. Her tone had been gentle, but there was something mocking in Riley's face—in the twist of her mouth or the angle of her brows. Or maybe it ran deeper than that: maybe it was lurking just behind her eyes. Heat roared in Kait, bullying her like a kite in beach wind, but she smothered the feeling behind a forced smile. Now was not the time to lose her cool, she reminded herself. She needed help—and Riley had been nice to her this far. Maybe she'd imagined that sneering look. Maybe she'd imagined everything.

"It sounds insane," she admitted. "But you didn't—"

"It sounds *drunk*," Riley countered. Again her expression softened—*I must have imagined it, after all*, Kait reasoned—and she put a hand on Kait's knee, squeezing it gently. "You had a little scare back at the gas station, and now you've gone and scared yourself all over again. But it's okay," she continued. "Sometimes the bad stuff comes back. Sometimes it happens to me too. Maybe it happens to everybody."

"But it..." Kait wavered. Riley blinked at her expectantly. "But it felt so real," she finished, her voice limp in her mouth.

"That's how it always is," Riley admitted. "Listen—I don't know what you heard, but if it makes you feel safer tonight, I'll come sleep in the bedroom with you. Would you like that?"

"I—" But before Kait could fully reply, her bedroom door creaked open and Alice emerged, blinking and squinting in the light. "Kaity..." she mumbled, searching the room for her. "You out here?"

"I'm here," Kait said in a small voice.

Alice's eyes found her and seemed to focus, zeroing in on her friend. "Are you okay?" she asked. "You kind of... took off, there."

"I'm..." Kait paused, turning from Alice to Riley, to Alice to Riley again. Her head spun, but she caught Riley mouthing 'yes' and aping a big smile. "I'm fine," she said at last. "I just scared myself, I think. It's nothing to worry about."

Alice nodded, half to herself, and then tottered on her feet. "I've had a lot to drink," she said suddenly. "Too much," she added. Then: "I'm going to bed."

"Good night, girlfriend!" Riley sang out. "I'll bring you some water in a minute. You don't want to get dehydrated."

Alice nodded again and wobbled across the den, past the ash-filled hearth before pushing open her bedroom door with her face and kicking it shut behind her. Kait rose to her feet without a word and padded into her own bedroom, sparing only a backwards wave over her shoulder to Riley. The truth was, she felt ashamed—but more than that, she was head-tired and head-sick. The room kept tilting sideways on her, and at that precise moment, there was nothing she could think of that would suit her better than a good old-fashioned coma. She shoved her door closed with her toe and collapsed into bed, feeling sleep clawing at her aching eyes. Moments later, the light clicked off and the crack beneath her door went dark—Riley getting ready for bed as well.

She's right, Kait told herself. *She has to be right. Lutz wouldn't come here. He's got to be done with me—and I'm done with him. And that's how the story ends.*

But as she wriggled under the blankets and squeezed her eyes shut, she let her right hand dangle to the floor, brushing her fingers along the smooth cool wood of the stock of the Model 94. Her fingers twitched, again full of a memory she could only half-claim, and before she knew it, she was swinging her legs over the edge of the bed and kneeling on the floor next to the big hunting rifle.

I imagined it, I know I did, she repeated to herself.

But just in case I'm wrong...

With sure, practiced movements, Kait loaded a single cold bullet into the gun in her hands and slammed the chamber closed once more.

* * *

Through a deep fog, Kait drifted—and through a gap in the dense clouds an image floated into view: a wooden doorframe, hanging in space, opening into darkness. A light flickered on just inside, and soon after Kait could hear voices drifting out across the void, the words wriggling painfully into her ears like squirming maggots burrowing into soft soil. Beyond the door, the scenario began to take shape, and Kait waited, suspended in the fog, for the curtain to rise and the show to begin.

"Wait right there," Lutz said. "There's somebody I want you to meet."

They were seated on the purple futon couch in Lutz's one-bedroom apartment downtown, Kait with her tennis shoes kicked up on the cheap coffee table and sipping a beer from the bottle. Lutz stood, stretched with a grunt, then ambled across the den to the door leading to his tiny bedroom and disappeared inside. Kait preoccupied herself looking around the bits of the flat she could see. She had never been inside Lutz's apartment before—their previous flings and flirtations had all taken place in her dormitory bedroom or in the backseats of parked cars.

The space in which she found herself now was almost comically masculine: hardboiled action movie posters crammed in cheapo plastic frames littered the walls, and the white laminate countertops were besieged by empty beer bottles and cans and half-empty bags of chips and pretzels. A set of adjustable dumbbell weights—something Kait was quite convinced Lutz had never used more than a few times— lay in a heap in one corner of the room, resting atop a balled-up dingy green towel. Aside from these ornaments, the apartment was entirely undecorated and under-furnished: besides the couch she sat on, the coffee table, the TV stand and television, and a pair of beat-to-hell folding chairs, the den was a furniture desert. Lutz's apartment looked like her then-boyfriend had just been robbed.

But what surprised her the most about the apartment were the two street signs hanging from the eggshell-colored walls, one above the entranceway, and the other over Lutz's bedroom door on the outside. The first read LUTZ CIRCLE; the second, VISA GARA BLVD. Kait—the real, dreaming Kait, not the fabrication waiting patiently on the hideous purple sofa—remembered wondering how he'd managed to steal them, and why he'd done it. She remembered all this through a deep and complex haze, and even the simple act of conjuring the images of the street signs left her head feeling like a wet paper bag.

"Hi, Kaity," said a voice from down the hall.

"Don't call me that..." Kait began, almost on instinct, but she paused, looking down the passageway towards the source of the voice.

A tall young woman with very dark hair was padding down the hall towards the den, dressed in a brown bathrobe drawn tight around her waist. There were dark purple-black bags under her eyes, but Kait's gaze was drawn quickly to the smile on her face, which was so lopsided and goofy, it reminded her enough of Lutz to guess at a family resemblance. But no—on second glance, the face was too long, the hair was too straight, the eyes too small... plus her skin was a full shade darker than Lutz's, who was whiter than bread mold.

The bathrobe slipped down around the girl's shoulders, and beer splashed down the front of Kait's sweatshirt as she jumped to her feet, stumbled, and sat back down again. There was nothing beneath. No clothes, no bra—only smooth, perfect, bronze skin.

"Don't call me that," was all she could think to say. "Only one person calls me that."

"I know," the woman replied, still grinning. "Lutz told me all about you."

"Is that a fact," said Kait, making an effort to stand once more while averting her eyes. "Yeah, Lutz told me a little something about you too. About how you—hey, Lutz?" she hollered down the hall. "Lutz? I'm panicking. I want you to know there's a very serious chance that I'm panicking right now."

"Well, *stop* panicking," Lutz called back, his voice muffled by distance. "There's no reason to panic."

"There's a woman in here who's wearing your bathrobe."

"Her name's Jill Cicero," came the reply.

"Fine—there's a *Jill Cicero* in your den wearing your bathrobe."

"She's in town for the week," Lutz called back, "and she's an old family friend, so they asked me to put her up a few days. She just got off the plane, but I wanted you to meet her now, before the school week started back up."

"Bullshit, she's from out of town," Kait spat. "Lutz, she's not wearing any *clothes!*"

"Does it make you uncomfortable?" asked Jill Cicero, still smiling that lopsided smile.

"You stay out of this!" Kait barked. She felt like she was losing control; reality was sliding though her grip like fine sand.

"She's from California," Lutz replied, as if this were answer enough. Then, after a deep sigh: "That's why I'm having you meet her now. I don't want you to think she's a threat. At least," he continued, popping his head around the corner of the hall, "not in, like, the existential sense. You know what I mean?"

"Try to relax," said Jill, circling the coffee table to plop down on the hideous couch next to Kait. Kait squirmed away, but her limbs felt like tubes of putty.

"You're all worked up over nothing," Lutz said, sinking down to sit on Kait's opposite side. His skinny, birdlike chest was bare, his black Iron Maiden T-shirt slung over one arm like a waiter. "I promised I would explain everything, didn't I?"

"I want the two of us to be friends," Jill added.

"Friends…" Kait parroted, removing her hands from her face at last.

But when Jill spoke, she spoke in Lutz's voice… Horror jolted through her like a crossbow bolt. *She has Lutz's voice. And now she had Lutz's face too.*

The lights flickered and sparked, the fog swirled threateningly, and Kait, the dreaming Kait, felt herself lifting, surging up and up and up towards the gleaming hard surface of the sea.

"I don't want you to think I have any kind of agenda here, Heart-Brecker," she heard Lutz's voice say, somewhere in the far distance.

* * *

"I'm just doing what I feel like I have to do."

Kait turned in her sleep, drifting up, out of the gloom, thrashing and striking out with an open hand—and at the height of her swing, her palm connected with a solid object. A chin, bristling with stubble, floating in mid-air above her bed. She recoiled with a yelp, but before she could wake enough to really scream, a strong hand clamped down across her mouth and made her swallow her cry. Her eyes flew open to see shadows scurrying crazily across the four walls of her little bedroom, cast by the white-hot light of a smartphone flashlight. And in these shadows she could see her own vague silhouette, dancing across flat space and bending like a postcard whenever it slid across a corner—plus the even vaguer form of a second person's head, just above or just behind her own.

There was somebody in the bed with her.

His weight shifted, bending the mattress beneath his knees; Kait could hear his heavy breaths, feel them hot on her cheek, ragged with the effort of controlling her mouth and head. A second hand tightened around her shoulder, the rigid forearm barred across her chest, forcing her to roll face-up. The shadows leaped, and she struck out with the hand that had found the intruder's cheek, but her blows hit blind air or were smothered against the bare, heaving chest. Her other hand was trapped beneath the blankets, pinned by the weight looming above her.

"You know," said a voice in the dark, "you're a hard woman to reach."

Kait screamed—but the hand over her mouth only tightened. She felt like the blankets were constricting around her, squeezing in like a cocoon. The pressure from above increased, and Kait, now firmly pinned beneath the weight of the intruder, felt a big smooth hand stroking her arm through the sheet, running down to the ticklish spot just inside her right elbow.

"I didn't mean to scare you at the gas station," said Lutz— only it *wasn't* Lutz, not his voice, not his weight, not his hands, all wrong, wrong, wrong. "Although, from the looks of things, you're plenty scared now, huh?"

Kait's skull felt like a hive of shaken bees: she couldn't move, couldn't speak, couldn't think, couldn't *breathe* around the hand across her face. She could feel the dull pressure of his hand moving down her arm to her hip and across her thigh; the cell phone light was pointed straight up at the ceiling now, swaying crazily with the motion of the bed. His shadow surged upwards, spectral and looming, expanding like a cloud of gas.

But then his weight shifted just right, and Kait's right hand squirted free of the blanket. Frantically, she reached down through the darkness, her fingertips dragging along the floor, searching blindly until—*yes*. Her fist closed around something cold and solid and heavy, and she brought it screaming upwards in a wide crazy arc...

"We're going to talk through this like reasonable people," Lutz said. "I'm going to show you I can be reasonable. I'm going to show you just how reasonable I can—"

The Winchester Model 94 struck him across the side of the skull with a sickening crack, and Lutz loosened his grip and seemed to drift sideways, moving as though through deep water, uttering only a low moan of pain as he fell. Kait rose, shouldering him off the bed as she swung off it herself, the stock of the rifle cuddling into her shoulder as though it had a mind of its own. Her breath came in sharp, gasping barks, and her chest ached as though there had been tight wire mesh squeezing around her lungs that had only now been stripped away.

The light from the phone had stopped bouncing, and just beyond its broad beam she could make out a quivering form on the floor just behind the bed, blood matted in the hair and trickling down one pallid temple. Another groan floated up from between the bruised lips, and Lutz's shoulders heaved as he attempted to stand, but Kait's fingers found the lever and pulled—and in the tiny dark room, the noise of the gun readying to fire sounded like the hard knock of thunder.

"Don't you move," Kait snarled, her chest heaving. "Don't you *fucking* move."

The form on the floor obeyed, sinking lower behind the bed as though it could disappear, just sink into the floor and vanish forever. She skirted the bed, circling towards the door where the light switch was. "How's it feel, huh? I've *got* you, you son of a bitch. How does it feel? How does it fucking *feel?*" Kait's right shoulder brushed against the wall; now she'd have to take her hand off the trigger to find the switch. She could hear muffled voices through the door, and the shuffling of sock-feet approaching.

Here they come, she thought to herself.

And then, crazily: *And a Happy Valentine's Day to you, Alice.*

Out loud, she said, "Here's how reasonable I can be. You

move, and I'll blow your fucking head off." And as Alice and Riley burst through the door beside her, Kait took her hand off the trigger guard just long enough to flick the switch up and bathe the bedroom in light.

But as her vision cleared, Alice and Riley let out simultaneous gasps of horror and rushed past her into the room—and Kait's heart dropped in her chest like a lump of lead. The body behind the bed was once again struggling to rise, but as the bruised and bloodied head reared into view, the face blinking in the sudden light did not belong to Lutz Visgara.

"I promise this isn't what it looks like," Ben gurgled through a mouthful of blood.

Chapter 7

Ben Alden Walks Under the Moon

– thirty minutes ago –

Ben barely made it through the bathroom door before the contents of his stomach churned, heaved, and beat a grisly escape up his esophagus and into the dark bowl of the toilet. He sank to his knees, pitched forward, his hands white-knuckle tight on the rim of the bowl, panting heavily and trying with all his might not to think about the slosh of his vomit hitting the surface of the water seconds before. He stayed there, kneeling as if in worship, for perhaps ten minutes, feeling the cold laminate beneath his bare knees as the dark bathroom swirled around him in dizzying circuits.

When his stomach quit tossing, he thought to himself, he was going to strangle Riley Loomis for doing this to him. Twice, if he could manage it.

Finally he stood, stifling a groan so as not to wake Alice, who was snoring in the next room. He hadn't heard her come in; he'd gone to bed in a blue drunken haze, his senses and passions dulled as though beneath a carpet of thick foam. But now that his belly was empty, the fog began to clear, and fractured images from the evening before began to creep in, each poking at the dying fire that was all that remained of his anger. Names rolled around in his head like small steel bearings, colliding, clacking together, sending off showers of sparks: Riley. Alice. Kait. *Lutz Visgara.* This last name he mumbled aloud, which sent up alarm flares. Why should he think of him now, of all times? When the name tumbled from his mouth, it was like finding a gun you didn't remember buying stashed in your sock drawer. Alarming at first, perhaps—but perhaps oddly fortuitous as well, if you were looking for a gun.

Ben flushed the toilet and staggered sideways to the sink, first running cool water over his hands, then cupping them and sucking the water into his mouth and swishing. It came to him just as the first needle of pain skewered his temple—the beginnings of what promised to be a barnstorming hangover. Where, exactly, had things gone volcanic last night? He could remember the sounds of shouting, feel them ringing bright and sharp in his ears, but he could barely recall a single word that had been thrown against him. Every minute past nine wavered in limbo, lost in the plane between memory and invention, a stark photographic negative of a night.

But still those four names rattled in his head, around and around and around.

Riley. Alice. Lutz.

Kait fucking Brecker.

He spat, cupped again, swished again, spat again. Kait—he could picture her clearly, standing on tiptoe, turning around with the hunting rifle cradled in her arms. He could feel, again, the drop of his stomach as she'd thrust the gun into his hands, his arms going numb with fear as he felt the terrible weight of the weapon in his grip. He saw her smirking across the dinner table at him, then again across the circle of bodies at Truth or Dare, saw it so clearly he could swear she was there with him in the bathroom, close enough to touch...

And now she was sleeping. Sleeping, while he shivered in the darkness, puking and trying not to wake his girlfriend—if she *was* his girlfriend anymore, after last night.

Ben's stomach churned, but the wave of nausea was quickly swept away by a new sensation: though the bathroom and the water on his hands and face were very cold, a small ember of warmth was beginning to glow deep in his guts, smooth and fluid and probing, pushing small tendrils of heat into his darker corners. Ben stood frozen, exploring this new feeling—but as the minutes passed, he began to struggle against it, though it was like wrestling with a bonfire. This warm thing inside of him, it wanted to grow. It wanted to take him again.

It wanted to show him something.

Ben's hands rose, switched off the faucet, wiped his lips. His eyes had adjusted to the dark at last, and the room suddenly swung into sharp focus. There was a mirror hanging just above the sink, and Ben could see the entire bathroom rendered in the reflection. But he could not see his own face. Only a dim blob where he knew he stood, only a vague shadow where his features ought to be. His limbs felt thick and heavy, as though his flesh was a suit of clothes one size too large, and there was no feeling in them anymore. But he could see, or at least sense, when his right hand swung up slowly, open palmed, and when it was right in front of his face it squeezed into a tight fist.

Never stop making her pay, Benji-Boy.

"Who's there?" he cried out—but the sounds would not come up. His lips rebelled, his tongue lay dormant in the groove of his jaw. But his body was in motion: He took two soft steps back from the mirror and turned, padding back into his bedroom, a passenger within his own flesh. The warmth had spread, pushing out into his arms and legs, rising even to the surface of his skin as it surged through him.

Alice had stopped snoring. As Ben moved past their bed, she let out a low sigh and mumbled, "Ben?" her voice thick and hoarse with fatigue.

"Go back to sleep."

Alice sat up—out of the corner of his eye, Ben could sense her broad silhouette rising from the bed, her hair clown-crazy as she yawned and rubbed her eyes. "Did you throw up?" she asked. "Sounded pretty bad in there."

"Go back to sleep, Alice," he repeated. His hand was inches from the doorknob.

"Did you..." Alice paused, seemed to steel herself. "Do you

feel better now? After all that?" she asked. "To get it all out?" And when no reply came, she sighed again and sank back to her pillow. "I want us to talk to them tomorrow," she murmured. "Riley and Kaity. To apologize to them, y'know? I can't get what Riley said out of my head." Still Ben said nothing. "Anyway, I'll talk to Riley, but you and Kaity..."

Another pause followed, but when Ben's fist tightened around the door handle, Alice said, in a small sad voice: "I want you to promise me, Ben."

At this, Ben turned, feeling his cheeks push up in a lopsided smile. "I'll talk to her," he said. "You're right. It's the right thing to do." He shuffled around the corner of the double bed, sitting down on the comforter next to Alice as she slid her feet aside to make room for him. His hand snaked under the sheets, found hers, squeezed the fingers affectionately.

"You know I love you," he said, "don't you, Alice?"

Alice shifted on the bed, her hand going clammy in his. "You've never said that to me before," she murmured. "You... I mean, do you mean it?"

"Of course I do."

"All right." She pulled her hand out of his grip, only to thread her fingers through his. "Then... Then I love you, too, Ben." And with that her grip slackened, and she rolled back over as if to sleep, though her breathing seemed to catch in her chest. "And... you'll talk to her tomorrow?" she asked, more confidently this time.

Ben leaned down and kissed his girlfriend on the cheek. "It's tomorrow now," he replied. Then he rose from the bed and padded silently out of the room.

The time was 3:08 a.m.

The den was gloomy but not dark as he swung the bedroom door closed behind him, easing the catch into place so as not to disturb Alice or wake Riley. There was a moon in the back window, a frowny-faced sliver of white, flooding the back half of the cabin with dull silver light that seemed to suck the color out of everything it touched. Riley lay sprawled on the leather sofa, a throw blanket with a fringe covering her body to the waist; even in the gloom, Ben's eyes could make out the swell of her bosom rising and falling as she slept, lying there on her back with one arm flung up just behind her head. Her blonde hair, rendered silver-brown by the moonlight, fanned out across her pillow like a hand of cards, and her other arm dangled off the sofa, trailing on the rug with her fingertips inches from a crushed beer can lying on its side.

But all this Ben took in with a mere cursory glance as he crept forward, shuffling his feet, avoiding creaky boards and crumpled empties with a cat's grace, even though his limbs felt like soft lead. In moments, he had crossed the entire room and found himself standing before the other bedroom door, staring above it at the empty gun rack. Then he leaned forward, pressed his ear to the cool wood of the door, and listened.

He could hear her breathing through the door.

Passion sprang up in him; his heart beat very fast, and chills scurried down his flanks and the insides of his legs, though the core of him, the warm point of twinkling light holed up in his gut, remained unaffected, like a candle shielded from the wind. His hands twitched. He wanted to throw the door open, to tear it off its hinges with all the cruel leverage his body could employ, but instead he pressed a palm to the knob, teasing the door open with only the quietest of clicks. Behind him, Riley stirred but did not wake, and no cry of alarm rose up from the bedroom beyond—and now he was staring into the darkness, at the double bed that stretched nearly the entire length of the tiny cabin room, and at its single occupant curled up in a tight ball beneath the sheets and breathing softly...

There he stood: framed in the open doorway, the moon at his back, cooling his heels on the bare boards. As the silence settled, he became aware of a clock ticking somewhere else in the house, and a little later, an owl hooted out in the forest. Soon his legs began to ache, but he did not lean against the doorframe or even shift his weight from one foot to the other. He let his breathing slow, matching the rhythm of the soft, steady breaths that rose and fell from the bed not four feet from where he stood. Time passed in easy silence. He breathed in; Kait Brecker breathed out.

And then, as if at some secret signal, he strode forward and shut the door behind him.

* * *

He heard the crack—and the pain that exploded in his left temple shook him like the impact of a tremendous wave. Ben tumbled through open space, feeling weightless and adrift until his shoulder bounced hard off a wall and he crashed, face-first, into the floor. Darkness pressed in from all corners: he tasted copper and something like sunscreen, and when he moved his lips to taste them they cleaved together, sticking like licked stamps. There was something tacky and stiff in his hair; his ears crackled and hummed every time he moved or twitched his head to the left or right. And though his skull felt like a bowling alley on league night, he could hear voices through the roar of agony—somebody shouting, screaming in a high ragged voice, the words crashing like surf over his head:

"Don't you move... Don't you *fucking* move..."

Ben's eyelids flickered: he'd had them squeezed shut and hadn't noticed. The room was beginning to take shape around him, slowly, as though through condensation that was just beginning to burn off under the sun. There was a bed, a nightstand, a window with the curtains drawn and only a wafer-sliver of moon slicing through beneath the gap. His body was wedged down between the bedframe and the wall, with the floor pressing up under his cheek and his legs all jumbled like a marionette's, and somebody was standing above him. Her breathing was raspy, almost shuddering as she moved towards him, inching along the wall on the opposite side of the bed from where he lay.

Kait—he knew at once it was her, both by the sound of her voice and by the feeling of her eyes on him. There could be no mistake. He'd driven ten hours with the girl staring holes in the back of his head. He knew the pressure of her gaze now, but never before had he felt such an abominable chill when she looked at him. And he couldn't even properly see her; the room was dark, and her body was only a shadow floating above him.

Ben's shoulders heaved upward as he struggled to rise, but the sound of a bullet chambering sent him sprawling once more. *Chuk-chok!* A noise he'd only ever heard in movies before this, but the sound was unmistakable—so quiet it was almost a whisper. Like the sound of a key turning inside a well-geared lock. And he'd seen the barrel of that hunting rifle out of the corner of his eye as he slumped to the floor, seen the moonlight glinting off the oiled tip.

The muzzle had been pointed directly between his eyes.

Ben's mind raced, but his thoughts were scattered by fear and the thudding pain in his head. He flicked his eyes from Kait's planted feet to the bedroom door, both dimly visible under the bed skirt. *Have to get away from here. Have to—no. No, have to warn the others. Have to wake Alice and tell her. Tell her that—unless...*

Terror struck him like a fast-acting poison.

Unless she got Alice already.

Unless she's saving me for last.

Ben pressed upwards once more, struggling to climb to his feet, but his trembling muscles betrayed him, refusing to lift his weight more than a few inches off the floor. Hot tears of pain and terror welled up—but even this response failed him. His body simply refused to cry. Instead, he lay twitching beneath the bed, a hundred terrible thoughts pinging through his mind like ricocheting gunfire, but none were louder than the voice of his father, repeating the words he'd said the afternoon Ben learned his high school girlfriend had taken up with another woman:

You should have seen this coming, Benji-Boy.

"Here's how reasonable I can be," Kait was saying. And the last thing that flashed through Ben's head was the ridiculous question of whether or not he should put his hands in the air while he waited for the end to come.

But the end *didn't* come.

Instead, the room exploded with light—and at first, Ben thought this was the impact of the bullet ripping through him, but then the door banged open and there were warm hands slipping under each arm and dragging him awkwardly upward. The hands struggled with his weight and only managed to hoist him into a half-crouch before he collapsed sideways on the bed, and there he lay in a stupor, his head reeling. The air was full of a thick soup of female voices, all talking at once very loudly, mixing in the air like a flock of startled birds.

"...get some water and paper towels, he..."

"...just came in and got on top of me, like..."

"...you could have *killed* him, Kait. You're..."

"...bleeding everywhere. Might even have..."

"...not *listening* to me. I couldn't *stop* him. I had to..."

From there, the conversation was largely muddled: there was blood drying in Ben's ears and over his eyes and lips, but now somebody was sponging it away and putting firm pressure on the cut above his ear, keeping his head still between gentle hands. He was staring straight up into the light on the ceiling, and with the pain in his head and the constant dizzying motion of the room, he felt like he was staring straight into the blinding eye of heaven.

Then his vision cleared somewhat, and he blinked once, twice, letting the wheeling room settle itself. There was a circle of faces staring down at him: Alice in center frame, flanked by Riley on her immediate left—it had been Riley holding his head straight, he realized. Kait looked down on him as well—sidelong, and from farther back in the room. She'd stopped brandishing the rifle, but she still had it tucked down in the crook of her elbow, her other hand white-knuckle tight around the barrel. Her face was flushed up to the roots of her brown hair, and her mouth was set in a short, hard line.

"Pig," she mumbled without moving her lips much, and Alice let out a low wail.

"Shush," Riley barked, steadying him as Ben tried to thrash out of her grip. "Easy, soldier. You're not bleeding so much now, but you might have a concussion. What's your head feel like? You took a bad fall—and a bad hit, too, from the sound of things."

Ben tried to reply, but all he could manage was, "Alice..."

"I'm here!" She pushed Riley aside, taking his head in her hands. Her face was bright red as well, streaked under her eyes, and her voice quivered. "I'm here, baby," she said. "I'm here. Talk to me."

"You..." *You look like an angel,* he wanted to say. *With that light behind you, you look just like an angel.* But instead, all he could gurgle out was, "You... look... good."

"Well, you look terrible," Alice replied, laughing through tears. "You look..." She wiped her eyes on a pink pajama sleeve, sniffing. "I'm just glad you're gonna be all right," she said. "We're gonna take care of you, okay?"

Then her face darkened; her eyes flicked away, to Kait, then back to him. "I just need to hear you say it. All right? Just say it was all a mistake, and—"

"So *ask* him about it," Kait demanded, scowling.

"Kaity..."

"Ask him!" It was almost a scream. Ben winced; Alice wilted, her face drooping as though it would melt off her skull. Even Riley took a step back, her face, smeared with makeup, set in a mask of alarm. But Kait—instead of pressing forwards, she had actually shrunk back into the far corner of the bedroom, holding the rifle across her body like a shield. Her face was still red with rage, but the look in her eyes was all wrong. Wet, staring, almost quivering in their respective sockets. Like she was under a spell.

Like she was afraid of him.

"I want to hear him say it," she said in a voice that trembled. "I want to hear the bastard say he didn't..."

She trailed off. Alice hesitated, looking around the room, but finding no respite from the faces around her, she returned her gaze to him and spoke quickly and breathlessly:

"Did you do it, Ben. Did you attack Kait in her bed."

He opened his mouth to deny it. He *wanted* to deny it. The pain written out on Alice's face—he would have said anything in that moment to take that pain away from her. But the moment she said those words, it was as though there was a flood inside him. His head still throbbed, but now there was a peculiar *feeling* rushing up his torso, down his arms and legs and into each toe and finger, pushing up to the surface of his skin. And with this new, terrible sensation came memory—not words or pictures, but memories of motion, of touch, of muscular contractions and nerve-responses and reflex actions. His body, it remembered what it had done, even if his head could not.

His body remembered everything.

A sudden wave of emotion squeezed the water to his eyes, and for a moment, he could not speak, simply weeping into the silence of the room. His face did not move, only the water flowed from beneath his half-closed eyelids. The ring of faces, rendered in watercolor by his tears, all looked down on him, but nobody spoke. Nobody moved. The stillness in the room was unbearable, and it only made him weep harder. His head ached abominably.

You should have seen this coming, Benji-Boy.

"Ben, I know—" Alice began, but he cut her off. One last time, his lips betrayed him.

"Yes," he said. "Yes, I did it." And speaking those four words made him wish with all his heart that Kait had shot him after all.

Chapter 8

Under the Gun

Kait had waited for the explosion, for the room to erupt with sound, voices crashing against voices in dense, crowded harmonies—so the lull that followed struck her cold. Ben lay belly-up on the bed, his face glistening with tears and sweat, breathing shallowly, his eyes half-shut and full of water. Alice kept hold of his head, but her face had gone rigid, like it might slip forward and slide off in one piece. Riley had interposed herself between Kait and the bed, her arms outstretched as though she would embrace her, but Kait knew from the look on her face that Riley was protecting the boy on the bed from her: the stock of the big hunting rifle had once more nestled itself into the hollow of her shoulder, and though the rest of her body felt like it could shake apart at any moment, the hands gripping the gun were steady as stone. Something flashed in Riley's eyes—a warning and something else besides, something softer, indecision perhaps, though Kait couldn't tell from such a brief glance. But the message was clear, nonetheless: *Nobody moves.*

But I'm faster than her, Kait thought, the alien bit of her, the dark half showing her face from the back of the theater. *If it came down to it, I could be faster with the gun.* The memory lived, cool and quiet, in her fingers and wrists, of how to draw up and fire in an instant, from the hip if necessary, how to be deadly from the word *go*.

But, no, she reasoned. She wouldn't let it come to that. Mad as she was, angry as she was, she was not going to push things that far. She had not come here to kill anybody.

Liar, clucked the whispering voice. *You're holding the gun, aren't you? And you loaded the shot in. If you didn't want to dance, you wouldn't have put on your dancing shoes.*

Alice broke the silence first, her stiff face beginning to crumple. "Ben," she began haltingly. "Ben, please..."

She let her voice die away, choking on the rest of her words. But what remained unspoken was abominably clear: that one word, that "please", held a whole life in its trembling, butterfingered grip. *Please don't say things like that. Please don't be the person they're saying you are. Please, oh God, please let there be some mistake.* Kait had been to services with Alice when they were both small, and she could almost hear the big girl praying with all the strength in her heart, though her mouth did not move silently like it did in church.

And in Kait there sprung up an outlandish compulsion to recant. Watching her friend's face fold in on itself was like watching a priceless Ming vase tumbling end over end towards a hard stone floor in slow motion. If Kait could throw out her hand and stop the disaster, catch Alice before she shattered on impact, that would be worth the lie—wouldn't it? She wouldn't have to say much, just enough to start the ball down the hill. The others would jump over themselves filling in the chinks in her story: That they did not want to believe her accusation went without saying. After all, nobody wanted to doubt Kait Brecker more than Kait Brecker.

But Ben offered no defense, no protest. His blubbering cut through the air, and every time he could catch a breath, all he could say was, "I did it, it was me, it had to be me," over and over again as though he were committing it to memory. Alice had finally broken out into bubbling, body-wracking sobs, and Riley had dropped her arms, looking defeated and drained and maybe even a little bored, fighting back yawns by flexing her jaw.

A strange sense of awkwardness took hold of Kait then. The Model 94 was suddenly heavy in her arms, but she was grateful for its weight: without it, she would never have known what to do with her hands. The urge to bolt, to flee the room, plop down on the couch or, better yet, in Alice's bedroom and dive headfirst into her music library was almost overpowering. What more could she do here? She'd weathered the assault already, and born what witness she could. Surely her being there, her physical presence in the room, was no longer necessary.

And Ben's mewling was starting to work her over—she was actually beginning to feel *sorry* for the bastard, a fact that made her almost as uncomfortable as his hands on her. She felt no fear, now, even being so close to him; the man who had climbed into her bed only minutes ago seemed leagues away from the wretched creature quivering in a heap on the sheets. Compared to that specter, Ben hardly seemed there at all.

"Kaity... What am I gonna do?"

Alice had sunk to the floor in a tangle, her face cast in shadow by her cloud of red hair, and when she turned her head up to speak, her face was demolished by anguish—yes, *demolished* was the correct word. Or *ruined*. Like acid scarring on a stone statue, the features present but blurred, almost nonfunctioning, a mere shadow of what beauty had been.

"We have to call the police," Riley said quietly. "That's what comes next here. I had a little cell reception last night, I can make the call, but you'll have to tell them what happened in your own words sooner or later. We can talk that through first, if—"

"You've done this before," Kait interrupted.

Riley shrugged, and answered simply, "Yes." Then she stepped forward, and Kait barely had time to lower the rifle to her side before she found herself wrapped up in a tight embrace that pinned her arms at her sides.

"You did the right thing," Riley said. "You came through. You *survived*. You—" She broke off; the hug convulsed tighter, and Kait heard her shaking voice say close in her ear, "I should have been there. Been in the room, been listening, heard him go past me in the dark, I should have should have should have..."

She continued on in this fashion for several moments, and

Kait, who could think of nothing to say in reply, simply let herself be hugged until it became difficult to breathe, at which point she shifted her shoulders to signal that she wanted to be released.

"Maybe we should get out of here," she said when Riley's grip slacked at last—but then, over the other girl's shoulder where her chin was wedged, she saw Ben rock forward as though he would rise. His body twisted, the muscles of his bare torso flexing, and he got up on one elbow, swiped at his wet face with the back of his other hand, and blinked, first at Alice on the ground, and then at the two girls grappling near the bedroom door. His face had been rosy before from crying, but now, under the tears, all the color had gone out of his cheeks. His eyes were perfectly round and seemed to protrude aggressively from his skull, and they swept around the room, searching for something seemingly only Ben could perceive.

"Where are you?" he cried out suddenly in a great hollow voice.

Alice picked her head up once more, but before any of them could react, Ben was on his feet and stumbling forward, his eyes now locked on Kait. Kait shook loose of Riley's embrace and on instinct hoisted the Model 94 to her shoulder, but instead of recoiling, Ben seized the barrel of the hunting rifle in both hands with supernatural swiftness—and pressed the muzzle right between his eyes.

"BEN!"

The scream tore loose from Alice's lips—or maybe the scream was Kait's own, such was her shock. Alice scrambled to her feet, but Kait was only dimly aware of the motion. Ben sank to his knees, pulling the rifle down with him, nearly yanking Kait off her feet. She quickly adjusted her grip, keeping her finger quite clear of the trigger. Blood roared in her ears.

"I need you to listen to me, Kait," Ben said very slowly.

"All right." Kait's heart turned over once, like a cold car

engine, heavy in her chest. "You've got my attention. What do you want?"

"I know you don't... care for me much," he began, his eyes locked on hers, staring up the oiled length of the gun barrel. "I know you don't. And it's no secret I don't like you either. We've been at each other's throats this whole trip. Alice's been on me for that, and I'm willing to take blame for it. But you've got to believe me—Kait, *I would never hurt you like this*. You understand that, don't you? That I'm not... not *capable* of—"

"But you are," Kait interrupted, suddenly feeling as though the world had turned itself upside-down. "You *did*. You came into my room—you admitted it, we all heard you." She looked around the room at the faces of the others, half-expecting them to shake their heads, to deny it—or worse, have their faces transformed, Lutzes all, like the faces of her dreams.

"I know I did," Ben replied, nodding against the gun. "And, yes... I came in here, but I wouldn't *do* that, you understand? Not consciously."

"Jesus Christ—then you were sleepwalking?" Kait sneered. "Is that what you want me to believe?" At this, Ben's grip loosened around the rifle barrel and he nearly burst into tears again.

Maybe I should shoot him, she thought. *Put him out of his misery. Or shut him up, at least.*

"Not that," came the reply at last. "Not sleepwalking. Not exactly. I only mean that I wasn't in control..."

"Bullshit," Riley murmured from a far corner.

"I mean it wasn't *me!*" Ben pleaded. "I can't describe it. But you've got to believe—"

"I don't have to believe *shit,*" Kait roared, flame rising in her chest. "You *threatened* me, remember? Just as soon as we got out of the car. I thought you were gonna pull some shit right there, you sick freak, but you waited. You *bided your time*. Why? What did you think was gonna happen, that you'd break into my room in the middle of the night and I just wouldn't tell anybody? That I'd *forget?*"

Suddenly her face mirrored Ben's: The tears welled up and spilled over before she could blink them away. Their weight on her face seemed enormous. "I promised myself..." she choked out, but a full-body shudder cut her words in two. "I promised myself, *never again.* That I'd never get this low a second time. That I wouldn't let anybody, and I mean anybody, put me back here again. And you made me break that promise, you son of a bitch..."

Kait shook her head, wiped her face on her shoulder, and pressed the muzzle of the hunting rifle into Ben's forehead so hard she was sure it would scar his flesh.

"So here's my deal," she told him. "You're going to stop talking, right now, right this *second*—because if you don't, on God, I will put a bullet in your head, Ben Alden. Do you understand that? I will shoot you like a dog."

Now the tears were really streaming. She squeezed her eyes shut, opened them, squeezed them shut again, trying to clear her vision to no avail. Looking down the barrel of the Model 94 at Ben kneeling on the floor, through the film of water his form shifted and blurred, becoming something like out of a dream, a dream she'd learned to savor each time it visited her. Her holding the rifle in her hands—and in the dream it was always a rifle, her hands not on the guard but flush to the trigger itself, full of deadly confidence—and instead of Ben Alden crouching at the other end of the gun...

"*It was Lutz!*"

Kait froze, her finger flexed tight against the trigger-guard. "I told you to stop talking," she said, but now all the heat seemed to have been sucked out of her voice. She couldn't understand the feeling that stirred inside her. Maybe it was that name, or maybe there was something in the boy's face, written in the dried blood caked onto his mouth. It turned her blood cold, whatever it was.

A thought, a horrible niggling *doubt* squirmed in her brain—she tried to shake it away, but it dug in, chewing into her, insidious and burrowing. "You don't get to say that," she breathed. "Not here. Not after what you've done to me."

But Ben ignored her, continuing on breathlessly as though the gun pressed against his skin didn't exist. His expression changed, all fear gone; in fact, he sounded almost surprised at the words coming out of his mouth—and each word struck home in Kait like a blow from a fist.

"I know it sounds insane," he said to her, "really, I do. But Lutz—he *made* me do it. Don't ask me how. Like he slipped me on like a sock and walked around the cabin, wearing me. Do you think I'd say something that looney unless I had no other choice? Are you listening to how crazy I sound? I could *hear* him, Kait. In my head. Like his voice was part of me. And when he talked..." Ben paused, a mote of fear returning to his features. "There are parts of yesterday I don't remember," he said, quieter now. "Parts of last night. Whole big chunks of memory, whole hours of my life, just... *gone*. But he left something inside me, too, and I think... I think maybe he left it there for *you*—"

"Shut up," Kait snarled. "You're lying. That's... That's *impossible*."

"I called you Heart-Brecker—"

"And you'd better not say it again."

"But how did I *know* to call you that?" Ben protested. "That didn't come from me. You *know* it didn't come from me. Is that what he called you? A, a pet name, or—"

"You heard it at the gas station," Kait fired back. "You were there. Maybe you listened at the door. Or you could have guessed it..."

But he couldn't, whispered the dark little voice from the back of her mental theater. *He couldn't have, Heart-Brecker. You know what this means. You know what's coming now.*

"It's a stupid joke," Kait insisted, shaking her head so that her hair whipped at her cheeks, her knuckles going white. "You wouldn't have to think that hard to figure it out."

"What about your ticklish spot? There, near your elbow— how did I know about that?"

The world flashed dangerous red. "You got lucky," Kait snarled.

"Then..." For the first time Ben seemed to flounder. "Then..." Suddenly his eyes grew wide. "Then how do I know the name Jill Cicero?" he said, infuriatingly triumphant.

In one lightning motion, Kait yanked the Model 94 from Ben's grasp and smashed the stock against his face. Blood squirted up in a high red arc, and he slipped back silently, mouth open in a silent cry. Alice and Riley both lunged forward, but Kait was already moving as well, tracking Ben's fall, planting her heel on his bare chest and pressing the muzzle of the rifle into his forehead once more. Rage and confusion and sheer, overpowering *terror* flooded every unlit corner of her mind—and the little crawling voice inside her was laughing, laughing, *laughing...*

"You are so full of shit," she seethed. "You... You don't know *anything* about me and Lutz. If you did, you'd have shut your fucking mouth when you had the chance, because now—"

"Holy *hell*, Kaitlyn..."

"Now I'm gonna make a *project* out of you."

"Kaity...!"

"I'm gonna show you *exactly* what smooth sailing looks like."

"Kaity, please—"

"Tell me we're not gonna have any more problems, Ben Alden..."

"KAIT."

"What?" Kait wailed, only it didn't sound like a human word when it left her mouth, only an animal screech, something dying in the desert, screaming vengeance at the sun. Alice had come up behind her, putting a hand on her shoulder—but also taking a firm hold of the barrel of the hunting rifle. Both hands trembled, but when Kait turned away from Ben to face her, there was flint

in the other girl's eyes.

"Kaity... Kait," she corrected. "I'm sorry, but you've got to put the gun away now..."

Alice, her flash of bravery seemingly spent, appeared to wobble on her feet for a second, pitching back and then forward like she would collapse into Kait, send them both crashing to the floor—but she did not relax her grip on the barrel of the Model 94. Her eyes were wide, her face pale and stretched; she was staring not at Kait but at some point beyond Kait's head, out the window, perhaps, into the night sky behind the drawn shade. Then the big girl took a breath and held it, held it like she never wanted to let it go.

"I'm really sorry," she repeated. "But you've got to put the gun down. Because I think I believe him..."

"Alice—"

"Because I think it's happening to me too."

Now it was Kait's turn to wobble. The whole room seemed to expand and contract once, like a single beat of an enormous heart, and the faces surrounding her floated off their moorings; they shuffled around, swapping places with one another in dizzying, arrhythmic patterns.

"Alice..." she whispered. "Alice, no, Alice you *can't*..."

But Alice only looked at her, almost pityingly, and when her mouth moved to reply, the swirl of the room swept her words away, drowned in a whirlpool of sensation and color. Kait felt curiously weightless, but the rifle was suddenly huge in her arms, the weight of a world pulling her to heel; it came loose, slipping through her fingers, sliding harmlessly to the floor, which seemed miles away and falling. And now there were arms beneath her, scrambling for purchase as she toppled back, as she felt herself drifting backwards into darkness, *Oh, come on, Heart-Brecker—don't be like that*, and the last thing she heard, from a great distance away, was the sound of her very own voice crying out in stifled terror as they eased her gently to the ground.

Chapter 9

Touch

And now Riley was talking, very fast and very animated, but Alice only half-listened. She kept looking back at the bed where Kaity lay sprawled, her eyes three-quarters closed and rolled so far back in her head that only the white showed under her lashes, and she kept thinking to herself, *If I fall apart now, they'll never find all the pieces,* over and over again until the words smeared together in her head like wet blobs of paint. Her rump was starting to ache from sitting, while Riley kept her feet, striding around the little bedroom and making big gestures in the air with her hands. The bed—and Alice's outstretched legs—got in the way of her pacing, so she had to make horseshoes instead of full circuits, but it didn't seem to slow her down much at all.

"So what are you saying?" she was asking. "How does it work—by touch?" Riley paused in her patrol, pressed palm to palm, showed Alice where they touched. "Bare skin to bare skin? That's the only logical way I can figure…"

"You'll have to ask Ben," Alice replied in a low voice, half to herself.

Ben was gone, mercifully, off in the other bathroom—throwing up again, Alice guessed. She could almost hear the splash of it, even across the cabin, an undercurrent to Riley's constant chatter. The thought of it turned her stomach. She felt like she ought to check up on him, but she still didn't trust her legs to lift her—and she kept imagining the sight of the open toilet bowl, the water in the bottom standing filmy, maybe with a single spittly bubble floating on the surface. And besides that: She did not want to be in the same room as her boyfriend right that second. That wasn't fair, she knew, but it was the truth—and Dr. Lehman had said that was important, hadn't she? To acknowledge what you were feeling, and why you were feeling it? But she'd just told Ben she loved him not an hour ago. Why couldn't she stand the sight of his face now?

The answer came without her bidding: *Because my boyfriend tried to rape my best friend.*

Because my boyfriend admitted *he tried to rape my best friend.*

Because my boyfriend got possessed by my best friend's ex-boyfriend, and then *tried to rape my best friend...*

Alice let out a stifled wail, pressing the heels of her hands to her ears as though she could block the awful thoughts out. The room was suddenly too big and too loud. She tried to focus on her body, on physical sensation, but it was her body that was betraying her now: heart still pounding, stomach knotted, face caked with tears and sweat... She felt *gross.* Gross and ugly and totally exhausted from all that crying. Her face was sticky with grief.

If she could just talk to Kaity, she reasoned, if the two of them could squirrel away in some hidden place and put their heads together like they used to, Alice knew they could dream up a way out of this craziness. But now? Kaity's eyes kept flashing across her mind, widening and going glassy just before she began to topple backward—the expression of anguish, of *betrayal,* of sheer brute-force horror making Alice quail as though she had been struck across the face. She stole a glance at her friend's limp form, at the one pale hand that had flopped over the edge of the bed, then quickly looked away again.

She probably hates me now. The thought skittered through her head like a rat through a hole in a wall. *And she's right. I would probably hate me right now too.*

She felt a shadow fall across her. Riley was standing over her, bowing forward at the waist with her fists planted on her hips. "You all right down there, girlfriend?" she was saying, pink around the cheeks and a little out of breath. "Come on, talk to me—I feel like I'm alone in the room over here."

Alice flinched, screwing up her eyes; the light was right behind Riley's head, and it was painful to look her in the face. "I don't know," she muttered at last, bring her knees up under her chin and wrapping her arms around them. "I'm fine, I guess. I can't—I mean, I don't know. I'm trying not to think about it."

"Oh, no, you don't." Riley crouched, both knees popping, and she took hold of both Alice's shoulders. She didn't *shake* her, not exactly, but the force of her grip moved Alice just the same—or made it known she could be moved. "Alice, you've gotta stay with me, okay? We can't go goofy on each other. Not now, not until we know for sure what's going on here."

"But I don't *know* what's going on," Alice moaned. "It's like Ben said. There's parts of yesterday I don't remember. That's all. Maybe it's nothing."

Her gut squirmed, and she looked past Riley's silhouette at the closed bedroom door, expecting Ben to walk through it. "Maybe I shouldn't have said—"

"Bullshit, it's nothing." Something like anger flashed in Riley's eyes—her grip on Alice's shoulders flexed, and for a second, Alice thought she might actually slap her across the face. But instead Riley released her and gathered her hands in her lap. "If there's time you can't remember, that's not nothing. That's a serious problem."

"We were drinking last night," Alice reasoned, shrugging limply. "I... I must have blacked out. Things got crazy. That's what it has to be. Because—"

Because, what? Because there's no such things as monsters?

Or because monsters aren't supposed to look like Lutz Visgara?

"Bull. Shit." This time Riley did slap her, only it was more of a nudge, a tap on the shoulder to draw her notice. "Don't talk like that," she urged. "Don't you ever talk like that. This wasn't your fault. You *know* something's wrong here, and so do I. Ever since we got out here, we've all been acting screwy. And you *felt* it, didn't you? I can see it on your face—but I can't put the words in your mouth, Alice. I need to hear you say it, do you understand that?" And when Alice tried to look away, she tapped her again, harder this time, on the cheek. "Look at me. *Look at me.* Do you believe Benjamin would do something like that?"

Alice's gut squirmed again. "I don't want to believe it."

"Neither do I," Riley replied. "But unless you can back up his story, we've got to go with what Kaitlyn's telling us. She's..." The other girl paused, glancing over Alice's shoulder at the shape of Kait laid out on the bed. "She's our friend," she said at last. "We owe her that much. I don't want to believe her creepo ex-boyfriend was wearing you around like a Buffalo Bill suit any more than you do—but what Ben said's got me scared to death. I think there's something seriously messed up happening here, but you're the only one who can say for sure now."

She squeezed Alice's hands, and Alice was shocked to note the lines of moisture underneath both of Riley's eyes. "Goddammit, I'm asking for your help, here. Don't you get that? I'm asking for you to save me."

"I wish..." Alice sniffed and wiped her nose. "I wish I'd never touched him..."

"Just talk," Riley pleaded. "Don't think about it, just talk. How did it feel?"

It felt so good.

Like a symphony—just like she'd imagined a hundred times. Even if it was over far too quickly—the sharp, hot spike of adrenaline, followed by the throbbing ache in her clenched fist as she stared at Lutz on the ground, nursing that bloodied nose. But that's when everything had gone wrong, hadn't it? She'd felt hot all over climbing back into the car, but as her pulse slowed, the uncanny heat remained. At first it was almost pleasant, like a kitten curling up in her lap, but then it sank deeper—she could still feel it in her gut, a phantom sensation, wet and warm.

Like fresh blood, she thought. *Like I was bleeding inside.*

"After the gas station," she began at last in a faltering voice, "that's when it started. When I started losing track of time. Like I zoned out in class, staring out a window—only I couldn't come back, you know? No matter how hard I tried. And then suddenly, we were here, pulling up to the cabin. I'd lost five hours: I know, I counted... I thought I was getting sick, but then I started remembering things. Little things, right? Little bits of time—like a few words of a conversation, or the feeling of a seatbelt digging into my chest when Ben stomped the brakes. But it was all coming through fuzzy, like I'd dreamed it. Or like my body was remembering instead of my head. But..."

But I couldn't have dreamed that voice, she wanted to say. *Because if I had dreamed it, I would've woken up screaming.*

Alice paused, hoping Riley would pick up where she'd dropped off, but the other girl knelt still as a stone idol, those wet tracks still glistening on her inscrutable face, until at last Alice knew she would have to speak again or the silence would crush her.

"It was him," she murmured, the words sending tremors throughout her entire body. "It had to be him. I don't know how—but when I punched him in the face, that's how he got me. That's how he got in my head."

She looked from Riley's face to the bedroom door, then back at Kaity, still unconscious on top of the rumpled sheets. "And do you know what the worst part of the whole thing is?" she whispered. "The worst thing is, I don't even know if it's over. I don't even know if he's gone, if he's really done with me. What if he's still here? What if... if he never lets me go?"

She fell silent, her arms limp at her sides. Riley cocked her head at an angle, and Alice could almost feel the pressure of her eyes running across her face. The quiet between them seemed to stretch thin like an elastic band, and it wasn't until Alice could feel the band tremble, about to snap, that Riley spoke at last.

"Then we'll force him to," she said. And then, in barely a

whisper:

"That's what it felt like for me too."

So the story came spilling out at last, and though most of what Riley said should have horrified her, to Alice it was like the liberation of a captured city during wartime. By the time the telling was over, both girls were shaking head to foot, and Alice felt so fiercely close to Riley that she could hardly contain it. They had never really been friends, she realized, not in the way she and Kaity had been friends—but now she felt prepared to kill and die for this girl, almost begging the world to give her the chance to prove it. Her pulse still roared in her head, but this peculiar kinship pulled up her cheeks, contorting her face in a confused and crazy grin.

"One of you must have tagged me," Riley guessed, looking down at her hands with a shrug. "You, or Ben, or even Kaitlyn, I suppose. I never went anywhere near Lutz—the whole thing must be contagious, somehow. I thought it was the alcohol at first, but I couldn't shake off that warm feeling in my belly, even when I went out in the cold for a smoke. What do you think he wanted with me?" She rubbed her chin with her knuckles thoughtfully. "I didn't lose as much time as you—only a half hour or so. But I'm used to blacking out. I didn't think anything of it until Ben started in with—"

"I don't wanna think about it," Alice cut in with a shiver. "You know, I always thought there was something scary about that guy, even before Kaity busted up with him. But I never figured... I mean, I never thought..."

"Stop that talk." Riley smiled, though it seemed to take some effort. "You didn't know. You couldn't have. Let's focus on what we *do* know, huh?" Alice nodded, and Riley straightened her shoulders, rising to her full kneeling height, about to deliver a lecture.

"Item one," she said. "We know Lutz Visgara can take over people's bodies. I don't like to think about it either, but we've just got to accept it and move on for now. Item two: I think he or whoever he's puppeting needs to physically touch you to get control. Meaning, he's not a virus. He's not in the air. This is good—that's what's going to protect us. As long as we stay away from each other, we're safe from him. You with me so far?"

Alice withdrew her hands, scooting back a foot from where Riley knelt, and nodded once.

"Item three, then." Riley heaved to her feet and began to pace once more. "I think he can only control one person at a time."

Alice cocked her head. "How do you figure that?"

Riley grinned and tapped her forehead. "I know my own mind," she said. "I've been drinking a lot longer than you have, I guarantee it. I know when I'm in the driver's seat and when I'm not—and right now, I've got both hands on the wheel. If Lutz was able to control us all at the same time, why wouldn't he? It'd make things a helluva lot easier on him, wouldn't it?"

Now it was Alice's turn to shrug. "I suppose that makes sense," she replied. "As much sense as anything has tonight." A thought struck her. "Item four," she continued. "We know what Lutz is after."

Both girls turned their heads, looked at Kaity, then turned back to face each other once more like a pair of pizza parlor animatronics.

"We need to get her out of here," Alice said in a low voice. The tight panic in her chest, quelled before by Riley's lively talk, began to quiver and bloom once more. "The sooner the better. We know what he's here for. He's already tried to…"

No. I won't say that. Not in front of her. I won't even think it.

"He tried to get at her once already" she managed to get out at last. "What's going to stop him from trying again?"

"Nothing," Kaity replied softly from the bed. "Nothing in the whole world."

Alice leapt to her feet, stubbing her pinkie toe on the corner of the bed. Somewhere behind her, she heard Riley stumble backward, bashing an elbow or a knee against the back wall of the bedroom with a sharp cry of pain. Kaity was sitting up in bed, a tangle of sheets drawn up to her chin, with one pale leg swung over the bed's edge as though she meant to stand. Her face was a blank, smooth shell—but Alice could see the gears and levers of panic working behind the mask. She knew, from a dozen Halloweens, that Kaity could scream and holler at a scary movie with the very best of them, but it was only when she went completely dead in the eyes like this that you knew she was good and truly rattled.

"You're awake!" Alice cried out, feeling immediately ashamed and stupid for saying such an obvious thing. "How long were you—"

"Long enough," Kaity said, her voice frosty. "Both of you, stay where you are."

Alice froze in her tracks, her pulse up and racing. She hadn't even realized she'd started forwards—but there she was, halfway across the distance to Kaity, her arms half-raised as if to embrace her. She dropped them to her sides guiltily, stealing a glance at Riley, who leaned against the wall by the door with her arms folded awkwardly across her stomach.

"Kaitlyn, you have to understand—" Riley began to say, but Kaity cut her off with a sharp look.

"Shut up a minute, will you?" she muttered, and rubbed her eyes sleepily. "I've been listening to you talk all night."

Alice's mouth clamped shut around a hundred hoarse pleas. Kaity didn't speak, not immediately; instead she yawned, rolled her shoulders, and slid her other leg out from under the sheets and planted her feet flat on the wood floor. And as she rose from the bed, Alice thought she saw something change in her eyes—a certain hardness, like the dull glint of black iron. But her movements were slow, unsure, deliberate to the point of caution; to Alice, she looked like a much older woman, one who'd just struck some terrible bargain and was only now beginning to feel the weight of what she'd wagered away.

"I need to talk to Ben," she said at last, inspecting the far corner of the bedroom through squinting eyes. But when Alice and Riley raised their voices to protest, she only waved them off almost casually.

"It's all right," she told them, her mouth creased by a hard flat smile. "I know what I'm doing." Then she cried out in a loud voice: "Ben! I know you're out there. I can see your shadow under the crack. Come in here, I want to say something to you." And when no reply came from beyond the door, she added, a little coyly, "It's all right. I'm not going to shoot you. I don't even know what they did with the rifle."

Then, almost like magic, the doorknob jiggled and turned; the door swung outward, revealing a sheepish-looking Ben standing behind it. He'd washed his face, but there was still some dried blood on his bottom lip and caked into his eyebrows and hair, and the cut above his left ear was badly bandaged and weeping a little. He looked wilted, and he clearly didn't know what to do with his hands. They twitched at his sides, slipping into his belt loops, then into his pockets, then crossing in front of his waist like a penitent schoolboy. His eyes were red and puffy, and his bare chest glistened with sweat and water.

He took a step into the room, but froze when he saw Kaity standing next to the bed. His eyes flicked from face to face, and he finally dropped his gaze altogether, turning red up to the roots of his matted hair. "I was trying to think of something I should say to you here," he stammered out. "And I think I had something, just a minute ago. Only now I can't remember what I was going to say..."

Kaity seemed to dismiss this with a shake of her head. "How're you feeling?" she asked.

Ben's mouth opened and shut like a fish. "My head hurts like hell," he said at last, and Kaity nodded, but would not drop her eyes.

"I'm sorry I hit you with the gun."

"Don't be," Ben protested. "I... You did what you had to do."

"No." Kaity shook her head curtly, her eyes never leaving Ben's. "I didn't. Not the second time." Her hands made knots in the sheets, twisting in circles. "So, I'm sorry," she said. "I shouldn't have acted like that. It wasn't your fault. Can you forgive me?"

"Really?"

Kaity nodded, and Alice saw her boyfriend's chest swell.

"All right, then," he said. "I forgive you."

He was facing away from her, but Alice thought she saw him stand a little straighter, a little taller—she felt the sudden urge to run up and kiss him, and it was only pure animal survival instinct that kept her from at least reaching for his hand.

But in the end it was Kaity that drew her gaze: again Alice saw the change in her, a hardness coming into her eyes and the position of her body—but now the hardness showed cracks. She was splitting wide at the seams. Now there was light pouring through all over, and Alice had to fight, to truly struggle against the will to rush forward and put her arms around her friend, to push her fractured pieces together in an embrace, to knit her whole with her love. Kaity had never needed it before, that kind of love. She had always been strong—but now, Alice was almost grateful for the cracks, though the thought made her ache with shame. Here, at last, was something she could do for her. A break she could fix. A great wide hurt she could kiss and make better.

Alice Gorchuck would do just about anything for Kaity Brecker.

"So you believe it, then?" Riley asked cautiously. "About Ben—and Lutz?"

Kaity shrugged. "My hands are tied," she said, as if this were justification enough. She wrapped her arms around herself, turning to face the window so that her profile showed against the backdrop of the glass and the night beyond that.

"There was something he used to say to me," she began, almost casual in her tone. "Lutz, I mean. Before he... When we were still together. He would tell me that sometimes he wished we were the only two people on the planet. Picture a beach with a million empty beach chairs and umbrellas, stretching north and south for miles and miles and miles—and us walking on the sand, always in the shade, always together. I used to think that was so romantic."

The sound of a single sob rang out—but instead of tugging Alice's heartstrings, it sent hot shafts of nameless dread plunging into her stomach. In one rough animation, Kaity's face had collapsed down on itself; the effect was almost grotesque, a parody of anguish, and now the air quivered with the sounds of her weeping.

"I'm sorry," Kaity was saying, scrubbing at her face with the corner of the bedsheet. "I'm so, so sorry—but it's too late. I can't protect you from it. He's not going to let me go. He'd rather die than let me go. But you're in the way—don't you understand? Now you've gotten involved. Now it's not me he's coming after. It's *you. It's all of you...*"

But Alice couldn't hear her anymore. She was thinking about that long empty beach, with those millions of umbrellas, and the miles and miles of warm, smooth sand all in the shade. She pictured them—her and Kaity, in bathing suits, or wrapped in matching towels, or wearing nothing at all, walking hand in hand through this lonely and beautiful world that woke up each day just for them. The water was calm, and the surf quiet, and the rows of seashell-colored beach houses stood empty, their dark windows staring. There were no birds in the sky, and time moved slow as sunset.

North and south. Sky and sea. Always together, always in the shade.

For the first time in her life, Alice perfectly understood how Lutz Visgara felt.

She wished for it, that lonesome world. She had always wished for it.

Chapter 10

Through a Wide Keyhole

Jill Cicero was thinking about houseplants.

Her mother had kept them, ever since Jill was a little girl. She would get them as gifts or buy them from the Home Depot on Sundays after church, and fill the house with them. There were bromeliads on the countertops, devil's ivy in the bathrooms in hanging pots, elephant's feet in fat, squat jars in the living room, and always a peace lily as the centerpiece of the family dining table. Her mother would feed them, Jill would water them—one of her first chores, and she did it well—and the whole family took turns shooing Patty-Cake the cat away from them when he tried to sidle up for a nibble.

And, one after the other, regular as the sunrise, the plants would always die.

It wasn't her mother's fault. She didn't have a green thumb, but she'd always managed to keep their garden plants green and healthy. They had tomatoes and bell peppers and fresh basil all through the summer, and their front walk was always guarded by rainbow rows of posies. But the plants inside the house stubbornly refused to thrive. No matter what Jill's mother did, after about a month's time they would wilt, turn brown, and crumble apart like something that had been mummified.

By the time she was ten years old, Jill was terrified of the plants. A dog, she reasoned, could bark and whine when it was hungry, or paw the door when it needed to use the yard or go for a walk. Cats were more self-reliant, but they could still meow and hiss and prod with a forepaw to communicate their needs. A fish couldn't, of course—but at least a fish could *move*. She'd heard stories about goldfish that leaped from their bowls, committing wet and gasping suicide on the floor below in protest against some secret agony of their existence. But a houseplant couldn't even stir its leaves. She imagined the peace lily on the dining table, already turning a little brown at the edges of its leaves, watching the rest of the family eating ravioli, silently screaming out for some unknown *thing* it desperately needed to survive. With every bite, she tortured herself with thoughts of what life would be like if she couldn't tell her mother she was hungry. Trapped in her seat—or potted, like the lily—watching her brothers and sisters gorging themselves, vibrating with need and pleading with her eyes, slowly drooping earthward as silent starvation devoured her from the inside out.

One day she shrieked when her mother walked through the door with a tall ficus, and after that there were no more plants in the Cicero house. The outdoor garden continued to flourish, and, eight years later, Jill packed off for Armistice University. And her mother, as far as Jill knew, went right back to buying and killing houseplants. But this was fine—so long as Jill stayed safely tucked away on the coast, where she could not hear the screams.

"You don't have to keep her in there anymore," the girl, Kait Brecker, was saying. "I mean—not if you don't want to."

A young man's voice chuckled, and a door creaked open. "I thought you didn't like her staring at you," Lutz Visgara replied airily. Their voices were close by, muffled by wood and darkness.

"Maybe I know better now," Kait replied. "Maybe I'm starting to understand."

Jill stared at the closet door, her back against a cushion of thick winter overcoats, her eyelids blinking mechanically every sixty seconds or so without her willing them to. Every so often, her left hand would twitch involuntarily, and her knuckles would scrape against something hard and crooked—the hook of an umbrella, she guessed, leaning in an urn. The closet was pitch dark, but over the hours her eyes had adjusted to the conditions; when light crept in through the slats and the crack under the door, she could see just enough to make out the dingy white of the faux wood three inches in front of her nose, and beyond that, the occasional dim, moving shape out in the hall. For twelve hours, she had seen nothing else—and for twice that long, she had not stirred once from the confines of the closet.

But Jill Cicero was not a prisoner. In fact, she wasn't even there at all.

Jill was thinking about houseplants.

Forty-eight hours back, now, counting back to the last moment she could remember seeing the sky. Through the windshield of her own Jeep Grand Cherokee, driving to the little apartment on the bay side of downtown, speeding the whole way through rain that turned to early flurries halfway there—and when the female cop pulled her over two miles from the parking deck, Jill had laughed in her face. All this she saw as if from some distance, peering out of the darkness, watching her life whirl by through the keyhole. Lutz had been in the passenger's seat beside her, laughing as well, hiccupping with mirth like he was going to choke on it, but she was only vaguely aware of him, in the same way she was aware of the nails on her toes or the hair on her head or her tongue in her jaws.

She no longer wanted to scream.

* * *

He hadn't knocked on the classroom door; he'd simply appeared, as if he'd always been there, as though he belonged, the door hanging ajar behind him. Three pages stapled together dangled in his right hand, and right away she knew why he'd come. Even across the room, she could see the maze of red ink on the topmost page, so right away she laid aside her satchel, half-packed and already bulging with work, and folded her hands on Dr. Kamaczek's desk.

For a moment, they merely regarded each other across

the room, expectation hanging heavy in the air with neither speaking. Then:

"Jill," he said with a broad smile. "That's a very pretty dress you've got on."

"You must be Lutz." Jill sighed, and Lutz nodded, still grinning. She gestured to one of the dozen or so fixed desk-chair combos arrayed in the classroom. "Go ahead and sit down, I guess, if you want to."

As he ambled forward, Jill realized just how strange it was that she'd recognized him on sight—considering that she'd only read his essays. But this shuffling, gangly youth could not have been anybody else. *Lutz Visgara*. The name suited him, somehow. He came toward her in a wobbling mosey that was almost a strut, the shrubbery of loose curls piled on his head tottering back and forth with every step he took. He didn't stink of money like some she'd seen on campus, but you could tell, by looking, he'd never had a hungry day in his life. His walk, his clothes, that stupid sloppy grin smeared across his face... it all made sense, in some ineffable fashion. *When was the last time you held out your hand and didn't get exactly what you wanted?* Jill wondered. *When was the last time somebody told you 'no'?*

He didn't sit. He came up to the desk with all the pomp of a young hotshot lawyer approaching the bench, case-breaking evidence in hand, his grin never wavering. He lifted the papers in his hand to chest level and let them drop silently onto the desk in front of Jill, who looked at the C– on the front page and the words *Graded by Jillian Cicero* written beneath.

"I don't get C's," Lutz said.

Jill pushed back her chair. "You're supposed to call me 'Ms. Cicero,' I think," she said, puffing a strand of hair out of her face and knotting her hands behind her head. "I know I'm not a proper teacher, but there's decorum in place. You know."

"You're Dr. Kamaczek's TA?"

"That's right," she replied.

"And you graded my essay?"

Jill glanced down. The essay, titled in bolded capital letters, read *A Swift Affirmation of Principles,* and she chuckled, remembering a joke Dr. Kamaczeck had told her the week prior: "Students who make puns in their essay titles," she'd said, "generally have dick else to say, and you can quote me."

"That's my name on it, isn't it?" she responded, pointing with a manicured forefinger.

Lutz splayed his fingers across the essay, shifting the pages as if to draw her attention to them. "I have a deal going with the world," he said. "I put in a certain level of effort, and I get back a certain kind of return for my hard work. I can't take a C lying down—it wouldn't be fair to either of us."

"It was a C minus," Jill corrected.

"More to my point, then."

"Fair, huh?" Jill tugged the essay out from under Lutz's hand and studied the first page. "Well, let's see. For starters, this was supposed to be a four-page essay."

"I thought I would get points for brevity."

"Your third page was your works cited."

"I'm a slow writer," Lutz replied with a shrug. "Cut me some slack, huh?"

"Lutz, your essay actually *supports* Jonathan Swift's *A Modest Proposal,*" Jill protested. "You realize it's a satire, don't you? He's talking about selling and, and eating the children of London's poor. What were you trying to do here?"

"I took a risk," Lutz said as if this explained everything. Then he shrugged again and rolled his eyes skyward. "My essay's satire, too, if that helps. It was all a joke."

"A joke." Jill rubbed her eyes. It had been a long day already, even before this incursion. "Well, I don't get it. Don't you want to be taken seriously here?"

"Of course." Lutz's eyes flashed—for the first time since he'd set foot inside the classroom, his big grin had slipped away.

Now his mouth was set in a determined line, only degrees away from a smirk. Jill could feel the heat of his eyes on her, and she straightened, almost unconsciously trying to appear bigger in the chair.

"I can't take a C minus for this," he told her.

"You're going to have to," Jill responded. "It's a C minus essay."

"Look," he said, drumming his fingers on the desk, "what scale are you grading by? I want to know exactly where I'm losing points here."

"Baily—Dr. Kamaczeck, I mean—has a strict system laid out," Jill began, trying in vain to think back to the syllabus she'd gotten by email at the beginning of the school year. "Certain proofs she looks for in each paragraph, things like that. I just follow the—"

"But it's still you grading it," Lutz interrupted. "Not her. So there's room for subjectivity on your end."

"Of course."

"Part of the grade could be determined by your personal opinion of the essay."

"I suppose so."

Lutz leaned forward, a single curl of dirty blonde hair flopping down across his forehead. "So I'm asking you to change your opinion."

"I can't," Jill said, then cocked her head and shrugged. "No, that's not fair," she added. "I could—but I *won't*. I wanted to fail this essay, do you understand? I hated reading it, I mean I really hated it. Your writing style is... pedestrian, you make only the barest attempts to support your claims, and your jokes just aren't as funny as you think they are. But the worst thing is: I don't believe you when you say this is supposed to be satire. This doesn't read like real satire. Part of me thinks you actually believe every word you've written here. I don't know what that means about you, and frankly I'm afraid to think too hard about it. I certainly don't want to believe it—what a terrifying human being you'd have to be, if it were true."

She rubbed her eyes again, shrugged again, and sighed. "Listen, maybe I could have taken a second look a week ago," she said. "If you'd brought it to me when you got it back—or better yet, to Dr. Kamaczek. But you've had this back since last Tuesday. Why are you only talking to me now?"

The grin returned, slotting into place on his features like a puzzle piece clicking home. "I just didn't think of it until today."

A feeling like distant thunder rose up inside Jill; she wanted to holler, to scream, to lunge across the desk and commit violence against this young man, at least to wipe that smug, satisfied grin off his face. *You thought you were going to get away with it,* she wanted to yell out. *You thought you had this licked. You're like a baby lamb that's learned how to bite, aren't you? And now you bite and you bite and you bite, because nobody can touch you—oh, look how cute and fluffy and tiny and harmless you are, you couldn't hurt anybody. Well, I've seen what hurt boys like you are capable of, Lutz Visgara. I've still got the screws in my shoulder. So today, you lose the game. Today you're going home empty-handed.*

"It's five-thirty," she said out loud. "I'm going home. If you have any other questions, email your teacher. I'm done talking about this."

She waited for his anger—for the eruption, the red face, the threats, the fist thrust into the drywall. But Lutz's smile didn't waver.

"All right," he said cheerily. "Then I'll walk you to the parking lot. It's already dark out there, you never know what kind of nutty types are lurking around these days."

Jill said nothing, stunned into silence, quickly gathering the rest of her materials into her satchel before latching it and hoisting it onto her shoulder. The strap dug in across her collar bone, and right away the nerve in her shoulder blade began to complain. It wasn't until she'd left the room and arrived at the building's front door that she finally said, "All right. Walk me, then."

"Consider it done," Lutz replied, but he didn't walk through the door. Jill paused halfway through the heavy swinging door, light bleeding out of the English hall and into the night beyond. She looked over her shoulder—*my first mistake,* she thought, staring relentlessly through the slats in the closet door. *I shouldn't have looked back. I should never have even turned my head.* Lutz had stooped, putting his lips to the water fountain in the hall, but when he looked up, his mouth dripping water, such peculiar terror cut through her that she couldn't help but freeze in place, examining this strange feeling quivering inside her. Lutz stared at her, an undefinable emotion writ across his features, looking her head to toe, his eyes slow on her.

"I don't really *need* to be here, you understand," he said to her. "That's why this is all so frustrating. It's a lot of trouble to go to, just to meet somebody. But I want you to know it's been worth it. I want you to understand that I don't regret any of it, even for a second."

Then he straightened and began walking toward her.

"You know," he said, "that's a very pretty dress you've got on."

* * *

Canned laughter trickled in, startling Jill from a doze. She had to nap standing upright, with her eyes open, and take her sleep where she could. She never knew when her body would begin to move, bearing her forward into the world beyond her coat closet, off to perform some arcane task while the other two forms in the apartment lurked on the periphery. She had cooked, she had vacuumed—she had cleaned herself in the shower more times than she'd eaten, always in lava-hot water, though the heat never penetrated, never truly hurt her. She could see the steam, hear the water hitting her back and shoulders, sense the pressure of it, but all she ever truly felt was a kind of swaddling warmth deep in her belly. Like a long, uncomfortable hug that never seemed to end.

Outside the closet door, they were watching a sitcom.

Sometimes Jill could not tell her waking from her dreaming. Sometimes the dreams would be trapped, like her body, in this dark closet, floating in the warm bath of silence. But other times, her dreams were not her own. It was as though somebody had crept into her projector room and swapped out the reels for their own strange home movies—and what movies they were! They began experimental, swooping arrays of color and shape and chameleonic form, but eventually the colors would grow subdued, the shapes settled, the forms condensed, hardening into monstrosity. Pulsating, squamous flesh arranged in mind-rending, eldritch structures and geometries, loping and tumbling across empty air, all set against a black sky that was not sky at all...

Or perhaps she never really slept at all. Perhaps even this was denied her.

There had never really been any doubt in her mind over what was happening to her. Once she eliminated the obvious options—drugs, hallucinations, hippie-cult brainwashing—only one possibility remained. This boy, Lutz Visgara, had total control over her body. The thought of it had terrified her only at first, but once she was made aware just how powerless she really was, her fear evolved, transforming into cold, calculating rage, something she could use. She wasted no effort or time struggling against him: her brain seemed to be operating on low-battery mode, her wattage still flowing but somehow sapped. And besides—there was nothing to struggle against. No bonds she could break, no puppet strings to sever. Lutz was in the driver's seat, but Jill wasn't even in the same car. She simply wasn't there at all.

Her left hand lifted, groped for the closet doorknob, twisted and pushed. Light flooded in; Jill's eyes thankfully squinted shut against the sudden assault, but she was already moving forward, swiveling into the little kitchenette, heading for the fridge, which she already knew was full of craft beers and little else. Her hand roved among the bottles like a cursor, finally selecting a funky brown ale with a yellow wraparound label. Jill couldn't decipher the words on the label, even though they were written in huge block letters. This imprisonment, this enslavement, this theft of Jill Cicero—it had somehow robbed her of her ability to read.

She grabbed another bottle from the shelf, watching herself take it, bring it to the den, where hands reached out and took them from her grasp. "Thank you, Jill," the girl, Kait, told her, and laughter pealed out. Her face and Lutz's were half-shadowed, lit up strange by the flicker of the TV in the dark room; their heads were together, her head on his shoulder, his arm looped around her and his other hand resting on her bent knee. And yet he was also looming above them both as well, standing just out of focus, wearing Jill's skin and watching over them with Jill's eyes—and Jill watched him watch, as though looking through thick glass, standing in the deep, heavy warmth of his shadow, hating him.

And she wanted to hate this Kait girl too. Kait, who knew her name. Kait, who watched her boyfriend walk around inside her, watched him steal Jill's life one step, one breath at a time. Kait, who Lutz called *Heart-Brecker*—never by her name, never by any other diminutive. Kait, who stared at her like she was one of the stuffed heads mounted on Jill's father's wall in his new house out west. There were times, usually in the middle of the day, where Jill's mind would go blank, and hours would pass by without her notice; she tried not to think about what happened to her and her body during those times, but she could not help imagining when there was nothing left of her but imagination. But though she tried hating this Heart-Brecker, the hate wouldn't come. She kept thinking of the peace lily on her mother's dining table. She wondered if this girl had ever heard something scream like a plant could scream. If perhaps she could hear Jill's scream, if she could be made to hear. If, somehow, she was even screaming herself.

"Do you think she'd like to watch with us?" Kait asked suddenly.

Jill watched Lutz frown—and she could almost feel his confusion as well, bubbling over soft heat. "What do you mean, like?"

"The show." Kait pointed: on the screen, Kramer had just careened through the door of Jerry Seinfeld's apartment, looking wild-eyed and birdlike. "Do you think she'd like it? Only, I suppose you'd know the answer already, wouldn't you."

To Jill's surprise, Lutz reached across both their bodies, grasped the TV remote, and flung it with all his strength at the wall on the opposite side of the room. She could hear, but not see, the battery case crack, and the remote itself clatter to the floor. Kait recoiled backward, her face pale in the TV's hospital glow, but Lutz only pressed his palms to his forehead, knotting his fingers into his hair in frustration.

"You still don't really understand," he groaned, pulling the flesh of his face down as he rubbed his eyes in grotesque fashion. "How many times will..." He paused, jumped to his feet, and marched around the coffee table to plant himself in front of Jill. Staring into his eyes was like looking in a dark mirror.

"She can't see me," he was saying, waving an open hand in front of her face. "She can't hear me."

"Then where did she go?" Kait asked, struggling free of the blankets to stand as well.

"Go?" Lutz turned, blocking Jill's view of Kait. "She didn't go anywhere. This is all there is. We're alone in the room. *There is no Jill Cicero.*"

The world turned around Jill as she turned on her heel, walking back around the corner to the coat closet by the front door. She could still hear Lutz and Kait's voices behind her, but the words no longer mattered. Jill had seen the light flickering, the candle lit at the top of the dark and spiraling stairs.

There is no Jill Cicero, he had said. *She can't see me. She can't hear me.*

She wanted to grin, to crow to the heavens. *But I can hear you, you son of a bitch,* she wanted to say. *I'm not supposed to be here — but here I am. I survived you. I bobbed to the surface. I* came back. *That means I beat you, doesn't it? Somehow, I beat your creepy little game. And I don't know how I did it, but I'm gonna do it again — and again and again and again until you have to let me go. Until you wish you'd never seen my face.*

She shut the door, facing backwards this time, looking into the deep recesses of the tiny closet, but now the darkness was a boon, the muffled quiet a knife slipped into her boot.

You're going to wish it was true, she said to herself. *You're going to wish there was no such thing as Jill Cicero.*

She said this twice over, and then twice over again, repeating it like a prayer. Then she shut her mind to the world, constructing inside herself a desperate scheme ordered toward freedom — and somewhere just beyond the closet door, she thought she heard the sound of rustling leaves.

Chapter 11

Glasspowder

And then, sudden as a heart attack, it was dawn.

Kait woke gasping for air. She sat upright—a throw blanket wrapped tight tendrils around her arms and shoulders, dragging her to earth, but she shoved it off, her breathing labored and dry, trying to shake the nightmare out of her head. She was on the red leather couch in the den now, and the whole room was awash in yellow light. Sun streamed in through the wide back window, disorientingly bright, momentarily just as blinding as darkness.

There was somebody knocking against the front door of the cabin.

"Kaity?" Alice's plaintive voice floated in. "Kaity, it's me—or, I think it's me? You said we shouldn't sleep past ten, and it's ten-twelve now."

Memories crushed in. The night prior flashed once in her mind in its entirety, like heat lightning in the guts of a cloud. The blanket had felt like hands on her, strong hands everywhere, clinging, sliding, feeling, their touch rough and their grip like jaws. She pitched forward, striking her fists against her knees; her breath caught like a bone in her throat.

I'm going to show you how reasonable I can be.

The room flexed inward around her, to smother, to suppress, but Alice's voice beat it back into shape, though now her knocking drove long spikes into Kait's skull. She massaged her temples, struggling to keep one throbbing eye open, and the pain diminished, fading into a far-away rat-ta-tap behind her pupil.

"Kaity?" Alice called out again from the porch. "Are you all right in there?"

I'm going to make a project out of you, Ben Alden.

"Peachy fucking keen," she groaned softly, to herself—then

louder for the benefit of her friend: "I'm fine, Alice."

"Okay..." There was a pause—Kait could almost see Alice wringing her fingers, shifting from one foot to the other on the front mat. "Then can you let me inside? It's got really cold out here, and Ben took the cabin key off his keyring..."

After a final groan, Kait heaved to her feet and shuffled towards the door, scrubbing sleep out of her eyes with the heel of her hand. As she skirted the sofa, the Model 94, now leaning against the couch's backside, swung suddenly into view, and the sight of it shocked her fatigue away like a blast of cold water. She shivered, looking at it, afraid of its power for the first time.

Last night, the dream had changed.

In the dream, her shot had only wounded Lutz, and the tear in his flesh would not spill blood. Instead, she held him by the hair and slit his throat open with a long knife, or perhaps a straight razor—she had not been able to look as she sawed away at his skin. His flesh had made horrible ripping sounds, like tearing burlap, and only then did he bleed: what came out was warm and thin and bubbling and redder than anything she'd ever seen, and Lutz had only laughed at her, laughed as she cried over the blood spilling onto the ground and pooling at his feet and soaking into her trembling hands.

Kait crept forward, but when Alice knocked impatiently, she froze, looking back at the gleaming rifle. She had been careful— hadn't she? She chewed her knuckles, almost breaking skin. Her instructions to the others had been rigorously exacting: Nobody sleeps in the same room. Nobody leaves their bedrooms until dawn, and not until everybody is awake and able to defend themselves. Bedroom doors stay locked at all times—and since there were only the two bedrooms in the little cabin, somebody would have to spend the night in the station wagon while she, Kait, would sleep in the den to enforce curfew. And while nobody seemed willing to say it out loud, the deadly implication stood: anybody caught out-of-doors during the night could only be under Lutz's control and should be considered an immediate threat to everybody else in the cabin—and dealt with accordingly.

They'd fought her, of course. On every point, for every inch. Alice, scared as she was, clung stubbornly to the notion that Lutz was after Kait and Kait alone, while Riley insisted she couldn't possibly be "a Lutz", though by that point in the night Kait was too fried to wrap her head around the logic of this enough to really protest. But Ben, out of a clear blue sky, had agreed to each of her demands in turn, and even asked that he be the one to sleep in the car. He hadn't looked her in the eyes when he said this—he almost seemed scared to speak, chewing his words, tasting something bitter on them. And while in the end he had looked so unsteady on his feet that Alice insisted she take his place outside, for a moment Kait had seen another face behind his glasses, and her guilt burned against her like a hot brand.

Now Ben's and Riley's bedrooms were closed, but she could see lines of light under both doors; she guessed they'd each been awake for some time now. She wondered if their phones had signal, and if they were talking to each other.

If they were talking about her.

"Get back from the door," Kait called out. "I'm going to let you inside now."

"Do you have the gun?"

Kait paused, her hand centimeters from the latch. "It's here," she said.

"I mean, do you have it in your hands?"

"No?" Kait searched the door for a peephole and, finding none, pulled aside the gauzy curtain and put a cheek to the side transom to peer through. She could see the vague shape of Alice's curved back, shifting nervously on the front porch, and beyond that, fitful snatches of Ben's station wagon, visible through a scrub of evergreen. "Alice, I'm not—"

I'm not going to shoot you, she wanted to say. But the words stuck sideways in her, wedged tight. That had been the insinuation, hadn't it? That she was prepared to defend herself—and the others in the cabin—with force? She'd pulled the damned thing off the wall, hadn't she? Loaded it, cocked it, shoved the barrel down Ben's throat... So why did the sight of it churn her guts like this now? What had changed inside her while she slept?

Don't worry, purred a soft voice from the back of her mental theater. *When the time comes, pulling the trigger is easy. It has to be, right? You've done it before. You were good.*

"I don't need it," she forced herself to say, out loud. "Not for you."

I hope they run, when the moment comes, whispered the voice. *Like ducks, breaking away over the pond. You remember how to hit a moving target, don't you?*

"Shut up," Kait hissed.

You need to lead them into the shot.

"Kaity?"

"I said—"

You've got this, Heart-Brecker.

"You'd better get the gun."

The record skipped. Kait's cheek, cold on the window glass, went suddenly numb.

"What?" she asked, followed by, "Why?"

At first there was only an animal sound, low, a moan of anguish. Then at last:

"Because I think we messed up. Because I think *I* messed up."

Kait's hand found the latch, and before she knew it, she'd flung open the door and brushed past Alice, stumbling out barefoot onto the cold gravel lot beside the road. She followed Alice's gaze—for a moment, nothing drew her eye.

Then she was choking on her scream.

The hood of Ben's station wagon was propped up, and a pine branch jutted straight up out of the tangled guts of the engine, impaling a deflated volleyball on its sharpened point. The branch itself was shorn of all tributary branches and stripped of its bark, while the ball was filthy, smeared with dirt and red paint—no. Not paint. The head, the maniacally grinning face drawn onto the surface of the ball, had eyes that oozed and ran like egg yolk, dripping down the cheeks; there was no nose, and its teeth were huge and square and crowding out of the cartoonish, dripping jaws.

It was rendered in what could only be fresh and gleaming blood.

Kait turned her head; she tried to drag her gaze away. She couldn't. The face's eyes were only smotches of dribbling red, but she could feel them, like a painting's eyes, tracking her around a gallery. Alice was still standing on the porch, listing to one side and shivering in the cold, her eyes wide and staring and unfocused. A hundred questions whirled in Kait's head, but all she managed to say was:

"When."

"I don't know." The reply was barely a rough whisper, carried on the wind. "I woke up, it was cold, the engine had stopped running, and—"

"No. God, no."

The words were tiny, barely gone from her lips before Kait turned like a wobbling top and stumbled back to the car. As she drew closer, she had to force herself to lean into the gaping mouth of the station wagon's open hood, avoiding the cockeyed gaze of the grisly effigy impaled just above her head. She looked down. She looked for a long time.

"Get Ben," she said at last.

Alice sniffed mucus somewhere behind her. "Kaity, what—"

"Get your boyfriend, Alice." Kait cut her off without turning, her voice sharp and cold as the air she breathed. "And for the love of God, don't *touch* anybody—and don't let anybody touch you. Now *go!*"

She heard the other girl scurry away and, seconds later, Ben burst through the cabin's front door, his face half-lathered in shaving cream, a forest green bathrobe clenched closed over his bare chest. He took the porch stairs in a tumble, landing heavily on his hands and knees on the gravel before scrambling to his feet. Riley pursued—at a safe distance, thankfully, skidding to a halt on the porch when Ben took his fall, with Alice close behind her.

"What's going on?" Ben asked, looking around the lot. "Alice said there—"

Then his eyes fixed on the car. On the face drawn in blood.

"Oh, God," he said. "Oh God, oh God, oh God..."

"The battery's gone," Kait reported, watching the color drain from his face. "I don't know what happened. Alice was in the car. She said it wouldn't—"

But before she could finish, before she could even think, Ben had crossed the yard, mounted the porch, and grabbed hold of Alice's shoulders.

"Let her go!" he bellowed.

Kait waited for Alice to protest, to struggle, but she only hung limp in his grip, letting herself be shaken without objection. Her eyes were round with surprise, but there was no fear on her colorless face, which showed every freckle—her mouth was a hard, straight line and remained shut. The pile of crimson hair, matted to one side by sleep, bounced to and fro as her head wobbled around on her neck.

"You let her go," Ben snarled again—but there was no biting power in his voice. Fear had stripped it. "You son of a bitch," he said, "you leave her alone. You don't get to do this to her, she hasn't done anything to you. Whose blood is that? You tell me, *whose blood is that?*"

"*Goddammit, Benjamin!*"

Riley pressed between them, tearing Ben's hands away by seizing hold of his wrists. They stared at each other, Ben towering over her, red in the face and puffing heavily, his breath fogging the cold morning air. Riley's eyes narrowed, and suddenly she raised her hand and slapped him hard across the face.

"Get hold of yourself," she hissed. "What's shaking her going to do? Huh? It won't bring your battery back—"

"*Fuck* my battery!" Ben cried, nearly screaming. Riley's slap seemed not to have reached him at all. "He hurt her. He made her make that... that *thing* in the car. Where did he get the blood?" He repeated this twice, looking over Riley's shoulders at Kait, his voice rising with every word. "The *blood*—where did he get all that *blood?*"

"It's all right, Ben," Alice interposed at last, raising her voice as well. "I'm... I'm me, for now. He hasn't got me. And I'm not hurt—at least, I think I'm not hurt..."

"Damn it all, that doesn't matter," Riley huffed, throwing up her hands. "Don't you understand? We had him *cornered*. We knew who he was driving. Now he's in the wind. He could be either one of you."

"Any of you," Kait corrected quietly.

Three faces turned toward her, slowly and in unison, like satellite dishes rotating.

"You touched her, Riley," she continued. "And you touched Ben." She felt loose, distant, almost weightless, like she was floating somewhere above this scene instead of standing in the middle of it. "You let him in—or you passed him on. Either way, any one of you three could be a Lutz, now. That's how you said it works, didn't you? By touch? Skin on skin?"

For the briefest instant, nobody moved—then Alice let out a high wail, and there was a shuffle of gravel as all three bodies leaped back from each other, eyes wild, throwing their hands out before them in makeshift walls. The scene looked like a Mexican standoff, only nobody was holding guns, though their bare hands, Kait thought, were just as dangerous as a bullet.

"Well... Well, it's not me," Riley said at last. "I'd know. I'd *feel* it..."

"That's what you'd have to say," Ben argued, taking a step

back towards the cabin. He gestured with a pointing finger, poking holes in the air. "That's just what you'd say. If you were. A Lutz, I mean. You wouldn't *admit* it."

"Well—neither would you! Maybe you're the Lutz," Riley protested, "and you're just trying to throw suspicion on me."

"There you go again," Ben sneered, panic darting across his face like a lizard scrambling across a brick wall. "How did you get past Kait, huh? Your room's got a window on it. Maybe you didn't need to sneak past her at all."

"Your room had a window, too, you bastard," Riley shot back. "And yours was closer. I'd *know* if I was a Lutz. I told you, I'd know—"

"But *how*, Riley?" Alice put in, straining to be heard above the other two. "You keep saying that—but *I* didn't know. And I did all this without even realizing it. There's no reason to say it's not still me."

"Wonderful," Ben said. "Just-fucking-wonderful." A crazed grin was spreading his cheeks, and he pressed his fists against his temples, leaving his bathrobe hanging open and his torso exposed to the air. "So you're saying there's no way to tell now?" he asked. "No way at all? That's *great*. That's just *perfect*."

"It doesn't matter," Kait said quietly.

"And now, and now we're stranded here in the middle of the fucking forest with—what?" Ben made a face like he'd caught a nose-full of something rotten. "All right. So what's *that* supposed to mean?"

Kait shrugged, twitching with cold. "Okay, so yes—there's no way to tell who's who," she said. "There was never going to be a way. He's been all three of you, and each time, we haven't been able to tell." She heard Alice start to protest, but Kait powered through, drowning her out with her own voice. "But it doesn't matter," she repeated. "Alice didn't do this. She didn't take the car battery out, and she definitely didn't draw anything in her own blood."

Ben squinched his eyes, searching her face. "How do you figure that?"

"Because..." Kait wrapped her arms around herself, looking again at the ghastly face grinning at her from atop the bloody spear. "Because Lutz would never let anybody but him draw Mister Face."

Riley, Alice, and Ben turned toward her, looked at each other, and then turned back to her. Somewhere deep in the forest, a squirrel chattered at a hawk.

"Mister Who?" Riley said at last.

Kait looked at her bare feet. "It was stupid. Just another stupid thing we did. My old dorm room had a white board on the outside of the door, and sometimes Lutz would come by to see me and I wouldn't be there—out at a class or something. He started drawing this stupid cartoon face on the board, always in red, and when I asked him what the fuck it was, he said, *That's Mister Face.* Like that was supposed to mean something to me. But it was cute, you know? He started drawing it everywhere, places I'd see it: classroom whiteboards, on the sidewalk in chalk... And every time, it meant the same thing. *I was here, Kait. Missed you by a minute. See you soon.* I think that's what it means now."

Riley crossed her arms across her stomach, lips twitching. "You think he's... *here?*"

Kait nodded. "And I think he wants me to know he's here."

"But why? And—and *how?*" Alice clasped her hands, unclasped them, and knotted them together again. "He couldn't have followed us from the gas station. We'd have seen him."

Kait shook her head. "He didn't need to follow us. He always knew where we were."

Ben's jaw worked; the cords of his neck stood out like ropes on a suspension bridge.

"*You knew,*" he said.

Alice sucked a breath.

"Ben... Think about this..." Riley said, but Ben only shook his head, growing pink in the cheeks, his glasses flashing.

"No. You knew all along," he repeated. "You had us for a while, playing dumb last night, letting us explain the whole thing to you—but the way you talk now, you know way too much. You've seen this before. You knew what he could do this whole time."

For a moment, Kait couldn't speak. The air froze in her lungs. Every eye was on her—including the bloody eyes of Mister Face. She could feel them, boring holes in her flesh.

"I'm trying to protect you," she said at last.

Alice's face crumpled like foil. *"Kaity..."*

"What was I supposed to say?" Kait exploded. "What was I supposed to tell you? That my ex-boyfriend was some kind of movie monster? That he could ride you around like a stolen horse just by touching you? You'd think I was crazy. That I was lying to your face."

"Because you've been so fucking honest with us already," Ben retorted.

"I told you, I'm trying to save you!" Kait cried, her hands shaking. "Look, this doesn't change anything. He's still got hold of one of you—but he's here in person, too, and for some reason, he doesn't want us to leave. I think whatever he was planning, we fucked it up, somehow. We can fuck it up again, but that's only if we don't tear each other to pieces first. And that means no matter how much it sucks for you, you're going to have to trust me."

"And what if we can't," Ben said.

All eyes swiveled towards him. He met their gazes, each in turn, but his expression did not change.

"Ben..." Alice pleaded.

"I mean it," he said. "What if we can't trust you. What happens to us? If... If you're the mole, somehow. That you're working with him on this. If what you said is true, that he's really after all of us, and you're working with him... Then we're in danger, right now. You're the one who knows how to use that gun, not him. Wouldn't we be safer if we just—"

Kait felt muscles flex in the backs of her knees and below her shoulders. "I really don't think you want to be talking like that, Ben," she said in a low voice.

But he only gestured to the bandage wound around his temple. "I think I'm exactly the person who should be talking like this."

The others looked at her, but Kait only saw Alice, her eyes wet and round and wavering at the corners. She was shivering, teeth rattling against each other in the cold. Or was it fear that shook her? How had Alice looked that first time Kait picked up the gun? At the time, her bead was drawn on Ben, but now the afterimage of Alice's face emerged from the fog, frozen, a snapshot of a single instant. Memory stretched her features: surprise became shock, fear congealed into stark terror—*and why shouldn't she tremble?* Kait's guts twisted like a pit of snakes. Why shouldn't she be scared? Hadn't she come clean to them? Torn the mask away, shown them exactly what writhed beneath?

Hadn't she just proven them all exactly right?

She drew a breath, resolve hardening like cooling iron in her stomach. She should have seen this coming. All this, it was inevitable, all from the start. She should have known there would never be a chance that people like these could ever look at her again, not while this knife was twisting inside her. What did they see? A shattered vase, lying on the floor. Jagged edges. Busted glass, ground into the carpet. Well, all right. She'd show her breaks. She'd *be* busted glass. She would rescue them from this—then she would disappear.

This was what they all deserved.

"You know damn well," she said, "that can't be true. If I was really working with Lutz—Ben, I wouldn't have stopped you last night."

The others gasped—Riley swore hideously, Alice raised her voice to protest, but Kait silenced them all with a look that had all the recoil of a gunshot.

"Shut up. All of you," she barked. "I'm done explaining myself to you. I'm *not* working with Lutz. I was *never* working with Lutz. But I know him. I know what he can do. I'm not going to waste time telling you what kind of a monster he is—you've all drawn your own conclusions already. But he's *here*. And he's inside one of you. There's nothing I can do about that by myself. But together, we can find him. Track his ass down to the ends of the earth and put an end to this. But I can't do it alone. You've got to save yourselves."

She paused for breath, feeling tears in the air like the threat of rain, phantom moisture on her cheeks. But she wasn't ready to cry, though she felt spider-webbed with cracks. Like the air itself might be ready to shatter around her.

"Riley?" she asked. "Alice?"

"You've got a plan, then?" Riley uttered sullenly. "How do we stop him?"

Kait shivered, feeling her stomach drop away. "The only way," she said simply. "With the gun. With a bullet."

"Jesus." Riley looked away, folding her arms under her chest. "Jee-zus, I don't know."

"He had you too," Alice said suddenly. "All that time—for four months. That's what he did to you. That's why you wouldn't tell me."

Her brows were up around her hairline and her mouth hung open, but Kait could detect something incongruous in her tone—a kind of lightness, almost approaching glee.

"You were a Lutz too," she said. "Weren't you, Kaity?"

Oh, is that what she thinks? clucked a quiet voice—but not so quiet Kait couldn't hear or almost *feel* cold breath brushing against her ear. *Oh, no-no-no. Tell her, Heart-Brecker. Set the record straight. Not you—it was never you...*

But Kait pressed her lips together and nodded once, then again vigorously, tears finally breaking surface, spilling between her fingers and down her cheeks.

"Oh, Kaity..." Alice pressed her hands to her face as well, but steel sparked in her eyes. "Get the gun, then," she said. "And I want you to promise me you'll get him. Promise me I'll see it when you... stop him. I want to see you pull the trigger. I want to see him die."

Kait shivered again, but she nodded, feeling numbness creep across her body.

"All right then. Riley, what about you?"

"Jee-zus," came the reply. The blonde shrugged, her face still smeared with makeup and set in a sagging mask of fatigue. "Jee-zus, Alice..." She shrugged again, shaking her head in resignation. "What other choice we got..." she said at last—or something like it. She bit down on each word as she said it as if she were trying to crush a wriggling insect inside each one.

"You'd better know what you're doing," Ben muttered. He had his bathrobe tucked around him, one fist holding it closed, the other stuffed down in a big pocket. He was staring up into the skirts of the pine trees, watching the sky—for what, Kait couldn't say. Perhaps he thought it would fall on his head. Perhaps he was praying for it, like she was. "You'd better be right about this—because if you're wrong, it's all on you."

"I need you with me, Ben," Kait said. But she couldn't look him in the eye, and when he opened his mouth to respond, no sound seemed to come out at all.

Instead, she heard another voice:

It doesn't matter, it said. *How long do you think you can lie to them? You cannot change. You know it in your heart now. Eventually the other boot has to drop—and then they'll find out. And they will find out. Soon they'll see just how much of you really is busted glass, and they're going to sweep you under a rug. They're going to grind you under their heel, Heart-Brecker...*

She wanted to protest. To object—but her strength was gone, crushed under by the cold. She had fought as long as she could, but there was no silencing this now. Maybe that, too, was inevitable. There was no way to shut her up, this ghost, this constant parasite, this passenger inside her empty inside world.

It was always there, this voice. The voice of that girl.

All that remained of Jill Cicero.

"You're right," Kait whispered. "I know you're right."

But I'm not going to let anybody else bleed because of me.

Chapter 12

Happy Campers

Riley didn't know when she stopped feeling the cold.

Somewhere things had got out of sync. There was a cigarette between her lips but she hadn't lit it, but she'd smoked it almost down to the butt, but she'd just ground the ember under her sole on the gravel. Everybody was talking at once, their voices jumbled, clanging against each other like pots and pans in an overstuffed cubbie. Kaitlyn said something in a low voice that got Alice and Benjamin nodding, and Riley sensed her neck moving her head as well, her field of vision bobbing and ducking as motor neurons fired in eldritch sequence. Overhead the wind rattled dry pine branches together, sending down showers of bark fragments that tumbled around their heads and rattled against the roof of the station wagon. But Riley couldn't feel the wind's cold breath, or the bark's weight tangled in her long hair.

She couldn't feel anything at all. Anything but the warmth.

She wasn't afraid anymore, not really. She was safe. Safe by this warm fire. Safe in the arms of a shadow, a shadow that bore her face and her form, that moved her and *within* her with the languid grace of a candle flickering under glass. Its embrace was soothing, almost soporific, its voice mellow and smooth.

It wanted to show her something.

"So—where do we look?" she heard herself say, noting with some dull surprise how her lips clung together on each word, sticking in the cold.

"North is to the lake," Benjamin replied. He hugged the bathrobe around his shivering shoulders, clenching his jaw to stop his teeth chattering. "We could make a fire-line in the woods. Trap him against the water—"

Kaitlyn shook her head, cut him off: "What else is out there?

Besides forest, I mean."

"We're pretty much alone out here," he replied, eyeing her warily. "You saw that as we drove in, trees go on for miles. There's another cabin, but it's in the opposite direction. My parents say nobody's gone there for years. I've never even seen it—it mighta burned down, or got a tree dropped on it."

"He could be there," Kaitlyn said. "That could be Base Camp One. He wouldn't just camp out in the woods, he's too vain for that."

"If he's here," Benjamin put in sharply.

"He's *here*," Kaitlyn insisted. "And he'd want some kind of roof over his head."

"Unless..." All eyes turned to Alice, who whimpered, "Unless he *knew* we'd think of that. Ben, you said he left something in your head. Maybe it goes both ways. Maybe he already knows where we're going to look."

"Well, he knows *now*," Kaitlyn muttered.

"Goddammit!" Ben's fist lashed out sideways, struck the side door of the station wagon with a metallic thud. "We can't win. That's all there is to it. We look one place, he moves to the other. End of story." He pressed his palms to his eyes and sucked cold air through his teeth. "Christ—what are we even talking about? I mean, what are we even *doing*?"

"Keeping our heads, hopefully," Kaitlyn retorted, but her voice was so low nobody seemed to hear, nobody but Riley, who shifted her gaze from face to face with a fascination that was approaching frenzy. Alice and Benjamin both began talking at once again, their voices rising over each other like a deck of cards being shuffled together, and Riley felt her cheeks pull up, felt cold air against her grinning teeth. Hot smoke compressed and eddied in her stomach; the grip of the shadow tightened, pulling her closer...

"He can't be in two places at once," she heard herself say, and when the others looked incredulously in her direction she repeated herself as though they hadn't heard. "I mean—yes, of course he can. But not in the way I'm meaning. Not in the way that matters."

A moment passed. Realization dawned on Kaitlyn's face first. "Oh, no. No-no-no…"

"Oh, what now?" Benjamin growled, slapping at his arms against the cold.

Kaitlyn's pale face kaleidoscoped from horror to indignation, then back to a duller terror as she fixed him with her gaze. "She wants us—"

"It's the only way," Riley cut in serenely.

"—to *split up*." Kaitlyn wrapped her arms around herself, casting a glance back at the unlit windows of the cabin. "You know why this is a bad idea, don't you?" she said, seeming to address nobody in particular. "You know what happens next."

"Yeah," Benjamin answered, shivering. "Either we freeze to death or we starve. Look, I'm not that psyched to go Scooby Doo out here anymore than you are—but I don't hear anybody else throwing out other options. So unless you've got a brighter idea, I say let's try it while the sun's still climbing. None of us brought up much winter gear … especially you, Kait."

"You're an idiot," came the reply. But the words were heatless. She looked at Benjamin like he was a blood-fat mosquito splashed across her windshield, but only for an instant. Her gaze soon wandered away, staring out among the trees, looking almost resigned.

"Two teams of two, then," she said at last. "We…we'll have to be even more careful, now, only one group can go armed, after all. That means you stay in eyesight of each other at all times, but you don't get close. Ten feet minimum…and for the love of God, don't *touch* each other. If you see anything—my body-snatching ex-boyfriend, for example—you call it in first. And check in every ten minutes for as long as you've got signal."

"I'll go with Kaitlyn…" Riley began to say, but Alice paled

and shook her head.

"No—I'll go with Kaity," she argued sharply. "It's my fault he's here, and it's my fault we don't have the car anymore. I've gotta do something to ... to make up for that."

Heat like a column of molten rock—Riley looked to Benjamin, feeling an objection rising in him, but instead, to her great shock, his face seemed to droop as a cold, cloudy breath hissed through his lips.

"Whatever," he murmured after a pause. "Uh ... Stay sharp out there, then."

He turned back towards the cabin porch, squaring his broad shoulders, with his back to the rest of the group. "I'm going to put some clothes on," he said. "And maybe eat something. Then Riley and me can hike up to the cabin. It's better if we take that side of things—I can lead us there."

And with that, he picked his way barefoot across the gravel lot and disappeared through the cabin's ajar front door, moving slowly, his shoulder muscles rolling under the bathrobe in fluid rhythms. Riley cocked her head, watching him. A flash of scalding hatred simmered quickly away, leaving behind a film of curiosity that gleamed so bright it was nearly blinding.

Instinct took hold. She followed Benjamin inside, leading the others. Their bodies filled their stomachs, fuel against the cold, eaten in thin silence. He wouldn't look at her, at Alice—his eyes remained downcast and half-lidded, lost in toast and oatmeal—and Alice would only look at Kaitlyn. Only once did his gaze lift, and then it was only to fix her, Riley, with a look as alien as the unblinking eye roosting in her bones. A smile touched her lips; the fire in her blazed contentedly.

There's your face, Benji-Boy.

Time took a wiggle—suddenly Kaitlyn and Alice were gone, and she was outside, trudging through thick fallen pine needles, listening to the dry crunch of Benjamin's footsteps off to her right as they threaded between the pine trees. He'd put on a sleek black pea coat with fake gray fur lining the hood, but not before he'd slipped a poofy green down-lined parka over her shoulders, muttering something about the wind through his teeth. She'd felt loved in that moment, wriggling under that brief and gentle touch—again she wished she could pin the sensation down under glass, peel back layer after layer until she could study what twitched beneath the tingling of her skin... Now the cabin had dropped away behind them, disappearing into the brown-and-gray maze of bark-stripped trees, and Riley found herself wondering how well he really knew these woods, though the thought came and went with all the heat of a lightbulb flicking on behind a closed door.

They had been walking perhaps ten minutes. Benjamin had not spoken once, not since the front lot; his directions to her were grunts and pointed gloved fingers, always up the next rolling hill, always south or south-west, and he had stayed a dutiful ten feet from her, his face perpetually hidden by the ruff of his hood or by some leaning tree-trunk. At the twenty-minute mark, Riley gave up trying to catch his eye and occupied herself slapping the cold out of her arms, marveling at the sensation of her frosty breath whooshing in and out of aching lungs. The fact that her arms and legs were moving without her ordering them was no concern; the voice of the shadow had explained everything in a tone as thick and clear as amber.

It was true, she wasn't in control. But she had lost nothing.

She had never been in control.

With her limbs and lungs and blinking eyes on autopilot, it left Riley's mind free to cruise: back through the sloping forest she wandered, until her imagination gazed down upon Alice and Kaitlyn picking their way down into a dry creek bed. Perhaps there was some slick mud at the bottom, or fresh winter ice—ice, yes, and Alice had descended first, offering a strong mittened hand to Kaitlyn to steady her down the steep slope. Their hands clasped only briefly, but Riley could feel the spark traversing flesh, and she thought of Alice's fingers combing through Kaitlyn's dark hair, the fingertips tapping along her slender shoulders, and all at once an upwelling of such confusion and rage surged in her like a great dark thunderhead that she began to shake almost violently, and when she looked down at her own trembling right hand she could have sworn that for the briefest instant the fist was clenched around a hank of curly auburn hair and caked in drying blood...

And then, out of an open blue sky: "It's you. Isn't it."

Benjamin's crunching footsteps had stopped only a few paces off, just beyond a slender pine tree. The top half of his face was obscured by a sheaf of brown, low-hanging needles, and his visible jaw was twisted up into a peculiar half-smile that still showed both tooth and gum.

"You're him, aren't you?" he asked. "You're Lutz."

Then, even before the shadow in her bones could move within her, he laughed forcefully, appearing around the tree with his hand pressed flat to his cheek.

"I just wanted to see what you'd say," he told her. "To see if you'd react. But I guess there really is no way to tell, is there?"

Riley felt her mouth kink up in bemusement, which she hid behind a cough into a curled fist. The furnace in her guts, which had sent up showers of ember-motes mere seconds prior, cooled as quickly as though it had been doused.

"Sure seems that way," she replied, wiping a trickle of mucus off her top lip. "But now you've got me curious. What would you have done? If I'd said 'yes' just now—just outed myself. Right here in the woods. What was your master plan after that?"

Benjamin scowled. "I keep thinking about that," he said with a shrug. "But I guess there's really nothing either of us could do, is there? At least, not until we catch up with the others."

"I suppose that's true," Riley said. "Picture this: I'm Lutzed, and I grab hold of you. Then *you're* Lutzed, but I'm free. Nothing changes. We still both know where the danger is."

"Pure stalemate." Ben's gaze turned wry, clouded by apprehension. "Unless you're not trying to contaminate me at all," he pondered. "Maybe Kait's right. Maybe you brought me out here to kill me."

Laughter bubbled in Riley's chest—she could feel it tickle, like pins pushing through a thick blanket. "That is what Kaitlyn said, isn't it?" she replied. Then, off Benjamin's look: "Oh, please. I'd need the rifle for that. I've seen you without your shirt—it'd be like hunting big game, I imagine. What's your thing, protein shakes? Multivitamins?"

Benjamin chuckled mirthlessly at this, the sound of it like stone sliding on stone. "Then maybe we've got it reversed. You Lutz me, and Lutz uses my body to kill you. Maybe I bash your head in with a rock. Or strangle you. Or..."

He paled suddenly, turning the color of a fish's underbelly scales. He turned his face away into the hood of his coat, and his hand, which had drifted back to rest against the trunk of the skinny pine, picked frantically at the flaking brown bark.

Riley's pocket buzzed, Alice checking in:

ALL CLEAR HERE SO FAR. SEE ANYTHING?

"Or what, Benjamin?" Riley asked, slipping the smartphone back into her pocket—and the other Riley, the Riley lying submerged under the deep, heavy warmth, mouthed the question as though it were a line in a movie she knew by heart. "I mean, Christ—is that what you've been thinking about?"

But Benjamin said nothing, only ground a handful of bark to powder in his fist.

"That's what you're afraid of," Riley persisted. "Isn't it. That he'll use you again..."

"I don't want to talk about it."

"...to get at us..."

"Riley, *stop*..."

"To get at Kaitlyn."

"*He's already done it once.*"

144

Five words that sounded like five blows from a fist.

Benjamin sighed—the force of it seemed to rattle his eaves, shuddering him like an abandoned barn. "I...can't get it out of my head," he continued in a smaller voice than Riley had expected. She crept closer, bending forward to hear. "The look on her face when the lights came on. I see Kait, holding that gun, and her shoulders are shaking but the barrel's steady as a fucking iron rail, you know? And I'm on the floor, and it's all blood everywhere—I'm looking up at her through this film of blood, but her eyes are still eggshell white. Eyes like drawings of eyes. And there's Alice, coming in behind her, and I don't even have to see her face to know what she's going to think. I can see how scared Kait is. I can *feel* it. Her terror's like moisture in the air. In that moment, you know, I thought I'd really done it. That I'd tried to..."

His voice choked off with a sudden squeak, like a faucet tightened all the way. Riley was a yard off now—she could stretch out, touch him with her fingertips.

"I thought she was going to pull the trigger then," he concluded, staring past her into the dense trees. "And I wanted her to."

Riley frowned, cocking her head, feeling her long hair slide across her forehead and cheeks, the bonfire inside her shocked down to hot coals for the moment. "Well, all right then," she said. "Do you feel that way now?"

Benjamin wrinkled his nose, joggling his glasses. "Who cares? It's too late. She saw everything. As if I hadn't been a bastard all weekend anyhow."

He straightened, looking into Riley's face with clear eyes. If he'd noticed how close she'd come, he didn't show any sign of discomfort. "I think she feels like she owes me love," he murmured. "That's how her brain moves—like that's the price of whatever I'm doing for her, somehow. But this'll snap her out of *that* for sure. Did you notice that when I was saying all those horrible things last night, nobody batted an eye? Nobody thought, oh, Ben's sure acting strange, I wonder what his damage is? And now if we ever get back to school, any time she'll touch me, all she'll see is the freeze-frame of me climbing on top of her best friend in a dark bedroom. It'll always be in the back of her head: Maybe I *am* that kind of person. Maybe it wasn't all Lutz, after all. Maybe I just hate Kait that much."

They were face to face now, so close Riley could smell sleep still on his breath. Alice buzzed in again, the phone's vibration insistent against her thigh:

EARTH TO RILEY – PLEASE CHECK IN, LET US KNOW YOURE OK

"She cares about Kaitlyn a whole lot, doesn't she," she said.

Ben looked at her strangely. "Oh, you picked up on that, did you?" he said. "You didn't know her before—it's like she's got some kind of grip on Alice. I really think if she told Alice to jump off a bridge, there'd be no hesitation at all. Just the sound of a splash, off-screen. I can't even picture Kait in a room alone without her now. And now that she's *here*, it's rubbing off on me—whatever *it* is. Look, I don't hate her, you know, or at least … I don't know what it is about her, but I—I hate who I am around her. But I can't stop myself. I say things, do things … things I wouldn't—"

Riley rolled her eyes and cut him off with a frustrated slash of her hand. "And how does Kaitlyn feel about her?" she demanded.

But for the moment, Benjamin said nothing. His eyes were closed behind his glasses now, but Riley could see the bulge of his eyeballs moving under the thin membrane of each lid.

"They were close when they were kids, weren't they?"

Benjamin nodded, angling his face towards the forest floor.

"Yeah… Since they were twelve. They lived next door from each other. She told me Kait's parents weren't home a lot, so they spent most of their time in Alice's house. Sleepovers, stuff like that. Park picnics. Whatever girls that age like, I dunno. It always made me feel weird when she talked about it. There's this one Halloween party she always comes back to—"

"Halloween, huh?" Riley tilted her head sagely, casting a glance over Benjamin's shoulder. They had been coming down a steep hill, and the sun was resting on the crest, skewered by the silhouettes of toothpick pines. Her jaw ached for a cigarette; her hand moved unconsciously, shaking one out of the box while the other produced her Zippo lighter.

"Take it from somebody who knows," she told him, taking a heavy drag once the cigarette was lit and in her mouth. "Girl friendships at that age, they get crazy intense. There's a word in Japanese for it, I think—God help me if I can remember it. But it's like an addiction. It changes your whole brain chemistry around. Your friendship becomes a little marriage, almost. Like there's nobody else on the planet that matters."

She paused, searching his face with the intensity of a scientist. "Some people," she continued, blowing smoke in his direction, "even mistake it for being in love."

Benjamin's jaw tightened. "I wish you wouldn't say that."

But there was no surprise in his voice.

Alice again, three messages in a row, frantic now:

RILEY ARE YOU OKAY? WE'RE WORRIED ABOUT YOU
WE'RE GOING BACK – MEET US AT THE CABIN ASAP
WAS THAT A CAR HORN?

"Is that Alice texting in?" Benjamin asked.

Riley ignored the question and stepped back, half-turning away from the sun. "Listen to me—you love her, don't you?" Out of the corner of her eye, she saw him nod his head. "Why did you think I wanted to search with Kaitlyn instead of with you? You're a good guy, Benjamin, and Alice knows it. She's a smart girl, give her some credit. Whatever happened this weekend, she'll forgive you for. It'll take a couple of weeks, but she'll get over it. I guarantee you that."

Then she turned her head, hiding behind the sweep of her

hair a grin that mocked all other human smiles. Ember rolled over ember in her belly, and when she opened her mouth her words tasted like hot, dry ashes spilling from her tongue.

"But she won't ever forgive you for not being Kait Brecker."

Benjamin made no sound—Riley longed to turn, to savor the phantom agony no doubt crawling hand-over-claw across his features. She was keenly aware of him, a sharp presence trembling in her wake like a shadow cast on the surface of a pool. But there was something happening inside her. The nicotine calm had already opened the sponge-holes of her brain, but now a secondary release was hitting her hard: it was like fists gripping every nerve ending in her body, and they were loosening their grip, finger by finger. There was a wave of intense sensation, neither pleasure nor pain—and then the bonfire blazing in her belly whipped away in the end, to hot coals, to ash, and then to nothing.

For a mere instant, Riley broke gasping to the surface.

"But you can't *listen* to me," she said, whirling to find him crouched against a raised root, his head in his hands. It was a struggle to form words; the world still seemed half-real, her movements sluggish and juddering as though in a dream. But she had to fight through. She had to warn him. She had to *come through.* "Benjamin, I didn't know what I was *saying...*"

"Stop talking," he mumbled, his voice sticky with mucus.

But before she could speak again, Riley's tongue froze in her jaw. The heat inside her, however briefly it had been suppressed, now blazed up with indignation. Her hand flew to her face, nearly poking her eye out as she snatched the cigarette from her mouth, holding it still smoking down by her hip.

"Listen," she heard herself say, her other hand laying a finger across her lips. "Do you hear that?" For the first time, the voice that spilled from her mouth did not sound like her own.

Benjamin picked his face up from his hands, twisting his neck to follow her pointing finger. Through the trees came a high, piercing cry from a long way off—at first it could have been a bird, but the second time it rang out, the sound could only be human.

It was a scream. A girl's scream.

"That's Alice!" Benjamin bellowed, lurching to his feet. He nearly tripped over the pine's root, but he maintained his momentum, already in motion towards the source of the cry. "Christ, we're far off. Come on!" He only looked back once to see if Riley was following him, but then he vanished behind the scrub of dry brown needles, his footsteps thundering up the incline.

So close, Riley-Bear. How does it feel to be the silver medal?

Riley shivered, tracking the sound of his footfalls with her eyes. The cigarette was still between her fingers, smoldering but not yet forgotten. At last she followed, but first she pulled down the collar of the down overcoat and twisted the ember-end of the cigarette into the soft exposed flesh just above her collarbone. The pain was sharp and instant—the ember hissed against her skin, and the smell of that small spot of girl-flesh cooking tickled her nostrils.

But she could not scream. She could only grin, the whole world cold against her exposed teeth while thin wet lines trickled down from her unblinking eyes, and the fire scorching her from the inside out burned hotter than Hell itself. Her phone vibrated against her hip; she fished it out, didn't even bother to read Alice's latest panicked message, typed out three words in a series of staccato, mechanical clicks:

SEE – YOU – SOON

Chapter 13

Welcome Wagon

There was a boy Cormac didn't know in the gravel lot in front of the cabin.

He punched off the music inside the Jeep with his thumb, then tilted his neck one way, then the other, touching ear to shoulder to feel the stiff vertebrae pop in sequence. The other guy, he'd come up through the trees on the other side of the gravel, kicking red sneakers through fallen pine needles. Now he loafed on the steps, chin in his hands, half-hidden behind the wood-paneled station wagon with the propped-up hood. He was close enough to hear Cormac's Grand Cherokee idling, but he didn't so much as turn his head: He kept staring off into the forest, cold as a sphinx, occasionally shutting his eyes and angling his face as though listening for something, some otherworldly signal coming through the trees.

Cormac watched him through the windshield, drumming nervous fingers on the steering wheel as he weighed options against each other. He'd hoped he'd see Riley first, make contact before he tried to smooth in with the rest of her crew. Her last two broadcasts had him scrambled: the first, a shaky cell cam video inside the cabin, audio all blown out, a wash of shouts and squeals as the camera swung around a ring of flushed, laughing faces. He'd begged the address—then, silence for two hours. And then at last, when he'd started kicking himself for blowing so much gas money on nothing, her strange truncated reply blipped in:

BEN'S PISSED I ASKED Y—

He'd mulled that one the rest of the night. There had to be more to it, he figured—he'd fired off half-cooked late-night texts himself after an O-Lambda boozer wound down... But instead of getting a straight answer out of her, he'd lolled in bed another two hours, thoughts chasing round and round like slot cars, until at last he sank into tossing, hot-breathed dreams. That ring of red faces circled him in his sleep, faster and faster, their laughter distorted into animal screams and grunts and cries.

She sent him the address in the morning, but by then he'd had time to question the position of all the stars in his sky—and now he was here, staring over the steering wheel at who could only be Benjamin Alden, his wind-tossed hair piled like lint in a dustbin, and he felt those old scratching anxieties come clawing back to surface. He thought about squeezing off a quick text to Riley, *Hey, come outside, I'm here,* but thought better of it.

You're here now, Caveman. You got this far. Go bang rocks together. Make nice with the big dog.

He feather-footed the gas, pulling into the lot at last, gravel grumbling under the Jeep's tires. Benjamin's head whipped towards him like a bird's—no surprise on his face, just a level studying gaze. Cormac killed the engine, slid his seat back, and swung out the driver-side door, wary of eye-contact. The cold hit him like a wall of force, but the silence hit harder. Icy dread splashed against his innards: Where were the others? Riley, Alice, that Kaitlyn girl? Benjamin's face stayed coolly neutral as he stood and began striding towards the Jeep, and panic scrabbled inside him, but as he thought about slamming the door and gunning it for the coast again, the other boy's face broke out in a broad, almost sheepish grin.

"Hey," he called out, "*you're* not supposed to be here!"

Then he put out his hand, grinning broader still. "You're Cormac, aren't you," he said. "I'm Lutz. Lutz Visgara."

Cormac reached, and nearly fell out of the Jeep. By the time he steadied himself, clumsily catching his weight one-handed on the car's roof, the other boy, Lutz, had already pumped his hand twice before retracting his own and stuffing it in his pocket with a sly look on his face. "It is Cormac, isn't it?" he asked, laughter creeping into his voice. "I didn't just fuck that up, did I?"

Cormac brushed something that wasn't there off his flannel button-down. "My friends call me Caveman," he mumbled. And then, unnecessarily: "I'm not supposed to be here."

Lutz finally bust out into laughter, which he smothered behind one hand.

"I bet they do call you that," he said, nodding. He rubbed his eye, shook off a yawn. "That's all right," he continued. "I'm not supposed to be here, either."

"Where are the others?" Cormac peered over the other boy's shoulder. The cabin's windows were dark and cold, but the front door had been left ajar, moving slightly when the wind picked up. "I'm at the right place—aren't I? Riley gave me the address, but my GPS crapped out a few miles ago. We're kind of in the middle of nowhere."

"Yeah, yeah. Middle 'o nowhere." Lutz mooched his lips in a weird lopsided smile. "We're playing a game of hide and seek," was his response. "They're looking for me, out in the woods, but I gave them the old run-around. They'll catch on soon, though."

Strange vibrations from this guy. Cormac couldn't figure the smirk in his voice. Every smile showed half his teeth—it unsettled him, somehow, set his own teeth on edge. But he seemed friendly enough, and this reception was a far shout from the unfriendliness he'd braced for on the trip over.

"Riley didn't give you the address," Lutz said. "I did."

Cormac blinked, once, twice. "I don't understand," he protested—but the other boy had already turned his back, ambling toward the porch, his sneakered feet making almost no sound on the gravel. Cormac pursued. "I don't understand," he repeated. "The message came from her phone. She gave me the number."

"That's true," came the reply. "Or, it may be true. I really don't know. But it was me that gave you the address, just the same." Then he turned again to look at Cormac, his face thin and grinning and flushed with cold. "Tell me, Caveman—what do you know about girls?"

Cormac felt his back stiffen. *What do you know about girls?* A locker-room challenge, leveled at his manhood—or something else? Only seconds to decide. He studied the other boy's face, nearly a foot lower than his own. He'd gotten jabbed for it his whole life: his huge frame, the meat hanging heavy on heavy bones; his feathery voice, his joy and rage forever jammed in his throat; the way his eyes would glaze and cross whenever he got lost in a daydream... Sure, in high school he'd grown into himself, sculpting his bulk into sports-hardened muscle, learned he was as fast in the water as he was slow on land. But he never forgot the feeling of eyes on his back, never managed to shake away the weight of a thousand cold assumptions.

Not until six days ago. Not until Riley.

You need to guess my name, she'd told him. *And if you don't get it right, you need to tell me something about you. Something nobody else at this party knows. House Rules.*

"I know they don't play fair," he said at last, smiling in spite of himself.

Lutz raised an eyebrow. "She's a riot, isn't she? Riley, I mean," he continued, off Cormac's stunned look. "You and her, huh. Very nice, Caveman, ve-ry nice."

"Lucky guess..." Cormac rubbed the back of his neck, suddenly shy. "Why'd you ask?"

"Nah." Lutz shook his head, the grin shrinking to a smirk. "I've been around these people forever. Feels like forever. No secrets between us, that kinda thing. She says you've got a dick like an Italian sausage. First thing she said to me this weekend."

The red shot all the way up to Cormac's crewcut. "She said that," he mumbled, a dull admission. *Damn it all—that's just the kind of thing she would say. Even as a joke.*

"Like I said—no secrets." Lutz shrugged. "It's kinda creepazoid, when you really think about it. What do you think?

Are we a freaky cult up here, or what?"

"Hey, look. When are the other's getting back?" Cormac glanced past Lutz's head at the darkened windows of the cabin, his teeth beginning to chatter. This was the furthest north he'd ever been, and he hadn't dressed for the wind or the cold.

"D'you love her, Caveman?"

Cormac felt the hackle-hairs rise on the back of his neck. He'd only taken his eyes off Lutz for a second, but now he was across the gravel lot, kneeling on the porch, facing him almost in supplication. The skin on Cormac's back began to crawl, a small patch down near his hip. The vibrations were getting stranger, like ocean waves rolling in reverse. Sand crashing against the water again and again and again.

But still he thought of Riley. Of a dark room in the back of Lambda house, a door discovered in a drunken fumbling, of the two of them sitting cross-legged on an unmade bed, the ember-point of Riley's cigarette the only true light source other than the milky moon coming through the half-cracked blinds. She never touched him, save for an instant her fingers brushed across his leg as they positioned themselves on the bed. The noise of the party was only a dull pulse through the walls—music and laughter and the occasional tinkling shout of breaking glass.

I'm going to tell you something about yourself now, she'd said. *Maybe something you know about yourself, maybe something you don't. But if I get it wrong—I drink.*

He heard, but could not see, frothy beer sloshing in a Solo cup. *And what happens if you get it right?* he'd wanted to know, his voice still guarded.

Nothing, she'd replied after a small silence. *Then I know something about you I didn't before. Then I know you a little better. Isn't that enough?*

"I'm sorry?" It was all Cormac could work the nerve to say. It was getting hard to think, all of the sudden, like the air was too thick, like gauze filling his head and his lungs.

"Oh, don't look at me like that," Lutz huffed. "Not in, like, the Biblical sense. I mean truly: Do you want the best for her? That's all love is, you know. It's a conscious thing. It's a *choice*. It's—" Then he paused almost mid-word, perking his head up like a dog after a chipmunk, angling his nose out towards the forest. Cormac followed his gaze, but only the trees stared back. "Well, do you?" he asked at last as if coming out of a trance.

"I mean ... yeah! Or, I guess so. Like, if that's all it is—"

Lutz tsk'ed over folded hands. "Such commitment. Weren't you listening? She needs your *support*, Caveman. That's all a woman needs from a man, my guy."

Almost unconsciously, Cormac was stumbling across the gravel towards the porch, not taking his eyes off the kneeling Lutz. "Aren't you cold, dude?" he mumbled. And then, out of the corner of his eye—a blob of white canvas, a flash of dull crimson ichor... "Muvver of God," he blurted, lips already numb with cold. "What happened to the *engine?*"

"She needs your support," Lutz repeated, his voice oddly hollow. Cormac whirled clumsily just in time to watch the other boy rise from the porch as quickly as if he'd been jerked on a string fixed to the top of his head. There was something in his hand, concealed behind his hip and by the drape of his hoodie jacket. "That's all a woman needs from a man."

"Whose blood is it?" Cormac asked, though the words felt ridiculous now—as though he knew the answer, as though he'd known all along...

Lutz snorted. "That's just something I picked up on the way here. You don't need to worry about that. It's not really important anymore."

"I... I think I'm gonna go inside and wait..." Cormac said, tried to say. But his legs were like wood posts, his thoughts turning slow and heavy in his head like taffy. His lips had moved, but he could not be sure if he had really spoken. "Are you sure... you're okay out here?"

"Aw, now, see? There's the concern! There's the *commitment!*" Lutz took one step toward him, then another. His hand came up into view — he held a small hacksaw by the handle in his clenched fist. There were wood shavings on the blade, which refused to reflect light. "I'll be fine, Caveman," the other boy said in an even voice. "Like I said, you don't need to worry about this. In fact — you don't really need to worry about anything. It's just not worth it."

Every muscle in Cormac's towering frame struggled to move. But it was shadow-boxing: There was nothing to fight against, no bonds to break. Only the cold — and this was quickly seeping away, replaced by fear that spread inside him like a warm pool of honey. Lutz's smile was no longer a smile. His lips were stretched tight around his mouth, ringed around a grin that was only two parallel lines of perfect white teeth.

"You know, I didn't plan any of this," he was saying, peering at Cormac through squinted eyes, gauging the distance between them. "I've already got a fish on the line, so to speak. But I love her, Caveman. And I guess this is what you do when you're in love."

A horrible thought stirred, cutting through the coiling terror. Cormac's lips moved again, sticking in the cold, sticky and slow as though they might never move again, all to form one single, desperate, terrible word:

"*Riley?*"

Lutz's face darkened like a thundercloud. He raised his fist, pressing the handle of the saw into Cormac's own hand, closing the fingers around it. "Actually," he sneered, "that's none of your fucking *business*, friend-o."

And then Cormac's hand raised the saw, turning the blade around, and he tilted his chin up towards the sky, to accept it, as though he was going to shave. But his hands did not shake. He felt liquid heat shoot up his arms and legs like agony as he sank backwards, being siphoned away by this warmth, drawn down into a deep and grasping darkness. Now there could be no more fear in him. Now there could be no more him at all. This moment seemed to suspend itself, juddering slightly like a videocassette on pause.

The teeth of the saw touched his neck, paused there, pressed against the skin.

Then somewhere through the shadow, a car horn bellowed out a single lusty note:

Hey. Come outside. I'm here.

Chapter 14

The Outsider

Alice reached the tree-line first, puffing from the descent, with Kaity close at her heels—and when her scream tore out across the gravel lot, at first she couldn't tell that the sound had come from her at all. It struck her numb, like a sour note struck hard in the middle of a complicated piano piece. At first there was no fear at all. Only that automatic shriek, and the echoes of it ringing back from the forest, and the sound of her friend's footsteps coming up the deer path behind her, and the terrible juddering beat of her heart in her ears.

When she looked down across the gravel, all she could see was red.

Behind the front left wheel of the station wagon was the beginnings of a grisly tableau: a pair of Timberland boots lay together on their sides, the ankles twisted at bone-snapping angles. Beyond that was what remained of the body. Lying stomach-down and almost completely naked, arms splayed drunkenly, broad muscular shoulders glazed with glistening blood, redder than red could be. And above that, the white pulp of the head...

No. She'd got it wrong.

There was no head at all.

Alice thought her lungs would bust. Affixed to the corpse's shoulders was Mister Face, the rust-colored painted grin twisted upward to face the bright noonday sky, the long wooden spike thrust down into the oozing stump of the severed neck. Now there was pus-colored stuffing pushing through split seams all over the ball, and the whole affair had deflated, caved in, with dents like finger-holds on a bowling ball almost forming a second face where large strong hands had seized hold of it.

She could almost hear the drone of flies gathering.

Alice stared, not trusting herself to blink, horrified at what her imagination would conjure behind closed eyelids. She listened to the sound of Kaity not breathing behind her. In a sudden flash, the urge to laugh surged like madness inside her— to throw back her head, to bay at the high, white sun and let the red creep in at the corners until it swallowed her up.

Lutz killed this person. Left him here for us to find.

Left him here because he wanted us to see.

"It's Cormac," she heard Kaity say behind her. "It's gotta be."

Alice turned, unconsciously reaching behind her to take hold of Kaity's hand—but when she looked in her friend's face, a new wave of confusion rolled through her. There was no dismay, no disgust, no fear that she could project onto that mask. Only boredom in the eyes, and something deadly close to mirth in the up-tilt of her chapped lips. Kaity was staring past her at the body with an expression dawning on bleak fascination, and Alice realized she had actually retreated a step backward, yelping at feeling a branch goosing her in the small of the back.

"Kaity..." Her mouth barely moved to form the words. "I... I don't understand."

"I warned you," came the reply in a tight breathless voice. "I told you what was going to happen." Kaity's eyes finally met hers, but they seemed not to see her, looking through her, filling up with red as well. "What do you all *want* from me? Didn't I say this would happen? Didn't I tell you what he was going to do?"

Without warning, she turned, balled her fist, and struck at a sheaf of pine branches hanging close to her head. Her first blow flailed pathetically through the empty space between the needles, and she struck them again and again, grunting with effort.

"Didn't I tell you?" she repeated with every whiffling blow. "Didn't I warn you? What do you want from me? What do you *want?*"

"Kaity, *stop*," Alice cried out in desperation.

But then came a horrible sound: Kaity's choking, sobbing laugh seemed to trickle out of her like sewage from a rusting pipe. Her face pinched up, flushed with cold, her jaw tight and her teeth clenched together in a rictus of mirth, but all Alice could see were her glassy eyes—dark and smooth, like a doll's eyes. And she could see the hunting rifle, cradled under her friend's arm, the barrel shaking as Kaity shook. Alice looked away, but there was only Cormac rotting in the gravel and the empty, bloody space where his head should have been. Even in the depths of their revelry the night prior, before things had soured, Kaity did not laugh like that. She had *never* laughed like that.

Alice had never heard a human being make a noise like that before at all.

She shook herself, shivering. No—she wouldn't allow herself to think like that. The fear, the cold, the fatigue from the hike, it was turning the inside of her head to candy-floss, scrambling her thoughts, stretching them thin… Kaity was her *friend*, wasn't she? Kaity was trying to *protect* her. If Lutz had left this for them to find, it had to be a message for *her*, not Alice. *You're next.* This was what she'd prepared herself for, wasn't it? What she'd been dreading these past months?

Wasn't this what she'd prayed would happen?

Don't deny it, spoke a voice from the bottom of Alice's mind. *You wanted this—to believe it was a monster that took Kaity from you, instead of a man. That's easier, isn't it? A monster you could fight and beat and kill, and take his head back to your friend on a dish. And when you did, even while you were wiping his blood off your sword, she'd be so goddamn grateful that—*

Again, she shook herself, banishing the thoughts. Her phone buzzed three times—a missed message. She thrust a mittened hand down into her parka pocket. A text from Riley: *see you soon.* So they'd heard the car horn too. Well, that was good. She and

Ben would be back soon, and it would be so good to see Ben now. Good to share this abominable feeling with another person—for even though Kaity was close by her, now leaning against a tree with her arms wrapped to the elbows around herself, the feeling that she was utterly alone in this wilderness would not stop pawing her.

Just when the thought occurred to her that perhaps she should warn her friends about what they would encounter upon their return, Ben came crashing through the tree-line on the opposite end of the lot, hollering her name.

"Alice!" At first he appeared not to see her, scanning first the porch, then the clearing itself, his eyes unfocused. "Are you hurt? Where's Kait? I heard screaming, and..."

His voice dropped away as his gaze fell to the ground. Alice watched his lips move, forming indecipherable phrases— perhaps a prayer, or something like it.

"Oh, God," he managed to murmur at last, almost inaudible at that distance.

Then he pitched forward and emptied his breakfast out onto the gravel at his feet.

Riley emerged next, panting from the run, so the howl of terror that flew from her lips escaped half-formed, an aborted wheeze crawling from her lungs. A host of emotions flashed across her face—horror, confusion, disgust, fury. She tried to scream again, and then again, but no sound emerged at all. So instead she brushed past Ben, still bent forward and retching horribly, and rushed forward to kneel beside the corpse.

"*Don't touch it!*" Kaity cried out, pushing past Alice to join the others in the clearing. But it was too late. Riley was nearly on top of the body, pulling at one splayed arm as though she would turn him onto his back, both hands already slick with blood.

"What happened?" she screamed up at Kaity.

Kait regarded her stolidly. "I think it's fairly obvious what happened."

Riley sent up a yowl, and Kaity stalked away towards the second vehicle in the lot, a white Jeep Grand Cherokee with a blue stripe painted nose-to-tail along the hood and across the roof to the back hatch. "Hood's warm," she remarked, laying a palm to the metal. "He hasn't been here long. Lutz was here — maybe minutes ago. We can still catch him."

"But how?"

Alice almost clapped a hand over her mouth. The sound of her own voice frightened her — she thought the sight of Cormac's headless, naked bulk had killed it away. She forced herself to take one step forward, then another, advancing slowly across the lot towards the body until it stretched out before her, limp and massive, like a beached whale. Cormac could have been over six feet, she thought. Even without the head. Maybe close to seven.

Almighty Christ — it was already starting to stink.

"How? How what?" Ben asked, wiping sick and spittle off his chin.

"How did Lutz... *get* him?" she replied. She could not make herself say 'kill'. "How could he? We said he could only control one of us. And how could he possibly do... this?"

She gestured vaguely to the corpse. Riley wailed, swatted blood off her hands, wailed again, but nobody answered. Kaity kept inspecting the Jeep, circling it, peering into fogged windows and putting probing fingers under the lip of the hood.

"Engine's cooked," she remarked, heaving the hood up and peeking down beneath it. "Same as the other one. That's why he had to—"

"Urm... Guys?"

Ben circled the station wagon, knelt out of sight, came up with something balanced in his hands. Alice looked, and quickly looked away again: the teeth of the hacksaw were stained in blood, but worse were the pale chunks of flesh and skin nocked in the corners of the saw, bunched like sheets piled at the foot of the bed. Instead she focused on her boyfriend's face, but the disgust and anguish painted there was almost as horrible as the sight of the blood and offal on the blade of the saw.

"It's mine," he said in a sickly voice. "I... I brought it for firewood. I didn't know how much we'd have, or if the heat would work. I... I thought..."

His jaw kept moving several moments more, but his lips formed no words, only flapping like a puppet's mouth with a hand inside. The hacksaw slipped from his blood-slick fingers— Alice heard it clatter against the gravel over Riley's thick, wet sobs.

"I think he made him do it," he said at last. "He took the saw, and..."

"Don't say it." Riley lurched to her feet, wobble-legged, almost drunken in her movements. "Don't you dare say those *fucking* words, Benjamin Alden. You're the one who didn't want him here. I don't want to hear you talk about him."

Ben stiffened, revulsion spinning swiftly into anger. "You're right," he said. "You're the one that wanted him here. And look what happened to him when he arrived."

"You son of a bitch—"

Riley advanced on Ben with a snarl, her fists raised, but Kaity cut them off with a shrill whistle through her teeth. One by one they turned to her—she was sitting cross-legged on the hood of Cormac's jeep, the winter sun over and behind her. In that light her face was little more than a black spot coming out of the sun, but Alice thought she caught something almost disdainful in the lift of her head and the queenly arch of her back.

"Do I have your attention now," she said.

They all stared, but Kaity looked away from them, the fingers of her right hand drumming against the Jeep's hood. The rifle lay across her lap, the barrel pointed off into the trees. Alice thought of an old soldier, staring off into a bloody, booming past, recalling various frantic, kinetic terrors with cold regard. A soldier, yes—a soldier, or a stone idol. Something unmovable.

Something *ancient*. Only an image, an emissary of a greater, unknowable whole.

"You knew what he could do," she said, still staring impassively out towards the road. "You knew what he wanted. What all of you mean to him now. And I told you what it would take to stop him. Did you think there wouldn't be blood by the end of this?"

"You knew this would happen?" Riley scuffed her heel in the gravel, pointing one manicured finger at Cormac's body. "You knew he'd..."

"I didn't know he was coming here," Kaity shot back, her head whipping around so quickly that her hood flew off. "I'm not the one that gave him the address. But you saw the blood on the ball and on the car. Where do you think he got it? He's already hurt somebody else—we just haven't found that corpse yet."

She slid down off the hood of the Jeep, hoisting the rifle in her arms. All three others jumped a step back, Alice included. She could feel something stirring within her—not fear, there was plenty of that already, but a deeper dread, clear and cold like snowmelt. She still could not see Kaity's face. It was a black, shapeless shadow framed by her dark hair.

"This doesn't change anything," she continued, her voice beginning to wobble slightly. "We still know he's here. And he's close. If we stick together this time, maybe we can—"

"Shut your mouth," Ben growled.

Kaity coughed, shook hair out of her face. "What did you say?" she said.

"You heard what I said."

Alice gaped at him—his eyes were opened so wide they seemed to bulge, like he was in a trance. "I don't want to hear another one of your fucking *speeches*," he uttered. "A guy just *died* here—doesn't that mean anything to you?"

For a moment, Kaity didn't speak. "I didn't know him," she

said, a shrug in her voice.

"None of us knew him!" Ben waved his hands at the rest of the group. "Nobody except for Riley. Have a little fucking humanity, huh? He's *dead*. Your ex-boyfriend *killed* him."

He flapped his hands as though he were drying them, pacing backwards a few steps towards the cabin, then back again.

"Tell me something," he said. "If you know so much about this—how'd he kill him? You said he was controlling one of us already. Do you expect us to believe Lutz talked him into, what, into sawing his own head off?"

Riley gagged, clapping a hand over her mouth as she glared at him, but Ben didn't even look her way. "I mean it," he insisted. "Tell the class—how'd he make it happen?"

Again Kaity was silent. Her hands twisted around the rifle, white-knuckled. Alice looked from her face to Ben's and back, feeling her heart shrinking into her chest like an eel vanishing down a hole. She wanted to tell Ben to stop, to *beg* him to stop— but another part of her wanted to hear the answer. Another part of her wanted to know for certain. Strange anger was rising in her gorge whose source she could not trace. But it felt old, older than herself, older than the hundreds of trees swaying in the cold wind around them.

It was old, and it demanded satisfaction.

"I'll tell you what I think," Ben said, his voice pitching up wildly. "I think you're wrong. I think he let us go a long time ago. We split up for forty minutes—he would have been alone with one of us all that time. Why didn't he attack then? I say..." He shrugged, an expansive gesture. "I say he wasn't there. *That's* how he tagged Cormac. That's how he took care of the Jeep. It's more important to him to keep us here than to kill us. It's all some kind of game to him—him, and whoever he's working with."

"Whoever he's working with," Kaity parroted. The shadow on her face squirmed. "All right, then. If you're so smart. Who's his man on the inside, then—me? Is *that* what you're trying to say?"

Ben shrugged, an awful sneer carved across his face. "You're obsessed with him," he stated. "He doesn't need to touch you to control you. *You* stripped the car. *You* put that volleyball on a spike. *You* sent us on a wild goose chase out into the woods—"

"Ben, this is *insane*," she interrupted. The shadow had melted away, but Alice could barely recognize the girl beneath: Kaity's face seemed to be twisting in on itself, her mouth corkscrewing downwards in disgust and rage, her eyes so wide and wet that they shone.

She looks like January Kaity, she realized. *The Kaity on my doorstep.*

The Kaity that Lutz sent me.

"If what... if that's true," she was saying, her voice like creaking wood. "Then I led you away... so Lutz could kill Cormac. Then it's like... it's like I killed him."

"Well. You are the only one holding a loaded gun."

Kait coughed again, and her grimace flashed quickly into a pained grin and back again. "Christ, you're serious," she said. "Christ, you're..." Cough, cough. "Guys, I would *never*..."

Her voice failed, and for the next few seconds, the only sounds she could make were panicked wheezes. "C'mon. No, *c'mon*, really. Tell me you don't believe it."

She looked from face to face in turn, her head whipping back and forth so quickly Alice thought her neck had to break, and she longed to comfort her, to tell her, *Of course. Of course we know you couldn't...* But the anger stopped her. Strange, alien anger that clamped her tongue and sewed her lips shut. Anger made her wait and see, to hold out for a terrible miracle...

"Alice?" Kaity said. "Riley?"

"You don't care that he's dead," Riley said suddenly. "Lutz got him because of you—and you don't even care. I can see it on your face. Goddammit, I tried to *help* you..." She kneaded her temples with her palms, her breath seeming to catch in her lungs. "What did we ever do to you, Kaitlyn?" she continued. "What did the *world* ever do to you? I can't even see you anymore. I mean, I'm not even supposed to be here…"

She trailed off, her hands falling helplessly to her sides, her face turning a sickly lime-green. "I didn't want to say anything," she continued at last. "But last night—I saw you get up. You came right past me, you had to, to reach the door. You had the gun. You didn't come back for an hour, and when you did, I heard the sink running. I heard you scrubbing something off. I didn't want to say anything," she repeated. "I really wanted to be friends with you."

"No. No." Kaity was shaking her head, slow movements, her eyes dead in their sockets. "No, tell them I wouldn't. I, I sleepwalk. Alice knows. Alice's seen it…" She was hugging the rifle to her now, cuddling it against her like a favorite plush bear.

Ben stepped forward, his mouth set in a hard line. "Give me the gun, Kait," he intoned. "It's over." And to the others, out of the corner of his mouth: "Get on either side of her. Be ready to catch her if—"

"*I said no!*" Kaity screamed. The words were barely words— what flew from her friend's lips was an animal shriek, the rabbit that sees the trap's teeth closing. "Alice, tell them. You know me. You know they're making a mistake. Just, just talk to them."

Now the mask broke. Now the tears rushed down, smearing down her face so that it glistened under the shadow of her hair. Her whole face seemed to split open, and Alice could feel tears welling in her own eyes, hot tears, the kind that stung and made you blink.

But the trap was already sprung. She opened her mouth to comfort her friend—but instead the horrible, ravenous anger seized hold of her, rushing up her throat like molten lava. And when the words came at last, they stung worse than the tears. They stung worse than anything had ever stung her before.

"You *abandoned* me," she wailed. "You abandoned my friendship—for *him*. Why?" She wrung her hands, tilting her head to peer under Kaity's bangs at her tear-streaked face. "What could he possibly do for you that..." Her breath caught in her throat as wind like razors ripped through her. "...that I couldn't?" she continued. "Kaity, I didn't hear from you for *months*. But I didn't care. When you showed up at my door, I thought this was finished. That you'd come to your senses, that we could go back to the way things used to be."

Alice sniffed, wiped her eyes, stared at the back of her hand and wiped again. Her lips cracked into a misshapen, painful grin, dry and sticking from the cold. *"The way things used to be,"* she repeated mirthlessly. "What the fuck is that? You slept in that monster's bed for four months. I don't even know who you are."

The wind howled. The trees creaked and bent. Kait didn't move—not at first. She blinked tears away, her breathing loud, full of snot. Her hands tightened around the barrel of the gun, her knuckles standing out pale on her hands, and as one man Ben and Riley surged forward, each grabbing hold of an arm.

"Drop it!" Ben was saying, "Drop it!"—*like he was reprimanding a dog,* Alice thought. *Like he was ordering a beast to heel.*

And when they got the rifle away from her and tossed her to the ground, she did not struggle or even cry out, not even when her head bounced against the gravel, opening a red seam along her right eyebrow. The blood trickled down, mixed with the tears on her face in streaks of pink and pale crimson. But no more tears flowed. Kait was silent, staring up at them, not even trembling in the cold now. If it wasn't for the movement of her eyes and the dull gleam of the blood on her face, she might have been dead, another corpse beside the headless horror lying not fifteen feet from her.

"Get inside," Ben intoned, his breath fogging. "We're done here."

They had to lead Alice to the door. She couldn't see the cabin or the trees or Kait lying on the ground or even the porch steps under her slow feet. Her eyes had filled up with red, and no matter how much she rubbed them, the red would not go away, and neither would the pricking sensation of Kait's bloody stare pressing into her, even when she was through the door, even when it was shut and locked at her back.

Chapter 15

Riley's Last Dance

She could hear their voices through the door. No hushed tones now—they didn't care if she heard them or not. Didn't need to hide the fact that they were talking about *her*, Kait Brecker, good old Heart-Brecker herself. There were curtains drawn over both transoms now, but she refused to press her eye to the glass to peer inside. She imagined the dim forms she would see through the gauze: dark, shapeless, distant. She imagined them moving in the shadows. She imagined the wracking cold of the glass on her skin.

"All I'm saying is, we shouldn't rule anything out."

Ben talking. Ben always *talking*—in full lawyer mode, each word sharp and penetrating. It hadn't taken him long to take command of the situation indoors. She could almost see him pacing in front of the dead, cold fireplace, striding across the burnt-red braided rug, poking holes in the air with his finger, gaining leverage inch by inch. It had to be him. She'd known it all along—when this moment came, it would be him at the other end of the wire. But this wasn't Ben Alden's fault. She'd done this to herself. An unforced error.

And now they were about to call the game.

She was sitting on the cabin porch, her legs folded sideways beneath her, leaning against the door. The blood from the cut in her eyebrow had dried fast, and when she raised her eyebrows she could feel it crackle and shift. She wanted to pick at it, to tear at the scab with her fingers. To pull and pull until she was tearing away living flesh instead of dead scab tissue, until she was all gone, until she had unmade herself the way Cormac had unmade himself. Until there was nothing left for Lutz to steal away.

"We're not going to talk about that."

Kait jumped. Alice's voice was just beyond the door, low to the ground, as though she was sitting against it. Kait could press a palm to the wood and be an inch away from her. The picture of it sank into her heart like strong fingers squeezing a stick of soft butter.

"Alice, you're not listening—" Ben began.

"I said we're not going to talk about that," Alice snapped. "I don't care what she did. We're not at that stage yet. We can't just—"

"I want to know why we can't talk about it." Riley now, sounding far off. Kait had to strain to catch her words. "We need to come up with a plan."

"That's not a plan."

"It's a start," Riley countered. "I want to know how we're getting out of here."

"The station wagon's toast," Ben said. "So's the Jeep—so long as Kait wasn't lying about that. We're three miles from the main road, and fifty from the nearest gas station or store, and we're running low on firewood. It's time to call somebody. To deal with this."

"You mean to deal with her."

"Alice, honey," Kait heard Riley say. "Look what she's already done. I know you two were close, but that body out there—she did that. Or she helped. No matter what else, that's on her. We need the police." There was a pause, like static between radio stations. "I'm sorry," Riley said, closer now. "I know you two were close. I know she was your friend."

"Yes," Alice said. "She was my friend."

Something cold and wet touched Kait's nose, and she looked up to see the first few fat snowflakes tumbling out of the sky. In moments, the air was thick with it: white whirled and danced before her eyes, and soon it was difficult to see the road from the porch. But she could see far enough—out to where Cormac lay, pale against the dark gravel.

She stood up so suddenly that blood rushed into her head, leaving her unsteady on her feet. She struggled for balance; she did not want to brace herself against the door, not while Alice was sitting there, not while the others were lurking just beyond the barrier. When her vision stopped swimming, she wobbled to the steps and padded down to the lot. The corpse slid fully into view, and then she was standing over it, peering down the length of the wooden spike shoved into the neck's oozing stump.

She tried to feel something. To dig down into herself, to conjure the appropriate sentiment. She scowled at Mister Face, then peered around at the surrounding trees. She wondered if she would hear Lutz coming. She hadn't before—he'd appeared in the door, unspeakably quiet, like dying in your sleep. She wondered what she would say to him, and what he would say to her. She wondered what they would do to each other when the time came.

On a mad whim, she angled her head down once more, regarding the body.

"Do you think I killed you?" she said.

I don't even know who you are.

Up floated a deep clear voice that sounded like it had emanated from deep within the chest cavity of the corpse. Kait's lips kinked in disgust, imagining the neck hole flapping like articulated lips.

"I'm Kait Brecker," she said. "Lutz Visgara is my boyfriend. Ex-boyfriend. The boy who... did this."

Oh. The syllable appeared in her ears like a sigh. *Well, I was holding the saw.*

"But you wouldn't have done this to yourself."

That's true. I didn't want to do this.

"Lutz made you do it. He can—"

Don't you think I know what Lutz can do?

Kait fell silent. The snow beat tiny frigid blows against her face.

"I'm sorry," she said.

Lutz didn't want to do this, either.

Kait's nose twitched. She'd seen it through the cover of the snowfall—the neck *had* moved that time. In her mind she took a step back, but the foot didn't move. She imagined looking down, seeing Cormac's huge hand wrapped around her ankle.

"Lutz never does anything he doesn't want to do," she said.

Not this. He's never done something like this.

"You're wrong." She looked back at the cabin's dark windows, feeling eyes pressing into her back. The curtains over the transoms didn't move, but she thought of dozens of faces swarming behind the glass. Hundreds of eyes, teeming like fish.

Never like this, said the deep empty voice. *Never this far.*

"You're wrong," she repeated. "You don't know what he's done, how could you know?"

He wouldn't unless you pushed him. The voice grew, reverberating like an empty room, spilling up and over like a pot of water on full boil.

And you pushed him hard, Cormac said. *And now look what happens. Look what happens when you put him in a corner. Look what you made him do—*

Kait lurched back as the corpse heaved forwards into a sitting position, every bone in the spine snapping like walnut shells under boot heels as the torso bent up and backwards, the wrong-elbowed arms rotating around to lunge towards her, the backwards-facing hands snapping open and closed as they thrust towards her to grasp and snare and crush...

Kait's mouth fell open in a soundless scream, but when her eyes finally flickered open, she was back on the porch, curled against the door, tears streaming down her face. Her lips were moving, and when she had finally shaken off the dream's cold, bloodied hands she realized that she was mouthing words as the real snow swirled around her. A single phrase, repeated over and over, like a curse: *"I'm sorry — I'm sorry — I'm sorry — I'm sorry."*

Somewhere deep in the trees, she could hear Jill Cicero laughing.

* * *

"Does anybody have eyes on her?" Ben called out.

Kait hadn't slept long — not long enough for the snow to pile up, but long enough for her lips and fingers to stiffen and numb. Perhaps she had only dozed off for a moment or two. Perhaps she had not been asleep at all.

"Where's she going to go?" Alice huffed from the other side of the door. "Without the cars, she's trapped here just like us."

"I don't like not knowing where she is," Ben replied. "That's all. Who knows what she could be getting up to out there?"

"Oh, put that thing down," Alice sniped. "You're making me nervous walking around with it like that."

"I don't like not knowing where she is," Ben repeated. But through the door, Kait heard the unmistakable sound of him laying the hunting rifle aside. *Against the back of the couch,* she thought. *No — that was a chair moving. He put it on the breakfast table. Where was the barrel facing? Toward the door? Toward the kitchenette?*

Was it pointed out into the middle of the room?

Kait flexed her fingers, then reached into her sleeve and peeled the glove off her right hand, her trigger hand. She examined the skin on her knuckles, which had split from cold; when she closed her fist, blood oozed up from the split, thick and slow. There was no pain, now, only a dull ache in the knuckle-joints, and the tight, stretched feeling of the dried blood on her eyebrow. She could still do it, she realized. For now. The motion was still there. That hand could still kill.

But the rifle was behind the door.

174

That didn't matter. Lutz would not come for her now, she knew. Not when he could simply watch from the trees or from inside the cabin as she slowly froze to death. A slow end. That would interest him. She wondered if he would feel anything when she crossed the threshold or if she would become like the others—empty meat, discarded, forgotten.

The cold was reaching long-fingered hands into her bones now. She quickly slipped the glove back onto her hand, jamming it down over stiff, numb fingers, then stuffed both hands under her armpits. What had Lutz called it? She shivered, struggling to remember. She could see the dance floor when she closed her eyes: there had been a masquerade on campus in November, a week before Thanksgiving, and she remembered a hundred dressy forms whirling around them as bleary orchestral music fell upon them like waves. One two three, one two three—the forms paired off, the girls in sequined dresses, the boys in sport jackets and dark pants.

Lutz was a bad dancer, but anybody could rock back and forth to a waltz. He led her slowly across the floor, occasionally treading lightly on her bare toes—she had kicked off her high heels an hour ago, the high wedges borrowed from Jill Cicero's closet. Lutz was still wearing blue jeans, but she had persuaded him to put on a brown suit jacket over his black T-shirt, and a handful of styling grease gleamed in his hair. Around them, bodies twined and whirled like water draining, and colored lights flashed in arcane symbols on the ceiling, switching to the gentle rhythm of the music.

Then like a clap of thunder, she remembered—*a forest*, he'd called it.

A forest of bodies.

That night the music never seemed to end. Her feet never got tired, even after dancing with a hundred partners. They were boys and girls, and they appeared in an endless queue, an identical question on their tongues: "May I have this dance?"

And then their lips would kink up a Lutz Visgara smile, a Jill Cicero smile, and they would whirl her away, cloaked in sweat and music and flashing rainbow lights.

"We're like hollow trees," said a blonde footballer with a square jaw.

"He lives inside us," said a nursing student with stripes dyed in her hair.

"We don't feel a thing," said a tall senior with a basso voice and thick dreadlocks tied back behind his head.

"We love him," said an Asian student with very red lipstick.

"Like the wood loves the carpenter," said a hundred shining faces.

"We are empty without him," said a hundred grinning mouths.

"We don't feel a thing."

"We don't feel a thing."

"We don't feel a thing."

A forest of bodies.

She remembered, briefly, seeing Alice Gorchuck among the masked dancers that whirled like sand in water around her, identified easily by her cloud of crimson hair—but she could not remember if she had danced in her arms that night. After a time, the faces had blurred together under the colored lights, the voices merging under the liquid rhythm of the waltz. After a time, all she saw was Lutz—and to her shock and horror, although a part of her hoped she had not danced with Alice Gorchuck that night, there was still another part of her that wished she had.

* * *

Time passed—the snow whirled, piling on the roofs and hoods of the two cars in the gravel lot. Kait strained her ears, but she could no longer hear the voices of her friends through the cabin door. Only the clinking of glass and the shuffling of feet, and occasionally a cough or a burp, coming from Riley, and the crackle of the fireplace. The new-fallen snow had silenced things, inside and out. The landscape was still, as though it had been smothered.

Then Alice's weight shifted against the door and she said: "Somebody should go check on her."

"Hey, whoa," Riley protested, her voice oddly thick. "You can't go out there—you *know* that, right? She's out there, probably right outside the door. It's too risky."

"I'm not gonna go *outside*," Alice fretted—Kait could almost imagine her knotting her fingers together in her lap or wringing them. "I'm just gonna look through the window. I wanna know what she's doing. We should be doing that, right? Keeping tabs on her?"

"What do you care what she's doing?" Ben muttered from further in. He had been pacing, stalking circles inside the cabin, the floorboards complaining under his heavy boots. "That's the whole point of her being outside, isn't it?"

"Somebody should go check on her," Alice repeated. "Anyway, it's started to snow out there, and—well, you saw how she's dressed. I just... I just want..."

"Just what?" Riley snapped suddenly. "Alice, for the love of God..."

But she trailed off, her protest left unvoiced. For a moment there was only heavy silence.

Then Ben heaved a sigh and his footsteps tromped back toward the door.

"You can give her my coat if you want," he said in a thin, flat voice.

Kait's ears pricked up as Alice sucked in a breath.

"Ben... Are you sure?" Riley asked.

"No," came the reply. "I'm not. So be quick, huh? Before I change my mind."

"Oh, Ben..." Alice breathed gratefully, and Kait scooted away from the door on numb hands and knees, emotion turning slowly within her. There was a shuffle of movement behind the door, and a tangle of whispered voices, but Kait couldn't discern the words. Her head was suddenly humming, and the light through the bleak snow clouds seemed to nearly blind her. But one idea cut through the noise inside her, over and over, like a heartbeat:

Even after everything I've done to them.

The words jumbled like puzzle pieces, rattling inside their box.

Even after everything I've done to them.

Even after everything we've done to each other.

For just a second, she let the hard knot in her stomach loosen and unravel. She let go, allowed her heart to soar, to hope—

Then Riley's voice rang out. "You'd better let me give it to her," she said. "Or at least, let me check through the window first. I don't want her to jump you when you open the door."

"All right," Alice replied slowly. "You want me to move?"

There was a smirk in Riley's voice as she said, "Well, I can't see *through* you, girlfriend." Suddenly, the squeal of flesh on glass—Kait turned to see one transom curtain pulled aside and Riley's face peering through, her nose pressed against the window glass. "She's still there," Kait heard her say. "Just sitting by the door. I think I woke her up."

"That's good..." Ben began to say, but then Kait heard Alice gasp in horror.

"What happened to your neck?" she cried out. "Riley—you're *burned.*"

The picture of Riley's face in the window froze a moment. Her eyes locked with Kait's; she could see tiny, inscrutable thoughts flicking across her features. She wondered what Riley saw on her own face, what horrors were written there.

But then Riley grinned at her, and Kait stopped wondering. Through the glass, she watched the other tug down the collar of her shirt, revealing a puckered, oozing wound under the cradle of her chin, a cigarette burn. Kait scrambled to stand, and she saw Riley mouth something at her, six words, her lips smeared against the window.

You don't want to miss this.

"Did Lutz do that to you," Alice continued unnecessarily.

Riley shook her head once, very slowly, her eyes never leaving Kait's.

"No," she said soberly. "You did this to yourself." Then, her face expressionless, she turned away from the glass and covered the transom with the curtain once more.

And then the horror began.

Kait was on her feet, mashing her face against the cold glass, trying to peer through the gauzy curtain. But all she could see were vague forms—the couch, the deer's head hanging on the wall, Ben's shoulders heaving as he stretched, and Riley's lithe silhouette padding away towards the center of the room, where Kait lost sight of her.

Then a dull thud, a muffled crack. Like an egg being crushed in a velvet glove.

At first, the cabin was silent—then the noise came again, and Kait felt all numbness drain from her like blood from a slashed artery. She had seen Riley's head wind back and whip forward, her hair fanning out like a fringe as she drove her forehead into a support beam running floor-to-ceiling near the center of the cabin.

Alice began to shriek.

"Riley, stop...!" Ben cried out.

There was brisk movement behind the door, but Kait put her lips to the keyhole, screaming through hoarse lungs. *"Don't touch her!"*

The movement stopped—Kait could hear panicked breathing through the door.

"Don't touch her," she said again. "He's got her. That's what he wants. You touch her, and he'll get you, too..."

"Shut up," Ben bellowed, his voice breaking like a stick underfoot.

But he obeyed. Nobody moved. For a moment, all went quiet.

Then Riley laughed, her voice wet and bubbling with blood.

"Hey," she said. "Hey, everyone. Stop me if you've heard this one..."

Whiff. Thud. Crack. Alice choked on a scream. Kait could not see the damage, but she could hear it—flesh slashing open, bone cracking, cartilage crushing under heavy trauma.

It made her want to claw her ears off.

"So a man walks out to a cabin in the dark forest..." Riley said.

Thud. Crack. Kait felt her stomach twist. She imagined pulped teeth, split lips, blood running down smooth cheeks into wide, unblinking eyes.

"...and of course he's shocked when a big *grizzly bear* opens the front door and steps out onto the porch."

Crack. Riley's voice was broken and spitting now. Alice's screams had devolved to wet sobs, and Ben was silent. Kait yanked the doorknob, but the door only rattled on its hinges.

Cheap construction. Heavy, but cheap. Maybe...

"So the bear says, 'What's the problem? I got sick of living in trees and caves. Can't a bear get a little real estate for himself?'"

Crack. Kait took a breath, then backed away from the door, measuring the distance in her head. There was no time for hesitation—and yet she paused, cocking her head at the voice in her mind:

They were going to let you freeze. They were talking about how to kill you, Heart-Brecker. You don't owe them this. You don't owe them anything...

But Kait could hear it through the door: the sound of Riley destroying herself. The sound of Lutz murdering the girl who had tried to help her. That was louder than Jill Cicero.

That was louder than anything in the world.

"And the guy says, 'Yeah, of course—I'm just shocked the wolf sold the place!'"

Kait sprinted forward, bracing for pain, names whirling inside her.

Then she drove her shoulder into the door.

Pain exploded all across the side of her body, pushing tears through the slits beneath her squeezed-shut eyelids—but the door gave, crashing down into the cabin as its hinges popped loose in one burst. She stumbled forward, clutching her injured arm, sweeping her eyes around the room. Alice and Ben had both whirled towards her, their eyes bulging with fear and anguish—Alice's were already red and raw from crying. Riley loomed behind them, lit up strange by the crackling firelight.

And there, lying on the breakfast table, the stock angled right towards her, was the Model 94.

Ben saw it coming first. He lurched forwards, hands outstretched, yelling something, but he was too slow. The rifle seemed to leap into her hands, and before Ben was halfway across the room she had it trained on him, aiming down sights right between his eyes.

"Back up," she snarled, sending him scrambling. "I'm done asking permission."

Then she pointed the gun at Riley.

The other girl's hands clutched the beam, spattered red and cracked from repeated blows from Riley's head. Kait could not look her in the face all at once. She focused on pieces—the ruined mouth, the broken nose. Blood applied like makeup to her skin. A face in deconstruction. Her beautiful features looked like they'd been strip-mined.

The bloody eyes flicked down, lit on the gun, flicked back up.

"Oh, come on, Heart-Brecker," Riley burbled. "Put that silly thing down."

"Let her go," Kait growled.

Riley giggled, wiping her nose and leaning casually against

the blood-spattered beam. "Or what?" she asked. "You're going to shoot me? That'll make them love you, Heart-Brecker. Really, great plan. A round of applause for you."

"She didn't do anything to you." Kait lowered the rifle slightly, watching out of the corner of her eye as Ben edged away. Alice had collapsed against the couch, her lips moving silently, almost comically, like a fish at the surface of the water. "You don't need her," she said. "It's me you want, isn't it?"

Riley grinned, or tried to grin: there were more teeth outside of her mouth than in it. "You're right," she said. "She didn't do anything to me. It's Thing Two over there that broke my nose. Wanna trade?" And when Kait did not reply to this, she continued: "You don't remember it, do you? The masquerade. You loved dancing with this body—you made me take her twice. But you don't remember her face. You don't remember her at all."

"You're lying," Kait retorted.

Riley's bloody face went blank. "I've never lied to you."

"What's the point of telling me that?" Kait blustered. "So I forgot her. So you remembered. Big whoop. Why do you care?"

It was almost imperceptible in the firelight, but Kait thought she saw Riley's face fall. "It was our first dance, Heart-Brecker," she said. "It was important to me."

"Oh, my *God*." The rifle quivered in her hands. "Get over yourself. We're *through*, don't you get that? Do you really think this, *all* this, is going to get me back?"

"No." Flame-light glistened in the blood on Riley's chin. "No, I didn't think this would get you back. I'm not an idiot."

"Then why are you doing it?"

Riley—Lutz—heaved a sigh.

"I love you, Kait. Nothing can change that."

Then her hands tightened on the wooden beam.

"I just need to show you what that actually means."

With a terrible crunch, she whipped her head forward.

Kait let out a squawk. She'd struck the corner that time, and the edge had opened a long crimson seam that split her forehead neatly down the middle. Kait aimed the rifle, but the gesture felt impotent. The rifle grew heavy in her hands, useless as lead.

"Let her go," she wanted to scream, but her lungs would barely whisper. Her throat was closing up. "Let her go—Lutz, please, I'll do anything..."

But Riley would not look at her. She peeled herself off the beam, whipped her head back, and struck again and again. Pain crossed her eyes, ragged in her breath, but that grin—that stupid, lopsided, *horrible* grin—never left her lacerated lips. Alice would not stop screaming, and now Ben was yelling "What do we do? Kait, what do we do?" over and over again. The air was a soup of sound, bubbling in her ears.

"I don't know," she breathed, each word threatening to choke her. "I don't... Lutz, I'm *begging* you—"

"Kaitlyn..."

Kait stopped breathing. Riley paused, halfway off the beam—a long strand of gore ran from her brow to a splinter in the wood, sagging like a spider's thread. She faced Kait in profile, one bloodshot eye juddering in its socket, struggling to meet her gaze. The lips moved slowly, sticking like wet playing cards can stick, slimy and suppurating: "Kaitlyn... Honey... What are you waiting for?"

"No..." Kait shook her head, her eyes suddenly heavy with tears. "No, it's a trick. This isn't her, you're trying to trick me..."

But Riley only moaned, her hands shaking on the beam. Kait thought she would shake the entire cabin down. "You know it's not," she replied, her voice like a dark, wet mountain cave. "You know... He's not going to let us go. He'd rather die than let us go. You know what you have to do, Kaitlyn—Goddamn it, *this hurts so much*..."

"But what if I'm wrong?" Kait wailed. "I can't do this, Riley. I can't. Not again..."

Riley coughed red, sniffed, coughed again. "I can't hold him," she gurgled. "He's going to come back." Under the blood, her face was pale as printer paper. "Kaitlyn, honey," she pleaded. "He's hurting me. *Please.* I've never begged for anything... But I want to... While I can still see your face..."

Kait sniffed hard, tooth grinding against tooth. She could barely see, but she could not take her hands off the gun to wipe her eyes. She peered blearily around the room. She could not see the faces of her friends, but she could picture them clearly in her head. They were all around her. They were all watching her.

Ben, who had tried to forgive her.

Alice, who had tried to save her.

Riley, who had tried to be her friend.

Jill Cicero, who made her promise —

"Kaitlyn...?" Riley breathed. Then her head pitched back...

You have to lead them into the shot.

Up from Kait's lungs tore a scream like a blast of wind. The rifle bucked once against the hollow of her shoulder — then thunder, like the end of the world.

Chapter 16

Help Me, Kait

Jill Cicero had been practicing.

The closet door was closed but not latched all the way. Werelight poured through the crack and through the slats in the door, forcing Jill to squint in the resulting quarter-gloom. She could hear the sounds of the other two returning: first Kait's high giggle, then Lutz's bleating laugh, approaching from down the hall, closer and closer. Soon they would reach her.

By her side, she flexed the fingers on her right hand, first one at a time, then all together in a tight fist, over and over again. Then the wrist: she rolled her hand around, testing the joint, the range of motion. And now the elbow, and the shoulder. She could never get past the shoulder—struggle as she liked, the warmth of Lutz still flashed there, and in the rest of her body as well, like yesterday's embers.

But this was fine. She had the arm. The arm was all she needed.

She had found her lever point.

Jill could barely contain her glee. She could not physically jump for joy, or even smile without Lutz's say-so, so the feeling had nowhere to go—it cooked inside her, like bottled lava, scalding her from the inside out. It had taken her two weeks to dream up the idea, and then another three weeks of practice before she could reliably manage the trick.

But now she had it. Her circuit-breaker. Her manual override. Her CTRL-ALT-DEL. So long as Lutz was not consciously driving her physical body, so long as his mind stayed elsewhere, she could make that right arm do whatever she wanted. And now they were coming down the hall, closer and closer, but Jill Cicero felt no fear. There was only excitement—excitement, and the plan.

There were five tiny screws in the meat of Jill's shoulder.

She didn't know how it worked—didn't know, and didn't care. But that shoulder was where she began, or Lutz ended, and that was enough. Sometimes when she concentrated very hard on the flesh just below the ridged scar slashing across her deltoid, she could feel them, actually feel the five hard points of the bio-absorbable screws lodged in her rotator cuff. She imagined them turning, slowly, as if suspended in her flesh, twisting in jelly-red space. She imagined them arrayed like a fence, keeping Lutz's warm power at bay, or biting into his fingers like tiny, threaded teeth.

She remembered the nightmares she got when the surgeon first drilled them into her—that the screws would come loose inside her somehow, tumble down into other parts of her body as though she were a hollow suit of armor and not a girl. That they would get lost in her inner machinery, like loose change or a slipped cog. She imagined looking down at her hands, seeing threaded metal cylinders pushing out beneath her fingernails, the points twisting and chewing free of the prison of her flesh. Oh, the horror she tortured herself with: watching dark, gleaming claws splitting her fingertips—*squeezing them out*, she thought, waking soaked in cold sweat. *Squeezing them out like she was birthing them.*

She could not remember the operation itself at all.

But she could remember what came before. She could remember everything.

I've seen what boys like you are capable of, Lutz Visgara.

His hand rattled the doorknob, followed by footsteps in the front hall. Jill's heartbeat rolled like thunder. The shuffling of shoes leaving feet, coats peeling off shoulders. Lutz said something unintelligible, and Kait's rasping laugh spurted out like a landmine going off.

"But what was her *name?*" Kait said, giggling drunkenly.

"She—oh, you *know* who I'm talking about. The one wearing that... cape-thing. Cloak. Cape."

"I don't learn their names," Lutz replied irritably. "My head fills up. There are only so many names a man can learn."

"You learned hers." Kait's soft footfalls padded into the kitchen, and Jill heard the hoarse whisper of the faucet turning on. "Whasname. Jill's."

"There are only so many names I can..." Lutz's voice trailed off—she could almost picture him scowling at the ceiling, his features clouding like a mountaintop.

"Well." The fridge opened, closed; ice-cubes splashed in a glass. "I liked her. The cloak girl. She was nice."

"I was nice," Lutz replied waspishly. "Honestly, Heart-Brecker..."

"I don't want to fight tonight," said Kait. "Tonight was nice. Let's be nice to each other, huh? Have a drink. You're making that face again."

"Maybe..." A rattle at the closet door—*his hand was on the knob.*

"Y'know... There's something I wanted to show you, Kait," he said slowly, so close Jill thought she could reach for him, reach through the slats in the door with her screwy right arm. "I've been thinking about it for a while now."

A pause. The knob turned a quarter-turn. Jill's heart leapt up into her throat.

"But I don't think tonight's the night for it."

The hand on the knob relaxed, and Jill watched Lutz's shadow pass the door and plod into the kitchen. Her free right fist uncoiled. *Fine.* She would wait a while longer.

Jill cast her mind outward, mapping the interior of the apartment before her unblinking eyes. There, she could see it now—the small linoleum-floored kitchen, and the carpeted den beyond, and around the corner from that the dark hallway that led to Lutz's bedroom. She calculated the volume of the space in lungfuls of air, the distance in footfalls:

Nine steps from the closet to the sofa. Twenty steps from the closet to the bedroom. Fifteen steps from the sofa to the bedroom.

And only three from the closet to the kitchen.

Jill had been practicing, there in the dark closet. Quick, powerful movements with her free right arm. With fist, with open hand, with grasping fingers—ready for whatever opportunity showed its face. She could not turn her head to look, but she imagined the wall next to her knuckles cracking, caving, bulging inward from her practice, from the brutal attentions of that callused right fist. She could almost feel his hair between her fingers, his nose breaking against her fist, his trachea crushing in her grip. She could almost feel the blood, really *feel* it, as it trickled down her taut and trembling wrist. And then, the instant his hold inside her broke, the moment she could use her entire body—yes, *then* she would act out the deeper fantasies, the things she could not practice in that closet, the thousand terrible revenges she could only dream of, there in the darkness.

Yes, she could wait for that. She could wait forever, if she had to.

Then the door swung wide. Light flooded the closet; Jill's eyes narrowed to slits as Kait leaned through the doorway, their faces so close that Jill could smell the other girl's breath. The two of them regarded each other for a long moment, Kait's face bobbing before Jill like a cork in a bathtub, Jill's own features a scowling mask that reflected Luz's own frowning visage. She'd gotten used to this by now, her face twisting into parodies of emotion on Lutz's moods.

"Hey," Kait said at last. "Jill—*why the long face?*"

She grabbed Jill by the shoulders and pulled her free of the heavy winter coats hanging in the closet and half-led, half-dragged her out into the intersection of foyer, kitchen, and living room. Jill's arms flopped limply by her sides like marionette's arms; Lutz kept her upright, but only just, and Kait giggled drunkenly, dancing Jill around and around in grand, sloppy circles, sweeping empty beer cans and a stack of magazines off a low table with one dangling hand.

And with every turn, Jill whirled closer and closer to Lutz.

He was lurking by the corner, watching the antics of the two girls with a slack look on his face. Jill could not turn her head or even swivel her eyes to track him, but she could sense his shape on the periphery—in the same uncanny, crawling way she could feel his warm grip inside of her. And she did see him, though his form was a blur, wiping by like the blur of a streetlamp through a rain-slick window.

And now he was seven steps away, eight, four, six, five, *two*, dancing closer and closer, almost within her reach…

"You'd dance with me, wouldn't you, Jill?" Kait was saying. "You'd dance with me. If I asked you too. My lady, offer me your arm, and we'll take a turn about the room…"

"You're drunk," Lutz said flatly as he blurred past them.

"I'm enjoying myself," Kait responded gaily, breathing alcohol into Jill's face. "I'm reminiscing. It was our first dance together—doesn't that mean anything to you?"

Out of the corner of her eye, Jill saw Lutz heave a sigh and roll his eyes towards the ceiling. "I'm tired," he uttered. "You're wearing me out. I'll be in my room—come in when you're done playing with your dolls."

"Tally-ho!" Kait went for a pirouette, nearly sending Jill's body crashing into the TV table. Lutz stretched, scratched himself, and turned on his heel and sauntered back towards the bedroom, humming something tuneless.

No—she had been so close!

But the bedroom door clicked behind him, and the muscles in Jill's right arm went slack. Well, it was for the best—she'd want to be alone when she carried out the plan. Wouldn't she? She wasn't certain how this Kait girl would react to the attack.

Would she react? Would she try to stop it?

Would she have to kill her too?

The realization struck her like a hook catching in her lip. She didn't want to kill this girl. She had tried to want it, Lord knows she had—but she had never managed the trick of opening the umbrella of her hatred to shade Lutz and Kait both. It would be easier, she knew, to hate both, to paint them both in loathing. A unified, faceless threat to vanquish. But Kait... She *asserted* herself, somehow. Showed her face in ways Lutz never managed. It made no sense, Jill knew—Kait was her jailor, just as much as her preening beau. But no matter how hard she willed it so, she could never look into the girl's face and see the monster. But perhaps this, too, was Lutz's power writhing within her. Lutz loved Kait, and Lutz was inside of Jill.

Transitive affection. Equivalent exchange, like alchemy.

The thought made Jill want to vomit.

"I know..." Kait breathed, panting from their dance.

Jill felt her skin crawl and scurry. Kait's mouth was next to her neck when she spoke, and her breath tickled when it moved her hair across her skin. Her lips twitched, the beginnings of a laugh—but it wasn't her laugh. She shuddered inwardly: she'd never considered that Lutz could feel what she felt. But it made sense: he'd carried on whole conversations as her before, watching through her eyes and hearing through her ears. Why shouldn't his command of her body extend to all five senses? Why shouldn't he feel Kait's touch through her skin?

"I know the name of the cloak-cape... girl," Kait continued, her words thick and sludgy.

And then she said something that turned Jill cold.

"Her name was Jill Cicero."

Jill could not have moved if she wanted to, even if Lutz had loosed his hold on her. She stared into Kait's face, her own face slack, her eyes unfocused. For a moment, Kait's eyes searched her features, gleaming with werelight, almost seeming to glow of their own power. Then the eyes flicked away—and suddenly

Jill felt herself drawn into a back-breaking embrace.

"The girl with the cloak was Jill Cicero..." Kait repeated. "The girl with the striped hair was Jill Cicero..." Her chin was tucked into Jill's shoulder, just under the curve of her chin, and she was shocked to feel something cold and wet trickling down her collarbone.

"The boy with the dreadlocks was Jill Cicero," she kept saying. "The girl with the really red lipstick... Hollow trees, all hollow, hollow, hollow..."

Kait's whole body shook against Jill's, and even though Kait's arms were locked around her, Jill couldn't shake the peculiar feeling that she was holding Kait, not the other way round, holding her up: that she might crumple to the floor like an empty suit of clothes. The skin on Jill's right arm began to itch, just above the wrist. The one place she couldn't scratch. She rubbed her wrist surreptitiously against the ridge of her hip, but it only made the itch worse.

And Kait wasn't making any sense. She kept mumbling into Jill's shoulder, strings of names, repeated phrases, nonsense syllables, bathing her in tears that flowed like blood. "Don't feel a thing," she kept saying, again and again like an omen. "You—Lutz says you don't feel a thing. But you'd dance with me, wouldn't you? *Wouldn't* you, Alice?"

Jill had not practiced for this.

But this girl Kait was sobbing now, trembling in the grip of something powerful and strange, something that seemed to command her body as totally and effortlessly as Lutz commanded Jill's. Trembling like she was about to tear in two, her hands knotting into Jill's shirt, stretching the fabric, her arms steel-trap tight around her torso.

No, Jill had not practiced for this—but still, she acted. Without thinking. Without considering the consequences. Her free right arm rose up, laying the open hand on Kait's quaking shoulder, stroking it. She ran untrimmed fingernails through the girl's hair, just scraping the scalp, as though she were combing her little cousin's hair after a bath. And for a moment, just a tick of the clock or two, Kait's tremors quieted. Her sobs died away to little gasps, and the hard, tight muscles in her shoulders seemed to relax as she pressed forward into Jill's one-armed embrace, registering the affection, wanting more of it.

For only a moment, their hearts beat together.

Then Kait came alive, thrusting Jill away with outstretched arms, her eyes wide and crazy, full of horror. Jill toppled away, unable to steady herself. Her right arm beat the air, trying to slow the fall she knew was coming—she only just managed to deflect herself away from the coffee table as she crashed to earth, whirling with the force of Kait's shove. She landed face-downward, her head cracking against the floor, and pain burst across her skull like the yolk of an egg. Everything spun and wobbled. She could feel her pulse in both temples, pounding like drums in the jungle, spinning out an alarm that sang like a scream in her veins. The carpet tasted like carpet, and she couldn't move now, not a muscle, not even her good arm, and everything was wrong wrong wrong *wrong*...

She couldn't see Kait, but she could feel her shadow moving across her, hear her breath coming in shallow, ragged huffs.

"You..." she said. "You..."

Then two bare feet stepped over her, running down the hall, towards the bedroom. A silent moment passed. The door opened, closed, opened again. Then the footsteps came back, two pairs of them, Kait's and Lutz's. "Don't worry about it," he was saying, his voice booming and enormous above her. "I'm going to take care of this."

He said something else after that, but Jill couldn't hear the words.

Somewhere far across town, the plants had started to scream again.

Chapter 17

Nobody's First Choice

Alice's shriek threatened to burst the windows, but to Ben, the noise of it seemed to come from a long way off, somewhere deep under the earth. The world had stopped moving, or had slowed to a honey-crawl, drifting somewhere between heartbeats. All he could really hear was the echo of rifle-fire, ringing in chorus in his ears, and the smell... Ben knew there should not be an odor already, but it tickled in his nose anyhow: the smell of cordite mixing in his nostrils with the terrible imagined *stink* of flesh and rot.

And all he could see was the pool of crimson spreading across the faded wooden floorboards where Riley's body had collapsed to the floor.

He yanked his gaze away, forcing himself to look above that ruined face, the head hanging askew on the neck, limp, like a half-inflated balloon. She had fallen on her backside, propped against the wooden column like a child's doll. One leg was splayed out and the other curled beneath her, the arms lying in her lap like they had been posed there. The curtain of her long blonde hair dangled in front of her face, and though he could not see beyond it, he could feel her eyes following him from beyond that veil—one glassy and lifeless, the other a dark, wet, oozing socket where the bullet had struck home.

So he forced his eyes upward, his gaze dragging up the red-streaked post, its white paint chipped away to reveal a dull damp brown beneath. Up past the globules of fresh blood snaking slowly down the corner of the wood, racing each other in a slow dash to the floor. He focused on the hole—mere millimeters across, surrounded by a ring of tiny red-and-pink splinters, like the labor of a carpenter bee in a back porch. All around this hole there was blood and matted hair and chunks of something unspeakable that clung to the wood like wet breakfast grits.

It was a bullet hole. Kait's shot had gone clean through.

Ben wheeled and bent double, and a long string of vomit spattered across the rug and down the back of the red leather couch. His stomach heaved again and again—the room spun, and dancing spots of black swarmed at the corners of his vision. Somewhere off beside him, Alice's cries had died away to small gibbering whimpers. She kept saying the dead girl's name over and over, insistently, like it would call her back, like it could summon her to life again. The syllables ran together like mud and sand as they bubbled from her lips.

Kait Brecker had not said a word.

Ben picked himself up from his knees, turning slowly as he rose, careful not to look at Riley's... *Her form*, he thought hurriedly to himself, but the word *body* jumped up anyway, larger than life, blown up full-screen before he could will it away. Her body. Her *corpse*. His stomach jerked again, squeezing like a fist, so he let himself drift, his eyes sliding over Alice's trembling shape to find Kait by the little breakfast table, one folding chair turned on its side just beside her, her body crouched in a tight ball with her heels off the floor. The rifle lay at her feet, and she was staring at it, her face the color of the pale belly of a leaf, as though she wasn't sure the weapon was really there at all.

Snow swirled through the open doorway, dusting the fallen wooden door, collecting in the divots in the carved panels, silent and pure and cold.

He tried to think, but his head seemed to be stuffed with the same soft cotton-fluff that filled his heart and his limbs. He felt cold all over, bone-cold that penetrated every cubic inch of his mass. He could not take his eyes off Kait. He waited for the hatred to rise up inside him—the acid rage that had consumed him not two hours before. But that part of him seemed to switch off, to short-circuit with a fizzling pop. There was a second image beginning to form before his eyes. The specter of Riley's limp-marionette's body hovered just above Kait's own hunched form, overlapping, like double-exposed film. And the face on the corpse was changing, changing—from Riley to Alice, to Cormac, to Kait, to Ben himself. But the wounds were always the same. They were open and weeping and raw, and redder than anything else he'd ever seen.

He forced himself again to look at Riley, to truly study the wounds on her face. The sound of her head striking the post played back in his head again and again—the dull wet thud of impact made his stomach cinch up. He tried not to imagine the pain, but the feeling overtook him nonetheless. He imagined what it had to be like: to be a prisoner in a body that was self-destructing, driven by the mind of a monster speaking in riddles while the blood flowed down his face and neck and his fingers dug into the splintering wood.

Yes—he would have begged for death, he thought. He would have prayed for it.

He would have prayed for Kait Brecker.

And so he looked back at her, the part of him that hated her lying dead and stinking in his chest. She had come to save them, he realized, and guilt like barbed wire twisted in his guts. Even after everything we've done to her. *Even after everything I've done.* Twice he tried to speak to her, but his throat was closed tight, squeezed off like a spigot, until at last he heard himself say, "What do we do?" His voice shook with dread—dread, and something else he couldn't name. "Kait... What *can* we do?"

But Kait didn't look up, only her head bobbed downward and her shoulders slumped a fraction of an inch, the only indication she'd heard him at all. "We have to call the police," she murmured. Ben opened his mouth to reply, but shut it again when she suddenly rose from the floor, continuing to stare at the rifle as though it were a venomous snake.

"That's what comes next," she continued in a very soft voice.

"I can make the call, but you'll have to tell them what happened in your own words, sooner or later..."

Riley's words. Something turned over in Ben's stomach. Riley's words in her mouth—beat for beat, line for line. Like she was reading off the script. Like it was Riley's very own voice, floating up from a stinking grave.

"You should talk it through first, you and Alice," Kait said. She turned her head towards him at last, but her eyes looked right through him. "Get your story straight between you. Make sure they know what... what happened here. What I've done."

"What you've done," Ben parroted. A split had appeared in his lower lip from the cold, and he flexed his jaw, stretching it out experimentally. "Kait, what're you saying?"

"You need to wipe your mouth."

Unconsciously, his hand rose, wiped dribble from his chin, then wiped it on the knee of his khaki pants. Still her eyes stared straight through him, wide and dry and haunted.

"And you need to know..." she continued. "You need to understand... Alice was wrong. Lutz never controlled me. Not once. He wouldn't, or couldn't..." Her voice quavered, and the end of each word sounded hacked off, as if from a blow from an axe. "No, I was never one of his hollow trees," she said. "But he got me, just the same. And now look what he made me do..."

With the toe of her sneaker, she nudged the rifle towards Ben. The whole weapon rotated on the floor like a game of spin-the-bottle until the barrel pointed straight at Kait.

"Take it," she said. "Before I..."

"Before you what?"

The words came out in a shuddering sigh: "You need to get her somewhere safe."

There could be no question who *she* meant.

Ben's eyes flicked over to his girlfriend: Alice didn't seem to be hearing a word they said. She was tucked up in a tight ball like Kait had been, staring through splayed fingers across the room at Riley's body, her breath coming in wet huffs like sobs, her cloud of hair wobbling like gelatin atop her head. He had never seen her like this, never in their four months together. "I can't." The words jumped out before he could stop them, but once they hit air, he accepted them as gospel. "Not without you."

"You have to," Kait barked hoarsely, her eyes flashing firelight. "Listen. Think about it—it's my prints on the gun. They'll find powder burns on my hands. They'll lock me up, and Lutz won't be able to get me. He'll leave you alone. You'll be safe, finally *safe.*"

"You don't know that," he insisted. He took a halting step towards her, careful not to tread on the hunting rifle. "Safe?" he asked. "Safe from *him*? Where's that? Where could I take her that's safe from him now?" He took another step forward, and Kait's mouth twitched, ready to bolt. "If you're so confident in my ability to protect her, give me an address—anyplace on this fucking *planet* where he won't touch her."

One more step forward. They were close now, only the length of the rifle separated them.

"I can remember it now," he said. "When he had control of me. I could feel what he felt—I don't think I was meant to, but it kept... *slipping through,* somehow. He hates her, Kait. More than me, more than Riley. More than you. He's got *plans* for her. And if he ever gets inside of me again, he'll..."

"What do you want me to do about it?" Kait hissed, twisting away from him, rage flashing across her features. Then her face went slack. "I can't help you," she said. One hand rose up, gesturing limply in Riley's direction. "I *tried*. And look what happens when I try."

"I'm not afraid of you, Kait."

An ineffable expression crossed Kait's face. She glanced at the gun at her feet, then at Riley's crumpled body, then finally her eyes returned to Ben, focusing on a point just above his left eyebrow. Her expression barely changed—the log on the fire popped, filling the silence.

"It's too late for that now," she said, almost kindly, though there was no light in her eyes. They didn't even reflect the firelight now. "And besides—it's a lie."

She took one swift step forward, maneuvering neatly around the rifle on the floor, and Ben flinched backwards, his heartbeat suddenly up and racing. Kait rocked back on her heel, looking up at him with a sad smile.

"You see?" she uttered. "Look at you—and you were so brave this morning. But I bet if I was holding the gun, you couldn't even touch me now." She raised one hand, and Ben flinched back again, hating it, hating himself for it. The hand snapped into a finger-gun, aimed between his eyes. "Not even if your life depended on it."

Ben stared down the "barrel" of her pointed finger, suddenly lost in memory—remembering that cold night when the gun had been real. Remembering the feeling of the cold steel pressed against his forehead, the warm trickle of his own blood falling in his eyes. Remembering the horror in Alice's eyes, the rage on Kait's face. The fear in his own shuddering heart. He began to shake all over, suddenly, uncontrollably.

He was afraid then, and he was afraid now. That was the terrible, runaway truth of it.

For as long as he'd known her—he'd *always* been afraid of Kait Brecker.

But now there was a small warm hand lacing its fingers through his own. Alice appeared like a phantom at his side, pressing close to him, squeezing his hand in hers. He angled his head towards her, and though she did not meet his eye, something unspoken passed between them in the grip of her fingers, like an electric current. He squeezed her hand back, and looked past Kait's finger-gun and into her eyes.

"All right," he managed to say. "You got me. I'm spooked."

This time Alice did catch his eye—her own eyes shone, still

glittering with tears. "But I guess I'll get over it," he said. "If that's what it takes."

And then, as one body, he and Alice stepped forward, pulling a startled Kait into a deep embrace. For a moment she stiffened, her rigid shoulder digging into Ben's chest. Then she fought them. She wormed in their grip, twisting and struggling, but never so hard that they had to fight her back, never with her full strength. And as she struggled she cried out, begging them to release her—but soon, these protests died away to ugly wet sobs that ran down her cheeks and down the front of Ben's shirt. Alice, on the other side of the tight circle, had positioned her mouth next to Kait's ear and was whispering constantly into it, and for the first time Ben did not care what he heard and what he did not. Even with him so close, this was a private moment, and he was content to let it stay that way. Or he would try to be.

It could have gone on an hour—but after what was likely only a few minutes' time, an unspoken signal went out and Ben and Alice eased their grip, letting Kait stand between them. Her face was pink from crying, but she had dried her smeary eyes on her sleeve, and she looked almost contemplative, gazing off past them at the stuffed deer head gawping down at them from the wall. Before anyone could speak, she retreated to her room, returning with the stained white pillowcase from her pillow. She crossed the room and knelt by Riley's side, knotting her fingers through the dead girl's own, and the hissing sound of her whispers carried across the cold room. Then she stood, but before she rose all the way, she slipped the pillowcase over the bloody mess of the head, carefully tucking every strand of blonde hair up inside it. Then she faced them.

"Lutz made a mistake," she said coldly. "He left us an opening. He was controlling Riley when I... When he made me kill her. But now he's alone. With her dead, if he wants to control one of us, he'll have to do it *himself*."

"Then what's our move?" Ben asked. To his left, Alice sniffed and nodded.

Kait's mouth flattened in a grim line. "We draw him out," she intoned. "We finish this. Hike for the main road—it's not far, but we need to make it out of these woods by nightfall. I don't like our odds against him in the dark. If we act like we're trying to make it back to civilization, he'll come for us. Then we'll take him."

Kait ran her fingers through her dark hair, shivering slightly as a blast of cold wind came rushing through the broken-in door. "Pack your things," she said. "Whatever you can carry comfortably—but don't leave each other alone, not even for a second. Go room to room together. You have to remember one thing: Riley died to give us this chance, but unless we all live through this, her sacrifice doesn't mean a damn thing. You've *got* to survive. You've *got* to stay free. For Riley. Do you understand that?"

She headed across the room once more, stretching her hands out to them, palms up.

"I understand," Alice replied. "For Riley." She took the hand closest to her and turned her eyes to Ben.

Ben gulped and nodded. "For Riley." He took the other hand, so cold in his own, and so much smaller. But the strength of her grip was almost superhuman as she gave each of their hands a last squeeze, then released them.

"For Riley," Kait said, like sealing a letter with wax.

Her lips twitched again, and for a brief instant Ben though he saw the beginnings of a shy smile grace her pale features, though it was gone as quickly as it had come. With slow, careful movements, Kait stooped to lift the hunting rifle—but before she could touch it, Alice's mouth fell open in soundless horror. From the other side of the room, there came the sound of rapid movements: a cracking, shuffling sound, the noise of flesh scraping across a wooden surface. Then a terrific crash, and the tinkling of falling glass.

Kait whipped around, raising the rifle to her shoulder faster than human thought. But Ben knew she was too late. The sliding back door of the cabin had shattered, and the glass lay gleaming in the snow on the back porch. He could see bare footprints, stained scarlet, bounding off into the wilderness, losing themselves in the swirling white vortex. And in the space where Riley's body had fallen, there was only a dim outline in dry, faded blood.

Riley was gone.

Chapter 18

Truth

"This can't change anything."

Mere moments had passed, but to Kait the frigid seconds—each tick of the clock, each beat of her thundering heart—seemed to stretch and pull like pink taffy. Alice and Ben stood on the rug in front of the dying fire, careful to avoid the crust of Ben's drying vomit. Kait paced at the back of the cabin, winding a pensive path from one corner of the room to the other, the rifle perched on her shoulder like a tin soldier and broken glass crunching occasionally beneath the heels of her Converse sneakers.

"I mean—it shouldn't change anything," she insisted. "We stick to the plan. Get out of the woods by dark. Find Lutz. *Kill* Lutz. Everybody goes home."

"But she must have been *alive*," Alice wailed for perhaps the tenth time, her head in her hands. "She must have survived it... the bullet... somehow. It doesn't make any sense any other way. He can't... Lutz can't drive a, a..."

"Please don't say it," Kait murmured, but Alice fumbled on unheeding.

"...a *corpse*. Can he?" She turned spotlight eyes to Kait. "*Can* he do that? I mean, has he ever done it before?"

"Of course he's never done this before," Kait hissed. "Don't you think I would have mentioned that? Now would both of you shut up and *let me think*."

Her friends' mouths both snapped closed, and Kait resumed her pacing, her one free hand pressed to her cheek, her mind whirling with terrible possibilities. She hadn't known—had she? How could she have predicted such a thing? The image kept flickering against the blank wall of her mind: Riley's ragdoll body rising from the floor, bones clicking into joint, the head snapping back into place like a bobblehead doll on its spring, the eyes rolling forward inside wide bloody sockets. She pictured the body sweeping forward, almost weightless, drifting across the floor, breaking through the glass door as if it were craft paper. She imagined the feeling of wearing the corpse—the sensation of that dead skin and muscle hanging from her frame like a sleeping bag, heavy and sagging and soft.

"That boy Riley knew..." she began at last.

"Cormac?"

Kait nodded. "Is he still in front of the cabin?"

Alice paled and scurried to the transom window. "He's still there," she breathed at last. "I can see... Oh, God, I can see his feet under the car."

"All right." Kait took a deep breath, squeezing the stock of the rifle to her chest. "We have to destroy the body."

Ben turned the color of beached seaweed. From the front of the cabin, she heard Alice's gasp of horror. "What... What do you mean, *destroy?*"

"I hit Riley through the eye," Kait said. "I saw the hole the bullet came out, on the other side. The shot scrambled her brains." She paused, letting the weight of her words click into groove. "Alice, I'm sorry. But that thing out there, that's not Riley anymore. I... I killed her. I've got to live with that somehow. But pretending it didn't happen isn't going to bring her back."

A terrible shiver wracked her body, like the feeling of cold lips brushing her ear.

"So we've got to face facts," she continued. "Lutz can use dead things." *A hollow tree, an empty corpse.* "I don't know how he does it, but *how* doesn't matter. I'm not going to let him do it again." *They don't feel a thing, Heart-Brecker.* "We have to destroy the other body: hack it up with the saw, or..."

"No!" Alice shrieked through laced hands. "We can't. Not with..."

Her voice trailed off, but the unspoken words were clear as

snowfall: *Not with the saw he killed himself with.*

Kait scowled, dropping her shoulders. "Fine. Burn it, then. Or..."

Her gaze fell on the braided rug in front of the fireplace.

"How far away from here did you say the lake was?"

"Not far," Ben replied slowly. "Half a mile, maybe three-quarters. Riley and I... We didn't make much progress there."

Kait scrubbed her tired eyes with the heel of her hand. "Do you think we could carry him there?" she asked. "Wrap him in the carpet, weighed down with rocks. Throw him off the pier so the water's deep enough. It'll take us out of our way, but..."

"I think we could do it," Alice put in hesitantly. "As long as we don't have to... I mean, if you think we really need to."

Kait nodded. "I'm sorry. But it's the only way to be sure." *The only way I can protect you.* She adjusted the rifle on her shoulder, which had begun to ache, a dull pulse of pain just beneath the skin. "Go on and pack," she said. "But pack light. Anything you can fit in a backpack. We won't be coming back here again."

Her friends shared a glance, then nodded in almost-unison, retreating to their bedroom—Kait thought she saw Alice cast a nervous look over her shoulder, but she couldn't be certain. She hardly trusted her own eyes now.

She returned to her own little room and closed the door behind her with a low moan. Her earlier surge of adrenaline was cold in her blood. Now pain like hot blunt needles dove into her right arm, into the shoulder she'd bruised against the cabin door. No, not bruised—this was something else. She had been able to conceal it from the others, but every so often, her right hand would twitch on the stock of the rifle. A finger would move out of synch, or her grip would tighten without her meaning it. Like the whole arm was rebelling. Like it had a mind of its own.

Like she had let something inside.

She lay the rifle lengthwise on the bed and clutched at her shoulder with the other hand, peering around the room. There wasn't much to pack: her big over-the-ear headphones lay on her bare pillow, and her backpack slouched on its side in one corner, still zipped closed. She bent at the waist to lift it—there beneath it hid four brownish circular stains sunk into the floorboards. Off-brown, she thought to herself, feeling faintly ridiculous. If white could be off-white, then a brown could be "off" as well. And that's what this was. *Off-brown*. The color of day-old blood.

Christ—*it had only been a day.*

Kait shook herself, reaching for the headphones, dragging the pillow towards her so she could reach. How many places were there like this inside the cabin? Or outside, on the grounds? Little signs, fading reminders of the nightmare. The flecks of blood here, the vomit on the rug, the broken glass on the back porch, the broken door near the front. The decapitated body out on the gravel. The silhouette of Riley's corpse on the floorboards, like a chalk outline. Even that had already begun to fade, but the mark would last a while longer, she guessed. Maybe it would last forever, preserved by the cold. Like a gravestone. Like a sigil of a violent death.

She shook herself once more, reemerging from the bedroom to find Alice and Ben waiting for her, looking at her expectantly. Kait gave them a nod and hoisted her backpack, propping the barrel of the Model 94 on her shoulder. She grit her teeth as red sparks of pain sizzled in her shoulder joint, struggling not to let the discomfort show on her face.

Don't you dare, she thought grimly. *Don't you fucking dare. Not now. Not when we're so close. Not when they've finally decided to trust me...*

Trust you, cooed the whispering voice of Jill Cicero. *You know better than that, Heart-Brecker. They chose the devil they know. But I bet you it could have gone either way.*

Kait ignored this. She led the others outside, Ben dragging the rolled-up rug from in front of the now-cold fireplace, and instructed him on how to lay it out beside Cormac, and where to position the stones so they wouldn't fall out in the water. Nobody questioned her, questioned how she knew the things she told them, all in a voice as level and cold as sheet ice. But she caught them stealing glances at each other—but whether it was confusion or pity or plain old fear flashing in their eyes made no difference to her.

Then she rolled the corpse onto the rug. She did this alone, insisted on it, even though her shoulder flanged with agony and her skin crawled to touch his stiff, cold flesh. Though it wasn't as stiff as she'd first imagined—Riley's hands had felt like living hands, only cold to the touch, but Cormac's skin felt artificial, somehow, like a rubber glove filled with water. He was laid out with his legs straight and his arms at his sides, which made him easy to roll, but he was still awkward and stiff and monstrously heavy, and it took her almost thirty seconds to muscle him onto the carpet. Then the others helped roll him up inside, one on one side of her and one on the other. Kait thought she saw Ben trying to catch her eye, but whenever she looked up, his gaze was always elsewhere—out in the trees, or across the snowy lot. She wondered, briefly, what he could be looking for. But the answer wasn't far behind.

Eyes among the trees, she thought.

One staring and glassy, the other a wet crimson hole.

It took the three of them a few tries to hoist Cormac's rug-wrapped body onto their shoulders. Once they dropped him, only a foot or so, when Alice's grip failed, but the second time he fell from Ben's shoulders, the head-end of the carpet sliding to the snowy gravel almost silently. The rug came unwrapped, and the oozing, empty neck sprang into view, tearing a shriek from Alice's lips. Even Kait felt a frustrated cry bubbling up in her throat. She turned her eyes skyward: the snow had stopped, but the clouds overhead were still very thick, and the temperature was dropping by the second. It was not so late in the day, but the dark would fall quickly on this kind of winter evening, especially out among the trees.

She tried not to imagine the woods at night. The white-gray of tree bark going ochre, then lead-colored, then black altogether, the beams of flashlights flickering among the looming trunks, the Model 94 useless in her numb hands. She tried not to imagine the sound of her friends breathing in the darkness, quickening with panic as fear crept in and the blood began to roar in their ears, loud but not loud enough to drown out the sound of stealthy footsteps somewhere in the snow—shambling, sliding footfalls, the gait of a corpse.

Or perhaps they would not hear Riley coming at all. Perhaps there would be no sound, only the faint glisten of one bloody eye-socket in the dying light of a flashlight or a cell phone screen—glistening like dew in a spider's web. Or perhaps she would turn around and one of her friends would be gone. Alice vanished, or Ben, without so much as a cry. Perhaps she would suddenly find herself alone, and then, only a few yards away, she would hear the hissing, ripping sound of a hacksaw working rhythmically against human flesh.

Her hand struck out, latching onto Alice's shoulder almost without her willing it. Her friend yelped and stiffened, nearly dropping her end of the rug a third time. "Kaity, what's wrong?" she asked.

"Did you see something?" Ben asked from behind the carpet.

"No, I..." For a moment, she couldn't speak, her breath like a lead weight in her chest. "We should tie this closed," she said at last. "We're... We're runnin' out of time."

* * *

Ben and Alice carried the body. They carried it like lumberjacks with a fallen timber, in a row with one on the right and one on the left, threading down through the trees. Kait led them down, the rifle cradled in her arms, occasionally steadying herself in the snow against one tree trunk or another and watching her breath fog the air ahead of her. The snow was not deep here, but the ground beneath was loose and muddy—twice her sneakers caught a slippery patch, and it was only by throwing her shoulder against a leaning pine and digging her toes into the dirt that she managed to keep from toppling over.

The atmosphere was nothing if not grim. The snow, which had reflected the sunlight in glittering waves in the early afternoon, had now begun to suck the color out of the air like a sponge. The world was a wash of gray and dull brown and dingy white, utterly silent save for their crunching footsteps and labored breathing, and the occasional low howl of the wind in the trees. Kait wished somebody would speak, but there was nothing to say. She could feel the strain in the air, held tight like piano wire between two outstretched fists. She was afraid to turn around, to see her friend's faces twisted by fear—or transformed altogether.

And she was losing grip, Kait realized. And it wasn't just the crawling dread or the pain in her right arm—she was slowing down. Maybe it was the cold, or lack of sleep, or adrenaline fatigue, but she was definitely coming unglued somewhere. Now every movement, every foot planted in the snow took precise effort. Her arms and legs felt full of cold slurry. She slowed her stride, hearing the others skid to a halt to accommodate her. Let them wait—just for a moment. Just long enough to recoup a little horsepower, to stir some warmth back into her hands and face.

If I fall again, she thought grimly, *I won't be able to catch myself. I won't even have the strength to pick myself up out of the snow.*

"We can stop for a minute," Alice called out hesitantly behind her.

"I'm fine," Kait said—or tried to say. The word came out in an empty breath.

"Lake's not much farther," Ben added. "Just past that bit of old fence there."

"I said, I'm fine." Kait's head swam. Something wasn't right.

There—a flash of black against the low white sky. Too small to be a person, but too big to be—

Shrunch.

The sound of crushed snow. And it was close.

Kait held up a trembling hand, her heart like a lump of ice behind her ribs. The others stopped without a word: slowly, she raised the rifle to her shoulder, the pain forgotten. There were soft movements in the snow just beyond the curve of a titanic redwood trunk—quiet, furtive sounds, almost stealthy. She sucked a breath through her teeth and held it, peering down the sight on the gun. Skirting sideways around the tree, careful not to cross one foot over the other. One, two, three steps. Her hand went to the lever action, the other resting with one finger just beside the trigger guard...

"*Raawk,*" said a strange, low-to-the-ground voice.

Kait felt her skin jump across her bones. It was a crow. A fat black crow, hopping comically around in the snow with its chest feathers all ruffed out and its beady eyes glinting in the late afternoon sun. "Jesus," she breathed, her hand pressed to her breast. "Jee-zus..." Behind her, she could hear her friends' breath whoosh out, their feet shuffling noisily in the crunchy snow. The crow cocked its head one way, then the other, twisting its beak sideways to look up at Kait, completely fearless.

"*Raawk,*" it intoned in that peculiar, half-human voice. "*Buhrawk.*"

"Scared the shit out of me," Alice hissed. She had one hand off the carpet on her shoulder, pressed to her heart in a mirror imitation of Kait. "Go on, shoo! Get!" She kicked at the crow, waving the toe of her boot in its direction.

"Hold on," Ben said. "Don't... There's something on its beak..."

But Kait wasn't looking at the crow. She took another step to the side, the rifle still leveled by her ear. There was more movement behind the tree. A flutter of another pair of wings, and another and another. Fluttering, and a strange repeated wet sound, and the sudden tickle of rot in her stinging nostrils...

"Don't look." Kait twisted her head away, shutting her eyes against horror. "Don't... It's... No further..."

"What *is* that," Ben said. "Christ—is that... is that..."

Blood. On the beaks, on the claws of perhaps a half-dozen flapping, hopping crows. They were circled around a tree with a low fork in its trunk, fluttering up to the fork and back again, tearing at *something* lodged in the split in the wood and squabbling among themselves as they floundered in a snow drift. There was more blood in the snow, so pale it was almost pink and sunk into dozens of tiny three-toed footprints. One of them was nibbling at a scrap of dark flesh; two more were having a tug-of-war with the front half of a pale, slippery human eye.

"Don't look..." Kait repeated uselessly.

She felt her gorge rise half-heartedly, her body too fatigued even to vomit. Cormac's neck had not been severed cleanly; the teeth of the saw had left a ragged edge like wet tissue paper dangling below the nibbled-over ears. The wax-colored skin on the face was mostly untouched, save for an almost perfectly triangular gash of cheek-flesh that had been stripped away by one sharp black beak or another, but the lips had been picked down to nothing. Teeth grinned through a haze of blood and masticated dermis, looming huge in the jaws without the curtain of lips to conceal them. The left eye had been gobbled out completely, leaving a shallow, red, oozing hole that dribbled blood and pulped eye-mush down the ruined cheek like tears. The other had rolled back so far into the skull that the veins flushed purple.

Kait felt like it was staring straight at her.

Behind her, Alice and Ben eased the carpet—the rest of Cormac still packed up inside—down onto the snow. Alice's hand landed on Kait's shoulder, even that soft touch making her hands tighten on the stock and barrel of the rifle. "It's him," she said. Her voice was air blown through thin grass. "It has to be him."

Kait could only nod. The world was slipping sideways on her. Her head felt like it was full of helium, and she caught herself listing to the side like a dead tree.

"Why bring it here?" Ben growled, his voice pulpy with disgust. "We walked half an hour to get here. Why would—"

"Mister Face," Kait murmured before she could stop herself.

Her friends blinked at her. "The volleyball?" Ben finally ventured.

"The meaning's the same," she replied, staring back into Cormac's single violet-veined eye. "It's a tag. A flare. *Lutz was here.* Left here for us to find, just like the rest of him."

"He knew we'd see it," Alice breathed. "He knew we were coming here."

"But how?" Ben demanded. "How could he know? These woods are huge! Even if he knew we'd go to the lake, how could he be sure we'd come here and see it?"

"Maybe he got lucky," Alice put in, but Ben only shook his head, his jaw set and his eyes staring past both her and Kait, out into the darkening trees. A peculiar shudder ran through his whole body, like a tree cut through at the bottom right before it starts to fall.

"Lucky," he spat. "Lucky. He's been lucky this whole damn *weekend.*"

Then he whirled away from them without warning, striding away towards where the trees were thickest, the shadows darkest.

"*Ben!*" Alice cried out. She stepped over the rolled carpet to follow him, but Kait shot out her hand, seizing her by the wrist. The bigger girl nearly jerked her to the ground, but she clung on with the little strength left in her slender body as Alice tried to shake her loose.

"Where are you *going,* you idiot?" Kait screamed after Ben.

He paid her no mind. He stopped behind a thorny shrub, leafless but veiled in snow, almost out of their view. "This is what it was all about—wasn't it?" he called back over his shoulder. "Drawing him out? Then let's *draw* the bastard."

Then out into the woods he hollered, at the top of his voice: "Come on! What are you waiting for? What do you *want* from us?" He stooped down, picked up a rock, hurled it out into the darkness. It made no sound when it landed. "We're *here*, you damned coward!" he screamed, his voice cracking like sheet ice. "If you want to finish this, you're going to have to come and fucking *work for it!*"

"Ben, what are you doing?" Kait screamed. Another wave of dizziness crashed over her, and she squeezed her eyes shut so she wouldn't see the horizon bob and bend like rubber. The mob of crows took off cawing, their wings beating the air with startling percussive thunder.

"He knew we'd be here."

Ben turned towards them, and even at that distance, Kait could see the gleaming whites of his wide eyes. "He knew we'd be here," he repeated, his face pale against the dark wall of the forest. "He always knows. No matter what we do, he always *knows*. He's always *there*."

"He got lucky," she repeated, the lie stinging her lips as it left. "Or, or he figured it out, somehow. I don't know. This is no time to—"

"Nobody's that lucky," Ben moaned, unhearing. "And nobody's that *smart*." His hands tore at his hair, swiped at his face as though he were tearing off a mask. "Don't you get it?" he howled. "It's one of us. It has to be one of us. How else could he see us coming? How else could he know?"

Kait stared at him. Her mind raced—she could hear Alice's breath start to quicken beside her, feel the darkness closing in, falling from the sky like descending fog. Ben took a step back from them, into the snow-covered undergrowth. Another step, or maybe another, and he'd disappear. *Oh, God, it was starting, it was happening already...* Kait flicked her gaze left and right, expecting to see Riley among the shadows of the trees, a hundred Rileys waiting in the darkness, watching through bloodshot, hollow eyes. She waited for bare arms to wiggle out from the shadows, to pull Ben away from them into a tight and unbreakable embrace....

"We're gonna die out here," he was saying, making fists in his hair. "God Almighty, we're gonna *die* out here..."

"*Truth or Dare,*" she blurted suddenly.

Ben's head whipped toward her. He was too far away now; she could not see his face, but she could imagine his expression, incomprehension written in the tilt of his head, the slack droop of his broad shoulders. His lips moved, but the snow seemed to swallow his voice. Only the barest whisper reached her ears, one single clear word:

"...What?"

"You think he's still got control of one of us," she said, holding her voice level, even though it took all the strength of her will to accomplish it. "Well, fine. Let's find out, then. Let's find out who it is."

Without looking at him again, she stepped over the rolled-up rug and eased her weight down onto it, trying to clear her head, trying not to think about what was wrapped up inside, trying hard not to picture Cormac's hole of a neck flopping like a fish's lips as his cold, hollow voice floated upward. Trying with all her strength not to look toward the crow-tree, where she knew that horrible, bloody head was watching her from the fork, slack-jawed and grinning its open-mouthed, lipless grin. She crossed her ankles demurely, patting the surface of the carpet beside her, an invitation.

"But I'm not going to play with you all the way over there, Ben," she told him. "We all need to be together. We all need to be close. It's what Riley would want. House Rules."

Ben's head tilted almost imperceptibly. "We're gonna die out here," he repeated, but his voice was thin, unsure. Wavering on the edge.

"We are not going to die," Kait said firmly. "That's not how this ends. Everybody lives. Everybody goes home. No substitutions, exchanges, or refunds."

Ben said nothing. For a long moment, he didn't even move. Kait kept her eyes down, but in the corner of her vision she could see him, a blank form wavering. Then, with uneven steps, he crossed the clearing. Alice sat down hesitantly on the carpet beside Kait, but Ben leaned a shoulder against a sturdy-looking tree trunk and crossed his arms.

"Fine," he huffed. "I'm here. Truth."

"All right," Kait said—then she froze. The words were there, but they had formed without her bidding them. Another voice, another mind, feeding her lines from just off-stage, from the next screen, the next breath. And they were the right words, yes... But she was afraid of the question. Afraid of the answer.

"I want..." she began again, haltingly. "I want to know..."

There's your face, Kaitlyn.

"I want to know why you hated me," she managed to get out. "Not on the trip. I know I've been a bitch to you. But before, in January... I know I never tried to be your friend, but you didn't even know me. We didn't talk. I don't think I looked you in the eye the first week I knew you. So what made you...?"

She trailed off, suddenly deathly aware of the silence. She kept her eyes on the snow under her sneakers, and if it wasn't for the sound of Alice's breathing beside her, there would be no reason not to believe that the nightmare was real, that she really was alone in the woods. She waited out the silence, one moment, two, wondering if he'd answer at all.

"I should have known you'd ask that," Ben said at last.

He straightened a little against the tree, his winter coat scraping off shavings of bark. Kait found herself straightening as well; she wrenched her eyes upward, but his eyes were elsewhere, staring over her head at something only he could see.

"I guess I have to be honest, then," he began with a nervous chuckle. "I... You're right. I didn't know you. I hadn't even heard of you when Alice and I got together. But then, there you *were* one day. Like you'd always been there. A part of our life. I didn't even realize it until then, but that's how I thought of it. *Our* life. Maybe it was too soon for it, but that's how I felt. But as soon as I met you, I knew Alice didn't feel that way about it. Even that first night, I could see the way she looked at you and I, I started... *imagining* things. Rotten things. Hateful things. I thought you were going to take her away from me. That you wanted to. That she would let you."

He rubbed his nose with the back of his hand. "I'm sorry for all of it. You're right. I didn't know you. It wasn't fair."

Alice let out a small sigh but didn't speak. She put out one mittened hand, and Ben took hold of it, squeezing it briefly before letting her go. That was enough.

"What about now?" Kait asked. "Do you? Know me, I mean."

Ben shrugged, then shook his head, seeming to make up his mind. "I'm sorry," he said again. "I wish I did. But I haven't really been trying very hard yet, have I?"

Something like a smile tickled Kait's lips. "All right, then," she said. "I don't think Lutz coulda come up with something like that. You're clear—for now."

She faked a playful jab at Ben's leg, and the hint of a smile that rippled across his features hit like the sun busting through clouds.

"Me next, then," Alice ventured, twisting towards Kait. "All right. Truth."

Again Kait hesitated. The next question was harder—but again the words seemed to thrust forward without her bidding them. And she could feel a strange sensation tickling along the skin of her right hand. It was like the pressure of another hand, knotting finger through finger, a hand with long fingernails and a warm, firm grip.

Ask, whispered a voice—not Jill Cicero's voice, and not so close. No, that wasn't true. It was closer. This was the wind. The breath in her lungs. The pulse of her blood.

Ask her. The truth won't hurt you. The truth can never hurt you.

See for yourself, Kaitlyn.

Kait closed her hand on nothing. "I wanted to ask this before," she said, shaking the cold out of her shoulders. "Last night, I was working up to it. I wasn't even sure if I wanted to know the answer, I just wanted to ask it for the asking. Alice, are you... angry with me?"

Alice's face furrowed. "For what?" Kait only shrugged. "Oh, Kaity... Of course not. I don't... I mean, I wouldn't be..."

A shadow crossed her eyes, and she didn't speak for several seconds.

"You were my best friend," she began again in a softer voice. "But there was always more to it than that, wasn't there? Even when we were little girls. We were never really equals. And I was okay with it. I thought, of course it would be like that. You were... you. And I was a mess. I depended on you, but you never needed anybody for anything. You were your own person in a way I could never be. But you always wanted me around you, and that made me feel like, like the luckiest person on the whole planet. And I loved that about you, that you could make me feel like that, without even trying to, without even realizing you were doing it. I... I think I might have even been *in* love with you, for a little while. I didn't know what it meant then. I still don't. It didn't have a name in my head."

Then her eyes hardened up, and she stared at the snow under her boots as though she would melt right through it.

"But then Lutz showed up," she continued, "and it felt like you'd cracked the world on top of my head. Suddenly I couldn't find you. You wouldn't call, wouldn't text... I never saw you in class or anywhere on campus. You left me behind—and everything I'd ever felt about you got all twisted up inside of me. I spent the first two months missing you, but I spent the next two *really* hating your guts. But I didn't hate you because you were sleeping with a monster. None of this had happened yet. I hated you because he wasn't *me*."

There were two wet tracks running down Alice's face now, but they stopped only halfway down, like the points of blunted teeth. "So—am I angry with you?" she asked. "What kind of question is that? When you came back, I thought I would feel… better. Better than this. But I just felt, *feel*, greedy. Like I want to keep you all to myself. Like I never want to let you out of my sight again. How messed up is that? I'm not angry, Kaity… But things aren't all right between us, either. Maybe they never really were."

Kait stared at her friend. The whole of her chest cavity felt heavy, swelling with ineffable feeling for this girl as time slowed to a silent crawl around them. She could not think of anything to say. There were a hundred things she wanted to say. Her toes curled in her sneakers, and she thought that if only one of them would look away that the spell would be broken, that she could speak and tell Alice Gorchuck everything, give voice to the cry of the strange and trembling *thing* clawing its way free inside of her. But Alice didn't even blink. She gazed back steadily into Kait's eyes, her cheeks glistening faintly—and it was only then that Kait realized her own eyes were streaming too. Her weeping made no sound; it only ran down her face like rain on a window, stinging and cold.

"I'm sorry," she said. She sniffed, wiped mucus, sniffed again. "I'm sorry I made you feel that way. I never knew you…" She shut her mouth on another lie, opened with the truth. "I wanted to make it up to you," she said. "I've been trying so damned hard to make it up to you. But I guess I never really understood what I'd done, until now."

"Well?" Alice said, a note of worry creeping into her voice. "Do I pass?"

Kait managed a nod. "You pass," she murmured. "It's you. It's really you."

It's always been you.

She caught Ben's eye almost by accident. His face was flushed red up to the roots of his hair, but when he caught her staring, he shrugged and offered a brave smile before averting his eyes. "Not that I'm not having the time of my life right now," he said, "but we should probably think about getting that thing in the lake, huh? Remember that we might have to break through some ice before we're done."

"I hadn't thought of that," Alice said, the spell broken at last.

She slapped her knees and stood, offering a mittened hand to Kait. But Kait didn't take it. Her head was still on spin-cycle, shaking her thoughts to pieces.

I think I might have been in love with you.

"Let's go, then," she managed to say, shifting her weight to stand.

"Wait a minute," Ben said quickly. "The game's not over. You never answered."

Alice blinked twice. "Oh... Right!" she said. "I guess that's fair. Truth or Dare, Kaity."

"Don't call me that," Kait replied automatically. Her face felt tight, like a blush but without any of the heat. "Sorry. Er... Truth, I guess."

She could hardly catch breath. The air felt too heavy to breathe. The cold had retreated from her, leaving her numb and slow and distant. She could hear Ben asking something, but the words had to trickle down through layers to reach her.

"It's the obvious question, really," he was saying. "One I've been trying to figure all damn weekend. How'd you end up with a creepo like Lutz Visgara, anyhow?"

For a moment her lips moved without her voice attached to

them; the words came on a delay, echoing. "He..." she tried. For a moment, she forgot the question. "He..."

But the world was tilting. The treetops slanted towards her, the darkening sky whirling overhead like a planetarium's bowled ceiling. Her eyes did not close, but her vision sealed off just the same, and then she was floating away into that dark gray sky, tumbling slowly, her senses fading into television static.

"Oh, my God..." somebody screamed. "Catch her! *Catch* her!"

She didn't know whose voice it was. She didn't know anything at all.

Chapter 19

Flesh

He was the Alice-body. He was curled in the front seat of the station wagon.

He was the Ben-body. He was sleeping beside her in the cabin's double bed.

He was the Riley-body. He inhaled sweet nicotine smoke under cold, unfamiliar stars.

He was the Lutz-body. He was waiting in the flesh among the trees, peering through frosted windows. He watched the empty world turn against him through another pair of unblinking eyes, and another and another and another.

The change was easy. A touch, a mental twitch, a chemical flashpoint—then the surging, pleasurable warmth of a new skin, eyes flickering open, the flesh smooth and welcoming. There was no effort, no expenditure of power. He had taken a dozen bodies this week alone, perhaps more. Now he would take one more, and one more besides, and then he and Heart-Brecker would come together and rest. Then the flesh would welcome them both. They would walk out together into the bright and empty world, and they would never come back.

He was the Riley-body, loping barefoot through the snow, sure-footed as a deer, not feeling the cold. The bleeding had stopped from the hole in the back of the skull, and the pain—the ecstatic, mind-scrambling *blast* when the bullet had passed through the brain case—was gone, but he could only see through the one eye. There was a hole in his vision like a cigarette burn. His Ben-body and his Alice-body were back at the cabin, empty and idling, like a car left running in a parking lot. They would keep. Or perhaps they had already started down into the valley to dispose of his Cormac-body, his fallen timber, the flesh ruined but not unusable. He remembered being the Jill-body, and he shivered in anticipation, deep in the flesh, in the hollow bones. Despite the cold, the Riley-body did not shiver with him.

The other flesh would reach the lake soon. Heart-Brecker would discover his gift to her, or she wouldn't. Perhaps she would be afraid. It did not matter. Night would fall just the same. Tomorrow would come. Valentine's Day. They would come here, rather than huddle in the dark forest. Their fear would rule these extraneous bodies, and Heart-Brecker would lead them straight to him. He would stake his soul on it.

There came a thunder of engines. Snow crunched under steel-belted tires, and a slate-gray SUV lumbered slowly around the bend, its headlights flickering among the trees. The Riley-body reached up, combed matted blonde hair over a vacant eye socket, and stepped out into the road, shading the good eye with an outflung hand. He could not see the driver, but the vehicle slowed, sliding a little on the snow as the brakes engaged. The SUV creaked to a halt, and he allowed the Riley body to collapse, bathed in the glory of the headlights.

The driver-side door swung open, and boots crunched on the snow, running toward him. The Riley-body lay motionless. He had learned patience these past two days. Flesh rebelled against that kind of patience, but he had learned to conquer the will of flesh, to bury it in himself, layer over layer. He thought of Heart-Brecker, leading bodies carrying a body through a world that did not know her. He would watch a while longer. Then he would join her. He would sew up the wound between them and wash his hands of the whole chore.

This all had stopped being fun for him a long time ago.

* * *

It seemed so long ago now—but he remembered, at first feeling merely frustrated with the whole affair. Heart-Brecker had thrown tantrums before, but they always fizzled out inside of an hour or at most a day or maybe two. Then she would return, ready to play the game again. But this had felt different. Like a window slammed shut on his fingers. His mind could not touch her, and she had run so far away this time, fled north to this bleak and hostile place. And she had brought the bodies with her. No... Heart-Brecker would say the bodies brought *her*, acting autonomously, as if detritus bumping across a windswept parking lot could *act*. Vehicles driving vehicles. Bodies driving bodies. He remembered thinking it was madness. She had never really understood, despite all his lessons. He loved her—but deep in his heart, he had to admit she could be a stupid bitch sometimes.

He knew he loved Kait Brecker. Could have loved her. If she had only let him try. He could have been any body she wanted him to be. Anything she desired: any shape, any flesh, any number of faces and voices and sensuous forms. Features in endless combinations. Infinite variety across infinite years, combining and re-combining, creating new flesh from old. That was the beauty of this empty world. What more was there? He would have given her the stars. But the flesh betrayed him. She abandoned his love for her friend. For another woman. Another *body*.

A body called Alice Gorchuck.

He remembered being heartbroken. He remembered being incandescent with rage, numb with confusion. He had never seen them in the same room before. Not truly together—only on that one Halloween night, and the Alice-body had been dressed in some absurd regalia, the end result of some vulgar spark of flesh-instinct. A costume born out of mutation. A mask wearing a mask. *Thing Two*, she called it. They had laughed at her that night. Then they coupled, and then they laughed some more. He had disregarded that body's worth, discarded the memory of the peculiar expression on the girl-flesh's face as he shut the door in it.

He had been a fool.

Because later, at the gas station... That should have been the end of it. It was the first time he had seen Heart-Brecker in over a month, and his heart had swelled with affection at the sight of her. They spoke, and she had felt it—the overwhelming pressure of his love. Their minds touched, it was like a symphony. Right then, they could have begun to heal. But the Alice-body, it intervened somehow. Against every conceivable possibility, he had actually been forced to speak with it, engage in *conversation* with the flesh. And he had played along, hadn't he? Played make-believe in the puppet show, pretending he couldn't see the strings, the hand in the sock. He had displayed the patience of stone—but when he tried to reach out to Heart-Brecker once more, the body attacked him. It *attacked* him. With strength enough to knock him down, to actually damage his own beautiful flesh-set and force him into retreat. Heart-Brecker scuttled under the shadow, and their minds did not touch again.

A nervous defense system. Something subdermal. A pre-rendered protocol, calculated to preserve the integrity of the flesh. Nothing more.

That's all it *could* be, he reasoned after, nursing his wound, feeling warm ichor drip down his broken face. But still, he felt irrational hatred blaze up within him. He had wanted to destroy it right then, take the offending girl-body and fling it onto the highway where a vehicle would strike it. He wanted to feel it fly apart, feel his consciousness scatter as the flesh broke up like a continent. But he had controlled himself. The destruction of the Alice-body would not solve the larger conundrum. He remembered being the Jill-body, and this cooled his nerves. He would regroup. He would try again. He would find another way.

* * *

He was the driver-body, hunched over the steering wheel. His

Riley-body crouched in the passenger seat, folded up for storage. Driving was easy—the flesh remembered the movements. Protocols stored in the muscle and nerves. He needed only to direct them where to go. He had done his homework, surveyed this part of the land, probing it for weaknesses. The boy-body at the gas station had a map in his car. This road wound up to the cabin, or it would take him down into the valley by a circuitous route. It would pass by the lake. There was a pier, and a dry dock. He could drive right up to the water.

* * *

It was only when he arrived at the cabin that he realized the depth of Heart-Brecker's confusion. He had tried something he'd never accomplished before, a hitchhiking maneuver. He left a piece of himself inside the Alice-body, to observe without acting, something that could be activated remotely later, a seed that could grow under the right kind of light. He transferred the seed to the Riley-body, then the Ben-body, all without taking full control of the flesh. It was an unusual experience for him, acting as a passenger, relinquishing control like that. But this status afforded him certain insights as well. He could observe Heart-Brecker anonymously, see her just as the flesh saw her.

What he saw enraged him like nothing else ever had before.

Heart-Brecker and the Alice-body—they *touched*. They were sitting at the dinner table, very close together, eating something the Ben-body had prepared. This other flesh kept twining fingers through Heart-Brecker's hair. She stroked it, idly scratching her scalp just like Heart-Brecker had done for him so many times before, and it was only then that he realized: this was no approximation, some mere effigy of affection, a copy of a copy. *It was real.* He could not touch her mind in this form, but he could tell just from the look on her stupid face that she liked this, this... this abominable *mockery*. The stomach of his flesh turned, thinking about it. For an instant he hoped against hope it was more play-acting, a joke for his benefit, another strange wrinkle in their two-hearted game. But it was not so. She did not know he was there. Heart-Brecker, his Heart-Brecker... She *liked* this flesh. It wasn't a parody at all. It was love.

That was when his rage boiled over, exploding inward like a collapsing star. He took the Ben-body in his anger, filling it with himself—but when the flesh welcomed him, something inside woke up and began to talk to him. Began to whisper. Not an intelligence, no, but a cluster of higher processes, nerve-center instinct, almost like a personality. And something in this alien signal in the flesh whispered like hatred, sweet and intoxicating and strong. This was when he made his first mistake. He *listened* to the whispers—and it almost cost him everything.

He needed to plan, he knew. He needed a timetable. Heart-Brecker had fallen down the crevasse, and she would need to be fished out before their game could continue. But the doubled hatred moving and flexing inside the Ben-body overpowered him, if only momentarily. It made him lash out: he laughed in her face, mocking the mockery, scorning the perverted dollhouse she had constructed around herself. He hurt the flesh's *feelings*, if such a thing was possible. And later when his anger cooled and he realized what he had done, he tried to smooth the waves kicked up by his tantrum.

But again his emotion ruled him. He made another mistake.

He exposed himself to Heart-Brecker.

And then Heart-Brecker exposed him to the world.

* * *

He remembered being the Ben-body. Heart-Brecker had nearly bludgeoned him unconscious, once before he relinquished control of the flesh, and once more after.

He remembered being the Riley-body, smashing the flesh

against the unforgiving edge of the wooden post. Living tissue pitted against dead tissue. Heart-Brecker had destroyed the body to prevent him from destroying the body. It defied logic. Perhaps he would never understand.

He tried to forget being the Alice-body. There was no telling what Heart-Brecker had inflicted upon that flesh while his back was turned, while his attentions were elsewhere. He would have to destroy that body himself, burn it down to ash, just to get the stink of that memory out of him. Would Heart-Brecker forgive that? Would she be able to forget her obsession and play the game as she had played it before? Yes—he believed she could. He held onto that faith, even after everything else. But the Alice-body was quite large. It would take a lot of burning.

He was the driver-body, and now the lake shimmered into view, brilliant in the late evening light. The water was frozen over, but the ice did not look thick. Sparkling liquid lay in puddles across the surface. The ice could be broken with a fist, he wagered, or by the weight of a body in a carpet. The SUV idled behind a thicket, crouched on the snowy road. He could see the pier and the dry dock—there were two tiny figures struggling across the road, carrying a long *something* between them. He adjusted the driver-body's glasses.

The Ben-body. The Alice-body. Heart-Brecker was not among them.

He considered, for a brief instant, calling out to them. They would not see the Riley-body in the passenger's seat from this distance, and they did not know this man-body's voice. He considered activating the dormant mind-seed he'd left in the Cormac-body. That flesh was strong, stronger than any he'd taken before. It could escape the carpet, especially cut loose from the autonomic limits that prevented flesh from injuring itself. He wanted to see the girl-body—this *Alice Gorchuck*—flail in terror as a corpse lumbered toward her. But Heart-Brecker was not there. Her suffering would be meaningless.

Instead he pressed the gas pedal, and the SUV began to creep forward, snow groaning under the steel-belted tires. His hands gripped the wheel, the knuckles going white from the pressure, and the Riley-body slipped sideways, its head falling into his lap. He thought of the Jill-body, but the memory only left him cold, like a mouthful of ice. The vehicle gathered speed, and the two forms by the water's edge did not look up.

* * *

Confusion would do him no good. Outrage would do him no good, nor wounded pride. This was not his fault. He could never have predicted that Heart-Brecker would do something so cruel, so *foolish*. He wanted to set the cabin on fire with all of them inside it. Let her burn with the bodies she loved so much. He wanted to disappear into the forest, drown himself in flesh, gorge on the emptiness of the world until he burst. Instead, he had dug in like a tick. He watched and he waited. But Heart-Brecker stacked injustice on top of injustice. She talked to the bodies, but she would not talk to him, even when she knew he was hidden among them. She plotted against him with the bodies. She announced that she would *kill* him, destroy his flesh-set with the hunting rifle on the hook—she told him this to his face, and he had been too stunned to respond. And every attempt at reunion he made, she thwarted with the precision and cunning of a suicide bomber. She harmed flesh to harm him. She harmed *herself* to harm him. She destroyed the Riley-body, and she wept over her sacrifice, over the devastation of beautiful flesh.

He wanted to weep too. He wanted to tear the whole stupid empty world into halves and watch the hollow bodies tumble out among the stars. He wanted to stop this feeling that followed him from flesh to flesh, body to body, form to form. He wanted to find another world to wander, one where the flesh did not have names. But he could not abandon Kait Brecker.

So he would have to show her. One last try. One last attempt at welcome. He would prove to her what his love actually meant, prove that she had only broken his heart and not his spirit. That he was still her mate, her *man*, that it was baked into his flesh-self, stamped onto his mind like a heart carved in the wood of a living tree. He would remind her why they loved each other. Why he was the only person on the entire planet she could ever truly love. Of course, he would have to clear the path. Hold the doors open for her at every juncture. He would do this for her. He would teach her one last time which direction the empty world really spun. He would take her by the hand and lead her where she did not wish to go.

But she would not take the lesson well. She had never taken his lessons well.

He would have to ram it down her throat this time.

Chapter 20

The More We Get Together

For one agonizing instant, Kait forgot how to scream.

The world went away—but then consciousness came surging back like a rush of cold water splashed in her face. Alice was shaking her awake, and as the eggshell of the dream cracked open, sudden fear gripped her in iron-toothed jaws and she lunged upward, seizing her friend's shoulders with such force that the other girl cried out in pain. But Kait herself could make no sound. Her mouth hung open, but the only noise that escaped her lips was a thin whistle, like air escaping a poorly tied balloon. Images fled her mind—no true renderings, but bizarre wipes and swaths of liquid, oozing color. Crude renditions of unspeakable violence, constructed from the dark reds and pinks and browns of human tissue, while the horror of real life flooded in around every corner.

"It's all *right*," Alice was saying to her. "We're *here*, Kaity. You're all right, you were only dreaming…"

Kait blinked, peering blearily past Alice's face: the straight trunks of trees thrust upward all around her, shooting off into the deep gray crush of the forest sky. She shifted her shoulders against the ground. Snow hissed and popped underneath her back, packed hard by her weight. The world looked like a painting of the world, rendered in broad, dark, impressionist strokes. She had slept. And night had fallen. The darkness was already here.

Something terrible was about to happen.

"How long…?" she managed to croak at last. "How long was I…?"

"Only a few minutes," Alice began in a soothing voice, but Kait was already struggling to climb to her feet, wrestling out of Alice's grip as she floundered on the ground, her hands searching the snow all around her like a blind man.

"You just... kind of... fell," her friend continued, letting Kait flop down to her knees in the snow. "We figured it was fatigue, from, you know. Everything. We tried to wake you up earlier, but you just kept talking in your sleep. The same thing, over and over—"

"The gun," Kait interrupted, panic springing into her voice. Her hands swatted the empty snow around her. "The *gun*, Alice. Where is it?"

"Right there, against the tree." Alice gestured with one mittened hand. "We didn't want you rolling over on... Kaity, what's wrong? What is it?"

"I..." Feeling began to return. The air turned knife-steel cold in her lungs. She took several shallow, quaking breaths through her nose, trying to shake off the throbbing ache in her chest. "I... I had a..."

A premonition.

It still didn't feel like a dream. She remembered when she and Lutz would sleep together, side-by-side on the lumpy double-bed mattress in his apartment, or collapsed against one another on the sofa in front of the flickering TV. She remembered falling unconscious with Jill Cicero's warm body positioned between them, the sound of the other woman's breathing slowing from its fevered pitch to a soothing, rhythmic hum, lulling Kait into slumber. Those nights she would always dream. The experience became less alien as time went on, but she never truly got used to it—holding conversations with her boyfriend, hearing his voice in her head while they slept. Sometimes she would wake up in the dark and hear him murmuring in his sleep; sometimes it would only be his lips moving, with no sound coming out. She would hear his voice just the same. And he would hear hers.

This had felt just like that. Like hot breath against her ear. Like a long finger tickling over the surface of her mind.

"I had a nightmare," she said at last, thinking quickly. "I saw... Everything was all tangled up. Riley was..." She let emotion overwhelm her, and for a moment she could only rock back and forth on the cold ground. Her face screwed up, but no tears would fall, and her weeping made no sound. "I dreamed Riley was still alive," she moaned softly. "And I had to... I *had* to..." She hated the lie. Hated herself for telling it. But there was no other explanation she could offer up. She had heard Lutz's voice again. She could still hear it, murmuring within her as though he had slept by her side.

It would take a lot of burning.

"Where's Ben?" she coughed, uselessly scrubbing her tired eyes with one gloved hand.

Alice shivered, slapping her arms. "Well—we couldn't move you and Cormac at the same time," she explained gently. "He's coming back. He's right behind me. He wanted to—"

"What do you mean, *coming back?*"

To Kait's great shock, Alice smiled down at her, her eyes glinting even in the looming darkness. "We got it in the water," she said, almost gleefully. "There was ice, but it wasn't thick. And he sank like a, well, like he had a bunch of rocks in there with him—that was a good idea, Kaity. And there's a *road*. Right down by the water's edge. Ben thinks it'll take us to the main highway." Alice's mitten-clad hands grabbed hold of Kait's own as though she would help her stand, but instead she simply held it tight, like she feared it would fly from her wrist. "You did it," she said. Her eyes shone in the dark, pinpricks of light held captive in the middle of her round face. "You *did* it. We're going home. It's over."

Then she did pull Kait to her feet, just in time for Ben to come crashing through the snowy underbrush. "You're up," he said when he caught sight of them standing together. He averted his gaze, his face flushed with cold. "We, ah. We were worried."

"Thanks." Kait looked from one face to the other, feeling her own face flush pink. Something had changed while she slept. She could feel it, loose and kicking in the air: Ben nudged a pile of snow with the toe of his boot and slapped his cheeks with leather-gloved hands, pointedly avoiding her gaze, while Alice shuffled her heels in the snow, looking embarrassed, caught-out.

Kait felt her heart sink. She knew this was no time to think such things, but her mind could not shake the feeling welling up within her. *I think I might have been in love with you.* What did this mean for them now? What would it mean after, when they were back in the world? Guilt like the cold weight of lead sank into her. Ben had known all along. He had seen more clearly than she had—and it had driven him to hatred before. But now there could be no pretending, no feigned ignorance. Now the same truth burned inside them all. Ben loved Alice, but could that love survive a confession like that? Did he want it to? Did *she*?

She studied Ben's face, a dark profile against the backdrop of the forest. In spite of everything, she could not help feeling some measure of affection for this boy. It was no romantic feeling, or even the sisterly love she'd felt for Riley—no, it was almost... *recognition*. Perhaps even gratitude. But for what? She could not reason it out, and so her guilt continued to gnaw at her, to peck at her heart like a mob of crows with raw, bloody beaks. She wished she could go back. She wished they could just keep on hating each other, or at least return to the comfort of that old, sullen, silent distrust they had enjoyed so much.

Things would have been so much easier if Ben Alden had not become her friend.

"Did I miss anything else?" she asked, breaking the silence. "While I was..."

She gestured vaguely to the Kait-shaped snow angel on the ground and shrugged.

"Nothing," Alice said. "Kaity, we were right there the whole time. We weren't..."

"We weren't going to let anything happen to you," Ben

finished for her.

Kait felt like crying again. Fatigue crushed inward like the weight of an ocean, and she felt what little energy she had regained slough off her like a heavy blanket sliding off her shoulders. This was backwards. It was *wrong*. She was supposed to protect them, not the other way 'round. But now she wondered if she would even have the strength to lift the Model 94, much less fire it. She turned at the waist, looking for the glint of the gun's barrel. There it was—leaning against a slender oak, just like Alice had said. She thought of Riley, wished she hadn't. She tried to focus on the dull throb of pain in her right shoulder, but the sensation there had vanished. The arm seemed to belong to her again. It was the rest of her body that rebelled.

"Alice said you found a road," she murmured. Out of the corner of her eye, she saw them both nod. "So let's go, then, huh?" She could not raise her head to look them in their faces.

"Night's comin' on," Alice remarked.

"It's here already." Kait flexed her hands inside her gloves and lifted the rifle to her shoulder. Even through the pads of the fabric, the metal and wood were deathly cold against her shaking fingers. Alice removed one mitten to flick on the flashlight of her smartphone; all around them the darkness seemed to leap as though to the rhythm of night music only it could hear, lurching in ever-tightening circles as the fragile beam of light swung in her grip. Human forms flashed against the trunks of trees— but it was only their own shadows, looming huge above them, projected nightmares loping and twisting against the wood.

But none of it matched the crawling, scraping dread that perched on the rungs of her ribcage like a stoop-shouldered carrion bird. She wanted to hope—oh, she wanted to dream of warmth, and a heavy locked door standing between her and her friends and all the horror and blood of the last twenty-four hours. But she could not shake off the terror of her dream. She could still hear his whisper in her crowded mind. It sounded like footsteps in the distance.

It sounded like the last grains of sand in the hourglass dropping into the bottom.

"Show me the road," she said over the clamor of her jangling nerves. "Please."

The snow was especially treacherous in the darkness. Now every crunch, every shuffle, every crack of a dry branch under their feet echoed in Kait's ears like thunder. Alice held her light as steady as she could manage, but every time her foot slipped, the beam would swing around crazily, making the dark surge up around them like a cloud of bats. Kait's eyes kept playing tricks on her: she saw shadow-people in the trees, phantom faces looming just beyond the fragile boundary of the flashlight's beam. Once an owl shrieked, and she jammed the stock of the Model 94 into her shoulder so forcefully it left a bruise, her heartbeat exploding out of her sternum. She wished one of the others would speak—something to fill the air, to plug the gaps of quiet in between footsteps. But the snow seemed to have stolen her friend's voices, and Kait herself couldn't think of anything to say.

When they finally crashed through the tree-line and emerged under open sky, to Kait it felt like the first breath of fresh air after being trapped under a frozen pond. And sure enough, there was the lake, with the wooden pier projecting nearly thirty feet over the ice, its wooden slats covered in snow and slush. There was a break in the clouds now, and the moon poured through: under its frigid gaze, Kait could see footprints in the snow, two pairs of tracks leading all along the length of the pier, as well as the thick track-mark of something heavy being dragged up to its edge and pushed over. She could not see the hole in the ice that Cormac had plunged through, but an image sprang into her mind, of Alice and Ben hauling the bulky carpet to the edge and slipping it through, watching it vanish into liquid darkness under that same moon. She pictured the rug unraveling below the surface, the huge body wrapped up inside drifting slowly upright to stand in the mud under the ice as it closed over him, angling back as if to peer up into the night sky. She pictured Cormac's raw head still wedged in its tree, pecked down to just the grinning skull now, staring at nothing forever, preserved by the cold.

They were standing in the road. Kait almost didn't notice it at first, but there was a narrow paved path under their feet, covered up by snow and winding away from the water, just wide enough for two cars to drive side by side. The lake was at the bottom of the forest valley, and the road rose up into the hills on both sides of them, vanishing into the dark woods to the left and right. The snow was smooth here, and in the newly uncovered moonlight it glittered like flecks of broken glass.

"Well, this is it," Ben announced, planting his feet with a dry crunch. "One of these has got to take us to the main road. I guess we just pick a direction and start walking? I mean, they both have to go somewhere, don't they?"

But Kait wasn't listening. She was staring up the leftward road, at the bend, where it disappeared from view beyond the wall of the trees. At first, even in the moonlight, she could only guess at the geography—but soon, light began to blossom along the crest of the first hill. One beam of light split into two headlights, and then the quiet snarl of a big engine floated down the incline towards them, along with the crunch of broad tires on snow.

Kait held her breath—it seemed too good to be true. In that moment, her entire reality felt carved from paper-thin crystal, as though the slightest sound could shatter it. She didn't dare blink, terrified that in that quick wipe of darkness the car would vanish or that she would wake again in that snowdrift, gripped by terror, Alice shaking her awake once more. But before her very eyes, a large yellow SUV lumbered over the hill, its headlights swinging up and over like long, outstretched arms. The vehicle had a roof rack strung with red, gold, and green bulb lights, and a drooping Rudolph nose made from red tinsel hung from the front grill.

"Oh, my God..." Alice seized hold of Kait's elbow—the bad right arm, and it sent bolts of pain scurrying up past the shoulder. But Kait didn't care: she grabbed Alice's arm, and Ben's, just to know they were there and seeing what she saw. She felt Ben stiffen at her touch, but when he spoke, his voice was jubilant.

"It *can't* be..." he said. Then he raised his other hand over his head and waved frantically, jumping up and down a little in the snow. "Hey!" he bellowed. "Hey, over here!"

"Oh my God, oh my God, oh my God," Alice said, pressing her knuckles to her lips.

With a hushed roar of tires on loose powder, the SUV braked about fifty feet from the three of them, bathing them in the gaze of its headlights. The driver's side window rolled down, and the dark shape of a man's shaggy head emerged, along with a plume of cigarette smoke and a tinny fanfare of alt-rock garbage pouring from the car's stereo system.

"*Hey,* now," shouted out a chilly basso voice over the gurgle of the engine. "Hey, now, are you kids in *trouble* or something?"

They all looked at each other, momentarily voiceless—and then, as if some secret signal had passed between them, each of them burst out into high, hysterical laughter.

Kait couldn't understand it—and yet, she couldn't stop the ghastly noise that bubbled up her throat like an insuppressible belch. Perhaps it was the appearance of their ridiculous, washed-out faces in the glare of the headlights. Or perhaps there really was something funny about the whole scenario. Maybe this kind of merriment *was* the natural human response to nearly freezing to death in a snow-hushed forest a hundred miles from civilization. Kait would never know, and didn't expect to learn. She doubled over, clutching her stomach, the barrel of the gun dragging a furrow in the snow at her feet. Each breath filed her lungs with thousands of tiny icy needles, but even this only made her laugh harder.

Trouble, she thought to herself as she held her aching midsection. *Yeah, no. No trouble here. We're fine, really. Nothing to see here. Go about your business.*

"Hey—what's so *funny* out there?" the man's voice hollered. "Hey, now, if you're not in trouble or nuthin', how about getting out of the road, huh?"

"We're sorry, sir!" Alice called out quickly, straightening and smoothing down her coat.

"We *are* in trouble," Kait added, hoping her voice would carry enough for the man to hear. She wiped her eyes, a last giggle wriggling loose from her lips. "We're stranded out here. We're trying to get to the nearest town, but we got lost in the dark. If you could just give us a lift out to the gas station or something, we can call a taxi service from—"

"You all the group up at the Alden cabin?" the man cut her off.

Kait nodded, realizing too late he probably couldn't tell she'd done it.

"The power got shut off," Ben explained. "And then... Ah, well, my car wouldn't start up, either. Kind of a bitch of a weekend, all told."

"Lot of that going around," the man replied evenly. "Sounds like you kids have had a time of it." Then his head drooped, almost in resignation. "Well, come on then," he said. "It's not like I can very well leave you out here."

"Oh, my God—*thank you!*" Alice's voice was almost a shriek as she bounced up and down in the snow. Her mass of curls drifted up and down with the motion of her body, and in the intense glow of the headlights there almost seemed to be a halo, a ring of golden tinsel around the silhouette of her head. "Oh, my God... We did it. *You* did it." She turned bright eyes to Kait— then, very suddenly, she leaned across the snow-covered road and pecked her gently on the cheek. Kait's face was so numb she hardly felt the pressure of her lips, but it scrambled her insides all the same. She felt hot under the skin, then cold, then hot again, then both all at once.

"You got us through," her friend was saying, suddenly bashful. She opened her mouth like she would say more, but instead she just turned on her heel and trotted off toward the SUV, still bouncing slightly with every step.

Kait didn't need to look up to know Ben was staring at her.

But she made herself look anyway, her feelings still wrestling back and forth inside her chest. His face was a wash of smooth yellow, lit from beneath by the headlights. His glasses were a mask of white light, rendering his entire expression inscrutable. "I'm sorry," she started to say. "I didn't want—"

But Ben cut her off with an airy wave, forcing a brave smile onto his face. "She's right, you know," he intoned. "You got us through."

Kait's heart dropped into her stomach. His smile never wavered, but there was no mistaking the break in his voice. The sound of a heart coming unglued, piece by piece. What had she done? How had she allowed this to happen? She wanted to say something, to defend herself, to offer some assurance to this boy, but she did not trust her own voice. "We'll talk about it later, when all this is over," he told her, turning away. "All three of us together. We'll work this out somehow. I owe you that much."

"You don't owe me anything," she whispered. But when Ben didn't respond, she could only nod and look away as well. "All right. Later, then." Kait felt like something inside her had burst a seam. She forced her gaze back into the powerful blast of the SUV's headlights, watching Alice's broad back moving away into the light. She raised her eyes, peering through the dark windshield of the vehicle: the man had pulled his head back inside like a turtle, and the window was rolled up. He was only a blob of motionless shadow behind the glass now. And it could have been a trick of the moonlight, but Kait could swear she could make out a second body in the car, a slouched form next to him in the passenger's seat.

Alice was only twenty-five feet from the car. Now she was twenty.

Then a pinprick of flame bloomed behind the glass. The jet of a cigarette lighter—and though the flame was tiny, it was just enough to illuminate a small sphere inside the cab of the SUV. Half the man's bearded face sprang into view, smiling coolly, his lips wrapped around the tip of a cigarette, his eyes locked on Kait's. And there *was* a second body in the car. All Kait could make out was a curtain of long blonde hair, almost covering a grin that mocked all human smiles—and the black oozing pool of an empty eye-socket.

"ALICE!"

The scream tore loose like a gasp, for that was all her aching lungs would allow. She coughed cold air, suddenly shaking all over. Her right arm tingled like it was crawling with hot embers. Alice did not hear her. She kept bouncing forward, almost to the SUV now. The flame from the cigarette lighter was gone: other than the bright needlepoint of the tip of the lit cigarette, the windshield was a mask of darkness. There was no time to think. There was no time at all.

She launched herself forward, the treads of her Converses struggling for purchase on the loose powder, the Model 94 swinging in her gloved fist. But it felt as though she was running through the thick amber of a dream. Her limbs crawled through the air, her muscles resisting every step, every movement, as she urged her exhausted body onward. She tried to call out again, not a word but a mere meaningless half-formed cry—and this time Alice did turn, slowly, as though she was spinning on a line of invisible thread. Kait saw her lips move through the haze of darkness, her face screwing up in confusion and concern, *Always concerned, always worried about her, such a dear, dear, sweet, apple-*

cheeked Alice Gorchuck...

The driver gunned the motor. The SUV lurched forward at impossible speed.

Kait found her scream at last.

The front bumper was wide enough to crush them both, but the driver yanked the wheel, aiming for Alice alone. But the ice had other ideas. The tires shrieked against the loose snow, grinding all the way down to the cold pavement beneath, the headlights slashing across Kait's body like a swipe from a long sword. The back wheels sent up a shower of powder that seemed to hang in the frigid air like a curtain, and in a sudden burst of speed, the entire SUV shot straight past Alice, only managing to hip-check her into the snow between the road and the trees, where she collapsed face-down with a soft cry, her limbs in a tangle. But now it was skidding sideways, an uncontrolled slide, gliding almost silently across the snow as it bore down on her. Kait could see the driver's hairy face through the side window now, his features set in an expressionless mask, even as the meaty, white-knuckled hands battled the steering wheel.

Maybe she could have run, or tried to dive out of the vehicle's path. Perhaps even an hour ago she could have managed it. But it wasn't just her arm now. Her entire body felt it belonged to someone else, like she was watching another girl standing on some other snowy road, some other body being destroyed. Each muscle was locked in place as if by some hidden protocol of the flesh. She thought of a gun jamming. She thought of screws falling loose into a vast, alien mechanism. She thought of a hollow tree swaying, about to crash to the earth. She wondered, in that brief instant before impact, if Lutz was right about it all, if it would really hurt so much to die. If she would feel anything at all.

It was funny—she wasn't even really scared anymore.

Then something heavy struck her from behind, tossing her out of the path of the SUV as though she weighed nothing at all. She landed on her hands and knees, the rifle spinning away across the frozen surface of the snow. The vehicle swung past her, skidding a half-donut on the snowy road. There was a dull thump, and the crunch of flesh. Ben did not even cry out — she heard something like a surprised sigh as the car struck him broadsides, carrying him away, out of sight. The SUV spun away almost gracefully, making no sound save for the almost-distant purr of its engine, gliding like a duck on a pond. Then it whirled into a tree, the metal of the back bumper buckling with the impact. A shower of loose snow plummeted down from the branches with a muffled thump. Then there was quiet.

* * *

Kait struggled to stand. Her brain whirled like batter in a mixing bowl. Whatever had locked her limbs in place had melted away as quickly as it had taken hold, but her arms were still almost too weak to push her weight up from the snow. The road was no longer silent. The SUV's engine had cut off, but she could still hear the idle ticking of the motor as it cooled, regular and rhythmic as the seconds on a clock, as well as the soft hiss of steam released somewhere under the vehicle's hood. Her eyes first fixed on the road behind her — her gaze tracing the SUV's careening tracks through the shallow snow. A ways up the hill, she could make out Alice's limp form, lying beside the road, her shoulders rising and falling ever-so-slightly with every breath.

Then she forced her eyes to follow the path the other way, towards the wreck. Here the tracks crisscrossed, and crisscrossed again, churning the snow into mush. It was white, then gray, then colorless, until it was bright scarlet under the glistening moonlight. Ben lay in a heap in the center of the road, not moving. She yanked her eyes away with a gasp of horror — his body didn't look like a body anymore. His torso was whole, but somewhere around his midsection he seemed to go all to pieces. His legs kicked out at strange angles, one knee seeming to bend inward on itself. He did not move when she screamed his name. Nothing moved. Even the shadows refused to flicker, and the snow swallowed her shout like a whale gulping down a mouthful of fish.

Again she tried to stand, but her legs refused to hold weight. She slammed her fists against the snow, slashing at it, throwing powder in the air and nearly blinding herself, howling in frustration and rage. The forest took that cry, too, unquestioningly. Finally she had to drag herself forward, pulling her weight along with the strength of her arms alone. She found the Model 94 halfway there, and clutched it in her fist as she crawled along, loping like a gorilla through the wet mush closer to the wreck site. There lay Ben, his eyes open under shattered glasses, one already swelling shut. She could hear him breathing, and hope boiled in her chest—but when he began to speak, it was like a light switched off inside of her.

"I think…" he said in a voice as soft as a warm bath and a straight razor, "I think we better have that conversation now."

Kait's insides twisted into knots. "No-no-no. Don't *say* that," she begged, stinging tears pushing under half-closed eyelids. She wrestled herself into a kneeling position beside him, and she pulled him towards her, though it took all the strength left in her body to draw him into her lap, ignoring the wet heat of the oozing blood sticking between the fingers of her gloves. "You're gonna be fine, you hear me? This wasn't… This wasn't in the Goddamn *deal*…."

But Ben only laughed—or she had to assume that the moist hacking sound that bubbled up from his mouth meant laughter. Blood trickled down from one corner of his lips, and she wiped it clean with her glove almost angrily.

"Don't waste… a bullet… on me…" he croaked.

"You son of a bitch." She wanted to punch that idiot smile off his face. She wanted to lie down in the snow and die beside him.

She couldn't see. The world kept fogging up, flooding from the corners of her eyes. She wanted to pull the world apart around her until Lutz crawled out from under, where she could crush him under her heel and watch him squirm as he died. "Why'd you do it, huh?" she hissed through her teeth. "You big dumb idiot—why'd you *do* something like that?"

Ben turned his eyes towards the hill, and the groan he let loose told her even this small movement nearly destroyed him. "Is she... all right?" he asked. Kait could only nod, her lips pressed together so hard that it nearly drew blood. "You need... to tell her—"

Kait cut him off with a vigorous shake of her head. "We're not doing that now, you hear me, you bastard?" she snarled. "I'm not gonna tell her shit. You're gonna tell her yourself. That's the deal. Everybody lives. Everybody goes home. Remember the plan?"

Ben nodded, beckoned her closer. She leaned in, turning her head so that her ear faced his mouth. His breath was cold as it left his lips:

"Take her... if you have to."

Kait almost dropped him. She sat straight upright, staring down at his sad smile.

"I mean it," he croaked. "Take her. Like him. If that's... what it takes."

"You knew?" she whispered. Ben shrugged, the movement barely registering. "But when?" she demanded. *"How?* You never said anything. Even when—"

"Jill Cicero," he said. He pointed one trembling finger. "In my head. In yours."

Kait felt her blood go cold in a sudden flash.

"You're not... like him," he told her in a shuddering breath. "Not really. Not where... where it counts. That's all... that matters... now. You can... save her. Promise me, Kait... Promise me you'll—"

"I already made a promise," she told him, shaking hair out of her eyes. "I told her—"

"Promise me..."

"But what if you're wrong?" Now *she* was shuddering, her entire body wracked with uncontrollable sobs. "I don't... I don't even understand what I..."

"Say it," he insisted.

What else could she do? She shook away her tears and nodded, feeling the trap close around her heart at last. "I'll protect her," she swore. "Whatever it takes. And I'll tell her..."

She sniffed, searching for the right words. Ben supplied them.

"...Until the very end."

His mouth opened very wide in a gasp, looking above her head at something only he could see. His jaw flapped up and down several times like a ventriloquist's dummy. "You..." he began to say, but then he refocused his watering gaze, looking her in the eye one last time.

"You're... a good friend... Kait Brecker," he said.

The forest was silent. The break in the clouds widened, and harsh, ugly moonlight pushed through, setting Kait and all the devastation around her awash in otherworldly radiance. Lit up under the moon's gaze, the world around her looked like nothing more than an extraterrestrial landscape, the snow glistening like bright crystal on the road and across the lake and among the branches of the trees. She would have felt at home there, despite everything—an alien in an alien world. That was what they were. That was all they'd ever been.

She held Ben Alden to her heaving chest. She held him a long time, and she wasn't even certain when she stopped hearing the sound of his breathing.

Chapter 21

Game

Jill Cicero watched Lutz heave the bedroom window open, and the cold night blew in, moving the thick curtains in billowing waves. The window stuck in its frame, and he had to struggle to push it up past the halfway point. But he was smiling. The moon leaned in through the aperture like a curious neighbor, and under its milky eye she saw his face in profile, grinning a hard, cold grin like the tip of a sharp knife. Kait was not in the apartment; before Jill picked herself up off the floor, the other girl had made her escape out into the hall, and the sound of her footsteps had been quickly engulfed by the heating system kicking into gear in the next room. Jill's mouth still tasted like carpeting, but she could not wipe the stringy fuzz from her lips.

Lutz crossed the room, moving towards her slowly, but with clear purpose. He didn't really seem to look at her. His eyes slid away from her as if she wasn't there. But when he stood before her, he raised his eyes to meet her gaze, and she watched that sharp, dangerous smile melt off his lips. He reached down, grasped her right wrist in his hand, and raised it to eye level. He dropped it: it flopped back to her side like a limp rag. He did this two more times, lifting her hand and dropping it, never taking his eyes off hers. His face never twitched.

She was not looking at a human being now.

Perhaps it had always been so—but now, under the peculiar effect of moon-rays and flickering streetlight, Lutz seemed... *transformed*, somehow. His flesh still cleaved to his bones in the usual way, but his movements were a half-step faster, a half-step longer. When he crossed the room, his strides stretched and quickened like his limbs were really longer than they appeared to be. Like there was another, larger boy under the surface, peering through the soft, pale skin as if it were thin gauze. She could feel hundreds of eyes on her, none of them in his head.

"What did you say to her," he said, without really asking anything at all.

Then he struck her hard across the face.

The blow exploded across her cheek, but she didn't fall this time. Her body took one quick step backwards to compensate for the impact, rocking back on some invisible axis like a buoy, and her face stung only for the briefest instant. The pain sucked down beneath her skin like water disappearing under dry sand, and Lutz withdrew his hand, wringing it out, sucking his teeth in discomfort. Then he laughed—she had grown to hate his goaty laugh, but this time the noise was like forks and spoons in an overfull cutlery drawer. Jill wondered if Kait had ever heard that laugh before. She wondered if she had ever seen her boyfriend scuttle across the floor as though he possessed twice the number of joints a human should possess.

"All right," he said, turning away from her. "All right, Jill Cicero."

He crawled onto his bed, plucking a cellphone off the filing cabinet he used for a nightstand. He tapped the screen a few times, then raised the phone to his ear. He waited: Jill could hear the soft, tinny purr of the ringing from where she stood. A cloud crossed over the moon. The streetlight beneath the window fizzed and popped, and abruptly switched off.

"Where'd you go, Heart-Brecker," Lutz said suddenly into the phone.

He waited again. Jill could not hear what Kait was saying, but she was saying a lot of it.

"Where'd you go," Lutz repeated. His eyes had gone glassy. More tinny chatter—the voice on the other end of the line sounded frantic, like a tape on fast-forward.

"I told you I would take care of it," Lutz said, almost bored. "Heart-Brecker... Listen, you're not making any sense. Now, I want you to come around under the window, the one by the back walk." He glanced back at Jill, who stared at a point just above his left ear, unable to shift her gaze anywhere else. "I want to show you something," he said.

Maybe some time passed. Jill's senses were deadened, her equilibrium drained away like the pain of Lutz's backhand smash. The ticking of the clock could have been Lutz's fingertips drumming the filing cabinet or water dripping into the sink in the kitchenette or any number of things. Her heart. Her imagination. The light outside the window did not change, and Lutz did not stir from his cross-legged perch on the bed.

Then the tinny voice from the cellphone spoke again, startling Jill out of her reverie. Lutz held the device away from his ear, holding it at arm's length, the speaker pointed toward her.

"I'm here," Kait said. "Now what."

"Stay on the line," Lutz replied, that knife-point smile spreading across his face once more. Saliva on his teeth gleamed in the moonlight. "I'm coming to the window."

But he didn't move—instead, warmth blossomed up from Jill's stomach, and she began walking towards the open window. Before she knew it, she had placed one bare foot up on the ledge, leaning through, out into the frigid night air. Wind swept under her, and the hem of the borrowed robe beat the air like a broken wing. She looked down—she did not want to, but the warmth forced her eyes, and far below her stood a lone figure in a square of cold moonlight on the winding concrete walk, staring up at her.

"Do you see the window?" Lutz asked. Seven stories below, the tiny shivering figure nodded slowly. "I told you to stay on the line," he said evenly.

"I see the window," said the cellphone's tinny voice.

"And do you see me?" There was another pause. The figure on the sidewalk cocked its head. The tinny voice said nothing. "Heart-Brecker, are you there?"

"Lutz, I... I don't understand."

A snarl of frustration—then the heavy clatter of the smartphone crashing against the wall beside Jill's head. Then the world whirled and tilted beneath her as she pressed against the windowsill, forcing her body through until she dangled over the edge, her weight supported by her outflung arms as she leaned over the maddening drop. She watched the figure on the ground press one hand to her mouth; the other still held the cellphone to her ear. Lutz's presence moved behind her: she could feel him, like pressure in the air, as he stooped and picked up the cellphone. Jill heard a crackle of plastic as the frame flexed in his hand.

"Still there?"

More tinny silence. Then: "I'm still here."

Lutz heaved a sigh behind her. "Heart-Brecker, I've tried... I've tried so *fucking* hard to explain things to you. How things are for people like us. I've tried a hundred times. But... I don't know. Sometimes I think you're doing it on purpose. Not getting it just to spite me. You know how much this *means* to me—don't you?"

He took a deep breath, holding the phone down by his hip while he massaged his brow with the other hand. "I suppose you want me to think it's my fault, then," he began again, raising the phone to his mouth. "My fault you don't get it. My fault you don't understand. Well, all right. I can take this one on the chin for you."

The tinny voice chittered agitatedly, but Lutz ignored it. He ended the call with a swipe of his thumb and tossed the phone onto the bed. It bounced once and clattered into a wall before tumbling to the carpet.

Outside, the winter wind picked up, buffeting Jill's hair around her face. She wished she could feel the cold instead of this terrible, swampy, soporific *heat* that clogged her veins and lightened her limbs. She knew she should be terrified, but she could not manufacture the requisite panic, even when her eyes swung down to the ground seven stories below. Her brain purred along at half-power, like it had when Lutz first took her, her synapses clicking sluggishly, pared down to basic flesh-functions. Breathe. Shiver. Blink. *Wait.*

Her neck craned forward, and her jaws moved: she heard her own voice come out, strange and stiff from disuse. "Are you watching, Heart-Brecker," she called out, and far beneath her, Kait Brecker took a step backward.

"Lutz..." she called out in a voice just as strange and stiff as her own. "What are you going to do with her?"

A smile slashed Jill's mouth open—she could only imagine that same knife's-edge grin on her lips, showing teeth that were not her teeth anymore.

"It's New Years," she said. "I thought we could watch the ball drop."

Then her foot pushed off the ledge, and the earth rushed up at her like a wave.

* * *

Jill felt the stock of the long hunting rifle punch into her shoulder, and the blast that followed seemed to crack the sky in two. She knew the shoulder would bruise—but in the moment, the pain was packed under layers of gauze as her heartbeat shuttled acid-hot adrenaline through and through her slender frame. Beside her, she heard her father's breath catch in his throat with a small *hup* sound, a noise he would make whenever he heard a piece of news and had not decided yet how he would react. Jill knew she shouldn't take her eyes off the valley, but she dragged her gaze away, looking at her father in profile. His thin, windswept hair tumbled out backwards beneath the flap of his rabbit-lined bomber hat, and his jaw was set like a statue of a jaw, rigid and angular and utterly inscrutable. He had the big field glasses pressed to his eyes, staring down into the tall scrub-grass at the bottom of the valley. For a moment he nibbled his lower lip, adjusting the focus on the binoculars.

"He's moving," he said in a voice as level as the horizon. "He's going to run, he's—no. He's down. He's down, Jilly. You got him."

The two of them were nestled behind a slanting white boulder that looked down into the wide golden dell, dotted with patches of scrub and the drifting amorphous shadows of clouds. The land seemed to fall away beneath them, stretching toward the pale horizon in every direction Jill looked. There was another low hill off to the right, and the rest of the herd was bounding toward it, heading into the low sun. Without the scope on the rifle, to Jill the pronghorn looked like blobs of cotton, bobbing only slightly with every long galloping stride. Their backs barely seemed to move as their powerful legs churned beneath them, bearing them to safety.

Jill's father rose slowly to his feet, adjusting his bomber hat atop his head. The field glasses hung at the middle of his chest. She waited for him to look at her, but his gaze stayed down-valley, his eyes shaded under the fringe of rabbit's fur. "Get your pack and follow me down. We're going to lose the light soon, behind that next rise. We don't want anybody to twist an ankle, do we?"

"No, Dad." She looked down the slope, realizing she had lost track of the tussock where her pronghorn had toppled out of sight. In truth, she had not even seen the animal fall at all. She had been on dozens of hunts with her father and seen more than a few beasts fall, but this was the first time she'd been allowed to carry the big Winchester rifle, at least while they were off the practice range. She had been preparing to pull the trigger all week, but in that instant, amidst the clap of mind-shattering thunder, she had been afraid to watch the animal die. Or, if she missed, that the pronghorn would turn and look at her before it bolted. That it would remember her face. Remember what she had tried to do.

"Will we butcher it down there in the field?" she asked, suddenly uncomfortable with the silence. "Or take it back to the truck?"

"Take it back," her father replied. "Don't want Mister Big Hat to catch us in the open with him, Jilly. Make for a bad birthday."

Jill followed the shape of her father's back down into the valley, watching where his big boots fell on the rocky slope so she could step where he stepped. The air was cold, but the ground still radiated heat; Jill knew from other trips that it would be another forty-five minutes before she began to shiver. They took a winding track down the hill, her father picking the path seemingly at random, but Jill imagined that each turn, each footfall was deliberate and precise, as though he could see obstacles before they became obstacles, as though he were forever one step ahead of the land, outsmarting it, guiding her through.

He only spoke once in the minutes it took to reach the flat of the valley. Without turning around to look at her, he said, "I never could have made that shot when I was your age. Neither could my father. You're very good, Jilly. I knew you'd be."

But it hadn't sounded like praise. It sounded like a headline, a mere reporting of fact. So Jill did not reply. Instead she adjusted her grip on the rifle, staying careful not to pass the barrel across her father's body. That was the first rule.

When the sun dipped below the rise to their right, Jill Cicero would be fifteen years old.

At last they reached the bottom, and the golden landscape around them had already begun to turn dull orange, running dull gray at the corners. Her father led her to a patch of thick, coarse field grass, beckoning with a jerk of his head. His eyes peered down into the grass as though it were a lobster tank, and he was picking dinner for a difficult guest. "You didn't see where he fell, did you," he said over his shoulder.

Jill's face flushed, and she shrugged under the heavy straps of her backpack. "No, Dad."

"You looked away."

Jill said nothing.

"If I hadn't been looking, we might have lost him. It would have been a waste. We don't do that in this family, do we, Jilly?"

"No, Dad."

Her father angled his head, and werelight flashed off the lenses of the field glasses around his neck like a second pair of eyes. "You'll do better next time," he said. "Look—there he is. In the matted-down grass, right there."

Jill took two steps forward and—yes, there was her pronghorn. The creature was lying on its side, its pale belly showing and its neck bent back around at a strange angle. In the near-darkness, its broad brown snout looked nearly the same color as its curving keratinous horns, and its eye was glassy and bulging, like a large black marble. She could see the hole her bullet made, glistening on the broad, tan shoulder. There was surprisingly little blood.

"He's young," her father said.

Jill felt a knot form beneath her sternum. "Younger than me?" she asked.

"Have to be," came the reply. "Pronghorn don't live but ten years, usually. Fifteen, sometimes, and that's in captivity. You couldn't have known. Not at that distance."

"I didn't want to shoot a young one," Jill murmured. She stared down at the beast, the rifle in her hands suddenly dragging her toward the earth, heavy as wet sand. "Ten years..."

"You couldn't have known," her father repeated.

Then the pronghorn stirred—Jill heard the sound of a gasping breath, its horns gouging a shallow furrow in the clay dirt.

"It's still alive!" she whispered, half-horrified, half-amazed.

"Not for long." Her father stretched out one arm, pointing in the gloom. "See your bullet hole? Center of mass. He won't get up from that." His eyes glittered coldly at her. "He's suffering, though. We don't want him to suffer."

His hand reached down towards his belt, came back balancing his old .22 pistol on his outstretched palm. "Like I taught you," he said.

Jill stared at the little gun, then back at the pronghorn laying in the bent grass. Suddenly that single black-marble eye seemed to be staring straight at her. Two more moist gasps burst like bubbles in the air, and she felt her stomach turn in on itself like a collapsing soufflé. She took a step back. "I don't think I can," she murmured.

Her father frowned. "He's going to die anyway," he replied, his voice hard and authoritative. "You made sure of that. And we're going to be careful cutting him up. We'll use every bit of meat we can from him, we owe him that. But he's hurting now, Jilly. That's not what this is about for us. He didn't want to play this game, but we didn't ask his permission, did we?"

He pushed the pistol toward her. "We finish what we start in this family," he reminded her. "That's the reason we're allowed to do what we do. The only reason."

Silently, Jill nodded. He was right. He was always right. She held the rifle out to him, and he traded it for the pistol without another word. The metal had been next to his hip, and felt strangely warm in her hands as though it were alive. Her father stood aside, and Jill walked up to the high grass and began to wade through. Soon she reached the pronghorn's side, and she knelt down, reaching out with the hand not holding the gun to gingerly touch its flank.

The fur under her fingers was thick and coarse, and the skin beneath was very hot, as though there was a fire blazing under it, eating away at the creature from the inside out. She stroked the pronghorn's fur, trying to tamp down the upwelling of feeling flooding her mind, wondering if the animal could register the affection and take any comfort from it or if it knew she was the predator that had felled it and would think she was merely toying with her prey before the kill.

"I'm sorry," she whispered to it. "I'm sorry you're hurting like this. I didn't mean for this to happen. But I'm going to make it better, all right? I'm going to make the pain stop."

The pronghorn's flank heaved under her hand, but then the creature lay still, save for one tawny ear that flicked idly, swatting at nothing. Jill mustered her courage and took hold of the pistol in both hands, pressing the barrel between the animal's eyes. She held her eyes open, bracing for the report. She would not turn away this time. She would not let herself look away.

"I'm so proud of you, Jilly," murmured her father's voice from above her.

She pulled the trigger, and this time the shot seemed to make no sound at all.

* * *

Lutz was wrong. Dying hurt like a bastard.

Jill would never remember the fall, the feeling of the weight of her body dropping away, of the icy winter air whistling past her legs, her bathrobe opening up like a rose in mid-bloom, lopsided and ethereally beautiful in the milk-thin moonlight.

But she remembered hitting the sidewalk like she remembered her own name.

The impact blasted away her other senses, forcing the tactile feeling of her body destroying itself to surface like a beach ball held under water. There could be no moment of shock, no merciful numbness, no brief respite: The agony rushed over her—just the pain, instant and complete, a finely woven net tightening and tightening across her entire body. The warmth blazed ecstatically within her, but even this offered no salve; it only prevented her from slipping into the balmy grip of unconsciousness, trapping her in a cage with her suffering. She couldn't breathe—every time her body tried, her chest would make a horrible sucking sound, and something sharp would stab into her lungs like a row of long teeth. Her heartbeat was no longer a beat at all. It was one long note, like a drumroll, constant but weak, a murmur deep in her chest.

Slowly, slowly, Jill's vision began to clear. She was lying on her back, each limb spread out at some madman angle around her, staring upward. At first the world above her was only a smear of dull liquid red, but then moonlight asserted itself, strong as a battering fist, sliding through the red of her half-closed eyelids like a thin, white knife. There was the long black finger of the streetlight, pointing accusingly into the sky, and there, at the border of her sight was the faint, blue, antiseptic glow of a police call-box. *All's well*, the steady light seemed to say. In the far distance, she could hear the noise of traffic, the noise of downtown coming alive.

She remembered, somewhere through the white haze of pain, that tonight...

...was December 31st. New Year's Eve. The world was starting over without her.

A dark shape fell across her prone form: she could see the fringe of her father's rabbit-fur cap before she saw his face. His features were still in shadow, but she could see his eyes, slate gray, staring impassively down at her from beneath the heavy brow of the bomber cap. She had not heard him approach. Perhaps he had always been there.

You looked away, Jilly, he said without moving his mouth.

"No," she wanted to scream. "No, I didn't. I wouldn't. You taught me better than that..."

You looked away, he said. The shape above her sighed, cocking its head. It made the earflaps of the cap pop out at strange angles. *You were going to kill him.*

"I was." Through the pain, another sensation pushed through—of her right fist chopping at the closet wall in the darkness, cracking the plaster. How silly that all seemed now, her dreams of violence. Her fantasy hunt, conjured in the dark. "But I didn't have a gun. I didn't have anything. Dad, what was I supposed to do?"

You didn't want to play this game, did you, Jilly.

"Of *course* not." Pain surged through her, bending her spine up into the air as her body took one sucking, shuddering breath. "He certainly didn't ask my Goddamn *permission* to—"

You looked away, her father said. *You're looking away now.*

Then his shadow began to melt away, to scatter into ribbons, into nothing.

We finish what we start in this family, he intoned, but his voice was worlds away. *That's the only reason we're allowed to do what we do.*

He was gone. He had never been there at all. It was only Kait standing over her now, her face a splash of alien features under the curtain of her brown hair. She was still holding the cellphone to her ear, but as she stepped closer to Jill, her trembling hand dropped slowly to her side. Jill's head twisted towards her, sending bolts of fury scattering down her spine as vertebra slid and ground against vertebra, and for a moment the two women regarded each other. Jill felt like she would sink into the concrete, that the earth would close over her, the black and red clouds at the corners of her vision converging to engulf her at last. Kait's face flickered between emotions. Her lips twitched curiously, rubbing against her teeth, and her eyes never left Jill's—though Jill could tell she wanted to shut them, shut them against the horror below her, to blink the other girl away like a stray eyelash.

"Lutz," she murmured. "Lutz... What did you do?"

And Lutz made Jill answer, her shattered jaw opening and shutting like a puppet's, each word sending rivulets of blood and spit streaming from the corners of her lips.

"Heart-Brecker," she—he—they said. "This... is... *incredible.*"

Kait paled and stepped backwards one pace, and Jill felt a flashbulb of anger go off somewhere in the back of her mind. *Don't look away*, something crazy inside her said. *He'll know if you look away. And you want him to love you, don't you, Heart-Brecker. You'd do anything for just a little piece of it, wouldn't you? Well, keep your eyes on the fucking prize. What's the matter — you've never seen anything die before? They say the first time's the hardest, but that's only if you can stop at one...*

As if in response, Kait knelt beside her, the knees of her jeans scraping the concrete, leaning over Jill's prostrate form. Now their faces were only a foot apart — Jill's breath turned to steam in the December cold, obscuring her view of the other girl. Jill wondered if Kait could smell the doom on her breath. If she could hear the plants screaming in the distance, coming closer and closer, closing in from every corner of her mind.

"You were never going to really understand," Lutz was saying — her voice, her mouth, her words. "I couldn't think of anything else. I thought... if I could just show you, maybe I could get it through your thick skull."

"Well, you could have warned me," Kait mumbled, her voice shaking from the cold. "I never thought.... I never guessed you would — "

"I improvised," Jill replied, a shrug in her voice. "Anyway, I thought you *liked* surprises. Happy New Year's, Heart-Brecker."

Kait chewed lipstick for a long second. The streetlight fizzed again, flickered on, flickered off once more. She swallowed, wiped something invisible off her chin. Then: "Tell me," she said, her lips trembling. "Tell me... what it's like. Please..."

"Oh, you're not gonna believe it," Jill choked out. "It's... It's like floating in cool water. And the water just gets cooler and cooler, but you never get cold. You just get numb to it after a while. All feeling just... slides away. It's relaxing. Like going to sleep in your own bed."

"But you *do* feel something," Kait yelped, sliding a few inches back from Jill. "You promised me—"

"It's all abstract," came the calm reply. "Of course there's a sensation to it. It's entropy. Matter turning into other matter. It's heat flashing away into the black. But there's nobody else here to feel it but me." Lutz rocked Jill's head back and forth a quarter-inch, a maneuver that nearly sent her spiraling into madness. "Nobody home," they said together, grinning with bloodstained teeth.

"Nobody home," Kait repeated slowly.

Jill nodded. "I can feel her slipping away now," she gurgled. "She's starting to shut down. Little bags of tissue in her gut stopping their churning, one by one. Like a countdown."

"But she doesn't feel anything?" Kait asked.

Jill bared teeth in a grisly grin. "I wouldn't let her suffer."

"All right." Kait's eyes flicked away and back, away and back. Her knuckles tapped the ground beneath her. "All right. Then..." Suddenly she reached out her hand, placing it on the side of Jill's neck. "Let me feel it," she said.

Jill's mouth could not drop open in shock, but the real Jill—buried under layers and layers of Lutz—felt the world freeze for a split-instant. "Are you sure?" she said. "I mean... Heart-Brecker, are you sure you want to—"

"I have to know," she said firmly, her mind made up. "I have to feel it for myself."

The blooming warmth within Jill flickered down, shrinking in on itself like a balled-up T-shirt. Cowed, uncertain. Almost... *frightened*. But when Jill spoke, her voice betrayed nothing.

"Of course," she said. "Just like we've practiced, then."

We finish what we start in this family.

Then Lutz shrank away, and Jill *lunged* like a hand bursting from a grave—

* * *

Who is this?

…

Who is this? Please, I can feel you there—
You know who this is, Heart-Brecker.

…

…

Lutz?
Do I sound like Lutz to you.
No. No, this is wrong. Something's wrong.
Nothing's wrong. This is exactly what he wanted. This was always the plan.
No, this has to be a mistake! Hold on, I'm going to fix this. I'm—

…

Why can't I leave?

…

Jill, why can't I leave?
So you do know my name.
What are you doing to me? Let me go!
How can I let you go? I don't even exist.
Please—I can fix this. He doesn't know. I—we—can help you.

…

Jill, you're hurting me.
Yes.
I can feel—oh, God. You're dying. You're dying. I can't— I can't—
Don't look away, Heart-Brecker.
What's happening?
You did this to me.
No. No, I would never… I never thought he would…
Did you honestly believe he was going to let me live?

…

…

You've got to let me go. I can still help you. I can stop this.
Don't lie to me, Heart-Brecker.
STOP CALLING ME THAT.

…

Jill.

…

Jill, please. I'm scared.
Lot of that going around.
I don't want to die.
Lot of that going around too.
What do you want?

…

…

Jill?
You can't save me.
You don't know that—
Shut your fucking mouth. I'm already dead. And unless you want to feel it when I eat that bullet, you're going to do exactly what I tell you.

…

Heart-Brecker?
Please don't call me that. I'm Kait. Kait.
Don't you like it when he says it?
I don't know. I don't know anymore.
You're a heartless, body-snatching bitch, Heart-Brecker.

…

…

Yes.

…

What do you want me to do.
Here's the deal. Swear to me you'll never do this again. No more pets. No more girls. No more dances. No more bodies. You never take anybody ever again. If you do, I'll know. I'll know, and I'll make you pay for it.
Lutz won't like it. He'll never agree to—
Fuck Lutz. I'm talking about you.
I never wanted this to happen. I never wanted to hurt anybody.

...

All right. I swear it.

...

Now please let me go.

...

Jill?

...

...

I'm going to let you out, Heart-Brecker.
Thank you—
But I'm never going to let you go...

* * *

Jill was standing up slowly. Jill was dying on the concrete.

Jill was wiping away tears, feeling a hand that was not her hand brushing a cheek that was not her cheek. Jill was staring up at the open window on the seventh floor. The curtains billowed out into the night like ghostly arms, and beyond them stood Lutz—or a shadow of Lutz, watching the sidewalk below. Jill was watching the cellphone in her hand ring, go to voicemail, and ring again. Then she dropped it, heard it crack as it struck the concrete by her feet. Jill was turning away, feeling herself turn, sucking cold air into strange, distant lungs. Jill was staring up at the moon, feeling her ribs stab into her lungs again and again and again. But there was no more pain to feel. She would never remember the fall. She was an ember from the fire, a piece from the shattered whole. A seed. A breath. A *thought*.

Jill Cicero was dead. Jill Cicero didn't exist.

Jill Cicero was fucking immortal.

Chapter 22

Lonelyworld

Alice didn't want to remember where she was.

She was crouched on the wet ground, a loose ball of limbs and tangled hair, and when she began to shake off her daze, the first thing she felt was ice-cold water soaking through the knees of her pants and the fabric of her gloves, and a dull throbbing ache in her right hip where—what? Had she fallen? When? She blinked sleepily, rubbing her dribbling nose with the palm of one damp glove. Snow. Wet snow. It was starting to come back. Little portions of reality, like water dripping into an empty bucket, stinging as they landed.

She was staring into the forest, where not even the bright moonlight bleeding through the clouds could penetrate the gloom. She searched along the edge for the footprints of her friends, something to anchor her to the present, but all she could make out was the uneven snow-surface, glacial and eerily beautiful, spreading away in either direction along the tree line. To her right, the white-glazed road rose up and over the first low hill, glittering like tiny glass shards under the moon's bulging eye. A set of clean tire tracks furrowed the surface, but further on the snow had been disturbed, churned to slush. She followed the markings with her eyes. The tracks wove back and forth across the road, carving crazy angles into the snow, and beyond that...

Alice felt her face go tight all over. The slate-gray SUV rested against a broad-trunked oak tree leaning over the edge of the road, docked against it like a boat in a harbor. The back bumper was crushed inward in a V, and both windshields were struck through with lightning-shaped cracks. Alice could not see into the front seat, but the passenger door hung ajar, and there was steam rising from one corner of the smooth gray hood. A marshmallow pile of snow piled on the roof, covering part of a roof rack. There was no movement from inside the vehicle.

Ben and Kaity were nowhere.

She fought to her feet—her head swam like it was full of soapy water, and her bottom hit the wet ground again before she realized she was falling. She slid onto her back with a wet crunch, letting the world spin around her for a moment, blinking moonlight out of her eyes. Then the rest of it came flooding back, playing on fast-forward: the SUV thundering down the hill towards her, swerving, nudging her off the road, Kaity screaming her name, and then Ben—

No. She would not think like that. It was all she could think about.

She must have imagined it.

She could remember it clear as day.

The crash. She hadn't seen it happen, but she could still hear the sharp, solid thud of impact. It played on loop inside her: the too-distinct noise of a body striking moving metal, then silence. This over and over, without ceasing, without variation. She wanted to cry out, but when she opened her mouth, all that emerged was a wet gurgling sound. She *had* to have imagined it. She struck the snow beneath her with her open hand, feeling the snow break and crunch beneath the blow. She had to have imagined it. The thought rang like a prayer between her ears. It couldn't be real. She hadn't wanted it to end like this. She hadn't wanted it to end at all.

A horrible thought struck her. *Had* she wanted this? Her stomach twisted, tightening like a constricting snake. After all... Wasn't this exactly what she'd wished for? To be *alone* with Kaity. The endless flat beach, the quiet world, the empty chairs and umbrellas and windows. All of it. Maybe, just maybe she had invited this outcome somehow. Willed it into existence—on the whim of a selfish, greedy, *jealous* little monster. She had loved Ben, yes, but what use was her love to him when she could throw it aside the second she tired of him? It chilled her to the very marrow. Perhaps this, too, was how Lutz felt about the world. Capricious. Impulsive. Cruel.

But even this could not be true. If it was—where was Kaity? Why was Alice alone in this silent, moon-washed world? If she was going to tear her reality down with a thought, why hadn't she saved the one person she couldn't possibly survive the end of everything without?

She got to her knees, peering around desperately at the snow-covered landscape. Nothing moved. The surface of the frozen pond gleamed like a broken mirror, and across that the dark wall of the forest towered up from the opposite bank. She prayed she would see something among the trees—a light, a house, smoke from a chimney. Anything to tell her she wasn't really alone in this great half-darkness. But nothing stirred, and no sound answered her silent cry. She thought she would weep, but instead she grew very still, curled inward on the snow. She remained like that for a long time.

Then sudden movement caught her eye. A person-sized flash of color flitted behind the SUV, just out of sight by the time she looked. "Kaity?" she whispered hopefully. There was no response. Then it moved again—closer, and quicker than before. It was among the trees, between her and the wreck. It was stalking her. Alice scooched backwards on her rear, kicking in the snow, her head still full of brine. Why couldn't she hear it? Her own movements crushed the snow beneath her like gravel under heavy tires. And there it was again, and again. Alice's heart leapt up into her mouth—but then, mysteriously, the movement stopped. Stillness returned to the forest. The moonlight dimmed as thick clouds crossed over. Alice released a breath, not even realizing she had been holding it.

"Hi, babe," said a male voice.

Ben was gliding across the snow towards her.

But Alice felt no fear. In fact, she hardly felt anything at all.

All emotion peeled away, strip by strip, replaced only with a kind of shallow melancholy that draped across her heart like thin gauze. Numbness settled into her skin, and the cold was suddenly but a distant memory. Even her hands and feet and behind felt dry—and then she could not feel them at all.

Ben's body was whole. She had not seen his injuries, but she had imagined horrible things: blood everywhere, his midsection pinched off, internal organs crushed to jelly or leaking out his lacerated flank. But there wasn't a mark on him. No blood, no bruises, no signs of violence on his beautiful face. Even his glasses were undamaged, gleaming in the half-light. Perhaps the skin was a little flushed, the lips slightly chapped. But Alice could forgive this. Deep within the armor of her numbness, her heart swelled, looking at him—and what was the harm in that, after all? Who was she hurting, taking a little happiness from this apparition. She understood implicitly that it would not last, after all. She had conjured this too. A comforting nightmare to keep her company while she succumbed to the cold.

But something wasn't right. Ben angled his face towards her, and when the light struck him full-on, his eyes were... *wrong*, somehow. Like drawings of eyes. Like the cutouts in a paper mask, glaring and empty. A thin finger of fear stirred within her but not enough to make her back away from the vision. She watched the ghost approach her, the tips of his boots just dragging the delicate surface of the snow.

"Aren't you going to say anything to me?" he asked, his voice deep and friendly.

Alice shook her head. "You're not real." Her lips stuck together with every word. "You're dead. I heard it happen. You—"

One hand drifted up, tapped the skin next to his eye with a forefinger. "Through the eye," he interrupted solemnly. "Did you think I would forget that?"

"No..." Alice's face screwed up in confusion. "You didn't get shot. A car hit you."

Ben waved her off. "Yes, yes. You'll have to excuse me. There's been a lot of dying happening around here. I guess I lost track." His glasses flashed moonlight, and beneath that, his horrible cutout eyes narrowed at her cheekily.

"Does it hurt?" she asked timidly.

Her boyfriend nodded. "Oh, yes. It hurts. You can't imagine it."

Alice looked at her knees. "I'm sorry."

"You let me go, babe."

She jerked her head up. "Please don't say that."

"Why not?" Ben drifted closer, looming huge in her vision. "We were going to have to talk about it someday anyway." He tapped his wrist, then shrugged. "Or, I don't know. Were we? What *was* your plan, exactly? Maybe you thought you could just disappear—leave me behind like Heart-Brecker left you. Wouldn't be the first time it happened to me."

"No!" Alice shook her head, trying to shrug the numbness away. "No, I would never do that. Not to you."

"But you wanted to," he insisted. He spread his arms out as though he would embrace her. "You thought about it, at least. I suppose this must be a lot easier for you. Now you don't have to worry about hurting my feelings anymore. Now you don't have to say goodbye."

"I didn't *want* this," she protested. "Don't you think I *wanted* to say goodbye to you?"

"But you *were* going to say goodbye."

"I..." Alice's face pinched up, uncertainty bubbling in her heart. "I don't know. Everything's so strange now. I don't know what to think."

"I love you, Alice Gorchuck."

She stared up at his blank face, not speaking, her heart in tatters.

"I want to hear you say it," he intoned.

"I did say it," she protested. "Remember? Last night, in the bedroom. Only..."

Only it wasn't you, she thought to herself with dawning horror. *It was Lutz.*

Right before he walked into Kaity's room.

Right before all this horror began.

"I want to," she sniffed. Again she tried to conjure the feeling within her, search it out like she had tried dozens of times before, in private moments, in intimate settings, after kisses before class or just turning out the lights in his bedroom or hers. Choose it, she thought. *Choose* to love. But it wouldn't come. The feeling would not rise, no matter how hard she struggled. She plunged the bucket into the well again and again, but every time it came up empty. "I tried, Ben," she moaned. "Why can't you understand that? I wanted to. I tried so hard." She felt scooped out, staring into the glare of her boyfriend's glasses. Like the knife-scraped insides of a pumpkin.

Ben angled his brows, turning away to show his profile. "Maybe it's not so easy for you after all," he sneered.

"Ben, *stop* it." She rose and took one imploring step towards him, then stopped. Another shimmering form had appeared behind him, just over his left shoulder. Then another, and another beside that. The air above Alice was becoming crowded.

"Who's there?" she asked, fighting the urge to retreat—to pivot and run, up the snowy road or back into the dark forest, to start running and never stop.

"It's so warm here," Ben told her in a peculiar voice. "Pleasant. We all think so."

Alice took one hesitant step backward. "Who's... Who's *we?*"

"Riley." He gestured to one humanoid glowing shape. "Cormac. And Jill Cicero—you'll like her, I promise. We're *all* here, Alice. All of us together. And it doesn't hurt anymore. There are so many of us now. I can't wait for you to meet them all."

As one man, Ben and the other glamouring shapes reached out to her, but Alice scrambled back, ice spreading over her heart. "Ben... I can't..."

"Can't what?" Anger crept into his tone. "Are you going to abandon me again, Alice?"

She stared at the shimmering forms. They all had Ben's eyes now, like eyes cut from a magazine. "You're scaring me," she murmured. "I... I don't like this anymore."

"There's nothing to be scared of."

Had Ben spoken, or one of the other ghosts? She could not tell one from the other now. They moved and shifted, swapping places and features like they were shuffling a deck of cards.

"We love the warmth," said the voice. "And we love him."

"*Who?*" Alice demanded, creeping backwards—but the shapes pursued, drifting swiftly over the snow, faster than thought.

"He protects us," said two of the voices in unison. "He would never let us suffer. We're like hollow trees. We don't feel a thing."

More voices joined the chorus, male and female, in swelling, terrifying harmony.

"We don't feel a thing."

Alice took another step back.

"We don't feel a thing."

She clapped her hands over her ears.

"*Don't leave me alone again, Alice Gorchuck—*"

"I DIDN'T," she screamed, and in her anguish she reached forward, grasping his hand in both of hers as tight as she could as if she could silence him, quiet his rage with even this superficial display. But as her hands wrapped around his, more stretched out and grasped her wrists, her arms, her shoulders—and awful, liquid, *wriggling* warmth slithered down her fingers and into her heart like a rat disappearing down a rat hole.

"Alice, *don't...!*" screamed out Kaity's voice, but the sound of it reached her as though across a great chasm. The other voices rose up, overwhelmed her—and Alice submerged herself in the tumult, submitting to the flame scorching up the veins of her arms like acid. She allowed the warmth to take her, feeling Ben close by, drawing her toward him, and the others as well. She was not afraid anymore. This was how it had to be. She was paying her penance.

She had finally come in from the cold.

Chapter 23

Welcome

It happened in slow motion, in the honeyed pace of a nightmare. But she was already too late. Kait let Ben's weight slip from her lap onto the bloodied, slush-slick road, but when she turned back up the path, Riley had already slunk free of the SUV's wreckage and was stalking towards where Alice lay, impossibly quiet, her long and crooked shadow stretching across the surface of the snow like a claw. Kait never saw the corpse's face—only the shape of her bronzed, slender shoulders bobbing as she crept toward her dearest friend, her bare feet hardly leaving footprints in the snow's surface. But she could imagine the huntress smile splitting those ruined lips, Riley's handful of remaining teeth bared in awful mimicry of Lutz's lopsided grin. And now Alice was looking up, turning just in time to see the dead girl almost upon her, her own face a beatified mask. She smiled in recognition, standing to meet Riley's approach, almost glowing in the moonlight.

A thought struck like lightning. *She doesn't see it. She doesn't see the train coming.* In that instant Kait was on her feet, fighting for balance, actually bracing her heel against Ben's rigid form to keep from sliding across the ice. Whatever her friend was seeing coming across the snow towards her, it wasn't a carcass. It probably wasn't Riley. It probably wasn't even real. She screamed Alice's name, jerking the Model 94 to her shoulder, but she was too slow by a shade. Her finger found the trigger guard, but the corpse was already stretching out bare arms toward her friend, and Alice moved forward into them, accepting the embrace as a gift.

Alice's eyes closed—and Lutz opened them.

There was no use for her scream now, but Kait could not force down one last shattering cry of horror and rage. It tore at her lungs as it left, leaving her ragged. Riley's body collapsed to the ground like a doll, and Kait watched Alice sway like a tree in a windstorm, momentarily off-kilter, a newborn deer wobbling on knock-kneed legs. Then she shook herself, vocalizing a few frosty nonsense syllables, and showed her teeth.

The Model 94 shook in Kait's hands. Even if Lutz himself had stepped out of the woods that very second—the real Lutz, not this false idol—she would not have been able to shoot straight. Her heart split down the center groove watching him gangling towards her inside her best friend's flesh, that stupid, stupid, *stupid* smile stretching across stolen lips. But there was nothing she could do. She thought of Riley Loomis, dashing herself to pieces against the corner of the wooden strut, begging for the bullet, and her stomach turned in her guts. Even that had not saved her friend. At least, it had not freed her. It would not free Alice.

So she let him come, glowering under her bangs, breathing cold air that smelled like nothing and death all at the same time. Hating him. Hating him like she never had before.

"Are you hurt, Kaity?" Alice called out to her.

"*Let her go.*"

The words burst out of her in an unexpected gasp, her voice hardly human to her numb ears. God help her—he had sounded just like her. It wasn't only her voice that sold the trick. It was her inflection, her expression, the concerned crinkle of her eyes, her... her *Alice-ness*. Everything, faultlessly replicated in real time. Kait had prayed she would be able to tell the difference now that she knew the change was coming. She wanted to find some seam, some loose stitch, anything to prove that the imitation was not total. But there was nothing to find. What had Lutz had to steal from her friend to create this mirror performance?

What had he sliced off her mind to steal her soul this completely?

"Let's try this again," Alice replied as if she hadn't heard. "Can't we, Heart-Brecker? Can't we at least pretend this is a happy moment for the both of us?"

Then her eyes fell on the rifle in Kait's hands, and a pained expression crossed her heart-shaped face. "Oh, for the love of— point that stupid thing somewhere else for once. You're going to give me a panic attack."

"Why?" Kait snarled, looking down the ironsights. "What are you afraid of?"

She still couldn't hold the weapon steady, but that didn't matter anymore. At this distance, there was no way she could miss the target, even if she shut her eyes.

"I don't want you to do something we're going to regret," came the reply. "Or—oh, what the hell." Suddenly Alice took two quick strides forward; Kait jerked the rifle up, but instead of moving out of her line of fire, the other girl seized hold of the muzzle with both hands, thrusting it up under her tilted chin.

"Déjà vu, huh?" she said. The grin returned, looking strange and awkward with her jaw pressed up against the cold metal of the rifle's barrel. "Well, don't do me any fucking *favors*," she said. "But we both know I can't really let her live. Not after everything you've done."

"Everything *I've* done?" Kait's teeth ground together. "You murdered my friends."

It was a struggle just to keep her tone level. Her eyes fixed on the spot of contact, just where the metal of the muzzle touched Alice's reddening flesh. Her hands began to sweat, even in the cold, and she moved her shaking finger away from the trigger with bottomless caution.

"You broke my heart," Alice replied in the voice one might use to order breakfast. "And I don't know what you're talking about. I haven't murdered anyone."

"You didn't...?" Kait's eyes bugged. "*Riley!*" she seethed. "Ben! Cormac!"

"You shot the Riley-body—"

"Stop *calling* them that—"

"You shot the Riley-body," Alice pushed through, gesturing with the hand not clutching the barrel of the Winchester. "I didn't force you to do that. You chose that. *Your* choices, not mine. And the Ben-body..." She shrugged ruefully. "That was an accident. Honestly. I didn't mean for that to happen."

"Cormac, then," Kait hissed. "You're not going to tell me he decided to saw his own fucking *head* off, are you?"

Lutz shrugged Alice's shoulders. "It's property damage at best, Heart-Brecker. I put my fist through a drywall. I'm sorry. Is that what you want me to say? I'm sorry."

Kait fixed him with a hard look, struggling to tamp down the white heat surging up inside of her. She could not lose control now. Not when she had so much to lose. She blinked, feeling her brow pop out sweat like beads of mercury. Not with Alice's bare throat balanced at the point of the gun.

"Jill Cicero," she managed. "You told me... You told me she wouldn't feel anything."

Alice looked down the length of the muzzle. "Would you believe it if I told you I actually regretted that?" she said softly. "I thought it would work. I really thought it would make you understand. But you just got more mixed up. I don't know what goes on inside your head, Heart-Brecker. But you're the only one like that. That's what I love about you."

Kait studied Alice's face, again searching for some sign of Lutz, finding none. "You regret it," she parroted. "Well, all right. Guess what. I *don't* believe it. You're not sorry she's dead—her, or any of them. I know better than that. You're just sorry I left. You're just sorry I won't play the game anymore."

Alice grimaced, her lips pulling down almost in a snarl.

"Well, it was worth a shot," she said evenly. "You need to give me the gun now."

Kait almost laughed. "Or else what?" she scoffed.

Alice stared at her incredulously. "Or else I walk out on the ice. Or I stand right here until this body freezes. Or starves. Or I come up with something worse." She shrugged. "Or... You give me the gun and the bullets you've got jangling in your jacket pockets. You get in that car and you drive us where I tell you to go. You *come home*. Do that, and I'll let her go."

Kait almost stepped back, but stopped when she realized she could not draw the muzzle of the Model 94 out of Alice's grip. "But you said that wasn't enough," she said slowly. "You said we *couldn't* go back to the way things were. What is it you want, then?"

Alice sniffed and stared off to the right, over the frozen lake. "I want to see you, Heart-Brecker," she said simply. "Face to face. Not like this. Is that too much to ask? I want to talk about the future with my girlfriend."

"I'm not—" Kait began to say, then paused, looking into Alice's eyes. There, at last, was Lutz. Implacable Lutz. Changeable and unchangeable, all in one. So instead she swallowed her protest and simply asked, "If I do what you say, you promise you won't hurt her."

"I don't have to promise you anything," came the reply. "We both know you have to trust me anyway. What other choice do you have?"

Kait's hands tightened around the stock of the Model 94, white-knuckled, almost bleeding from the tension of her grip. Two monsters regarded each other across the length of the gun. Kait stared into her friend's eyes, wishing with all her might she could believe Lutz, that there was any sacrifice she could make that would keep Alice Gorchuck unharmed, any price she could pay—no matter the cost to herself. But it was false hope, and she knew it. For the briefest instant, Lutz had revealed himself, and she had peered down into the dizzying depth of his hatred. Maybe he really believed there was no Alice inside that body, but it didn't matter. He would destroy her just the same.

She was not brave enough to see that. Her uncertain finger twitched along the loop of the trigger guard. She hoped she would not hesitate. She prayed Alice would forgive her cowardice.

"What's your answer, Heart-Brecker?" Alice asked.

* * *

She had to move the driver's body out of the front seat herself.

She tried not to think about how the bearded man had died. She focused on the physical task of moving the weight, of getting his seatbelt unstuck and hooking her slender arms under his thick, hairy ones to hoist him through the open SUV door. But she could not help noticing that the man had no wounds. His face was bruised, but there was no blood inside the cab, and no bones seemed broken. It was as if the man had been forced out of his body, somehow, or as though it had been empty the entire time. Eventually she had to dump his bulk onto the concrete; her hand slipped, and his weight crashed into the snow beside the front wheel with a wet crunch. Alice watched this from the back seat, holding the big hunting rifle under her own chin now, Kait's spare bullets bulging in one jacket pocket.

Kait climbed into the front seat. The keys were still in the ignition.

"Start it," Alice ordered. "Take us back the way we came. Up the hill and into the forest."

Kait did as she was bid. It took a few attempts, but eventually the SUV's engine turned over; the headlights came on again, bathing the snowy road in twin cones of yellow light. Kait's stomach turned when she saw Ben's stiffening corpse lying in his bloody snow-angel to their immediate left, his head turned away from them staring endlessly, the way Cormac's head would stare endlessly. The heat began to churn out, and Kait guiltily thrust her hands over the vents, greedily lapping up the warmth spilling out through the slats. Then she pushed the gas and cautiously maneuvered the SUV off the shoulder and onto the road itself, steering around the corpses on the road and angling the spotlights towards the first hill.

They drove in silence. Soon the air inside the cab was warm enough that Kait didn't need the heat on full blast. Without its roar, the quiet inside the SUV was maddening. She kept glancing into the rearview mirror, hoping to catch some glimpse of her friend's face, but the back seat was dark. All she saw, every so often, was the flinty flash of gunmetal, but that was it. Occasionally Alice would give her a direction, a turn to take or the instruction to speed up, but when Kait tried to reply, she was met with hostile silence.

"I'm going to get you out of this," she said once, turning to speak over her shoulder. "Just hold on a little longer. I'm—"

"Stop talking to her," Alice cut her off in such a harsh tone it made Kait blush. "I've indulged that enough, don't you think? Just let me enjoy the ride."

Kait's mouth snapped shut, and silence returned—but a few moments later, she heard her friend suck in a breath.

"I always hated this body," she murmured. "Even before I knew about your... little perversion. The shape of it offended me somehow. I thought about destroying it from the very first moment I saw it. It—or is it 'her', now? Now you've got me all confused."

"Maybe you're right," Kait hissed. Her hands squeezed the steering wheel like she would yank it from its post. "Maybe we shouldn't talk after all."

Alice sighed. "All right. I don't want to be angry with you."

Kait ignored this and drove.

"I love you, Heart-Brecker."

Kait ignored this too. She could hardly see the road.

* * *

They had been driving for perhaps ten minutes. Alice instructed her to turn onto a side path leading back towards the lake, pointing over Kait's shoulder, and Kait pulled the car into a gravel lot almost identical to the one fronting Ben Alden's cabin. There were two other cars in the lot: a pricey-looking blue sedan, and a beater Nissan Sentra with two hubcaps gone. The structure beyond was less a cabin than a small house—the front porch was built out of sturdier wood, and sported two rocking chairs and a built-in bench swing, both dusted with snow.

The front windows were lit, and as Kait put the SUV in park, a boy's shadow crossed behind one rolled-down shade. The inside of the vehicle squeezed in like a tightening fist.

"Let's shake a leg," Alice said, and kicked open the back seat door, and Kait followed dumbly. She watched the windows, but the shadow did not return, and she was so preoccupied she almost didn't notice that the wood of the porch under the snow was flecked with dried blood.

Alice seemed in much better spirits now. As they mounted the porch, she tossed her head and tried to blow rings with her frosty breath, and drew strange markings in the snow with the toe of her boot. "I hope you like what I've done with the place," she mused, flashing a half-smile back at Kait as she led her to the front door. "I've had this... *nesting instinct* ever since you left. I dunno how else to describe it. It's been fun."

Then she opened the door, and the horror within struck Kait like an open-handed slap.

The bodies were posed as though in freeze-frames of their lives. A man with thick-framed glasses and a wonderful curling, gray moustache sat on a plush, brown couch in front of the flickering television screen, a paperback novel open in his lap. Beyond the sitting area, Kait could see into the kitchenette where a grandmotherly woman bent over the running sink, a blissful smile seared onto her face. The third shape she recognized—the acne-faced youth from the gas station, crouched over a handheld game on a beanbag chair in the far corner of the main living space, under a tall floor lamp. For the first instant, Kait almost couldn't tell they were not alive. But they didn't blink, didn't move... The only movement in the room was the older man's flyaway hair ruffling in the warm breeze of the heat pump.

Their clothes were all stained with blood.

"The place came furnished," Alice was saying, trotting daintily into the room. "But I added my own little spin to things." She tapped the carpeted floor twice with the butt of the Model 94. "I'll be out to join you in a few minutes," she said. "Don't touch the thermostat—or Pops'll get mad." She cocked her head at the gray-haired man on the couch with a wink and an oafish grin. Then she crossed the room to the far wall, propped the rifle on her broad shoulder, and seemed to switch herself off.

Kait peered around the room. The sitcom on the television was on mute, so the only sound came from the running faucet in the kitchenette and the gentle thrum of the heating system. Her skin crawled—none of the bodies were looking in her direction, but every time she caught sight of one out of the corner of her eye, she thought she saw their heads twist toward her, or felt their eyes at her back. She imagined hearing a scuttling sound, turning just in time to see the pimple-faced youth scrabbling across the carpet towards her on all fours, his face transformed into Lutz's face, her ex-beau's lopsided grin full of only slightly too many teeth.

She kicked off her red Converses, then crept across the carpet floor towards where Alice stood like a tin soldier in her toy-store box. Her friend was just as motionless as the corpses posed around the room—only the gentle rise-and-fall of her breast told Kait her friend was alive at all. She didn't even rock back and forth, stabilizing herself. She stood as if suspended in clear glass, a girl on display, a museum piece. An exhibit. A charade. Kait briefly considered tearing the gun out of the other girl's hands, but she suppressed this urge, digging her nails into the palms of her fists. It didn't matter who had the gun—Lutz still had Alice. Plus, she did not like the mental image of reaching for the gun only for her friend to snap alive like a marionette and yank it away from her, or put the barrel under her chin once more.

The quiet lasted five minutes, maybe more. The backs of Kait's hands began to itch. The wind began to moan outside, died away, began to moan again. Then a door down the hall creaked open and shut—and then he was in the room with her.

The suit was too big for him. Gray worsted with a white shirt and a dark blue-and-gray striped tie, the hems of the sleeves dangled past his fingertips, and the cuffs of the pants dragged beneath his heels, bunching up around his ankles when he stopped walking, his hands on his hips. His mound of loose curls was slicked back with a handful of styling grease, revealing a tight widow's peak on his forehead that she had somehow never noticed before. His nose, broken by Alice not two days prior, was completely healed, but Kait hardly realized. The lines of her ex-boyfriend's face had changed, subtly but significantly. He looked trimmer, if such a thing were possible. He looked lean and hungry, like a jungle cat just before the end of the hunt.

"Bone of my bone," he uttered, his eyes full of emotion. "Flesh of my flesh..."

"That suit looks stupid on you," was the only thing she could think to say.

"I'll grow into it," he replied—then his mouth kinked up in a chuckle. Without waiting for her to reply, he crossed the room in four swift steps and took her hands in his. "It's really good to see you, Heart-Brecker," he said. "I'd almost given up hope this would ever happen."

"Just tell me what you want," she drawled, trying to keep the tremble out of her voice.

His features darkened. "Oh, stop it. Please? Can't we just talk a while? Like old times. We used to have such great conversations, remember that?"

Kait snatched her hands away. "You didn't force me out here just to talk."

"I didn't force you to do anything," Lutz protested, throwing up his hands. "I *can't*—or did you forget that too? That's another thing I love about you. You're independent."

"Why are we here, Lutz," she said as evenly as she could manage.

He stared at her a long moment—then sighed and turned away from her.

"I had to see it for myself," he said at last, crossing to a dark window. "When you left, it made me curious. Curious about *you*. What you were really like when I wasn't around. Even after all that time together, I still didn't know very much about you. But I never imagined it would be this serious."

"What would be?" Kait asked, curious in spite of herself.

Lutz glanced over his shoulder. "Your delusion."

Kait felt her fists ball. She wanted to break something, but as she cast her eyes around the room, the most fragile things there were all human. So instead she struck out with her foot, kicking the back of the sofa so hard it made her tear up. "I can't believe I'm having this conversation with you again," she hissed through the pain. "I shouldn't have to *tell* you this. I shouldn't have to convince you that... that other people *exist*."

Lutz folded his hands, his back still to her. "You're right," he said coldly. "You shouldn't." His shoulders shook with anger, and for a moment he said nothing, gathering his composure. "I wish I could hate you," he nearly whispered. "I want to, I really do. It would make this so much easier. But I just can't get away from you."

"All appearances to the contrary."

"What do you want me to do?" He whirled, red-faced, and stalked across the room towards her. "I can't just ignore you. You're the only other person on this whole empty planet who's like me. We're the only two real people in a world of...

of *imposters*. Hollow men. Flimsy facades. Excuses for people. Copies of copies of copies..."

"That's not true," Kait retorted, but Lutz only shouted her down.

"It is true!" he roared. "You just refuse to see it."

He looked down at the toes of his too-large shoes, seeming to gather his thoughts. "I *know* you remember it," he said in a lower voice. "The place before this. The formless place. You couldn't possibly forget—being ejected out into the cold. Tearing through endless, cavernous darkness, with every star in the void staring into you, through you, gleaming with life... But when I got here, the world had already moved on. The bodies, the flesh, all wandering empty. Hollow trees swaying. A dying world, running on fumes."

His fists opened and closed at his sides like anemones splaying their tentacles. "Tell me you remember," he begged her. "Tell me you saw the *stars...*"

Kait shook her head, staring back at her ex-boyfriend almost sadly. "I remember birthday parties," she replied. "I remember parks. Sleepovers, car trips, holidays. My friends, my parents—I remember being a child. Or something like a child. I remember feeling *loved*, Lutz. A hollow tree can't do that." She glanced quickly at Alice's form, looming in the far corner of the room. "They can't love you back."

Lutz looked like he might be sick. "You're right," he snarled. "They can't."

Kait scowled and turned away, feeling her hands tighten into fists. "I know we're different," she murmured. "I've accepted that. Of *course* we're different. How couldn't we be? But that doesn't mean that we're..."

Superior, she wanted to say. *Better*. But instead she simply shrugged her shoulders.

"I'm not like them," she said. "But that doesn't mean I have to be like you, either."

Lutz moved into her line of sight again, a pitying look on his face. "You're mixed up," he insisted. "You've always been mixed up. But I can help you now. I can fix this. Now we'll never have to be apart. Now you'll never have to be confused ever again."

The room squeezed like a ventricle. "What are you talking about," she whispered.

Lutz's breath quickened. "I've *discovered* something," he told her, his face opening up like a flower. "I found the method at last, the only method—a way we could share everything with each other. Our minds. Our thoughts. Our body. *Everything*. Perfect communion. Perfect synchronicity, forever. We wouldn't be alone anymore. You'd still have—"

"You want to take me," Kait interrupted, realization dawning like the shadow of a mushroom cloud. Her mouth contorted in disgust and horror. "You... You want to *take* me."

"I would *never* do that to you," he protested, spreading his palms defensively. "Or at least, I can't. Not without your permission." He wrung his hands excitedly, his eyes gleaming and wild. "Think of it like, like we're moving in together," he said. "I finally figured it out. Yeah, I'd have a hand on the wheel, but so would you. We'd *share* control, just like if we were married. You'd still be *you* all over—the good parts, at least—but..."

Again he seized hold of her hands, squeezing them with almost fanatical passion. "But then you'd finally see the truth," he said, his face like a spotlight pointed into her eyes. "Then you'd finally see things *my way*."

She yanked her hands away and shrank back, Lutz pursuing her every step.

"You're insane," she said. Her pulse exploded in her ears, each beat of her heart like a knock on the door of madness.

Lutz's jaw tightened, his face going red again. "You ungrateful *bitch*," he growled, still advancing. "Do you have any idea what I've done for you? You feel so damn bad for Jill Cicero—well, that was supposed to be *you*. But I couldn't take you. Believe me, I tried, but I couldn't. That's when I knew you were special. That's when I knew you were like me."

Kait whirled away, desperate to escape his eyes. "Don't you think I know that?" she cried out. "I knew what it meant the minute you brought her home. But I didn't do anything, and now I've got to live with that for the rest of my life."

Her foot brushed the beanbag chair where the pimple-faced youth sat cross-legged, his handheld game blooping softy in his freeze-frame hands.

"So this is what all this was about," she uttered. "You didn't ever really want me back. You just want to control me—just like you control everybody else."

"I want to help you, Heart-Brecker."

"You should have stayed at home," she replied. "You came all this way for nothing."

She could not see Lutz with her face turned, but she could feel his rage darken, like he was sucking the light out of the air itself.

"I'm not giving you the choice," he intoned in a voice like steel dragging across concrete.

And to her right, Kait heard Alice chamber a bullet in the Model 94.

Kait's vision flashed white. "If you hurt her—" she snarled, but Lutz cut her off with a scornful, barking laugh.

"I'm going to blow her empty little head off," he sneered. "What are you going to do? Kill me? It's a hollow threat. And even if you could, even if you *really wanted to*, you couldn't do it on your own. You'd have to take somebody. You'd have to break your precious fucking vow to Jill Cicero—or didn't you think I knew about that? Honestly, Heart-Brecker. It's like a knife swearing not to cut." He shrugged, spreading his arms in exasperation. "Did you really believe that promise would change you?" he demanded. "After everything you've done— did you *honestly* think that playing make-believe would erase *what you are?"*

"You're a monster," she growled. But she could feel the room closing in like a cage, the corner swiveling shut on her, jaws prepared to swallow her up.

"I'm *in love*," Lutz said. "That's what this means for people like us. And now I'm finally going to make you see that, whether you like it or not. I'm going to drag you into reality kicking and screaming." He thrust his hands toward Kait expectantly, palms up. "Now come here," he said breathlessly. "I love you so much it hurts—but I'm done waiting for you to catch up."

Kait stared at Lutz—stared past him, at Alice's shape across the room, out of focus through a veil of fresh tears. Her thoughts raced circuits inside her skull. She wanted to cry out to her, to tell her things would be all right, to bring some emotion to that inscrutable mask of a face, but anything she said now would be a lie.

"I want to tell her goodbye," she whispered. "I want to tell her I'm sorry."

Lutz shrugged impatiently. "Go on, then."

"No." Kait shook her head. "Not like this. Let her go, just for a moment. So that I know she can hear me."

His lip curled, showing the top row of teeth. "Don't insult me, Heart-Brecker."

"At least let me touch her, then," Kait said suddenly. "I need to know for sure you'll let her go. I'll... I'll feel it when she gets free. And if you do, I'll..."

She took a breath. Every cell in her body screamed at once.

"I'll do it," she said, her fists shaking at her sides. "I'll let you in. I'm yours."

Lutz stared at her, his face expressionless, searching hers with his eyes. A single bead of sweat moved through Kait's hair, trickling from her brow and down to the point of her nose— and though there was no clock in the room, she swore she heard ticking, softly, as though through a wall. For a long moment,

Lutz didn't speak. Then: "Fine," he muttered, shifting his eyes away. "I don't care anymore."

Without another word, Alice tromped towards them, the Winchester rifle still thrust up under her chin. Kait didn't need to look to know that her finger was just above the trigger. "Put your hand on her back," he said. "And give the other to me. Be quick about it."

Kait did as she was told. Her left hand slid under Alice's shirt, feeling the warm skin beneath. She stroked it, running her fingernails lightly across the skin, praying that her friend could somehow feel the touch. She thought of Halloween, of the two of them sitting on the futon side by side, the entire future spread out before them like a broad white road stretching into the far distance. How had things gone so *wrong?* she wondered, blinking away tears that stung like birdshot. How had she failed her friends this badly?

"I'm going to make this up to you," she said aloud, her voice like broken pottery. "I'm going to make this up to you if it kills me."

"Your *hand*, Heart-Brecker," Lutz demanded.

Kait took another breath, held it, let it out. Then she lifted her trembling right hand and placed it on top of Lutz's. His fingers laced through hers, and she tried not to feel his hand, shaking as well, to feel his palm sweating with anticipation that weighed as much as a world. She tried not to think about what was coming.

Instead she thought of Alice — and the rest was easy.

"You're Thing One," she whispered so low only she could hear.

Then she opened the door, and Lutz blazed up within her like hellfire —

Chapter 24

Lover

—and Alice opened her eyes.

The sudden rush of sensation disoriented her, and for one heart-stopping instant she felt as though she were falling. The heady, soporific warmth that had flooded every crevice, every cell of her body slid off her like a hand dragging sheets off a bed, replaced with a focused, liquid coolness that spread through her from the feet up as though she were a glass filling with cold water. But she did not fall—the coolness bore her up, steadying her, like a friendly, familiar hand between her shoulder blades. It was pleasant, this sensation. It welled up inside her like a mountain spring, clean and pure and smooth.

It wanted to show her something.

The world came back, booming into existence around her. For the second time that hour, she did not know where she was. She didn't recognize the room she was in, nor the woods beyond the dark windows. But she recognized the faces. Alice watched with a mix of amazement and horror as Lutz Visgara stiffened and lurched two steps towards her like a mismade, shambling corpse, then toppled forward, his eyes going lightless, collapsing to the carpeted floor where his body bounced with a muffled thud and did not rise. Alice took one quick step back, feeling a shriek rising in her throat. She stared at the body. Lutz did not move—and yet, he didn't look dead, not *really*. His head was twisted sideways, his cheek flush with the carpet, and his eyes were open and glinting dully, as though he had fallen asleep with them open.

And there, standing just beside where her ex-boyfriend had fallen, stood Kaity, her face stiff with shock and some other ineffable expression. She blinked twice, staring down at her open, trembling hands. "It worked," she breathed, her cheeks spreading in a horrible grin that showed every tooth. "Oh, Jesus—it *worked*." She clapped her hands over her mouth, twirling giddily in place as though admiring herself in a mirror. "Oh, this is gonna be good for us, Heart-Brecker," she giggled in a voice that did not seem to belong to her at all. "You'll see. Once you get used to the custody arrangement, I'm sure you'll..."

Then she froze. Her body stiffened like Lutz's had stiffened, only she didn't fall. She stared down at the limp body on the carpet, her mouth opening and shutting, the look of joy and disbelief on her features melting away, contorting into horror.

"What've you done," she whispered, her eyes swiveling toward Alice. "Heart-Brecker... *What've you done?*"

And it was Alice's own voice that answered.

"I made a choice," she said, without even thinking the words. They seemed to pour from her lips, the natural extension of the liquid coolness trickling down inside her. With a jolt, she realized she was still holding the gun. The weapon seemed to squirm in her grip, alive and dangerous, but quickly her hands took over, moving without her instruction, swinging the big hunting rifle around and slotting the stock into her shoulder joint with near-inhuman precision. Her fingers moved blindly along the weapon's length, slipping through the trigger guard, and her eye lowered to the ironsights, squinting down the length of the muzzle.

It was pointed straight at Kaity's heart.

"I made a choice," she repeated. "And I chose her."

Panic splashed across her like ice water. She struck out blindly, struggling against the cold, alien *thing* moving within her, recoiling from the nightmare playing out before her very eyes. But then she stopped. She stopped and she waited and she listened. There was somebody else there with her. The cold, liquid movements, they had a *consciousness*—like the warmth that had fled before. Something she could feel, something she could touch the surface of with her own mind. And when it spoke to her, it didn't whisper like the warmth had whispered.

Don't worry, Alice, it said in a dark, clear voice that was almost familiar to her. *I'll take things from here. I know what I'm doing.*

For a moment, Alice was too stunned to reply. But then she asked, in a voice that echoed off the walls of her innermost self: "...Kaity?"

And the little voice inside her laughed ruefully.

Yes, it said fondly—and a little sadly as well. *Something like that.*

And then the rest poured out, before Alice could even think to answer.

I don't expect you to understand, the voice of her dearest friend said. *Maybe it's better like that. I don't really understand it myself. But, Alice, you can't imagine how sorry I am that I never told you. You always trusted me—but now, I've put you in danger, and I've got to fix it. I've got to do something I swore I'd never do again. I don't know what's going to happen to me now, but I don't want you to be afraid anymore. I promise this'll all be over soon.*

"Kaity..."

Remember that I love you, Alice. No matter what happens next, remember that.

"Kaity, *don't*—"

Remember—and the rest will be easy...

Then Alice's mouth moved, and her faraway voice came tumbling out once more.

"Goodbye, Lutz Visgara."

Kaity gawped. A host of indescribable emotions fluttered across her features—then she opened her lips, and Lutz's peculiar goatish laugh rang out across the den.

"You wouldn't," her friend scoffed, rolling her eyes towards the ceiling. "You wouldn't dare. Think about it, Heart-Brecker. If you were gonna kill me, you would have done it a long time ago."

Then, in a slightly louder voice, "Besides. You don't want to do this. I'm... You know I'm the only other one like you. Maybe in the country. Maybe in the entire world. Think about what it means for you if I'm gone. You'll be alone. Is that really what you want?"

But Alice made no answer, and fear began to creep into Kaity's eyes.

"This isn't funny anymore, Heart-Brecker," she said. "I can't leave this body. The door you opened only swings the one way. The other one, it's *fried*, inside out. Scorched earth. That's how it works. You shoot me... You can't ever take that back. You'll wake up missing me some lonely night, and you won't be able to take it back. It'll be all your fault, all over again, every time you think about me. And trust me, you will think about me."

And when Alice still did not reply, the fear in her friend's eyes bloomed into panic.

"You understand what this means, don't you?" she hissed. "You'll be stuck too. You'll be trapped in that... that *husk* forever. You'll be a prisoner. Don't do this to yourself. All right. You hate me. I understand that now. But I'm, I'm not *worth* it, Heart-Brecker. Listen to me."

Then panic flickered into anger, hot and swift. "You planned this," Kaity snarled. "Didn't you. Tell me the truth. You knew I'd follow you here. You knew what I wanted. You've been behind everything from the jump. Admit it. Admit it was you."

This time Alice did respond, and when she did, her lips kinked up in a mocking sneer.

"Not me," she said. "Never me."

"Just tell me what you *want*," Kaity burst out suddenly. Her hands beat the air like moth's wings, clenching and unclenching. "Damn it all to hell—just tell me what you *want*." Her face screwed up in an agonized grimace, mucus running from her nose in slick lines around her lips. "Heart-Brecker... Heart-Brecker, I'm begging you. Don't do this. I didn't mean for any of this to happen. I didn't mean for anybody to get hurt." Her voice rose to a fever pitch, almost a scream. "Goddammit, Kait, *talk* to me. I... *I don't wanna die!*"

Alice cocked her head at him. "You want to know what I want?" she asked.

Kaity gulped and nodded.

Alice took a slow breath. "I want you to understand something," she said. "I was *never* alone."

Kaity blinked. The two girls stared at each other, not speaking. Then understanding dawned on her friend's features—and she lunged forward with blinding speed, arms out, hands reaching for Alice's throat, mouth gaping open in a soundless howl of terror and rage.

The gun went off. The world exploded around them.

Then Kaity seemed to pause mid-lunge, her eyes bugging from their sockets. A long scarlet jet of blood twirled away from a gash in the side of her neck, followed by smaller spurts that bubbled down the side of her neck and shoulder like fondue, running across the slick surface of her winter jacket and soaking into the fabric of the hoodie underneath. She stumbled forward, clutching at her bleeding neck as though her fingers could not find purchase. Alice—or the stranger inside Alice—let out a strangled sound, and she did not speak again. Kaity did not seem to hear. Her mouth moved mechanically, her jaw working, opening and shutting like a nutcracker's maw. She took another step forward, then another.

"Hhhhk," she said, pale pink saliva oozing from the corners of her chapped lips. "Hhhhk." Her eyes met Alice's, pale and bulging with terror.

Then, like a hollow tree falling in a silent forest, she slithered to the floor and lay still.

* * *

And now it was only an hour before dawn. Alice had not stirred from the corner of the den. She sat cross-legged on the floor next to the beanbag chair. Kaity's body was in her lap, curled like an infant, her head propped on her broad shoulder. Her hand stroked the corpse's hair; she smoothed the blood-stiff locks, and she traced the lines of the pale, tender face with one trembling finger. Her lips would move, but no words would come out, only a high keening wail every so often, like the cry of a bird. Fat tears rolled down her cheeks without ceasing. She had not slept. Or perhaps she had. Whether this was fiction or reality had ceased to matter to her a long time ago. Kaity's weight felt light in her lap, lighter every second, as though she might blow away, as though she might have never been there at all.

Dawn came at last—and outside the lake house door, there came the sound of sirens in the distance. Alice tilted her head to one side. After a few moments, the crunch of tires on snow joined the fray, and a chorus of tramping feet and shouting male voices as well. They were coming; soon they would be inside the cabin. Alice rose slowly to her feet. She gathered up the Model 94, letting Kaity slide from her lap into a heap on the carpet. She stood in the back of the room for a moment, listening, the noise outside growing closer and closer. Then she turned and walked down the hallway to a dark back bedroom of the house and shut the door.

Chapter 25

Suspect

Detective Trent Ymir hung up the phone. The searchers had found another body.

He leaned against the two-way glass of the interview room, massaging his forehead with a finger and thumb. Mental arithmetic: three on the road by the lake plus five in the lake house made eight so far—now nine. It was turning into quite a morning. They'd had to fish this one out of the lake with pole hooks after a local uniform spotted a flash of red carpeting through a hole in the ice. He was a big bastard, and young, maybe twenty at the most. He was naked to the waist, bloated from his time under the ice, skin gone all colorless.

They were still looking for the head.

Flash on the run-up to the crime scene: He remembered breaching the front door of the lake house, seeing the tableau laid out within like a Renaissance painting. Mom and Pops and Junior all posed like wax statues, their guts scooped out like the beginnings of a Jack-o-Lantern. He hadn't even realized they were dead until the woman at the sink fell over at his touch, collapsing into a boneless pile on the polished linoleum. Then there was the girl, shot through the trachea, leaking the darkest blood he'd ever seen on the shag carpet. He couldn't say for certain, but he guessed from a hundred other crime scenes the bullet hadn't killed her outright. A wound like that, she'd asphyxiate on her own blood before the bleeding really got hold of her. If she was lucky, she'd go into shock first. Really not feel much of anything past the initial jolt.

What really got him was the other boy. There wasn't a mark on him, unlike the others, and his eyes were open. The look on his face gave Ymir the heebie-jeebies. It was not a look a corpse should make. He prayed the medical examiner would tell him something else, but the nameless horror piled up inside him anyway—that nothing had killed the lad at all. That he had just... stopped. Like he'd been *removed*, somehow. Like he'd been sucked out of his own body.

He tried to clear his head, focus on the other girl. They'd had to get her name off ID after they relieved her of the hunting rifle they'd found her with. *Alice Gorchuck.* No priors, no record at all. Student ID from Armistice College down south. They'd already bagged up the five bodies at the lake house by the time they heard the sound of her weeping down the hall. Stealth up to a bedroom door hanging ajar: pitch black beyond. That's where they found her, curled in a ball on the floor, cradling a Winchester Model 94 to her chest like it was a doll. No visible wounds on her, but there was a spoonful of blood-spatter dried on her face, and more down the front of her chest and stomach. She didn't even seem to notice them as they entered the room, and didn't resist when they pulled the weapon from her grip and put her hands behind her back for the handcuffs. But she wouldn't talk to them. She kept mumbling a name over and over again, the blood on her making her lips stick.

Kaity Kaity Kaity.

Ymir's mind puzzled it, worrying it like a dog at a rawhide bone. Maybe the girl on the carpet, or the halfway-naked corpse they'd found at the edge of the frozen lake. Neither had ID. Maybe somebody from the school could make them. A teacher or a friend. Maybe this Alice girl could tell their names. Ymir guessed the medical examiner's office would tell him they'd died the same way, that the bullets had both come from the same gun. They'd already dug one out of the back brick wall of the lake house, but had come up empty on the other. Chatter was, the other girl's body had been moved after she died. A third crime scene, maybe, with more bodies to unearth. Ymir didn't want to think about it, but he almost hoped they'd find more bodies. One better corpse, perhaps—one that told the story clearer than these mute horrors. He felt as though he were stumbling in the dark, grasping for a light cord he only half-recalled being there at all.

He remembered almost guiltily shutting off the running water in the sink before driving back to the police station, Alice Gorchuck muttering softly in the back seat of his cruiser. He thought of the old tube TV squatting in a corner of the living room, gone to static. It made him think of the boy-corpse's strange empty body, and a chill crackled through him like an insect scurrying across his spine.

He pressed his nose against the two-way glass, looking through: Alice was cuffed to the table with a small Dixie Cup of water sitting undrunk before her. He was stalling, ashamed as he was to admit it: Soon, the chief would get off his phone call with early forensics, and then he'd have to go in and interview this girl. He could not explain the dread he felt. She wasn't a small person by any means, but he was not afraid of her strength. He had handled himself around suspects far bigger and meaner than her. But halfway into the trip from the woods, she had started to talk—not mutter, but actually talk, in full sentences in a loud, clear voice.

And something had answered her.

He'd almost swerved the cruiser into oncoming traffic. Another girl's voice had rung out, muffled by the shatterproof plastic between him and the back seat, but still clear enough to make out the words. It was a normal human voice, but something about it made him go tense all over—mostly because there was only one other person in the squad car with him. The voice only spoke twice: once to ask, in a hushed voice, "Do you want me to ask him for you?"

The second time it addressed him directly. "Detective," it said. "How much longer will the drive be? I have to use the restroom."

His eyes had flicked up to the rearview mirror, but the girl behind him had slumped over in her seat. He could still see the shape of her shoulders and the back of her hair rising from her head like a red tide, but her face was hidden from him. He answered her, but he had not been able to hear the sound of his own voice over the roar in his ears. Then he'd flicked on the siren and really booked it all the rest of the way to the station.

And now, as he watched her through the glass, she had begun to talk again. Her mouth moved, and her eyes cast about the room animatedly, looking for phantoms in the dark corners. He thought about turning on the monitor speakers, broadcasting her conversation for everyone in the hall to hear—but it was just him, now, alone. The rest of the station was still out across town at the crime scene, dealing with the bodies and the press. He was afraid that if he turned on the speakers now, he would hear that voice again, that clear female voice that did not belong to Alice Gorchuck. He was afraid it would speak to him again, and that this time he would not be able to refuse whatever it asked of him. No, he would wait for the chief to return from his phone call, and then he would go in, and then he would step in the parking lot and call his wife at her work and tell her that he loved her very much.

His wife. He thought of her at home, holding his breakfast for him in a clipped-closed paper bag as he rushed out the door. He would never be able to explain this to her, nor to his daughters. When she asked why he'd had to leave so suddenly in the morning, he'd make up some story about a Mexican standoff in a gas station. Their lives did not need nine dead bodies in them. They did not need that picture in their heads, of a family posed like waxworks, their eyes not dead but only empty, as if they could spring to life at any moment, just waiting for the word Go... He would hold this story inside himself where it belonged until he could find a more reasonable explanation for the whole business, and then he would file it away with the rest of the joy and horror of this job.

He wished Dooley, his old partner, had not retired. He could have talked this out with Dooley. They were buddies, and had seen their share of mayhem together. But it had been four long lonely months now, and Ymir felt them weigh between his ears in a way only a cop really understood. And now here was another story he would bear alone. One more dose of misery he would have to swallow. He stared through the two-way glass, watching the light change in Alice Gorchuck's eyes. Back and forth, back and forth. On and off, like a light switch. He watched her lips move silently, watched her smile and laugh and slap the desk at something only she could ever possibly understand.

Kaity Kaity Kaity.

Perhaps he envied her.

The thought struck him crooked, making him grimace at his own reflection in the glass—and yet, he could not dispute it. He envied her. He had always envied anybody who could talk to themselves and get a straight answer back, even when Heloise Dooley had still been his partner. He'd seen hop-heads and speed freaks and all manner of other crazies crammed in the station holding cell, talking to the walls or the floor or even a smiley-face drawn in blue ink on the palm of a hand. They all had one thing in common: They understood what this Alice girl understood, that the world was huge and lonely and cold, that sometimes an imaginary friend was better than no friend at all. That even a voice in your head was preferable to silence.

Ymir reached for the doorknob of the interview room. The chief could get his brief later. He would talk to the suspect now, while they could not be disturbed. Suddenly, even in the middle of the warm police station, he felt curiously cool all over. The feeling spread across his body, but he did not fight against it, not even when his limbs began to numb as though he had plunged them into icy water. He opened the door, stepped though, and closed it with a firm click. He was no longer afraid. He already knew precisely what he needed to ask.

COSMIC EGG
BOOKS

FANTASY, SCI-FI, HORROR & PARANORMAL

If you prefer to spend your nights with Vampires and Werewolves rather than the mundane then we publish the books for you. If your preference is for Dragons and Faeries or Angels and Demons – we should be your first stop. Perhaps your perfect partner has artificial skin or comes from another planet – step right this way. If your passion is Fantasy (including magical realism and spiritual fantasy), Metaphysical Cosmology, Horror or Science Fiction (including Steampunk), Cosmic Egg books will feed your hunger. Our curiosity shop contains treasures you will enjoy unearthing. If you have enjoyed this book, why not tell other readers by posting a review on your preferred book site.

Recent bestsellers from Cosmic Egg Books are:

The Zombie Rule Book
A Zombie Apocalypse Survival Guide
Tony Newton
The book the living-dead don't want you to have!
Paperback: 978-1-78279-334-2 ebook: 978-1-78279-333-5

Cryptogram
Because the Past is Never Past
Michael Tobert
Welcome to the dystopian world of 2050, where three lovers are
haunted by echoes from eight-hundred years ago.
Paperback: 978-1-78279-681-7 ebook: 978-1-78279-680-0

Purefinder
Ben Gwalchmai
London, 1858. A child is dead; a man is blamed and dragged
through hell in this Dantean tale of loss, mystery and fraternity.
Paperback: 978-1-78279-098-3 ebook: 978-1-78279-097-6

600ppm
A Novel of Climate Change
Clarke W. Owens
Nature is collapsing. The government doesn't want you to know
why. Welcome to 2051 and 600ppm.
Paperback: 978-1-78279-992-4 ebook: 978-1-78279-993-1

Creations
William Mitchell
Earth 2040 is on the brink of disaster. Can Max Lowrie stop the
self-replicating machines before it's too late?
Paperback: 978-1-78279-186-7 ebook: 978-1-78279-161-4

The Gawain Legacy

Jon Mackley

If you try to control every secret, secrets may end up controlling you.

Paperback: 978-1-78279-485-1 ebook: 978-1-78279-484-4

Readers of ebooks can buy or view any of these bestsellers by clicking on the live link in the title. Most titles are published in paperback and as an ebook. Paperbacks are available in traditional bookshops. Both print and ebook formats are available online.

Find more titles and sign up to our readers' newsletter at
http://www.johnhuntpublishing.com/fiction

Follow us on Facebook at https://www.facebook.com/JHPfiction

and Twitter at https://twitter.com/JHPFiction